THE MEDICI MEMENTO

THE MEDICI MEMENTO

Luc Louis de Lairesse

Waterside Productions

Printed in the United States of America

First Printing, 2021

ISBN-13: 978-1-954968-59-2 print edition
ISBN-13: 978-1-954968-60-8 ebook edition

Waterside Productions
2055 Oxford Ave
Cardiff, CA 92007
www.waterside.com

THE MEDICI MEMENTO

Luc Louis de Lairesse

Does the mind know the difference between a real and an imagined event or are they like twin sisters in the same constellation?

Characters:

2018: ***Florence, Italy-Geneva, Switzerland-Paris, France-Washington DC, USA***

GianLuca (Jean-Luc) Médecin, a writer
Isabel Lieverkussen, Time Travel Program Inc. (TTP) Director
Florian de Trèsloin, TTP lead scientist
Elizabeth von Weitweg, DoWell Director
Siegfried Freundreich, her husband, DoWell vice president
Gertrude, her mother
Désiré Lesclau, a detective
Simon Averardo, DoWell CEO-President
Judith Mannowsky, art collector, friend of Elizabeth and Siegfried

Eveliebe & Géraldine, DoWell secretaries
Izquierdo, Derecho, Dritto, scientists/spies
Jacqueline Kissmet, a Hollywood actress/spy
William Lawless, a Hollywood actor/spy
Angelo, his boyfriend
Harry Khope (HK), shadowy Politician/war criminal
John & Bernice, his personal assistants
Galessa Padrone, Osteria Medici (39 of age)
George, doorman of Von Weitweg-Freundreich. (59 of age)

1473 Renaissance; *Florence, Italy – Les Cathars, France*

Lapo Buontalenti, salesman-banker
Andrea, his son
Fiammetta & Agnola, Lapo's daughters
Giovannino, their page (14 of age)
Marco Farini, an astronomer, their friend (70 of age)
Lorenzo de Medici, called the Magnificent (24 of age)
Giuliano, his brother (20 of age)
Lucrezia Tornabuoni, their mother
Angelo Poliziano, their friend, a poet & philosopher (19 of age)
Galessa, daughter of 'La Caccia' tavern (39 of age)
Beppe, an Innkeeper
Bruno, a servant at the Fiesole Villa
Leonardo da Vinci (21 of age)
Clarice Orsini, spouse to Lorenzo de Medici
Lucrezia Donati, mistress to Lorenzo de Medici
Vincenzo di Lucca di Pistoia, merchant

TABLE OF CONTENTS

FOREWORD

Spiralling Reality (Poems choreographed from *Different Worlds*) was written in Florence, while living in the cradle of the Italian Renaissance. Home became an historical building in walking distance of the Piazza della Signoria, where the legendary sculptor Donatello was born. I was greeted, by a noble family, in front of his gigantic statue, Via San Egidio. Within its three-feet thick walls, some of the rooms were decorated by the great Bernardino Poccetti, the painter of the *Corridoio di Vasari*, an elevated enclosed passageway connecting the Uffizi (city offices) with the Medici's Palazzo Pitti. Today, the corridor exhibits the museum's famous collection of self-portraits from the Italian masters to the Flemish-Dutch school including Rubens, Rembrandt and their contemporary colleagues including, my own ancestor Gerard de Lairesse.

My *Nobile ospiti* (noble hosts), Donna Barbara Baldasseroni-Corsini and her daughter, Donna Vannozza bathed me in this unique *Cinquecento* ambiance. Their generous hospitality took me to their Tuscan estate, Querceto Baldasseroni –Panzano in Chianti, a splendid time of real inspiration and fairy-tale magic.

Back in the city, enjoying a chocolate nuts *Torta Medici*, I felt as if another timeline was calling, and I was unsure if my imagination had gone wild over the copious local dessert. Surrounding voices brought a title instantaneously:

The Medici Memento. The next day, guided uphill towards the Fattoria di Maiano I was struck by a most unusual event. I saw myself in Renaissance outfit galloping on a horse. I could do nothing but run behind this *fata morgana* (mirage). Halted, I almost froze in front of the closed gates of the Villa Medici in Fiesole.

Propelled to write, I returned for several visits, while I continued to develop an unexpected story based on real 1473 historical facts with twenty-first century chapters kicking into what would become a time travel novel. During an exciting nine months of visiting the vestiges of the Medici Family in Cafaggiolo, Careggi, and at their Via Larga home (now the Palazzo Medici Riccardi museum), the place I resonated with most, was Fiesole's ancient walls whispering their secrets into my eager ears.

Years of studying the *Art of Astrology* helped me to figure out many old manuscripts, books and letters and uncover hidden truths. Letters by Piero, *Il Gottoso*, the father of Lorenzo and Giuliano de Medici offered more insights as did the poetry by Lorenzo, Il Magnifico and the emotional works by Angelo Poliziano confirming the poet's deepest feelings for his mentor and lover.

An extensive survey by the Office of the Night shows that in Florence, homosexuality was not officially appreciated, even when not on public display despite being very much a part of daily life. The Renaissance artists or philosophers of the likes of da Vinci, Michelangelo, Botticelli or Poliziano are duly noted in those city records and all these prodigies were protected by the powerful Medici family.

Though on display in their artwork, these celebrated artists covered up their sexual preference well. The Maecenas of that Golden Age welcomed them into their homes, but many were simply abused like toys of the ruling elite, often still an unchanged fact of our present society. Those in power have often corrupted the world of entertainment for their own benefit.

Internationally, on the bigger political chessboard, incomprehensible decisions are made and we do not have the slightest idea of what is really the truth. Nothing is what it appears to be, and we can only set boundaries and discern for ourselves the truth we wish to live by. As such, this novel does unfold as a tapestry for the different realities created around us. The poetry of *Spiralling Reality*, my first book, is almost a prologue for this, my first novel.

Most chapters therefore offer a brief poetic excerpt with a hint at a theme addressed in that particular chapter.

It took me quite some years to gain the confidence to have the Medici Memento published. This novel is dedicated to all my friends who have encouraged me to never give up this project. My lasting gratitude to Colin Day, for your steady friendship and financial support to facilitate the editing, first with Patrick and Ana Gabriela, and principally by the Aussie magic of Adrienne Casey, an equally gifted painter who created the additional artwork! Rudi Devolder, since your exquisite work on *Spiralling Reality,* you remain a leading graphic artist and I am forever in your debt. Thank you Sean Stone for introducing the excellent Waterside Productions and their kind and always helpful Senior Publishing Associate Josh Freel. Lastly, my gratitude to Marc, Mari, Matthew and my loving hubby, James, for your unfaltering care and patience to keep me from Mercury-retrograde flavored anxiety attacks!

Healing is nothing more than reinterpreting
what you believe happened to you!

PROLOGUE. FIORENZA, 1469 PALAZZO DE MEDICI AT VIA LARGA

Dear Angelo,

You will forgive my Latin, unworthy to the educated eye! My writing will be less eloquent than any speech you will expect from me. Since our first encounter, we both felt we knew each other since ages. Therefore, it will be most appropriate that we have a more frequent correspondence. If it weren't for the ill health of such vernacular (and even here I fail in countless aspects) and for other good reasons, why don't we meet more frequently?

My brother Lorenzo had taken notice of your first letter to me last summer. Though very formal and less poetic than usual, he measured your vocabulary as most impressive. After all, you are but hardly a year younger than me. I love and admire my brother who only just turned twenty. He has knowledge and wisdom way beyond his years.

I have only turned fifteen, impatient to be sixteen next October. In his residency in Careggi, Piero di Cosimo de Medici, feeble and bed-ridden, usually forgets his sons' birthdays. But then of course like my grandfather Cosimo, he suffers greatly from gout, and he desires action from his immediate heir. I'm truly sorry for him and for the weight on Lorenzo's shoulders, and I am worried that Babo isn't going to make it through this year.

Lorenzo is now taking on so much work that there's hardly time to guide me when he has been like a mentor to me since early age. Will he disregard me – his best friend and brother? Even the simple progress of my horsemanship depends on him. You may recall, as childish as it may sound, that I do aspire to knighthood.

Did I mention that Lorenzo sent me off to meet the known astrologer Marco Farini, a man of rare wisdom? They had met at the residence of our friends, the Buontalenti. This Marco knows more about the stars than my forefathers knew about banking.

During an entire afternoon, I basked in this sage's pool of life experience. What he told me of both Lorenzo and of me personally is truly disquieting. Even before such intense an astrological reading I knew Lorenzo was destined for greatness. Yet Marco, an adept of Plato and Aristotle, confirmed that even I possess great potential.

As for the career at the Vatican my father projected for me, Marco confirmed it would not be the best option. From his reading, he concluded that I had a 'Scorpio-like' obsession with the fairer gender explaining that under the sign of Scorpio, passion often matches drama and more of a compulsive behaviour toward any gender. He is right about my tendencies to fantasize on numerous women, and it does appear to distract from my studies. My brother and I were mildly shocked by some of his disquieting statements about our careers and family.

Marco Farini who cited verses in both Greek and Latin, had compared our Medici family to the ancient power-hungry dynasties on a continent called Atlantis. He insisted that Lorenzo and I were born with exceptional leaders' abilities to influence and change our present society but that the planets indicated we also could end up as real offenders of the Tuscan laws. Our lives would be often in danger. Lorenzo had many doubts, but he also knew that the Vatican had taken astrology very much to heart. The Monarchy and the clergy were unwavering about this prophetic art; and wars were never fought without checking the planetary movements. Fortunately, you have greater talent to understand more of the art of reading the stars than I do.

The day our father passes, Lorenzo will need me beside him for how can any man possibly carry a republic? There is so much I still have to learn. Yet who will teach me when he starts to govern?

Well, forgive me for such long and selfish reflections. I am looking forward to our study lecture with Master Ficino, next Wednesday, at our Careggi residence. Marco Farini has been told about you and he will see you as soon as you both deem it possible. I must recommend his reading highly, for with help of the stars, your father's death must be decipherable! I only wish you the best and please you must not worry about any payment.

There's so much more to write about, but I wish this letter still be delivered tonight and my brother's servant is bringing it to you before our evening meal.

Most confidentially,

Your friend,

Giuliano di Piero de Medici.

Giuliano called upon the young man who was faithfully waiting in the hallway for his new task. Piero de Medici's son had told him to deliver the letter and to wait for an answer.

Back at his large desk where study material had piled up massively, Giuliano, like his brother Lorenzo, realized his interests and passions were extensive. They would both age quicker than their mother could foresee. He glanced at her portrait. That afternoon Lucrezia Tornabuoni returned from Rome with news for the forthcoming wedding between her firstborn and Clarice Orsini, and she would have the festivities planned carefully but elaborately.

1. FLORENCE, 2018 GIANLUCA

Squirming codes of intertwining wires,
unchecked by incoming voicemail
speaking louder than the buzzing discontentment
of troublemaking chips for
cryptographic methods wiping out, in depth,
all clarity in a worldwide network of sleeping minds.
(Masterminding Minds)

Any irritating situation accompanied by odd voices in his head was a warning to avoid the maddening crowds. The annoying *mal di testa* (headache) was like a pest for GianLuca's overactive mind. Migraines always returned when he got worried, even though he wasn't sure why he confused stories from his dream state with the present. Walking through Italy's past left him with a similar perfume as Louis XIV's Versailles at the King's exquisite gardens by Le Notre, the celebrated architect. He chuckled, feeling his collar too tight, his pants too loose and his crown absent; the subconscious always plays a game and he was aware of the attention he gave it.

In the big cities, he felt the need to escape from what his dad used to call a nine-to-five invasion. GianLuca's rescue remedy was simply to avoid crowds. He'd sit on a bench in the park or on the grass chatting up his own shadow. At first rather anomalous, he got used to it because it seemed so real. In the mood for socializing, he was drawn to a charming restaurant close to Piazza Santo Spirito, in Via Seragli, yes, the one that served the infamous *Torta Medici* (Medici pie), all nuts and chocolate.

Today, he was open to the idea of one of those pro-social jaunts. He sat there happily looking at the white table cover, framed by the sprinkles around the Chianti spots in a dance of capricious breadcrumbs, scattered around his first and last glass. Pepper and salt unravelled their Disney-like playfulness as, *'the couple that had heard all others complain about spending their life savings on blooming pharmaceutics, while they, Mr Pepper & Mrs Salt, well, they would be forever happy and healthy, they would never divorce, not like the clients that shook them so violently, dangling them over prying pasta plates.'* The toothpicks, by contrast remained stifled, unmoved by all the drama, and rarely, if ever made their ever-dwindling point in their enigmatic existence.

He popped out of his cartoon scenario. Since his childhood, words had foreshadowed unpredictable scenarios and he often thought he had missed the boat in not becoming a successful author. Gone were the days he would value those simple pleasures; joyful meals and laughter amidst cloudy tobacco rings flirting with the no-smoking sign right next to the once vanilla-cream painted toilet door. No more 'no-smoking' signs ... anywhere.

He felt better, and in a way that was obvious only to him, his shadow had now departed and GianLuca finished his meal, quietly watching the bartender's wife in front of him, as she ever so proudly sliced today's orange peel crusty cake. He had turned down the whipped cream, homemade of course, but she generously added it anyway. Her hands on her hips demanded respect and obedience. A real character she was, straight out of a loud Sofia Loren-Marcello Mastroianni scene, the movies his parents used to love.

With the tiny *café espresso,* words of deserved praise rained down. Four generations of cooks were celebrated in a family that was revered by even the International Guide Resto. The 4-fork rating was awarded for, 'every meal orchestrated with the wealth of a da Vinci-like inventiveness.'

She smiled away the honours, and for a moment GianLuca was fearful of the mad crush she seemed to have developed since the first time he had visited this celebrated eatery, months ago now. That day, she had crashed into him, cake and all, berries dripping from her generously welcoming bosom and right into his summer shirt. It clearly had been an excuse to unbutton that designer shirt right there, in her kitchen, whilst cleaning it all up in detail, ogling all the sweetness of his chest whilst forgetting the bulk on her husband's waistline. She loved a handsome foreigner: *finché è un vero uomo* (as long as he's a real man).

I wonder if such an overbearing nature stems from their family tradition, he had thought as she had disrobed his Hawaiian shirt minimizing the last bits of chocolate from his youthful looking torso, ever so slowly.

She didn't ask him to do the same, but he guessed
than the present showcase to invoke plenty of his childh
this local beauty turned around, no veils were dropp
mouth to an empty coffee cup...

The deep, smoky voice roared, "... *un altro caffè macchiato* (another espresso with a cloud of milk)!"

And it reminded him he drank too much of the dark stuff and yes, that little cup did get emptied in an instant. She knew his smile confirmed and the barman giggled as his wife kicked her hip in place with self-confessed lips pouting to her eyelashes' chorus, an operatic happening. The caffeine came around a second time, and his eyes wanted to sing a hymn to that trembling cleavage; could he turn back to being fourteen once more? Her nipples had hardened under her tight apple-green summer dress, embroidered with a lace matching the *Osteria's* (Italian eating establishment's) tablecloths, delightful as a Mediterranean coast's stand-up dessert, another treasure unrivalled in all of Tuscany.

He shrugged once again. A few whistles from the younger guys at the bar echoed the *padrona's* (mistress's) provocative step forward while one of them covered his crotch amusingly in shy pretence. "*Prego* (please), *il conto per favore.*" GianLuca's Italian was nearly perfect, so she thought. With his gentle voice, he added a piercing look over her almost strapless shoulder. The bill took a quick peek from underneath the silver nails contrasting those podgy fingers. For a moment, he expected a kiss. He quickly ruffled some Euro bills from his pocket; "*Grazie tanto* (thanks so much)," forgetful of the size of the tip with a habitual gaze in her sharply outlined dark eyes. As usual, she pouted her sultry lips, for a moment regretting age and then another goodbye.

That wave again, a kind of exotic sensuality pulling me right down to the chair and then I'm pretending to pick up the book I hadn't forgotten, not yet.

"*Arrivederci* (see you later)," he smiled.

2. FIORENZA, 1469 LUCREZIA

Where is there ...
another mirror;
mirror off the wall,
who is the neediest of us all? (Mirror off the Wall)

Of all Rome's wealthiest and most influential families, Lucrezia Tornabuoni had clearly chosen Clarice Orsini, her first son's future bride for all the right political reasons including a maternal uncle at the Vatican, the politically savvy Cardinal Latino. It all sounded too good to be true and of course it was clearly one of his mother's uniquely calculated manoeuvres *cum laude*! But how would such a manipulation affect Giuliano and his relationship to his brother after the engagement to a young woman from such a prominent family?

I guess mama's decisive factor is our father's health, Giuliano had mused. Maybe all that attention will put their wishes for my own non-existent clerical ambitions into an impenetrable drawer. No Vatican for me. He shivered while his mind wandered off to the last poem sent just a few days ago by Fiammetta, the charming daughter of the Buontalenti family he indeed fancied.

Rome nor the Vatican proved of any interest to Giuliano! His love for traveling was unfit for a Cardinal's cap, his charmer's ambition an inhibition to all. More, it meant a life of pretence while fishing for the pope's throne as required by each dynasty. All great Italian families wanted a high priest at this sacred court of holy corruption. He recognized Lorenzo had accepted Clarice as his wife to secure a powerful alliance with a 'royal' family, rich with many estates in the Kingdom of Naples. It was just another traditional tactical move on the Italian chessboard.

Giuliano just needed to talk to his mother. Lucrezia was indeed a true role model for the whole family and one of the loveliest women in Florence: *Questa*

Donna è un *esempio* (this woman is exemplary). Extremely preoccupied with her husband's health and the future of the entire Medici family, she sought no excuse for her extended visits at the baths of Volterra securing her own healing before taking care of the Medici political dynasty. While she adored Giuliano, she remained the most influential with Lorenzo. Mother and son shared the same intellectual and strategic objectives for the grandeur of their family tradition and future history. They aspired beyond state and country.

Certainly, this family has enough health problems, Giuliano reflected on the hereditary gout his grandfather and his own father Piero had suffered, and all men seemed threatened by. *It will be safer to spend as much time as possible in nature training my body like a true knight and to discipline my mind like a Greek sage.*

He suddenly spoke out loud and to his own surprise with much dramatic flair throwing his arms around like some athletic warrior. And did he ever have time to be a happy youth and not being groomed as another Medici family treasure? His mind had wandered off.

I guess if I want my mother's attention, I had better wait for her in the chapel. She never fails to visit the Madonna before even addressing the family.

It was cooler in the courtyard and he swiftly unfastened his cape, walking up the stairs to contemplate in front of yet another family gem, the Chapel of the Magi. This magnificent place of worship was a true *capolavoro,* a true masterpiece.

It had taken nearly ten years for the widely reputed and respected Benozzo Gozzoli, Fra Angelico's pupil, to paste the walls with the wet plaster before glorifying the power and wealth this family had acquired over the last century, through the most vivid and miraculous looking frescoes. An immense work had emerged, one that had fascinated feverishly the little five-year old Giuliano, then secretly hidden behind the scaffold while the workers brought all images to life with their brushes dipped in multi-coloured painting pots. He spent so much time there that Donna Lucrezia got worried her youngest son would develop a taste for the art of the canvas.

To divert his mind, she got him a donkey. Recreating the stature-riding showcase his grandfather Cosimo was known for in Florence, the young boy was admired by many during his humbly playful outings through the city. The little Giuliano imagined himself to be a knight in shining armour, equipped with stories from the Crusades as told by his illustrious *nonno* (grandfather) on their weekly visits. Parading straight like royalty on a proud stallion his sisters accompanied him in the Florentine streets, giving allure to the little prince in the making.

In front of the chapel's altar, Giuliano once again fixated on Filippo Lippi's *Madonna* lingering in a self-imposed silence. Shining in innocence and lacklustre expression, devoid of all sensuality; that was the perpetual feeling he got when he studied these painted virgins, galactic beauties and virtuous muses to these great masters. He envisioned the very essence of the word 'virgin' and remained stunned by such unearthly purity radiating from her eyes. The theme of the Immaculate Conception scratched the surface. Was this really possible, a visiting angel or a symbol of a visitor from another world? Since an early age, of course influenced by Cosimo, his beloved grandfather, he had been enticed to study a mythology where the gods had always been very active in the field of procreation.

Before his engagement to Clarice Orsini, Lorenzo and his brother were notorious for their nightly outings and visits to more than one married woman. He grumbled at his own impure thoughts invading the family's chapel, the holiest place in the Casa Vecchia. Fondling women's breasts was a balm to his libido. He would not go to confession and for a brief moment he dozed off, wrapped in the arms of a mysterious beauty apparently escaped from one of the frames.

3. PARIS, 2018 FLORIAN & ISABEL

Your library has enveloped in that foreign morning mist,
all of the mysteries I wanted to invent from your gloved hands (The Screen)

The library certainly looked overloaded, and its high walls seemed ready to break down in an avalanche of ancient editions of manuscripts, rare books of history and some original hardcovers.

Maybe this décor (suitable for a play featuring 'a Sherlock Holmes lost in time'), left Florian de Trèsloin, bathing in a superb afternoon sunlight, on the second floor of this ancient mansion on the Isle St Louis. It had once belonged to his distant grand uncle, but was now his own favourite, well-hidden, safe haven. If anything, he could live right here, his nose stuck in another literary masterpiece every day of his life.

When Isabel strolled in, sipping on an exotic flavoured iced tea, he paid no attention. It was obvious his focus was kept limited to the subject he just dived into. She wondered if he had forgotten their meeting about the trip that they were about to take or was he in an AI travel mode? After all, since they started Time Travel Program Inc. (TPP), life had taken a very different turn. Suddenly, time traveling had become their priority. How could they convey their research worldwide, to help science understand the past to forward the future?

She peeked over his shoulder at the book and gently pulled his earlobe. No reaction whatsoever. "You cannot deny the importance that Cosimo de Medici gave Marsilio Ficino, if we make it to the exact year 1473; maybe you'll meet him in a priest's robe."

He looked up and realized the sarcasm in her remark. But she wasn't flirting; not with that look she usually gave him when you 'know what's next'.

No, her mockery had a touch of seriousness to it even if the silken blouse was prettily unbuttoned.

"Well, we don't exactly know when he was ordained now, do we?" He hit the ball ever so gently back into her court and she grinned.

"How in the world was he capable in that period, to be so eloquent, so precise with the translations he made for Cosimo, his illustrious patron?"

"Indeed," she continued, "and that was just Plato. What about that endlessly long study on triple Hermes?"

He chuckled. "Triple Hermes you called him, like a double espresso? Ha-ha, not very Ficino." They both laughed but *The Corpus Hermeticum* could not be joked about for long. Its ancient knowledge, comparable to the Hebrew Torah and the Kabbalah had commanded much attention since centuries before Christ. "If the gods had delegated Hermes from their Olympus to the Nile, Thoth, his Egyptian counterpart must have merged as an alchemical twin." He responded vigorously. "I remember so well how Miss Young taught us the difference between the magical realms, the new-born alchemy and of course our capacity to bypass our own reality as we believe it and move on and into our own divinity!"

"In *The Journey of the Soul*, the explanation as the gods seemed to have channelled to our humans, may well be full of lies." Isabel threw in her five cents.

"Now show me your sparkling wisdom of the universal mind and how we are making that big adventure pay off our years of hard work."

"*Tout à fait d'accord mon petit chou (*I totally agree my little cabbage)." she smiled.

"I am not 'petit', and I am certainly not your 'cabbage,' *ma Princesse* (my Princess). It's time to grab a bite and finalize our plan. Have you decided to make a stop in Geneva or to get straight to Florence?" Florian asked, "Is your glamorous half-sister still living in Geneva?"

Isabel nodded as she got up and the thought of seeing Elizabeth von Weitweg, maybe the only family left, made her smile. They had no contact for decades. She avoided losing her focus, a seasoned super model crossing her legs while walking towards the windows overlooking the river Seine and Paris's royal treasure, Isle St Louis.

She was pleased that her friendship with Florian had never suffered from any romantic disasters and he always remained the perfect gentleman whenever she brought around yet another girlfriend. As for their professional relationship, Florian was thriving, and she trusted him to be once again the perfect navigator on their upcoming voyage.

It had taken less than a decade to find out he was able to create a program altering time.

His shaman uncle had guided him well and from his teenage years he understood we live in a free will zone with the option and ability to jump through time. How to correct the time continuum and find the right equations to return ... was indeed the key that very few could master. On more than one continent, deeply hidden government programs had tried; mostly unsuccessfully.

But together, Florian and Isabel well, they had it well-planned and to them this time traveling adventure could change the course of history. Florian opened a small case and took out two pairs of over-sized glasses, an Italian designer-look for sure, yet certainly a lot more than that. They had dropped their pink-coloured *lunettes de soleil* (sunglasses) way back, in the good old college days when, together with their best friend, Jean-Luc Médecin, they had seen the enemy hidden in plain sight.

4. FIORENZA 1469 GIULIO

Hi me, how are you?
Still bragging about how great you are – have been – will be?
Oops, bet that's a weightless lifter of truth's fifth Chianti glass?
Oh, you don't mind. Good. (Talking drunk with truth)

Theatrical graces framed Lucrezia's noticeable entrances, a courtly manner simply following her thoughts into the monarchy she wasn't born into and all audiences were convinced she was a *principessa* (princess).

"Giulio! Figlio mio, sei qui (My son, you are here)."

"That is such a wonderful surprise. No doubt, you were praying for the improving health of your father," she gesticulated in her familiar grand manner.

"Piero did send word to Lorenzo that he seemed to be feeling a lot better and he will dine with us. He will no doubt speak to his sons about the drill worthy of a future ruler of the city," she continued, "and you have returned and well, your looks are of real health!" Giuliano smiled, "Yes mama ... matching your blush." He had her almost bewitched with his cheerful beaming. She shivered at his delicate princely approach and refined touch.

Holding both his hands tightly: *How handsome he is becoming, my little Giuliano; no longer just a little prince! What a pity that Lorenzo cannot compare to this beauty, a beauty that is of course so similar to my own. Oh, Santa Madonna, there's no second to my vanity! Thoughts that should take me to confession!*

She shrugged, embarrassed at her silly girlish reflections. An instant prayer to be pardoned, muffled by the ancient walls while she scanned the chapel; no one had overheard her insubstantial, fickle thoughts. "Yes, I have spent two days in the magnificent baths close to Volterra," she answered with a big smile, whimsically unbuttoning her emerald-green velvet cape with royal gesture.

"I feel so replenished, with more youthful energy and vital strength than ever."

As they descended into the courtyard, she told him more of her trip. And then with even more excitement in her voice she announced that Giuliano would be the honoured knight to travel to Rome. He would bring back his brother's bride for the June festivities prior to the wedding in the Cathedral of Florence.

"You mean my brother isn't making this trip?" Giuliano asked, astounded.

His mother shook her head. "No. He really has to take care of the family business and we must prepare a long list of guests! Ah, what a grand assembly with ambassadors and nobility, yes even royalty is expected!" she announced in a singing voice, extending her arm movements in glowing pride. "But run along my sweet Giuliano and go and see your father. Tell him the good news while I go back up and refresh. I almost forgot to thank the Madonna for my safe return and this exalting wedding celebration."

She kicked her robes behind her short but muscular legs to glide back in front of the gorgeous saintly painting. *That beautiful face, oh Lippi,* she thought conceitedly as only she could do, while kneeling down like the best of performers at the height of all Greek tragedy; *I know I inspired you and you may have even loved me more than God could allow!*

Giuliano walked the long stairway up but found his father sleeping with a snore that might keep up the entire household. He slouched back down in a contemplative mood.

I guess it's an honour and I do love traveling. Maybe I'll get a new horse for the occasion he mused with youthful hope. *And maybe I'll meet a few Roman beauties on the way.*

A low voice brought him back to earth. "Master, master!" Bruno, their young servant had returned and proudly held up a small paper scroll, bowing with melodramatic flair. Giuliano gently thanked him and quickly opened it. As he had guessed, the message came from the young Poliziano. Appropriately dramatic in style, it read:

Blessed Brother to Lorenzo, Magnificent Giuliano,

Oh, kindred writer of such well-hidden poetry of the heart, with your warmth most touchingly represented in the simplicity of your prose. Blame yourself not now, nor ever for I am in debt to all of your family.

That blessed moment my mentor brought me to your family, just days after the horrible, premeditated killing of my father. Here I was drowning amidst battleships of emotions when he who had seeded my soul had forever left. My mentor was convinced your genitori (parents) would protect me and indeed they did.

When I lifted my eyes upon your youthful, majestic beauty, I knew our friendship would be sealed as the greatest gift I could ever receive. But how would I deserve such honour, to be adopted into such an illustrious family, the pantheon of our own gods?

Oh, forgive me my dearest Giuliano, for I write in such metaphors, Latin's spicy sisters, a language the gods may have bestowed upon me in this literary land where I reside in permanent bliss.

If you wish, I will gladly bring corrections to your own written Latin, with only the slight shortcoming in that you have dedicated yourself, as your great brother Lorenzo has, to the splendour of the most colourful of Tuscan vernacular.

As beautiful the latter may appear to be, there isn't always a perfect congeniality between them.

Thank you for your suggestion of this meeting and your intervention with such a Master of the Art of the Stars. Now forgive me for the brevity of my letter but your servant silently pledged my patience, and my hand does not write as quickly as yours, for in your honour, I like to make each phrase as beautiful as a miniature design from the accademia (the academy). Again, allow me to remind you that the lecture of Master Ficino was to be in two weeks, but it will not take place because we will all be on the Piazza Santa Croce, in a trance admiring your courageous brother at the tournament. I wouldn't miss it for anything in the world.

Nothing will please me more than to await your answer as I look forward to our next encounter. May all the Planets in the Universe bring you good fortune and may Apollo and his twin sister, the Moon Goddess, take you on their Chariot into the sweetest of realms and illuminating dreams.

Your devoted friend,
Angelo Ambrogini.

Giuliano's laugh brashly crashed into the last paragraph and then he read it again. He now realized he had not given any attention to . . . *Lorenzo's tournament!*

Oh, thank you my sweet poet for reminding me! He sighed. *How could I forget? It is in a fortnight and I haven't talked to Lorenzo to ask if he needed help. Of course, Lorenzo has it all planned and organized, as always. He's working like a horse pulling our Medici family carriage. I mustn't complain, instead I must help and assist him.*

He put the letter away, briskly jumping up the stairs to his room.

5. FLORENCE, 2018 GALESSA

No saint I was born, nor free of longing have I been, yet you shot others with cupidity and in spite of all venomous animosity, their hunger lessened not. (Envy Not)

Galessa moved like a dancing witch. With the tilt of her head, gloriously superior to all foreign command, she put the money on the counter and not where most males would have predicted. The cashier never missed a moment and by then, Flavio's eyes had followed the entire scene into her cleavage, one that had caused a stir in many a customer. But she was after all *la mia moglie* (my spouse).

Since day one he had treasured and trusted his woman, her humour, her southern sexiness, her prehistoric 'Hollywood-y' jokes, her laughter; it had never changed and would it ever? Jealousy wasn't a card he had played even with his overweight belly he knew his wife didn't want another husband nor a boy toy. He hadn't dreamed either that the great movie director Federico Fellini would come by their restaurant where she could have inspired him effortlessly. He gasped in a gentle manner; his eyes as enamoured as they were that first day.

"Galessa, you knooow," Flavio sighed with exaggerated puffing, "she's way overrrr seksie seeksty!" In a fat Tuscan slang, he repeated that she is still the most popular item on the menu, of course one she conceived all by herself, since the day they re-opened the restaurant.

GianLuca had finally closed the door behind him, a chill up his spine, he wondered what it would be like to be over sixty right now and take that woman right on the kitchen table amongst the yellow long-tailed zucchini, stark red *pepperoncini* (chilli peppers) and those shiny *piccolini pomodore* (tiny cherry tomatoes).

A summer breeze above the dirty green Arno River gently caressed his face. Almost twisting an ankle on the ancient pavement, he stumbled out of a familiar fantasy, fresh as any pubescent fancying waitresses. He laughed out loud and the little *nonna* (grandmother) crossing his path stared at him with accusing eyes that couldn't diminish his happiness when reflecting his college days of dating young waitresses, open shirt seductions with shiny pecs and improvised six-packs. His nostrils gave way to an itch and a busty tourist wetted a pair of pouting lips, flirting openly at his moving hand.

His pace quickened while he scanned an almost dried-out riverbed below his favourite Florentine bridge: the Ponte alla Carraia. A sweaty stream trickled at equal speed under his burgundy-red leather backpack. He walked even quicker to avoid the daily, massive afternoon invasion at the Piazza della Signoria where stood the world's most famous copy: the statue of the 'perfectly circumcised male,' Michelangelo's *David.* Perfect proportions and looks, envied as from a screen star; but does attractiveness equate with happiness?

He gestured at the tourists that nearly kicked him over. This David introduced the Piazza della Signoria to the herds of foreigners, admiring what had once been the seat of Florentine civic government, a symbol for the defence of civil liberties embodied by the Renaissance republic. Threatened from all sides by many powerful rival states, under the early hegemony of the Medici family, the eyes of David gleamed with a warning glare towards Rome.

GianLuca slowed down his steps and his slightly heavier breathing had stopped as in a slow-motion promenade on Via Maglia Bechi. Since his very early childhood, he had been enamoured with Fiorenza. Once again, the Basilica of Santa Croce was rising regally, and in front, the gigantic statue of Dante, or *Durante Alighieri,* the poet of the 'Divina Commedia', had turned his back to the most stunning thirteenth century edifice, the largest Franciscan church in the world and a religious town hall for Italy's elite families.

His father, a true historical connoisseur, had introduced him to such a rich past instructing his son personally till he had left for college. He had learned how this unusually shaped cathedral was built like an Egyptian cross, and in the nineteenth century it was transformed into a mausoleum for those who served the powers that be! Their imposing pantheon of painted and sculpted creations by Giotto, Vasari, Donatello, Canova and Brunelleschi housed the tombs of the legendary Michelangelo, Machiavelli, Galileo and Rossini; a loud cry out in an unequalled synthesis of art and historically manipulated spirituality. Their works, paid for by a glorified monarchy or a head of state, remained a living proof of the wealthy paying their outstanding debts to their political gods and/or respected and favoured 'elite' servants.

GianLuca reflected on the loving attention from both his parents when, as often was the case, in a midday hot summer sun, there was that flash. He had experienced it before as in a haunting dream. Some kind of a stroke landed him in maybe a superhero Hollywood production crossing the thick veil of existence. It threw him off, far away from where humans have no access and it pinched him right in the occiput area the upper neck.

And there he was, lost in broad daylight, alone in the square with a woman who looked every inch a Renaissance Venus. He rubbed his eyes again and again, as seconds became minutes. He moved in slow motion, trembling as if he were in a dream state induced by ayahuasca, the South American psychoactive brew. And the square at Santa Croce now appeared strangely empty.

Did my head start spinning because I'm getting overheated? He adjusted his neck with a loud crack, like welcoming a much-needed chiropractic intervention. But reality seemed absent. He had rubbed his eyes more than once and of course the square remained empty. But what kept him spinning in all directions in disquieting confusion while spiralling down?

The square fragmented and transformed itself, so very differently than only moments ago. Now an overpopulated piazza full of loud merchants in eclectic colourful attire painted an escape into another dream. With more stumbling, nearly fainting, he couldn't stand up, yet he seemed embraced by Venus's touch, unveiling all sensuous recollections from days of old, yes, a very old Renaissance distilled.

Sliding down to both knees, emerald green and aquamarine silks had covered his eyes, swathing him in a golden chorus of coded particles, with billions of tiny stars scratching an invisible surface. *Sweep me down on a lustrous staircase shining in all of its strangest gleaming like the abyss in a dream lived thousands of times before.* In that chorus of tiny voices and angelic whispers, in all absence of a familiar world, that choir stuck to this head, till, on a broader stage in one instance... all lights switched off.

6. FIORENZA, 1469 JOUST

I'm brains, before I'm boobs.
Like most of my genetic kind (BBB)

"Vedi! Bravissimi" (Watch! Bravo)

"There they are!" A handful of kids repeatedly shouting from the carmine and beet-red tiled roofs around the Borgo dei Greci attracted more than one disapproving eye.

"How did they get up there?" a heavy breasted wet nurse cried out loud while pulling her locks into a more 'elegant' hairstyle, so she thought.

"Come down from the bloody roof you rascals, before my mistress gets the *bargello's* (prison's) guards to throw you all in Fiorenza's favourite jail!" another local of the 'better kind' added to the palette of rambling delights by picking her left nostril amusingly.

The streets were spiralling with excitement and people were largely hanging out of their windows. It had been years since this wealthy family spent their gold on a big public festivity. In celebration of the marriage of the son of Piero di Cosimo de Medici, the Tuscan capital's future yet uncrowned Prince, this was indeed a long-awaited event.

"There she is, there she is!" A full populus chorus had claimed the Tuscan beauty as their own. The same high choirboys' voices now lost themselves in the crowd streaming towards the Santa Croce Piazza.

"Si, eccola è veramente lei (It is really her)?"

"Yes, there she is! It's her all right," the two harlots loudly confirmed while they mumbled vulgar comparisons of the madonna's waistline. Chewing some kind of repulsive plant that couldn't have been tobacco, they ran as quickly towards the square as their fat little feet could carry them, waving their chubby arms in an over-excited manner.

"The queen of the tournament," another one of the 'lilies of the night' screamed. But the busty one with the huge red lips and the blue green made-up eyes declaimed loudly the operatic effects to her friend. "He's marrying an Orsini, but the rumour goes he's topping la Lucrezia, La Donati ... ha-ha, they're all the same those rich pigs!"

"Such filthy language," cried the red-head, laughing as she matched it with a multi-coloured spit.

"... Holy cow that bitch! You know she's also doing it with that Niccolo." The fat one loudly roared, sneezing forcefully at least three times and nearly into her friend's face. Her podgy fingers vowed a 'V' as if to confirm all that her last words were the truth and nothing but the truth (so help her ... an equally gossipy neighbour who only last night gaudily told her the story!)

She spat as far as her lips could propel her venom. "Hey there, you slut! Watch it ... that's my face." Ferociously fixing her greasy hair as if she herself was the bride to be, her spluttering without any fixed target had yet to be stopped. "Do you believe it? When I was younger, and of course a lot slimmer ... I had him once, that Niccolo, ha-ha, years ago and ..."

"Shut up *befana* (witch), the only man you ever did is that disgusting pig of a husband of yours ... when he is not banging your neighbour's daughter and ..."

"*Vaffanculo maledetta, faccia da anatra* (fuck you, your damned, ugly duck face)." That dismissed all further lack of evidence, at least for her. The husband? Well, he wasn't worth thinking about, not for one instant.

"Look at her! *Sei stupido, inconsciente* (You are stupid, unaware)! La Donati, she is a beauty and you're a chubby, jealous and stupid *vacca* (cow)," her only friend sniggered, enjoying all previously unexpressed disrespect.

More and more people pushed to get closer to the throne area where a resplendent, goddess-like Lucrezia Donati had indeed taken the honorary seat of the 'Lady of the Tournament', while a parade of no less than eighteen of the most eligible young bachelors from the finest Florentine and Tuscan families drew more and more women to the square.

Three young priests tried to greet the agitated citizens in their customary way. While bumping into many, one elderly lady enjoyed a rambunctious landing in their arms. She grinned but felt a bit funny thanking the Holy

Trinity. Wittily sniggering 'my Father' and more witty responses brought light to their devotedly serious faces.

"Thank you, you young Saints," she said with dry mockery, "... for saving an older woman from kissing Fiorenza's bricks."

And while she rearranged her robes, two of the brothers gently gathered the bread and fruit back into her basket. With twinkling eyes, she unrepented her jolly remarks with all the charm born of a lifetime of feeding the nest of the too many children she had never asked for.

"When *I* got married, ah, now sixty years ago, like the Orsini girl, I was as young or even younger, I think sixteen." She shook the dust from her dress. "I must say, I can't remember much now, ha-ha, but I was as pretty." She stabbed her right foot with force onto the cobblestones till it hurt, "But I married a man from this town, and I gave him seven daughters and five sons," she yelled out loud.

"Now for that greedy 'Medici family'... our daughters aren't good enough any longer! Wait, those bankers think that an alliance with the richest families from Rome will save them from their destiny! We know better, don't we? Ha-ha, we do, don't we ... ugh ... hey Father, has God betrayed those of modest living?" The black-robed trio stepped back, astounded at the little brittle *nonna* (grandmother) running along back home, uninterested in the bread and games that would keep the masses quiet.

"So it is, and she is right indeed. Remember our Holy Father never bestowed a cardinal's hat to a Medici." One of the pastors nodded but his smug voice was quickly washed away in an abrupt explosion of trumpets and enthusiastic screams. All three heads turned around to a distant festivity growing into a loud commotion in honour of the most influential family in their city.

In a whirlpool of extravagantly embroidered standard-bearers depicting stories of flowered nymphs and mythical animals, elegant heralds, feisty trumpeters and musicians from all parts of Italy, all visitors and citizens were wearing their best and most extravagant dress. Children of all ages intertwined with their concerned mothers attempting to keep them at their side, while a few broad-smiling soldiers gently moved in and brought some order to the daylong festivities. In the midst of so much gaiety and applause, the roaring throng welcomed the bravest of knights in their most glittering armour. Many garnered admiring sighs for their feathered helmets and for the finest of horses, some especially commissioned by Lorenzo, a precious gift from the *Duc of Urbino* in Naples, bred in the healthiest of acclimatized stables close to the Neapolitan court.

"The horses! Look at those horses; and they're wearing dresses with pearls and diamonds, and crowns!" some of the children shouted, their astounded little voices getting louder and louder. These were magnificent stallions in ornamental velvets, trimmed with gemstones and the emblem of each horseman's family. At the end of the line of eager young knights, Lorenzo de Medici appeared sedate on a charger, another personal gift from the King of Naples. His face, fearless and proud, shone below a black velvet cap with a big octahedron diamond, and rubies and plumes of golden thread. He wore a white silk cape ornately embroidered with French lilies, precious stones and gold. His scarf, embellished with hand painted roses and his personal spirited motto, *Le Temps Revient* (Time Returns) caught the rays of the sun as if Jupiter himself had come down from Olympus to consecrate the event in Lorenzo's honour.

The standard carried in front, featured a golden sun and a rainbow on white and purple taffeta – painted by no one less than Andrea Verrocchio. Lorenzo's motto 'time returns' and 'centuries were renewed' suggested perhaps this elitist family simply repeats the past? For Lorenzo, a golden age had just started, but he was not eager to repeat anyone's past.

Pages and servants had prepared his armour, yet another exceptional present from the Duke of Milan. Preceded by his standard bearer holding up his personal homage to the Lady of the Tournament, Lorenzo proudly acknowledged how great popularity had now become his due. Cosimo's grandson could not deny that this glorifying event was set up to show off this most privileged son, to each citizen and to his most powerful allies and enemies.

An entire crowd excitedly applauded their new heroes' scintillating entrance. Lorenzo was riding right behind his good friend Dionigi Pucci, himself one of the favourites of this long awaited *giostra* (tournament*)* for which Lorenzo had paid no less than 10,000 gold florins out of the family's treasury. In the contest he wore a helmet with three tall blue feathers and a huge diamond that shone from his magnificent shield. To keep the animals well-balanced, his two main horses wore silver-engraved harnesses weighing over a hundred pounds, all of the design by celebrated artist, Antonio Pollaiulo.

"A king, he is truly a king," many agreed fully admiring the Medici's first son's striking presence. "Like his grandfather, Pater Patriae, he too is humble and he is generous!" they cried like a Greek chorus. Not only the female audience was galvanized by Lorenzo's charismatic persona and athletic appearance, but so too were the many of his grandfather's admirers who had come to support their new hero. The family of the young prince knew only too well that the *popolo* (people) did not live without heroes. If you want to rule them, you had better live in their highest esteem. That instant they witnessed that Lorenzo had indeed become their hero.

Meanwhile, Giuliano had joined an exclusive group of citizens who had accompanied his brother to the *Piazza* (plaza). Before the tournament commenced, he seated himself between his mother and his friend Angelo, as authorized by Lucrezia. It was an amicable but tender touch as he took the young poet's arm. She knew how sensitive Angelo was since the recent murder of his father.

Never without premeditation, his mum thought of her clever move. Once a Medici always a Medici! If he has to have a friend of his age, he might as well benefit from him. Angelo has such astounding Latin that it will well serve our youngest. But what if one day he does get elected Cardinal? Lucrezia had contemplated and she had conveyed the same thought to her husband. We are a privileged family after all, Grazie Madre Santa (Thank you Holy Mother!)

But the surging sea of people hungry for entertainment, watched in a trance. Unruly, and unknowing of the veiled visions their superior leaders were building, they entered the trap of bread and games! They discussed loudly, compared forcefully and admired the power by which the knights fought their way through the many turns, scoring points without shedding a drop of blood. The runt of the family had raised his voice in support of his brother. It was obvious though that there were stronger contenders for the gold than Lorenzo. Giuliano more than once held his breath, yet some kind of magical aura kept Lorenzo on his horse at each forceful attack. Next to a very concerned Lucrezia, a glowing Angelo remained convinced that his hero would win this tournament.

"He is Mars, he's Apollo," Angelo kept repeating in Giuliano's ear while remaining in total awe. "I am convinced he'll win. He's a true god," he had bellowed in ecstasy. Not everyone had shared that view. And throughout that day a few envious members from the Pazzi family, Florence's second wealthiest, were hoping that only the improbable would happen ... if Lorenzo could be massacred in an accident before his marriage was celebrated in June, the chance for his family to gain in popularity would be greatly reduced.

But food and wine had swept every citizen off their feet and this grand spectacle was unequalled in elegance and craft, a magic trick for all of Florence. Most knights demonstrated great courage and strength during this sporting and not savage event, and Lorenzo received the glorious Martian helmet taking the winner to an Olympian height of power and beauty.

While Giuliano comforted his brother for his unyielding love of the beautiful Lucrezia Donati, his sixteen-year-old future wife, Clarice and her sisters were in Rome religiously praying for Lorenzo's protection and victory at the. But no visitor would come from Tuscany until it was decided that Giuliano would ride Lorenzo's winning horse to Rome ... appropriately the stallion gifted by the Orsini family friend, the King of Naples. Giuliano would escort Clarice, his future sister-in-law and her large entourage of family, attendants, and maids-of-honour to the most celebrated of wedding banquets that Tuscany's capital of Fiorenza would ever come to know.

7. PARIS, 2018 ISABEL

... and the sun has shone since hours
On the layers of your reddish hair.
And I am still watching the painting come to life.
Again and again ... (Your Lips)

There was no reason Isabel Lieverkussen wanted to ever let go of his hand and Florian felt exactly the same. The Notre-Dame cathedral took on a mystical guise and the left bank suddenly seemed the most romantic place on earth. The Seine ran her undisturbed waves lightly in the full moonlight. The *bateaux mouches* (tourist boats) were absent, and all the tourists were somewhere hidden in the City of Light's manifold hotels. When they looked in each other's eyes, everything faded away into a nothingness that might make time traveling a holiday entertainment. Earlier that evening, after their favourite soup, his *crème de tomates* and her *soupe à l'oignon*, and of course, some Pinot Noir and French cheeses, they had studied different maps of the Renaissance streets of Florence, or Fiorenza as it was known in the 14th and 15th centuries.

Isabel had obtained the architect's plan of the Medici Villa in Via Larga. The original buyers, the Riccardi family and later the most recent owner had made countless changes. Florian had access to an unusual computer program used by MI6; one he had helped to build. He still had a few good friends in the London 'higher intelligence' milieu, who allowed them to calculate and compare the time and distance for the travels between the Tuscan capital and the Fiesole hills they planned to visit. There would be horses – no cars and of course no traffic jams.

They smiled at the extraordinary designs of the first 'time travel seats' that Florian's decades of work had produced. Yet – they would transport the apparatus via the simplest of ways.

"The advantage of remaining friends with your ex," Isabel joked, "of course can bring a lot of surprises in this century – like a big van with dark windows." He loved her for her zealous approach to their 'duo show' of creating the travel program that would once again take them to places they felt familiar with. This trip would provide them with the necessary key to advance their agenda and even if they imagined there could be some controversy and unexpected hardships, they were as confident as an 'Avengers' revival after Patrick McNee and Diana Riggs had enchanted the 1960's TV public. She yanked him out of his reflective mode with some funny high kicks.

"Just when you thought you were the only one with a few friends in influential positions," she joked.

"This will be quite a journey," they both said at the same time and once again broke out laughing.

"Let's finish the Pinot," he said as they walked up.

Unbuttoned was his shirt within an Olympic speed limit; pants had dropped, and she ran off in a concert of giggles.

Like a slow-motion athlete, he took silent steps, barefoot and naked throughout this seventeenth century residence. When he reached the bedroom, he found her lying, laughing at him on his bed in some yoga pose, holding her leg up next to her ear. He crawled back briefly, looking at her as if some revelation had hit him. She lowered her eyes, surprised by his sudden change of mood. 'Umm' wasn't a convincing start but he quickly resigned any doubt about being honest. She laughed and her exit was dramatic as she ran to the door and then, ever so slowly, she turned her head towards him, fixing him with her gaze as she entered the bathroom. She entered the shower, and he almost wished he'd sunk to his knees as if lost in a rainforest of exotic flowers, where droplets of tender love could reach his lips while he devoured hers. No this was a past long gone and he smiled at the thought that his former lover remained his best friend and travel companion extraordinaire.

8. FIORENZA, 1473 AGNOLA

Fly your vehicle, this body in 3D.
Fly where you can master,
A sole captain to your vessel,
no longer waiting in aisles of advent
for popping balloons in rabbits' global villages. (Inner Voice)

Was GianLuca's brain intact? Doubts were invading a time-drugged mind, or was this only a bad dream?

Still in Italy; in twenty-first century Florence?

It must be a staged event; I'm in an opera.

It certainly looks like a big production, maybe a Franco Zeffirelli movie?

Scattered, GianLuca is lost in a very slow motion, downloaded translation.

This wasn't an inner voice repeating itself.

"Sir," she said, "who are you? Are you from the north or where are you from?" Loud giggles followed.

"What kind of... an interesting bag you are carrying on your back?" More tittering.

"Are you a poet? You look like one, but, oh... in such amusingly cut pants?" The sisters snickered with pleasure!

This must be an opera – Mozart comes to mind – Così fan tutte?

His hands grappling for anything to hold on to, his scrambled mind left to even more confusion and suddenly a soft silk-like mass offered the solution.

The perfume is one of flowers; oh yes, a female delight, he babbles.

"Easy now; the sun indeed may have hit you strongly. It happens often in our Florentine summers. Obviously, you are not from here. Maybe from the north?" she repeated herself.

"Sir, your dress code is indeed of the strangest kind; and your shirt made of a silk I've never seen before? Remember, as from the orient, a thick silk." The giggles morphed into chuckles.

Huge eyes fervently approached, and GianLuca sank even deeper into the aria of lost pebbles.

"I have never laid my eyes on such rare design and the under-laid flower motif, how unusual for a man's dress?"

"Oh, how handsome he is," she whispers to her fellow soprano.

Girls, I heard you.

"What might be your name, fair stranger? Are you from the far land Marco Polo traveled?"

I'm staring at this beautiful woman and never-ending questions pop up.

So, is it you Galessa, my restaurant's bacchante disguised in some fancy green evening gown?

Please holy noises let there be a cell phone alarm.

"Did you just say my dress is strange? *Dio Benedetto* (Dear god)! What about yours?" the one called Agnola whispered rather harshly.

Help, here is the chorus again, definitely an opera. This cannot be a Venetian summer carnival with Sandro Botticelli's ladies stepping out of his 'Primavera' painting.

Faces blurred and the rays of a midday sun hazed all vision.

"You're mumbling sir, a very strange language." the older one told her sister.

"It isn't ours. Agnola, I heard it once before at the Palazzo Vecchio. Last spring, there was a foreign delegation from the Court of... yes, the Court of England. It was at Lorenzo de Medici's banquet. That's indeed what it sounds like doesn't it? Are you listening Agnola?" and the other beauty poked Agnola.

What an unusual name for this century.

And what century are we talking about here? By now the first one is shaking her sister's right arm persuasively.

"*Sorella ascoltami* (Sister, listen to me)."

The second face approaching is even younger, and yet as lovely. My Italian slang hampered by the absence of my small dictionary with its unique phrase finder... unfair, unfair! Ai, my pants are torn; got to get up, get out of this valley where I feel so miniscule, so small! How can I be so tiny?

"*Non ti muoverti* (Do not move)," the second face twittered. "*Aiutami me Fiammetta, è disturbato* (Help me, he's disturbed)!" She urged.

I cannot believe my ears. I'm not disturbed. Boy, what's wrong with me? Ouch my head... what is going on?

Flabbergasted, both young women relentlessly stopped GianLuca from straightening up to his full six feet two. By the time they had slowly lifted him from the ancient bricks, not without pain, they had wrapped the stranger in a humongous shawl trimmed with tiny pearls.

This is an erotic dream, of course.

How else could I be in front of Santa Croce? It is Santa Croce, right? And we're shopping on a market with such seductive creatures. I will be brave when you undress me ladies!

"*Venerabili Donne, non posso correre. Vi prego lasciatemi solo per un momento* (Esteemed ladies, I cannot run. Just a moment, let me go)."

Speechless, *due Venerabili Donne'*(two esteemed ladies*)* stared at him with wide-open eyes.

"He speaks! The man speaks, and in our language," the surprised women continued.

"Are you hurt Signor and what is your name?"

"*Prego, mi chiamo GianLuca. La mia mama è Toscana, di Volterra*!" He smiled at two smiling stunned faces, repeating himself now in almost perfect translation.

"Yes, my mother is Italian, born in Volterra where the health-springs are!"

At least, I lied up front, my mum wasn't Tuscan, but we ate in plenty of Tuscan restaurants, so for now that'll do. I can see why these young women are both even more stunned. But my instant lie is a hit: if I'm from that area that must really help. Ouph!

"*Vieni con noi, siamo vicino casa, appena dopo la chiesa* (Join us – we're close to home, right behind the church, Via San Christofano)."

"Oh *si,*" he mumbled, with eyes finally checking out the present reality. "*Grazie* (thanks)."

They've giggled again. I could swear they did.

I'm listening to their continuously whispering voices; oh, I do hope they are real!

"He knows his way?" the youngest one asked with broadening eyes, while they follow him.

But his head was spinning out of control.

What if this isn't a carnival? Of course, it isn't. What if... I've been drugged by some Chinese spy, the man seated behind me in the restaurant?"

But – wait a minute, where is Dante's statue? Oh no, stop it; I'm not going there. He continued rubbing his eyes.

What a time travel scheme, just like in the good old college days when we believed anything was possible. Right, let's open an agency: dive into your past: our summer special to a 'Buxomly Renaissance Tuscany'!

When they arrived at a huge mansion, a grand portal opened to a vast inner court and a heavy lady, armed with a mop and broom, loudly welcomed the young women.

She is neither their mother nor the maid, he observed; maybe some kind of nanny like in days of old. Days of old? OMG, am I talking Renaissance slang?

Now how's that for a reflection?

As the large and imposing wooden door closes, three heads blur into one. In no time, and all at once in perfect syncopation with their girlish titter, they try to put him at ease.

I'm their prey... smiling stupidly, my adult dreams morphing once again. So, it is an erotic dream after all? Nice. *OK... just undress me, I'm ready, ladies.*

But the next voice is a baritone and so isn't this an opera after all?

"You must be the English man. We've been expecting you." A commanding voice that was. It took little sign language to bring him through the attractive patio into a very large room with little furniture but a stunning portrait of a noblewoman... perhaps unfinished.

He wondered if it is by...

"Lippi?" A stunned GianLuca spoke forcefully.

"*Si, è di Filippo Lippi* (Yes, it's by Lippi)," the same charming baritone confirmed, "mama has posed for him. *Sono Andrea* (I'm Andrea), and I will do my best in your language."

Andrea is indeed a very handsome man with a proud nose and dark wavy hair.

Must be in his late twenties, I guess, a model from Milan and he's reading my thoughts?

What in the world is going on? Nobody was that loud in my dreams.

"I briefly studied with a mentor from the English Royal Court in London. But sir, *il vostro travestimento non è convincente.*" The man called

Andrea continued in a broken English, "Sorry, *I mussta say your disguiaze iz not very conveencing.*"

He was smiling reassuringly and GianLuca was charmed; the strong pronunciation, like that of his cherished Italian movies.

"You looked as if you're ... let's say, as if you are wearing a *sottovestiti* (underwear*)* how do you English men call it at court – underneath clothink?"

His thick accent was heavy but quite understandable and disarming.

"Underwear?" GianLuca didn't smile at the description of the twenty-first century 'ready to wear' summer pants and matching shirt, of course by an Italian designer.

But Andrea's tone grew more solemn.

"I'm glad my sisters found you before anyone else could pick you up. Market days are busy; we were all lucky ... as were you."

"Please sit down; you do look tired. *Un po' d'acqua* (Some water)?"

"I ... well yes, thank you", a briefly choking GianLuca was looking for any words at all, and now in another language, a different Italian than he was used to.

"Young man, there must be some kind of a mistake," GianLuca finally mumbled.

This is some kind of a bad dream and I will step out right now. That's what I always do when I have a scary nightmare: I stop it and get out and it doesn't come back ... though this isn't such a bad dream, not with those good-looking people.

He squeezed his eyes even stronger, again and again.

When I open them, I will be waking up in my own bed, my head on my Swedish pillow, at the house in Maiano, which I have been renting for three summers now. All will be just fine.

But the very slow peek he took at the three very amused faces still sitting around a heavy, dark, wooden table studying a very strangely mannered foreigner, left him in greater doubt.

"You are indeed a funny man. Maybe you are a court jester of some sort?"

Great, a stand-up comic, I must be losing my mind. Time for me to question.

"OK. I'm really sorry. I am not getting this right, am I? Two questions for all of you, gentle people: first, what year are we in ... and second, when I got up from my fall, why was Dante's statue missing from the front of the Santa Croce Basilica? Or am I mad?"

I'm sorry my voice sounds harsh, almost unpleasant and you're all very sweet; but this cannot go on. I'm going slightly mad!

Agnola slowly raised her posture, depicting old Renaissance nobility. All three remained astonished as the younger sister slowly, and without raising her voice, responded wryly.

"There is no statue in front of Santa Croce. There never was. And sir, we are in the year 1473. Whatever you may suspect, we are not pranksters."

Oh, oh ... now I'm spluttering!

"Durante Alighieri, known as Dante, the poet." GianLuca's voice, frenzied and panic struck by the second as he looked at his watch; it had stopped. He looked at the face staring at him and he pushed his wristwatch under his sleeve. "I must return to the square at once and check again. I mean it was there this morning!" The tone had taken on an angry arrogance wrapped in utter confusion.

Andrea had risen by Agnola's side to seek out why their visitor was so upset and confused. Who might this man really be? Is he the lost traveler from a recent dream?

"Sir, please do sit down, relax. My page will bring you some more water. Maybe the sun has made you somewhat delusional. You'll feel better after you have a good rest."

Yes, in my own bed, not in this foreign prison. But this rude reply wasn't blurted out.

Ever so briefly, he admired the more mature of the two beautiful women, the one called Fiammetta; her light, silky robes swinging around the table, framing her classical Italian beauty. Caught in the wink of an eye, their eyes briefly touched ... a hair-raising impression, as if she recognized him, and her cheeks turned reddish.

But this wasn't a continuous scenario; it was quickly interrupted as she stepped forward and he felt dizzy once again. In a strikingly unexpected move, she put one hand on his right shoulder. Her grip showed strength and her intense stare had him pinned down. He gulped. The brief pain inevitably took his eyes to her lips, so close ... GianLuca shivered. But kissing is not of the order of the day.

"Listen Signor, we have just saved your life," Fiammetta raised her voice slightly and her large, dark, brown eyes impaled his. "You mustn't move from here but remember that our home is not a prison. Instead, we are protecting you, nothing more. But do go out in the streets right now because within an hour you will be in a real fifteenth century prison. Just look at your outfit! You obviously have no idea about how to dress in the year 1473, in Fiorenza, and you have no idea how to behave. Even a peasant has better manners!"

"Once again, sir," Andrea paused, "you're tired and please do believe that we have been expecting you; at least I have. Do trust us for we mean no harm."

Expecting me? Really? But the nightmare continues, and these are all wizards?

"May I ask you, how well do you know the Alighieri family, and the great poet Dante, who has been in the public eye for more than a century and a half, and who remains an exemplary inspiration to all poets. His *Divina Comedia* is a masterpiece and he has greatly inspired many including one of our friends. There is another equally amazing man born in Tuscany. Of course, I'm speaking of our own Lorenzo di Piero de Medici, a poet of no lesser kind."

Dumbfounded, GianLuca stretched his eyelids. His chin nearly hit his sternum as he tried to yawn away all the discomfort of centuries old jetlag.

"I ... ugh, I do not know the Alighieri family, but yes, I have read their son's major book the *Divina Commedia.* He's a legend, worldwide and ... oh, forgive me ... this just cannot be," and for a moment he desperately hid his face in his hands. Tears were about to spring from his tired eyes. Both women stepped back. "Is this really true? If all of you are real and there are no cars in the street ..." he shook his head. Summer chills froze his skin and he trembled all over while three pairs of very attentive eyes continued to watch his inner chaos surfacing.

There were no cars. There was no statue ... my mind goes on racing.

Andrea kneeled closely while both sisters approached. Agnola covered GianLuca's shoulders with a large off-white, cotton-silk cloth. "What do you mean, sir?" Andrea asked unobtrusively. "You needn't be sad, GianLuca, we will help you." Fiammetta broke the silence ever so gently. "I am not sad. I feel ... ugh, actually rather well in your presence. I assure you I am so surprised by it all; but maybe even more by your kindness and warm-hearted manner, that lovely complicity amongst the three of you. It is quite different where I am coming from."

"Cars, you mumbled," a quick-minded Agnola insisted rapidly, "Did you mean carts or if not ..." Her sister continued in a joking manner, "What are carrrrrs?"

"You really must rest ... ladies do leave us for a moment," Andrea's voice lowered, "Let me take you to our guest chambers. The afternoon is still young." He gently touched GianLuca's chest. "Rest for a while; yes, you need rest. I will order my page to prepare you a cool bath. You'll find your *stanza* (room) refreshing from the heat of the outside walls. We'll talk later, at dinner. Does that suit you GianLuca?"

A guest room ....

GianLuca continued mumbling, "You're so right young man. That does sound like a good solution. I'm eager to know what has happened to me. Maybe you'll have quite some stories to tell me. Please make sure your sisters attend."

"Oh yes, they will. Surely you will be the one telling us a story! While our father is abroad you are indeed a most entertaining visitor to us all. By the way, my sisters are not betrothed you know, not yet," he answered with an adolescent smile!

A proposal upon arrival ...?

And they all walked up a long and widening staircase ... wider and wider it seemed. Weightless, GianLuca, once again floating, but where to?

The late lunch and Galessa, the padrona from the Trattoria, now Fiammetta ... not that Galessa had anything in common with this lovely young woman, but her Renaissance name. What if this isn't a dream? Where have I landed, in a parallel reality? Have I fallen into a time hole just by walking onto the Piazza? That didn't happen yesterday. The bathtub yes, water will help and some rest and later on, all will be clearer; or was it ever ... clear?

The family's pageboy had followed and was surprised when GianLuca was about to close the door behind him. He bowed and so did GianLuca. He smiled and so did he; no foreign language could have helped this exchange. He wasn't holding a towel, but something similar like a big sheet, neatly folded and hanging from his arm. The kid may well have stepped out of a Caravaggio painting, but it dawned on our foreigner if this is indeed 1473, well, we'd have to wait another century for that great painter to be born.

GianLuca shook his head in disbelief and the young kid, maybe thirteen or fourteen, acted equally confused. "*Prego* (please)," and he humbly gestured him towards a rather big bathtub right in the middle of a smaller anti-chamber, no doors on either side. GianLuca was a little uncomfortable to undress, and the boy did not attempt to turn around.

"*Prego, girate dall'altra parte* (Please turn to the other side)," GianLuca demanded in his best Italian.

What a relief it will be to slide into this lukewarm water, perfumed with rose petals and some kind of exotic oil … chuckles at the absence of all bubbles … I bet this is the wrong century for a bubble bath. It must have been quite a job bringing up all these buckets to fill this big a tub. There is that kid again, shuffling forward with that grin.

"*Sono Giovannino* (I am Giovannino)," the youngster told him, with that pubescent twinkle in the eye that makes any child affectionate at any moment of the day.

I can just think what comes next as he approaches with the soap. Oh no! At court, they wash you. No way. Your own personal page is there at all times and for wherever, whatever you need him for: bringing a confidential message to someone, running an errand, getting your clothes, preparing your bath. Oh no, I don't think so, not me I'm not a court person … never was, never will be. Oh, dear voices, please leave my head!

A minute later he had almost passed out, his line of thoughts wed to a lavender, oily rubbing … a vigorous sponge on his tired back.

"*Grazie, no* (Thanks, no)," provoked more than a sad look in those young eyes, as GianLuca grabbed the hard sponge and continued his own ritual.

Did the kid back off? No. For heaven's sake, he's pouting, head down, sitting on the floor. I'll take a dip and hopefully time-jump about five and a half centuries! It seems that I am also talking to myself a lot more these days. I haven't really focused on the outcome. And I have my wristwatch right here. Certainly, that will provide the necessary shock. It reads almost midnight, July 26th; it's a full moon. And that watch has stopped!

Fully raised in the tub, Giovannino is standing on the tips of his toes to cover GianLuca, with what seems to be no longer a sheet but yes, an extremely large sheet. Of course, it's their version of a towel.

His attempt to dry him off is welcomed with a new wave of unwanted resistance and this time the kid is running out of the room in a rage of some seriously insulting words. Within minutes there is an insistent knock on the door. Wrapped in his new white gown, with the doorknob in his hand, GianLuca's eyes drop right into a youthful cleavage, a macho habit he'd stopped being proud off.

And no, she's no waitress, you disturbed mind! For a Renaissance girl, woman, donna . . . she doesn't look too shy . . .

Briefly Fiammetta inspected a differently muscled body than the very few she'd seen. There was that flash; then a polite conversation; then just at that moment, all he could see was a queen. Her chest had taken on another breath, but her pride, sweet smile and good manners *(and this isn't the twenty-first century)*, had been reserved for an apology and an explanation about her brother's page. The little guy, Giovannino, was indeed the orphan he expected him to be. His parents had abandoned him after discovering that his real father was a nobleman. His mother nearly strangled, ended up disappearing. The way Fiammetta told the story, her voice enchanted him and GianLuca flew back quickly from his own sensuous flight in an instant. He had felt the kid's pain and he wanted to repair the little damage; after all he hadn't meant any harm. It resembled a tale from Greek mythology, Chiron the Centaur abandoned by Saturn, the god and his mother the nymph in horse dress-up.

In my century, counselling is a big hit. I'll simply beg her to explain to the boy that I'm just not used to being waited upon.

Fiammetta confirmed that she would convey his message. As she turned around, her head inclined ever so slowly, as if asking him why he is not used to being served. Before he could find an answer, she silently and unobtrusively skimmed the marble floors of a seemingly endless corridor. Within an instant, like a phantasm, she was gone. The ebony door closed, and he finally landed into the canopy bed. The richly dressed bed engulfed his male pride and he dozed off very quickly in a cosmic jetlag and a new dream tattletaled its way in.

9. FRANCE, 1473 THE CATHARS

The tower of innocence is still in place,
even fiercely hidden away, dungeon-deep
to most of us,
so long . . . forgotten. (Tower of Innocence)

A long braid adorned an upright back, dressed in hues of dark purple velvet. The red silk hair matched unfailingly the embroidered seam of the long, thick cotton skirts that seemingly gave way into a flying carpet, had it not been for the appearance of another proud body underneath, neighing happily. Isabel briefly tightened the grip on her vigorous stallion and the four-legged friend stopped right on the hilltop, only whimsically taking a peek at the rough dirt road still ahead. She felt proud and adventurous riding this fine Arabian whom she had baptized, Feu, because of the brown reddish mane and his fiery gait. She smiled at such an inspirational landscape. On a clear day, you could skim the horizon for long-forgotten villages shooting skinny towers between the endlessly undulating hills. She missed Paris, but this landscape was a painter's paradise.

Isabel contemplated the many more miles she had to cover in a day when the sun had not had a fair game with the budding clouds. The forest she had just left behind, had turned magical in the misty rays . . . rays that penetrated even further into the emerald greens. She knew how to reach her destination before the skies turned their purplish red into the next day's forecast of more summer heat. There was indeed something uniquely magical to time travel and knowing how history had unfolded and now, with the help of actually a good number of toys, she could help make the difference and maybe change the outcome, and history books could be re-written. She was wearing an ingenious pair of large framed goggles that Florian had created. They allowed her to command all messages vocally and to look at the entire reality around them from a very different angle. The virtual technique had been a secret for decades and yet a few young geniuses had broken the codes. Florian had researched everything in great depth and together with his friend GianLuca, he had been, since their high school days, amongst the very few true inventors. But the latter had disappeared, she contemplated, where to?

Well, we do have a good number of toys to play with and now a limited selection on this side of the reality frontier, no techno dancing here, she smiled. So where is Florian? When leaving 2018, he had in mind to play Sherlock at the first Cathars' abbey he visited. That Scorpio rising . . . always the detective!

Of course, that was one of his talents. He would be there soon, and she wanted nothing less than his presence. After all, they had only crossed that very morning; it would take some more days to get used to this century's cosmic temperature. A shiny, glimmering yet brisk dawn took her into the timeline she had visited once before and she loved the southwest of France. Her intuition would always rescue her and being in the moment was more than a motto, it had been taught since childhood.

They halted at a smallish pond where the cool water was clear and unpolluted; the ultimate refreshment for Feu, her happy stallion. Her lips painted a ponderous smile. Florian was still on her mind. She wondered what disguise her stubborn companion had chosen after his landing at Rennes-le-Chateau. If her attitude blossomed of innate pride, her intentions were of a quieter simplicity. She never felt more important than the mission she was leading. For an instant, contemplation closed her eyes. She could feel him approaching and Florian knew that she was on her way to the village of Montfroid where they were expected to meet their first contact, a 'timeless insider'; simply a spy in monk robes. This resident of the ancient abbey was one of those unique people who since birth, recognized that life was lived on more than one timeline. Florian remembered the land well and therefore she gave no second thought as to why he wanted to stay a day longer at the city of Rennes. After all, they were a team even if they both had different ideas after landing, on this time traveling adventure.

Isabel popped an aspirin-like pill; her 'French Pill,' nothing but a language program that did overnight miracles. Convenient to her highly trained brain, this pill activated just another program. But what an add-on it was!

She could rewind her mind like a tape and jump to past events recalling every detail. It was like one of those former MK-Ultra language program substitutes that many government agencies had trialled, initially on a few students to prepare them for an anti-communist training agenda.

In the sixties under a very protective government umbrella, her mother had been one of their first volunteers. Later, she had accepted being in a more advanced experiment, believing in the promised integrity to 'protect their great nation'. And yes, she had aimed to be the 'cleverest girl' on campus. Soon after, she had found herself pregnant with no recollection of the generous donor's name or any detail of the pleasant event of conception. She had befriended Nick, a well-informed colleague, an insider to one of the secret agencies. She confided in him and he veiled her from disgrace. She promised to never contact him nor reveal his identity. After some serious and often painful work, that man certainly got her through the mind-boggling training program.

Indeed, it was the first time Nick Skul had spread his hidden superhero wings. Isabel's mother had a grateful and loving attitude to him, but he had advised that she should move to France as a foreign university student. It was at that very moment, she decided to raise her daughter on her own. Nick got her a new identity and from then on, she was Miss Lieverkussen. Her daughter was born the year before she graduated from the Sorbonne University and like her mother, the baby appeared to be precociously bright. Before the age of five, Isabel could play word games in three languages. French remained her favourite. She expressed herself slowly and when she did, it made her feel that she was growing in a somewhat lady-like stature.

A brief chuckle escaped and then she laughed out loud about it all, while her four-legged companion delighted in her patting. Checking the saddle, she grinned at the chessboard design she had picked and then at the rather humongous, yet somehow ingenious twenty-first century combo of skirts and pants, that would go by (hopefully) unnoticed, even though a later day Italian designer would have been envious! She nibbled on some dry nuts from the small leather pouch dangling from the saddle. In the distance, Florian's uphill gallop increased speed, as Feu's nostrils flared.

This was about the time she had expected Florian ... a handsome name perfect for this century, she thought. She expected him to bestow, in a chivalrous attempt, a list of excuses as to why he was late. Within seconds, that's exactly what happened. She had turned her head away and looked slightly down on him. In this dimension the density was, oh so different, and the tilt of her head warned him she wasn't about to laugh. And then, of course, he claimed her gloved hand and kissed it. She looked him straight in the eyes and for a tiny moment both of them had forgotten the timeline they had crossed. His heart started pounding and his lips stumbled through "*Isabel, pardonnes-moi le retard* (pardon me the delay)," and she cracked a smile and mounted Feu in one swift move.

"Remember," she answered rolling the 'r', "we are here for the game, not a continued romance. On this timeline, our interventions need to be brief and accurate. This is a very different movie than where we just left!"

Oh, I just love it when she does her bit of tragedienne (drama queen), *Florian thought. Let's play along.*

"Well now, regarding Rennes; I know Frère Eustache is cool and no doubt he will adapt the necessary records rapidly and add whatever new data we bring," Florian responded, eagerly thinking of some old Robin Hood movie. "Milady, am I the only one to have remembered our past, our first encounter at Montfroid and our escape on the same shining stallion?" His eyes ravished her beauty. "That was quite an adventure we had two years ago. Oh, come on, I know you had a great time. I see you had no trouble reinventing yourself once again, nor have you lost your sense of dramatic fashion!" he joked, raising his voice in an equally stagy way.

Right this moment, they felt like melting away in the wealth of the intense colours that made up this cosmic wall of medieval branches like a cobweb of thinly veined translucent cells that might trap them in their twentieth century love life forever. It's risky for a couple to leave their 'reality home base', yet this harnessed duo knew how strong they grew instantly. If for an instant they believed this was more than a program, they would be prisoners stuck in a virtual reality. It was a pressure she had become used to – or so she thought. After all, their real bodies were still in the Fiesole Villa. Like gazing through a veil in the midst of flashing thunderbolts, a searing headache stirred her iris. Suddenly their concentration floated, almost lost in this silent film of an unrequited love.

She spun out of her daze instantly, nearly hitting an ancient, troubled-looking oak's desperate branches and reaching out to space, she plunged a few feet away from Florian. Her gallant knight stumbled backwards, in utter surprise at the abrupt end of his own dream. But he caught her and held her tight for longer than he'd remember.

This landing was nothing compared to the blinding dust explosion that their arrival had caused. She shook her robes back into place with a turn and a twist, more fitting to a silent cowboy movie. As for her cavalier, he was glad his own horse hadn't run off.

"Let's cut the memory bank to the minimum, OK? I don't want to land on my head!" she joked in a high-tech 'Minnie Mouse' voice.

In the first hours of their time travel journey, Florian was able to control their thought patterns easily. He read her lines reminding him of their last night together, about seventy-two hours back in the Fiesole Villa before they had intercepted a new trio of unplanned assistants. Isabel read his mind and smiled. Their horses shook them right back on track before *une autre pensée* (another thought) got a chance to come in between them and their goal. This mission needed full concentration and no emotions could distract them.

That stunning palette of heavenly hues of pink and lavender set onto an enticing fairy dusk, seduced them to a whole other game that would find no stage to play on till they reached Renaissance Tuscany and its magnificent capital, Fiorenza. Before their gallop took on full speed, they looked at one another with a mutual grin that blew forth an echoing laugh, enchanting all creatures of the valley.

10. FIORENZA, 1473 GIOVANNINO

Your credit is up.
I'll get myself another Higher Self.
Anyone home on that mountain? (Talking Drunk with Truth)

Waking up as from a cosmic jetlag, GianLuca bounced back from the too many pillows on this huge bed. The canopy with its fine brocade and transparent draperies hovered like a surreal cockpit over his head and *dove sono* (where am I) poked his head; a Mozart opera could have been the foil for this scenario. *Where am I? But no, I'm not flying, and I have no jet lag.*

A soft but persistent knock anticipated a door opening slowly. Giovannino's big smile walked in. Right behind, with one hand on his shoulder, Andrea gently pushed the boy forward.

I must look like some Roman mercenary draped similarly above as below.

"My sister and I have explained to Giovannino that you are from a very faraway country where children do not serve. Am I right?"

"Of course, you are right," GianLuca answered in an equally gentle manner.

Though there's a lot more to that subject, at least in that other century, he mumbled.

Before turning to GianLuca, Andrea gently ordered Giovannino to 'run along' in the most charming vernacular. "We expect you for our evening meal in a little while. You will join us?" Andrea asked.

You bet I will, GianLuca smiled*, I'm starved.*

About 15 minutes later, GianLuca appeared in fresh and rather unusual dress. Andrea described the couture details, explaining the make and fabric, which was a blend of cotton and silk, as worn only by high officials.

"*Benvenuto* (Welcome!)." The campanile had just rung their bells seven times.

"Welcome handsome stranger! You certainly look a lot better after your siesta." Agnola almost sounded solemn but the tilt of her head spoke differently. Both sisters outclassed all possible period movies in their light summer dresses, covered by some gauzy golden thread up to their necks ... very Roman fashion he'd been told.

"By tomorrow, our maid will have washed your clothes," Agnola said. "We hope this feels more comfortable. Do you also wear loose clothes where you are from? Your pants were ..." she chuckled "... very short." Their journey was not.

"Now sisters, no more questions till our guest has enjoyed our food and our wonderful wine."

It's better I do not resist the table delights, but I had better forget that I am sort of a vegetarian.

The timeline difference seemed to have made a very strong impact on his stomach. After what appeared to be a long dinner, the handsome trio walked him to a hidden roof terrace. He remained spellbound by the clear skyline, where only a few fluffy clouds cloaked the full moon and left him exalted with superlatives ... perhaps a vernacular somewhere between the Italian and the English.

I'll do my Shakespearian best not to sound too modern, but then again, what could be modern to these gentle people: a mountain bike?

After a brief silence, Andrea offered the opening challenge, "From which one of these magnificent celestial miracles do you visit us?"

GianLuca's head was still spinning*! These two women are as eager to get answers to the many questions they all have. Must I give them a simple rundown of my twenty-first century life? My childhood, the yearly vacations with my parents, the many travels back and forth between the USA and Europe, the airplanes, the boats, trains and subways ... almost five hours have now passed. And then, shall I ... show them my watch?*

While the campanile now announced midnight, Fiammetta might have scanned his thoughts. "That metal bracelet you were wearing at the Piazza," she was about to argue "... and you want us to believe your mother is from Volterra?"

Andrea's eyebrows danced their way up as he gestured to her to lower her voice, but Fiammetta felt no reason to do so.

So Agnola intervened on her sister's behalf. "Sorry GianLuca, maybe this is from your distant world, from behind the horizon, where our ships cannot reach … the stars?"

GianLuca remained stunned at the unavoidable discussion and only Andrea kept his cool.

"Sisters, please," Andrea implored in a discreetly gentle manner, all his own. "Look, I am now 34, Fiammetta; and when you were merely a very small girl, I was often sent abroad to study with men of a rare wisdom and knowledge. They had seen much more than even our own *genitore* (parents)! You may remember that our grandfather invited astronomers from far away to lecture us. One of them told us that our world was round, round like an apple." His almost rhetorical tone sounded funny.

As in a Renaissance painting come to life, the two young women, swathed in silk, attentively listened and admired the foreigner. GianLuca's story of his many travels was genuinely touching . The latter remained charmed by Andrea's enthusiasm, open mind and overall warm-hearted attitude.

"I am not surprised to find out that near the end of this century, this great city had some equally great spirits, not just famous bankers."

Would GianLuca's attempt to lighten the ambiance lead to a deeper conversation?

"You have guessed rightly. We are, of course, a family of very successful bankers," Fiammetta said, "but like most of our much conspiring competition, as you might suspect, we aren't driven by greed," Fiammetta followed up waving her arms in a balletic movement maybe familiar only to their guest.

"Please, we must all be in some kind of a shock. What has happened this afternoon and what we are now seeing around us, right here in 'your present', well, it has already happened. It is the past. Oh, how can I explain this to you?"

GianLuca smiled at three eager faces, delighted and slightly scared. "To you, I come from your future though I have no explanation yet as to how I got here." He sighed. "How to prove this? Let me think. For example, if you haven't heard yet, I will prove to you that in your 1473, a man born in a land north of Germania – one day celebrated as Copernicus – will show the world that the planets revolve around the sun and that our Terra turns from West to

East on its axis and that's the simple reason why we see a big movement in the heavens!" GianLuca continued.

The silence matched the night sky in all of its magnificence, but the air was thick with anticipation. They were stunned at what their guest had just said but they couldn't wait to learn more. Their foreign guest was anxious to tell more.

"Another Italian by the name of Galileo Galilee will confirm this, while many other stunning discoveries will amaze the masses and upset your Vatican. The Holy See will do everything possible to break this man of genius. From that period, we will retain an ugly part of our Western history that will be known as the 'Inquisition'. Not only will books and art works be destroyed, but people will be tortured and burned for their beliefs!"

"It is scary but truly exciting to hear you speak," Andrea softly whispered "I have been waiting for this moment and I hoped that some proof would be given to us that there are indeed many different worlds." He smiled innocently. "My father and I have always agreed on this subject."

"*Dio Benedetto, ti prego fratello* (My god, I beg you brother)," Agnola exclaimed, "My god, I beg you to be careful about what you are saying as such statements can be brought against you, you know the counsel at the Signoria..."

GianLuca prepared for a stronger statement as he replied to their own eagerness to know more. "Well then, look at your local de Medici family's history. It is written in blood." Andrea, Agnola and Fiammetta inhaled audibly... then held their breath. "You will lose one of your own finest men, for in about five years, in an attempt to murder both illustrious Medici brothers, Giuliano will be butchered. Lorenzo will escape and the Signoria will order the murderers to be punished in the most horrible of ways. The leaders of the Pazzi family will be hung from the balcony of the Signoria. I can tell you much more, but it really is a rather ugly story." Fiammetta had jumped up and she had covered her mouth while Agnola nearly stumbled over as she pushed herself up from the table, a slow weeping sound followed, and Andrea was about to break the silence.

Right, I could have just shut my big mouth!

"Thank you for your uncommon explanations, dear visitor from wherever you are calling from. But know that Giuliano di Piero de Medici is the most beloved man in this illustrious family. He is also our friend and he has actually shown interest in Agnola's poetry these last months. You see, both share the same age and he comes here often and sits right at that table," Andrea remarked. "Then again, I am not surprised that he and especially Lorenzo, who was pushed to the political foreground since childhood, are far from safe. Much jealousy reigns amongst the great and wealthy families ruling our lands and the pope – probably the whole Vatican – cannot be trusted."

Fiammetta spoke up-fiercely, "I beg of you, brother, please avoid such speech. How could our Holy Father be involved in any plot especially of such a low kind?"

Shall I put in my five cents? After all, why did I land all the way in an Italian Renaissance scenario? Maybe just to pass out a few cards from an unknown deck? It mustn't be for some nice long holiday anyhow, that's for sure!

GianLuca wasn't about to inspire laughter. "Your Holy Father's clergy is still, forgive me the expression, raping little girls and boys of the age and likes of your page, Giovannino. The church is fighting so-called holy wars only to fill their own already overloaded pockets. And the church is also stealing ancient knowledge from sacred grounds to keep it from the world! They will create more wars and there's going to be a big revolution at the end of your century, but history will take us into the twentieth century before true explanations and proof will be given about their lies and deceit, world-wide."

Andrea's eyes were now shining with a renewed confidence. *Finally, someone after my own heart and knowledge, he thought.* "I knew it, I always felt it. Let me tell you something dearest sisters!" Both women stepped aside in disbelief, horrified at what might follow GianLuca's scary revelations. "You know that when I traveled with our father to Germania to meet our printers in Hanover, they asked us the first day if all men from Florence were sodomites. Imagine the insult to my father. That's how they call us, the males from the city of Florence. Our fame embroidered by these strange, unhealthy ways of relating to the children, often like the Greek and the Romans did in the darkest of hours, yet in full bright daylight. At times, I am ashamed that I'm born here."

His throat slightly tightened as he launched a long and intense monologue.

"Our family does not share such tradition – of that I can assure you. Men of power always had a male slave trained from childhood on, and sisters, you are mature enough to know. I bet you've even heard of it. In Venice, Rome and Fiorenza, many men are sodomizing boys and young adults and what GianLuca is saying is the truth. The clergy has a truly vile history. What is really happening at the Vatican is scandalous. The pope himself is said to give personal attention to the upbringing of some very young boys, for so-called higher purposes. Now, how can such foul purpose be of high purpose when older men, some of the ugliest and most cruel kind, take a child's innocence?" He sighed.

Andrea had risen to his feet, a new confession ready to truly jolt both his sisters, nervous beyond all expectation. "Yes," an angry Andrea said. "I can tell you that as a child I was pulled underneath a priest's robes, onto my knees, in the sacristy, to unconvincingly perform 'a service to God'. I was nine when father found out from our mother in whose lap I cried for months before she confessed to her husband that awful truth! The next day Lapo Buontalenti, our father and a man of impeccable faith, journeyed to the Vatican." GianLuca noticed how both sisters covered their faces.

Andrea continued: "Thanks to father's genuine reputation, and of course many past donations, he was finally received by the so-called 'Holy Father,' God's representative on Earth. He requested from the pope that the priest be punished, convicted and banished. And in Rome he found out a lot more. A silent cardinal later confirmed many deaf or dumb born boys were being abused daily, sometimes taken to a dungeon and even sacrificed alive. Within the same month, the pope had the priest brought back to Rome to redeem his sins. It must have been quite a hoax of a trial, for soon after he was promoted to a position at La Cappella pontifical at the Basilica di San Pietro in Vaticano. Of course, my father never heard anything back from the Holy See. The only rumour that was confirmed a year later, was that the 'handsome priest' had become a very private devotee of the Holy Father himself; in other words, a personal slave for all 'unholy needs'!"

The story is rather familiar to the Western hemisphere. Nothing like getting some first-hand testimony, GianLuca watched growing outrage on the faces of both women.

Andrea's voice lowered, and he regained his composure quickly. He was adamant that there had been enough reading from the book of pain. "I believe it has been a very long day and a most revealing night. Let us retire for a good rest and turn to those stars to heal the many wounds we endured and help us refrain from more repeats." He wiped the tears from his eyes, before Agnola slipped her handkerchief into his hand.

She lifted a hand, maybe to contradict her brother about closing off so suddenly. But he insisted and somehow, the tone of his voice had turned bittersweet. "*No, cara sorelle* (dear sisters), I will gladly let you conduct the next discussion when the sun is at its highest; for now, adieu and good night. I will accompany our guest to his room."

Fiammetta and Agnola bade goodnight to GianLuca; their hands touched briefly while their smiles grew from a place of utter innocence. While the ladies glided down the narrow stairway on the opposite side, Andrea, a torch in one hand, accompanied GianLuca to his quarters.

"Thank you, dear new friend of old," he voiced with some hesitancy. "Your visit has lifted a burden off my shoulders. Our mother did die of shame when she found out how her trust in God and the Church had been betrayed. And our father, well since that day he has not stopped traveling, hoping to find more proof and possible explanations as to why such ugliness invaded our lives and destroyed our beliefs in what we were taught was our creator."

"Dear young friend," GianLuca answered warmly. "You are right about continuing the discussion tomorrow whenever you like. I will be up early. Good night to you and my sincere gratitude for your hospitality. Truly, in my century, in my own world I have hardly been received in a more gracious manner!" Andrea led the way to the guest room and GianLuca quietly whispered,

"One last thought to take to your bed of dreams; there is always an inner voice that knows what story to invent as tomorrow's challenge breathes around the corner. From there we can move on to become the witness to a cosmic miracle, called life."

Andrea opened the door and for a moment he glanced into his guest's eyes. "How fortunate an encounter this is", he smiled "we are all grateful for this visit and you will love our father's arrival, very soon."

11. FIORENZA, 1473 ANDREA

Yet suddenly, a must,
new open doors, a gate real near
and finally, an unpredicted trust
letting go of all we fear. (Reflections)

Andrea slept very few hours. A full moon had taken a permanent residence right above the Buontalenti residence and that morning no rays of the sun were needed to wake him up. He sat still and reflected on yesterday's encounter. Till the very moment of his meeting with the foreigner, Lapo's son had trusted two of the finest men: his adored father and their astrologer friend Marco Farini. The latter became like a mentor, an elder who had fled the former pope's court with a bag of too many untruths, he had instantly joined the endangered species. Andrea's parents had arranged for their neighbouring friends, the Bellini family, wealthy landowners outside the city walls to graciously house the man.

Marco rarely came into the city, and when he did, it was mostly after the sun set below the western horizon. So, Andrea had sent off his personal page to fetch him as tradition demanded, with some of last night's freshly baked bread, fruit and cheese. The message was indeed a simple one; he was expected for that same day's evening meal. Andrea was excited to hear his explanations of the current events in the sky, and above all, he was looking forward to challenging his new guest in revealing his true identity.

After the unfortunate series of events in the sacristy, the very young Andrea had cut god, and any suffering hero, from his beliefs. It made no sense to him that a so-called messenger of love and truth had been nailed to a cross to get His word 'a-cross', or was 'that' word manipulated from the beginning, and the story invented?

To Andrea, as to his father it was all dipped in falsehood. How well-planned history appeared; where the Roman Empire halted, Christianity and ... the Vatican took over! All this in a veil of symbols. Lapo had taught and explained to his son many of those historical lies.

Marco had remarked that since the beginning of time, the meaning of the 'cross' had been manipulated so the ruling class had an easier control over the people. To him the cross symbolized something quite different: life itself. It was the union of heaven and earth. In this union, spirit meets matter and the divine unifies within the human heart. For centuries, crossroads had been an eminent point to find one's way on the roads of life.

Yet on that sign, on that central crossing point, the Church had nailed a very sad figure. 'The Son of God', tortured and whipped, a bloody and dying body hung from that very cross! How pathetic a ritual was this? Why – if He had existed at all, why not a happy Jesus face, an inspiring one, the face of someone who supposedly taught others to be compassionate and good to all mankind? Andrea had always been annoyed at a story he considered being the most misleading fraud ever, the lie of all lies. It never felt right that a god created men and women as equals so that they would become his servants or was god a dictator? And why should humans be limited in their intimate relations and choices? Andrea allowed an old phantom to pop up to the surface, and his fist hit the table. The two cups tumbled down – but landed in his quick hands.

GianLuca had appeared so unexpectedly in their lives but it was perfect timing. Ah, indeed his father would be equally pleased. Tonight, he felt good about this surprise visit. Wherever GianLuca had landed from, Andrea felt this would prove to be most revealing for all in attendance.

Fiammetta paused briefly, and her long index fingers joined her bejewelled thumbs, all in a refined action to lower the sleeves from her pale shoulders, revealing the kind of beauty that many a foreign court might have envied. Behind her, Agnola giggled her way into tickling her sister in her own uniquely childish way.

"Lighten up", she laughed. "Father will be here soon, and all will be perfect, you'll see."

Fiammetta switched her focus to her sister's image. "Surprised?" she teased Agnola, while playfully waving an opened letter. "Yes, tonight Father sent a message and I intercepted it. Only we know, though Andrea has surely felt it," she added with a smile.

Hum, she contemplated. Did he read the message first? "That will be a meal for the higher mind, I'll say," declared Fiammetta who turned around stunning her sister with a rather unexpectedly low-cut neckline.

"You like him, the foreigner, do you not? He's older than our brother. I think he's rather thin though muscular, not in that soft muscle tone that will keep Andrea from ever looking old. Oh yes, you guessed, I watched him undress yesterday when he turned his back to Giovannino."

"Sister, how could you?" exclaimed Fiammetta in a girlish mocking mood.

"Well, Giovannino had forgotten to close the door and I watched. I'll admit to one thing – only to you – he inspired more than self-pleasuring. What do you say?"

Like some naughty tittering pubescent dance of genderless innocence, the sisters' cheeks embraced, and they ran with tiny, speedy steps through the hallway, like six-year-olds searching for their favourite doll.

Their laughter caught GianLuca's attention. When he pushed open a weighty door, his toga-clad appearance bumped into Fiammetta. He lost his fabric to the big black and white marble tiles while she almost slipped away from him, like a queen on a chessboard. He held her back from leaving, just in time, in a move worthy of a seasoned tango dancer.

A Renaissance tango?

She clung onto his shoulders and caught a skin perfume as strong as the passion that could send off thousands of flames through her veins. Recovering her composure, she showered him with a stream of apologies.

"*Prego, per me è un grande piacere* (Please, the pleasure is all mine)," he smiled.

Agnola hadn't disappeared within the walls and watched the whole scene with a smile.

"*Che bella coppia* (What a nice couple)," she quipped, grinning courteously.

GianLuca instantly posed with a grand smile.

They don't know what a camera is! The joke won't go anywhere.

Fiammetta withdrew proudly, not without scanning her present hero down to his toenails. Her sister had been right. By all means, he was sensuous, and she suddenly realized that yes, she was attracted to this visitor. She was ready to be swept off her feet as quickly as in the little incident a moment ago, '*but please land me in his arms*'.

No more silly remarks and Agnola got lifted swiftly off the floor by her valiant brother. He had coped with all her innate silliness since childhood and he loved her for it. *'A scene straight out of Romeo and Juliet,'* their guest remembered from a ballet performance he once attended at the Royal Opera House in London.

Andrea commented quietly, "GianLuca, in just a few hours you have brought back laughter to this place. Now how was your first night at our home? Quiet I hope?"

Both young women dashed along, disappearing downstairs, still a Renaissance teenagers' act, and Andrea hugged GianLuca amicably, making him feel like *famiglia* (family). "*Grazie, ho dormitto molto bene questa prima notte* (Thanks, I have really slept well this first night.)"

GianLuca chuckled at his American accent that might harm this beloved language.

"Take your time to come down. The cook is baking some fresh *pane di semi di lino* (flaxseed bread)."

"I hope you do not mind the fresh new clothes Agnola has left for you in your chambers. They were mine of course, maybe slightly too large," he said in a friendly whispering manner, "but, as mentioned before, made of the finest silk and pleasant to wear in this summer heat, I assure you. We weren't planning to keep you locked up here," he frowned.

When GianLuca opened the heavy but artful stained-glass windows, he actually inhaled for the first time that fresh and unpolluted air. If this was a dream or another timeline, he certainly seemed alert and fully aware, while breathing uncontaminated air in this Renaissance Tuscany. He scanned the clear blue skies suddenly free of those disturbing chemtrails, another phenomenon the press didn't write about, apart from the alternative websites or rapidly disappearing magazines. But for now, unmistakably beyond all logical explanations, here he was in a conspiracy-free Florence; at least so it seemed. The amazing City of Florence (so familiar from all the history books he had devoured), was indeed under the reign of the already notorious, exceptionally gifted young leader, Lorenzo de Medici, soon to be known as *'Il Magnifico'*. Yes, Lorenzo The Magnificent would change the face of his country.

12. FIORENZA, 1473 MERCATO

Framed
are the entertainers' memories
of what I never suspected
to bring me back alive. (Worded scent)

GianLuca glanced at this Tuscan *prêt à porter*. Uncomfortable at the prospect of changing into Renaissance clothes, he just didn't want to look like either a ballet dancer or a cloak and dagger hero. When he walked into the breakfast room, the oven welcomed a hankering stomach. He started to take a real liking to those three smiling faces making him feel at home as if he had always belonged to this household. That morning, only the bells ringing from the campanile reminded him time didn't always move that fast and the stories the young women told, full of lively descriptions of the colourful Florentine life, were as enchanting as any good book he could get hooked on.

A loud pounding on the front door interrupted their fun and another young woman joined both sisters. A brief gossip led their curious eyes to the stranger upstairs and off they went to the *mercato* (market). GianLuca tried to picture the Piazza de la Signoria without that famous *David* statue and without his first choice of any tearoom ever – *Rivoire.* He so often had indulged in his cappuccino addiction *solo la schiuma* (only the foam of the milk!) and oh, their specialty cheesecake, the very best in all of Florence! To compare centuries of evolution, the way this city had changed throughout the last centuries, how would these familiar streets now look car-free? And in the absence of all tourist shops, museums and uncalled-for monstrosities like concrete buildings housing telephone companies or post offices... this magnificent city would now still be wondrous. There would be no vacationers buzzing around, noisily clicking away, no more free-for-all and no culture-for-any attitude. That pandemonium of mostly superficial beings from all corners of the world in tasteless dress, vulgarly voiced, pushing about in masses of slumberous excessive weight, lost at the absence of their fast-food chains, landing their obese butts down in some cheap pizza fast food joint as if they hadn't left their own living room. Sucked in by their irrelevant, uninspiring television programs, they were pulled into a delta state of unproductive boredom. He sighed at his own negative judgement, but he knew that here no ears would be 'plugged in' or fingers whipping cell phones.

No, this Florence was the original version and to play the 'undercover tourist' he had better fix his disguise well. A gentle hand took his left wrist and Andrea asked: "The bracelet you wore yesterday was, of course to us all, very unusual. Can you tell me something about it? It isn't a decorative piece ... is it maybe, like your travel tool between different worlds?" He said this in a somewhat childish way that made GianLuca smile.

"Well, it does have something to do with time. I'll confirm that gladly. It's called a digital watch. A clock run by a system you could compare to the energy of the sun contained in a small 'chip', that is like a little container of energy; something like a flat pea that keeps this little device going for at least 365 days. Well, that is, ugh, until I came to your century." He smiled, projecting his own worries. He balanced his words on a miniature scale, making sure he didn't speak some voodoo language and that it made sense to a man living in a time where painter-artist-engineer extraordinaire, Leonardo da Vinci's great findings weren't public yet.

Andrea smiled back at him. "I knew you'd bring new information to our rather insignificant lives and, with your permission, to some more good souls. Maybe my father and tonight's surprise dinner guest ... ah you'll get along with him alright ... will find you more than entertaining," Andrea announced in a theatrical but humorous way. "Any invention that hasn't come through the city council, or wasn't at least introduced by Lorenzo de Medici, could cost your life. Therefore, I suggest you leave your bracelet here ... that is if you plan to walk around in the city." He remarked intuitively, "unfortunately, I will not be able to accompany you. It will not be safe for either of us, so better not to attract attention to your relationship to this home. Alone as a foreigner, you're but one of the many and you'll go by unnoticed, at least when dressed appropriately. I on the other hand am rather well known here."

GianLuca felt he'd be playing blind-man's buff by walking out of the monumental door; just opening it would attract attention. He wanted none. It seemed that after all, he had become a witness of what seemed another magnificent Franco Zeffirelli production of yet one more Renaissance story. He was thinking of sneaking out till a joyous Giovannino appeared out of nowhere, waving his arms. He followed the youth to a small door showing an exit behind a series of closely fitting trees. The door closed rapidly behind him and there he was, alone in 1473 Florence.

The new outfit was simple and fortunately not as theatrical as he had feared. It made him look more ordinary and his long hair brought a bonus to a now rather commonplace appearance. Pretending to be a craftsman of some kind wouldn't go over well; his refined looking hands and manner would suggest the contrary. He was glad his new friends had dressed him so casually and the long sleeves (of Shakespearean theatricality) were covering his more muscular arms. He avoided looking at the women, some of them fair and rather beautiful; some were rather heavy ... Juliet's nurse in the ballet version of Verona's ageless love story came once again to mind.

While curiously cruising the smaller streets for Renaissance discoveries, he noticed how narrow some of those alleys really were; an advantage with such summer heat for the many citizens in heavy dress. Strange, how easy life now seemed as he realized the absence of stores, the countless tourist traps, the banks and pharmacies. He was about to cross his favourite Piazza Santa Croce, a colorful market busy, as in a *Romeo and Juliet* ballet scene. Scanning the magnificent buildings once again, he remained mesmerized by the absence of Dante's statue. If he had any doubts, this really was the ultimate proof that he was no longer in the twenty-first century! When a few horsemen galloped right past him, he jumped to the side and nearly landed into a fruit stand. He bowed to the busty-looking saleswoman, and he didn't bother to risk his own 'outer-space' Italian as he bowed in a very gallant, almost balletic way, while she laughed out loud and clapped in spontaneous applause ... so much for getting by unnoticed.

He moved on quickly through the crowd until, hidden in the shadow of the cathedral, he noticed a few men, dressed in hues of dark burgundy and black ... all Renaissance-like suits. More suited to a grand opera's dress rehearsal, they appeared clumsy, causing GianLuca to suspect something was not right. He could not read their faces.

Are they looking for me? This makes no sense.

Hiding behind a stall, he overheard the tallest man whose English was tainted with a heavy American accent. "If she's here man, you cannot miss her. Isabel, with that head of red hair, not one of these women can compete with her beauty and then there's also Florian … no doubt he's on the lookout for her. I wonder if they traveled separately."

Florian, my goodness. Well, there must be more than one man by that name … but linked to a redhead called Isabel, well they must be talking about my old friends. Well, I haven't seen them since … my own unfortunate disappearance years ago. Hmm, we were all scientists in the making at university. So, these rascals may well be from … my century. That could become a fun adventure.

As these unfamiliar voices moved up the market square, GianLuca followed them as closely as he could. While checking out the stands, a younger voice spoke vividly. "Derecho, I don't believe our friends are in the province yet. Remember they needed to get to the abbey first and since they can't just simply use the cell phone …" he joked in a very New Jersey styled slang, "and you've closed off yours … ha-ha, well they have to ride for at least two days, on several horses for what would take less than a night by a high-speed train. But they only have the four-legged friends to count on!"

The third one with a gentle tonality and a huge smile up to his even bigger ears insisted they change the subject. "Maybe we need to look into Fiesole; wouldn't it be cool to visit the place we just came from?" And as GianLuca wanted to step forward and tell them he wasn't a Renaissance 1473 Tuscan either, two rather amusing women rushed into him.

"You're not from down here handsome! Where from?" urged one of the busty local saleswomen; she wore a deep orange, golden frilled dress that didn't hide nature's expansive gifts.

The second woman made it even easier to guess their professional occupation as she lifted up her green skirts so quickly that no trained eye was needed to catch the absence of all other garments. This short event reminded GianLuca of his Princeton years, always looking for a little afternoon adventure. He had some more obnoxious thoughts almost causing him to break out into hysterical laughter, when the first harlot almost grabbed him right between the legs so with utter surprise, he topped a high note. She shut him up by covering his mouth with hers, as if breakfast had no end.

Great . . . Like I need the attention!

The diminutive salesman from the little tent across from the opposite stall, had already alerted several clients that there was a scene to be watched. Fearing a 'reality show' outcome, GianLuca chose to escape. With an obscene gesture, he made his way through a crowd just thick enough to dive into an escape of unwanted popularity. The church now seemed the closest solution and just then he ran right into the arms of an obese, jolly-looking man in . . . robes. Friar Tuck and Robin Hood flashed into GianLuca's mind.

"Son, are you running to or from God? He's always waiting for you; wherever, whenever and yes, I can give you a hand!" He smiled, "Such a handsome lad looking for His Divine Guidance, hey?" and he grabbed GianLuca's hand with a firm grin on his big face. GianLuca immediately picked up his latest trick of playing dumb. It got him into the Basilica quicker than expected and after Santa Croce, there was no better hiding place to be thought of. The monk continued with unexpected enthusiasm in an atrocious vernacular.

A time traveler should never leave the ship without knowledge of any of such lingo.

"God has always been good to me. Indeed, I was just thinking how I could use a strong helping hand to assist me with cleaning His house! You came down from the Heavens, so unexpectedly, so quickly . . . this is indeed that kind of miracle that keeps our faith growing stronger every day we live under His divine guidance. What do you think, son?" he asked in a strangely humble voice while holding his wrist in an even tighter grip. GianLuca nodded with a consistent humming and faked a handicap, playing dumb with an annoyingly exaggerated humility.

The three English-speaking lads he had spied on were still on his mind. They all came from that same 'other world'.

Unusual sounding names: Derecho, hmm, that name is familiar, but where from?

He felt as if he blanked out. *That jetlag sure keeps me going*, and he shrugged. Before the monk could ask any more questions (and would one suspect from the fine attire he wore he wasn't a handyman?), GianLuca probed his limited acting talents and he grumbled, ached and pinched his belly till he was taken into a tiny room in the back of the sacristy near the garden. God's servant showed him a hole in an un-tiled floor while chuckling and pinching his nose tightly. He pushed the dumb boy finally into this toilet paper-free space.

GianLuca wanted to laugh out loud to have no paper in sight; not even *La Republicca (*Italian newspaper!).

He waited for the monk to get back into the front room and as soon as he did, GianLuca sneaked out and forced his way from the 'holy of holiest toilets' through a smallish window, tumbling upside down and right into the garden. He found an exit onto a small convent linked to the church by a corridor, a somewhat familiar territory from his youth.

Of course, he had visited the place countless times even if the century was a different one. In the back, he heard the friar's thundering voice and he quickly backed up when the door flew into his face (or almost), conveniently covering him up as the father ran by him looking for his now lost recruit!

Here's the real miracle Holy Father, "Now you see him, now you don't."

He swiftly closed the door and stormed through God's rather empty house, emptier than he would ever see it on his own timeline. Right before rushing to the main entrance of the Santa Croce Church, he scanned the big and empty space, his eyes searching for the tabernacle. Dumbfounded and shocked he hadn't immediately noticed, the few statues proudly representing Renaissance society did not compete with any of the legendary artists. Michelangelo's tomb was indeed absent, because he was still very much alive. The famous poets, writers, and inventors he remembered gracing the hall, all the recognizable signs of prominent Illuminati, were still absent from what was to become the *Tempio dell'Itale Glorie* (the temple of the Italian Glories).

Chills cemented him to the marble checkerboard floors, frozen down for a moment to an altogether unexpected reality. This was the Renaissance after all! God forbid this was a one-way ticket.

Get out right now and get a beard, he thought. Not a bad idea. Yes, I must get a beard. Definitely will make me look like one of the Medici family. What if someone pulls it . . . ?

He sighed and stopped the chatterbox before his head was turning into a melting pot of nonsense.

Sometimes I wished I wasn't such a Gemini*,* he contemplated, as he quickened his steps and exited with his eyes on that Piazza, void of the statue he had been so familiar with: Enrico Pazzi's 'Dante', and he smiled at his own disbelief.

13. FIORENZA, 1473 LAPO

Wondering mind
slides by perturbing over-questioning
while questioned brain resides in the doubtful reasoning
of the untrustworthy slide my heart just took
while excluding all simplicity of the intricate web
I shall not grab the essence from ... right now. (Complexities)

The market square was buzzing with loud, sassy salesmen. GianLuca, still avoiding the crowd, noticed the two harlots still hanging around the same stall, too active to even notice him. He'd better make sure he'd find his way back to Andrea's house. His steps took on quicker speed till he reached the back alley. He was relieved to find the little door open, and in an instant, Giovannino proudly jumped out holding a dagger to the newcomer's throat. GianLuca swiftly lifted him above his head then caught him in a grip of strength.

The young kid held on tight to his shoulders and there was a gentle comfort that gave the whole orphan story a new meaning. "*Sei forte Signore* (Sir, you're strong)!"

He couldn't refrain from speaking out loud, bouncing back to the grass with that permanently big smile.

GianLuca yielded to that happy energy the Buontalenti family conveyed at every moment he walked onto their premises. He entered the house finding Andrea in a pensive mood at a small desk near the window that gave way to an inner courtyard, framed by ancient trees in each corner. Right at that moment as he walked towards him, his host had turned around to another elegant, yet older man who walked towards a living space, maybe more like an office, with a magnificently aligned cross vault. Father and son dived into a deeply felt embrace while their guest watched their warmth envelop; their little page Giovannino watching from a close distance.

"*Prego GianLuca* (Please Gianluca)," Andrea said, in a happy voice. "May I introduce you to my father? He has just returned from a very long voyage – far earlier than expected."

"Any friend of my son's is a friend of the family," and Lapo Buontalenti's deep voice gave away an innate quietness and his firm handshake inspired confidence.

"GianLuca's mother was born in Tuscany," Andrea said, "and the only problem is, well, she wasn't born in this century, so it seems." He laughed in an unexpectedly high pitch.

An avalanche of skirts ruffled along the quick steps and "*Papà sei qui* (Papa you're here)," interrupted their unfinished introduction as Agnola jumped around her father's neck with all the charm of a teenager.

Her sister followed, as usual, slightly more dignified and yet, she equally melted in her father's arms. GianLuca observed this man in his late sixties, a mop of wavy grey hair standing up from a square yet open face. His proud manner showed a quality all his own. It struck GianLuca immediately; this man was truly loved by his children ... this family sticks together at all times. Whilst the Buontalenti patriarch might have dreamed away the afternoon with the playful sun through the leaves, all four turned to him and announced a *brindisi* (a toast), to his safe return home.

In no time, Andrea's father had received an update on their unusual visitor. They sat down in the garden and the young women draped the grass with their gowns to resemble a painting of an almost mesmerizing majesty. Only GianLuca saw Andrea's head in Fiammetta's lap like a kind of mature Raphael portrait (the as yet unborn master painter) of elegant simplicity; both sisters gliding definitely into one of Botticelli's masterpieces.

How could I ever reconsider returning to my own world, when such beauty cages my willingness in veils of a Renaissance seduction?

Just then their father turned to GianLuca. "Young man, you truly could be another son to my family. There's even a certain resemblance between you and Andrea and yes, Agnola turn your head profile, will you – see both of you – yes, very much so. Well, you are indeed welcome at our home and I am not surprised to find you here," Lapo spoke in a deep voice,

"… because I actually had a dream about such an unexpected visit only a few weeks ago."

"It stayed with me," he explained vividly. "It was on a big market square, similar to the one at Santa Croce, that you appeared the first time. I dreamed of *un gran festa* (a big party) and in the middle of much turbulent dancing, while hundreds were spiralling their happy *abbandonno* (the letting go), a man appeared with those exact dark locks framing a longish, handsome face."

Lapo continued, "He spun faster than the crowd and he moved through them as if he could fly through the walls while earth had no impact on him. He carried some kind of green leaves, like a bush of sage, dropping them on our house, and in his left hand he had something resembling a crystal wand. At least Morpheus introduced a Mercurial messenger to me."

"The dream state can bring us quite some surprising answers, sir." GianLuca tapped into a tentative monologue with dutiful respect. "Indeed," and as if Lapo hadn't noticed his guest's interception, the noble man continued, "… indeed, indeed there's quite a symbolic meaning to this. Because you knocked on our door, again and again, and nobody opened, because it wasn't … closed!" His laughing voice had taken on a very excited tone.

"Well sir," GianLuca responded, "if I may, hmm, there's quite a bit more to it all, though there's really very little I can explain, at least not right now. But together we may well find some revealing answers. I will try, or better than trying I will explain. I mean, if you like me to of course … you must be exhausted from such long a voyage."

That sounds a rather unconvincing introduction. That word 'trying' always annoys me … trying instead of doing. Certainly, one of our human failure programs – not easy to delete. Which twenty-first century philosopher said that trying implied the possibility of failure?

Andrea had read some of his guest's reactions. He was well connected to understand an almost gentle intimidation his father projected; sedate he seemed, yet awe-inspiring, as was his innate wisdom. Andrea had mentioned before that their friends almost worshipped him at their monthly gatherings.

Lapo Buontalenti proceeded in his own gentle manner. "We have a monthly gathering here where some of our visitors demonstrate their worldly skills and, shall we say, search for a deeper understanding of the human mind! Actually one of them, an astrologer, will join us shortly. We always prepare the evening meal together and during the discussions, he always comes up with some fascinating explanations of how the planets are influencing us in this very moment, etcetera. No doubt you've felt last night's full moon?"

Quietly withdrawn, GianLuca refused to interrupt Andrea's father's very animated monologue. He simply nodded at someone who seemed to have stepped out of the mirror he had just glanced in, while believing only to be looking at himself.

"Sir," GianLuca wanted to make a point, "I have searched – without a doubt even through more than this life – for the essence of my being, for the reason of coming to this 'Terra', and I have felt challenged daily by a prime issue; the power we humans possess and how to use it!"

"*Caro* GianLuca, if I may just call you by your first name – and please call me Lapo – I can relate to the passion in your voice, for power in this city has been 'our prime issue' in Tuscany and Fiorenza," he answered rapidly, "and I have contemplated many times as to how we've been dependent upon so many gods, the hierarchies from Egypt, Greece, Rome and many more, never truly knowing nor using our own power. I believe someone must explain to our people that such power resides inside of us all and at La Signoria – from where the local government rules – we should all have our say!"

Agnola's face cramped up; she squeezed her eyes. "Father please ..." she murmured, "you could be condemned for such speech." But the tension faded away quickly with Andrea's laughter. "Sister, you know our father. He's wise enough to only speak of such subjects between these very thick walls." Andrea continued with a smirk, "Or ... in many empty fields!"

Fiammetta watched the familiar family game and her sister lifted her eyebrows and stretched her eyelids while Lapo burst out loudly, joining his son at their very personal entertainment. At first a little uncomfortable, GianLuca smiled at the whole scene while Giovannino ran in, very excited, announcing their other dinner guest had arrived. When a stately figure by the name of Marco entered, both girls rose, and father and son clearly approached him as yet another member of the family. Introductions were made swiftly, and they all moved to the dining area.

GianLuca wasn't at all surprised that no vegetarian meal was being served. He looked almost embarrassed at the roasted boar that lay shining, butt up in the midst of what seemed a huge fruit salad, some sort of mashed berries … indeed a very tasty looking dish. His tongue took a peek and his nose recognized the scent of rosemary and sage. His mind wandered off in search of the non-existent refrigerator.

But this animal must have been hunted yesterday.

"A feast for us all," exclaimed Lapo. "Right before I reached the city, in the Foreste Casentinesi, this magnificent animal was waiting for me; you are getting your meal fresh from the woods."

Lapo turned around with his big smile and answered to GianLuca's lack of enthusiasm that he was only an occasional hunter and he wanted to welcome his visitors with an exceptional meal. Both guests answered him with a smile and silver cups filled up with a local red wine; a memorable evening awaited four wise men and two gorgeous women.

14. FIORENZA, 1473 MARCO

... closer, closer to grab the brilliance
"they" gave you to show us
how unique we all truly are and ...
yet we still need that screen to remind us:
we are the windows
and we can also be the gate. (A Bill for Windows and Gates)

"I see the art of studying the heavens is of your interest?" Marco declared somewhat solemnly as he finished his fourth cup of luscious wine.

"What a poetic way of describing ... hmm, the study of the heavens." GianLuca returned his smile, "in my youth I was taught that astrology allows us to find out more about seasonal shifts and how the celestial cycles are signs of a heavenly communication," GianLuca continued, "so, I've done my best to learn from the movement of the planets and their inevitable influence on our daily lives. There is not a day goes by without my being stunned at the fact that all important events in life can be retraced through such a study."

The silence confirmed the knowledge not unfamiliar to Marco Farini and it kept the small audience spellbound. Dresses shuffled around the open fire in a competitive dance with the bursting flames. Andrea and his sisters sank down once again as from one of the paintings GianLuca had so often admired at the city's Palazzo Vecchio. The men's skin gleamed like oiled parchment as if Michelangelo himself had time-jumped. Only the big torch at the entrance door fought the breeze from taking even the slightest attention away from the now blazing fireplace. The silence had invited their thoughts aloud.

How strange, in the middle of the summer, it's really almost cold in this house. Of course, these enormous thick walls keep out the heat.

A whimsical Fiammetta rested against her brother's back, and before Andrea had a chance to move a few more velvet pillows his way, Agnola threw herself victoriously on her brother's lap, sliding down in a careless bounce to a rather hard wooden floor. Naturally, a musical suite of giggles and tickling ended only when Andrea moved away, leaving both young women at a needle-point pillow fight, while the men savoured a *vino santo,* very much like an old port; one of Italy's popular after dinner drinks. GianLuca was fascinated by Fiammetta's beauty

'Do I not know you?' For a moment a rapturous embrace came to mind and some more erotic ideas framed an imagination that lacked all decorum. Long eyelashes suddenly whipped a thrill, enticing eye contact. Desirable, she was, indeed, and GianLuca's brain translated in slow sensuous motion. She smiled at him a bit gauchely and he beamed back, clumsily. The beauty he so admired took him floating between the stars till his eyes flirted with her one more time. He moved away from the hot fireplace only to be kept from a permanent trance of silent bemusement. Then Lapo called him back to the moment.

"Are you getting a bit tired?" Lapo asked in a deft manner as GianLuca's interest for his elder daughter didn't go unnoticed. "Maybe our bewilderment with the stars in the heavens has thrown you off schedule, and wisdom and science should be laid to rest till tomorrow morning?" Andrea said. He put down his cup and got up lifting his younger sister back to her feet and hurrying her off. She smiled through a brief curtsy picking up her fine dress without revealing so much as even an ankle. She then pinched her sister in the cheeks and left her father showered by her kisses. She waved at Marco and GianLuca with the indifference of a spoiled girl whose many dolls are sitting desperately awaiting her in bed. Both Andrea and Lapo exchanged a warm – hearted *Buona note* (good night) and while Marco decided to take a walk in the garden, GianLuca offered to walk Fiammetta to her room. *This isn't the century of instant romance. A one-night stand in the house of your host will not be welcome.*

From Agnola's room he heard a sweet voice singing something of a ballade, or so it seemed, and soothing it was to his ears. "She has a lovely voice", Fiammetta said, picking up the sound from his eyes. "She has written the aria herself; it's inspired by one of Lorenzo di Piero de Medici's poems. She plays the *liuto* (lute). It's a song often used at the carnival." She almost whispered.

They stood for a moment in front of her room as they feigned listening to Agnola's soft rendering of the poem:

"Come, be gay, while we may,
Beauty's a flow'r despised in decay;
Youth's the season made for joys,
Love is then a duty."

In his century there would have been no reason to part, but GianLuca, had no other choice but to retire to his own quarters and so he did.

15. FIORENZA, 1473 BUONTALENTI

Hand me your cell, sell me your hand
lesser your program of instant recall.
Breaking news speeders digest,
make sure you take no rest
in our Orwellian vision your spectre passed the test. (Scary Traps)

The early morning was swept away by the sun sneaking in through one of the smallish windows, painting the left wall into a picture gallery as if decorated by precious 'light-scrapers'. It reminded him that in some mysterious way, he did land back in the Buontalenti guest room. While refraining from turning his shirt inside-out from more erotic reverie, he dove back into the broidery of the surrounding pillows.

There was a repeat of a knock he thought had belonged to his dream. He knew the birds chanted to convince him the night was indeed over. He got up and opened the door and found himself facing the brother of the woman he had slept with in his dreams, and he detected a glimpse of disapproval … *but then, why would Andrea judge me? His behaviour seemed not at all fifteenth century-like.*

He discarded more unnecessary visions in his left-brain by this familiar friendly arm grip denying any further rumination. Andrea shook him amicably and GianLuca was now fully awake; not back to the future, back to the Renaissance.

"She's indeed beautiful, *una fiamma* (a flame), a truly burning flame; I am glad you aren't moving too quickly in your seductive actions," Andrea said with raised eyebrows. GianLuca looked perfectly unapologetic or at least slightly less guilty.

How can I leave this timeline ever again and return to a century where even my body might crave her presence? My heart will be left in total solitude, but in this Renaissance home?

"You have brought more life and light to our home than anyone has, since ... well since our mother passed away. Like her older daughter she was a passionate, amusing and a socially active woman full of light and our father's closest friend; a rarity among spouses. She cared about her family more than about her own appearance. Of course, she was a gorgeous woman and envied by many. She needn't even think about the word 'beauty'..." Andrea stared at the floor. "Well, I mustn't sound to you as if I was about to propose her hand to you. It's supposed to be the other way around ... what about in your world? Oh, GianLuca, I can tell from your look that it isn't the same."

Giovannino, who seemed to appear out of nowhere whenever needed, asked if he should bathe their houseguest upon which Andrea broke into a series of cartoon smiles GianLuca could relate to. It put him in an equally funny mood.

"If you don't mind, I'm having horses saddled," Andrea said, "We'll meet my father and Marco a few miles out of town in the hills of Maiano. That is after you have had a chance to change out of your night skin." He smiled and gently pushed the pageboy to get the warm water the kitchen had prepared ahead of time.

Andrea really is a prince; he's so thoughtful, gentle-mannered. He always has everything ready in the most unintended speed and in the most gracious way.

The hot bath dozed him off, till a rather hard brush brought him back as if he was an old horse greatly in need of a yearly cleanse. It invigorated him and a little later, he was riding next to Andrea, uphill, leaving behind the old city he thought he knew so well.

On their first brief stop, GianLuca was stunned once again at the Florence he had known and loved ever since his first visit in the mid-seventies.

Questa Fiorenza (this Florence), free of misty clouds, no fuming cars or a loud Vespa breathing down the narrow back streets ... it captured him like an old mistress who turned out to be a *strega* (real witch). It reminded him of the many hikes he took with his father in the hills of Fiesole and Maiano; those welcoming mountains and these giant ancient rocks from the caves of '*Pietra Serena*' (serene stone), or the place where Italy's legendary sculptors dug their 'holy stone'.

At each small church, Andrea called out the names of saints the pope had lured into local history; mostly professional martyrs, he joked. After about an hour in a firm gallop, on a vast open space with only a few olive trees to relieve the summer sun, they met Lapo with Marco by his side, both in a terrific mood. Not that GianLuca had expected them to be different, yet today there was, well something really ... yes, something totally different going on.

Marco had a scroll exposed on a velvet cloth. They all got seated in a tight circle around what looked like some sort of a detailed map with some coloured marks, and not GianLuca alone showed a lively interest. The other three men stared at him for the first time as if he was a true stranger and Marco broke the silence. "No doubt where you come from," his smile directed to GianLuca, "the map of the sky is far subtler in detail, and I imagine, far more complete. My teachers took me way back to the Persian astronomers. I actually met one myself and he also taught me how this wonderful palette of stars is the best mentor you can dream off. I sit and look at them and then, yes, I let them talk to me!"

"What a pity, what a pity," GianLuca exclaimed. "In my home, well, that is out there somewhere." He giggled, "I have a computer, that is ... ugh, a rather intricate device a kind of flat box," he hummed.

"Like your bracelet?" Andrea interrupted jokingly.

"Oh no." GianLuca smiled, "far bigger, more complex and versatile with countless, let's say menus. If you only could understand where we have come to in our century ... but let me not dwell on what your eyes cannot perceive, at least not in this life."

All eyes were on the new Italian drama. "Astrology is my first hobby, um ... that is actually what I do in my free time (that's what we call a hobby). When I'm not working, you know, like earning a living, I am very occupied with astrology. It will be fascinating to hear Marco's own revelations." GianLuca continued, "look, there are so many planets and asteroids, as Marco may well have told you. They're named after the Greek or Roman Gods like Jupiter, Saturn, Neptune, Venus, the Sun and the Moon of course, influencing our daily lives tremendously."

Guess I can't explain about Pluto since that planet wasn't discovered yet.

"In my century, we became aware of much more and we have also acknowledged asteroids. I like to think of them as an extra perfume to the study of our behaviour." He spoke with his customary passion for the theme and continued in greater detail to three very attentive pairs of eyes. "The twenty-first century you mentioned?" Lapo and his son whispered.

"Yes, ha-ha ... sorry, I'll explain more about that period later. At certain times of the year, the planets form alignments that can stir us in the most unexpected of directions. Chiron's return, a bit of a prelude to Second Saturn Return is like an important wake-up call to ..."

He looked at his trio of new friends who seemed to have stopped breathing during his rapid monologue and GianLuca dug his head jokingly into his lap. "I truly apologize; please proceed with your own discovery. I didn't mean to try to impress you, please forgive my rudeness."

But Marco arbitrated gently. "Your knowledge is not an intrusion; please do not stop. You are like a messenger, just like Lapo said ... and ..." The latter's voice thundered through with a cloud full of laughter. "*Caro GianLuca* (dear GianLuca), we are but beginners and we can hardly wait for your remarks and observations. Marco does have a little information to share and your comments are greatly appreciated! We are here to learn and discover so much more and this day turns out to be a unique one."

Their discussions took the afternoon to its unwanted ending and Andrea was only too happy to see that his new friend had brought yet another tool, less scary this time, as he related clearly to the soft paper notebook where GianLuca penned down his many remarks with a pen that needed ... no dipping in ink! The three Renaissance sages sat in awe, smiling like children with a new teddy bear that also could talk!

Astrology remained their common subject and Marco's knowledge was far from superficial. He offered some very in-depth information and a notebook in which to write it down. Lapo and Andrea had thrown logs on the small fire that was now slowly losing its glow, while the cool air topping the hill reminded them that they'd better leave soon as another great dinner awaited them. Earlier, Lapo's daughters had proudly announced there might well be a couple of other guests. GianLuca and Lapo rode together for a while and Lapo shared a few thoughts about the beauty and the good-hearted nature of his children. Lapo wasn't nodding just because of the horse's movement ... a permanent smile effortlessly masked his spoken age.

16. MAIANO, 1473 FIAMMETTA

... in realities no painter can ever veneer
in that pool of Universal consciousness where All that Is
will not exclude the power of the Light nor Dark ...
and all is game. (Lost Flavours)

As early as 1145, Florence had conquered Maiano and from its hills, the view was indeed, magnificent. A few days before, on a weekly bus ride to the di Maiano, GianLuca had stopped for lunch at the *fattoria*, a workshop place he cherished. And now he was looking down from that same spot without that oil factory; the view of Florence was even more breathtaking.

Admiring it from a different angle and, of course in another century, it was sparsely populated yet fewer houses left the impact the same. Still at a loss as to the events of the last forty-eight hours, he had felt ecstatic while riding down the valley; neither in a car nor bus, but on a magnificent horse that carried him like an obedient, friendly servant. He wondered if getting stuck in a time loop would be just the thing to hope for. Worse, he was enjoying himself. While his companions unsaddled their horses, Giovannino gently took that task from him.

Strikingly beautiful, Agnola, now in a simple white gown, was waiting in the courtyard. Taking GianLuca by his arm, she now addressed herself freely to her houseguest, glad to be whispering personal feelings about the obvious attraction between him and her sister Fiammetta. She had guessed well, and she shamelessly asked if he was considering marriage. GianLuca was nearly trembling at her unexpected excitement and an almost modern boldness.

No more erotic dreams in the next round!

With a blush he confessed to Fiammetta's beauty, but he explained: "I come from a world where marriage is not decided so quickly." And then, just then, she interrupted him with her almost disarming enthusiasm. Nearly ignoring his remarks, Agnola announced that maybe she could now dream up a double marriage ceremony, for she too, was equally in love.

"Wait," she smiled, "you'll soon meet the man of 'my' choice, and the one I adore above all noble men in Florence, yes, even the entire country." She ran off in her typical girlish way. Fiammetta had watched them from the second-floor balcony. He felt her presence and waved back at her in a gracious pirouette. The more he thought about the present moment, the more he felt confused. It seemed impossible to consider a relationship with any of these people, especially Fiammetta. He wasn't even sure in which reality he had landed ... trapped in time?

During his teenage Buddhist days, he had studied a lot and acknowledged the Universal Law of Energy. His teachers had taught him that on whatever timeline, whatever he would do, these actions would ripple along onto other lines of time. He had believed their theories and had acquired extensive knowledge, with a passion, about the eastern philosophy on the theme of life and death. He remembered these courses well, specifically those he had taken with a Colorado-based, female philosopher who claimed to channel a collective from a faraway galaxy. She also filled a void for wisdom, while a manipulated New Age world professed 'Love & Light', refusing to see the victimhood humanity still inflicted on itself.

"Does the mind know the difference between a real and an imagined event or are they like twin sisters in the same constellation?" she had once asked him with a Confucian wisdom.

He also started to wonder if this young Tuscan woman had any relation to Galina, his last girlfriend when he was living in the Massachusetts' Berkshires. There were no physical similarities ... none, yet the passion and the balletic lines she had drawn in his dreams last night were rather familiar. Before he had the time to walk up to his room, she stood right in front of him.

"I must give a hand to Agnola," Fiammetta halted. "She is the one who thought it would be fun to invite the de Medici brothers for supper." Slightly nervous, Fiammetta's eyes met his, uncomfortable behind the pupils. "It appears that Giuliano has accepted but we do not know if Lorenzo will come. Personally, I doubt it very much, since he's a man always working extremely late and he has to take care of the affairs of business related to his family. He is much admired by us all. As you may have guessed, my sister has a fondness for the brother of one of Italy's most powerful men." She ramped up a rapid voice, rolling her eyes.

Her speech had the charm of a chatterbox. Once he had walked into his room and dropped down on his bed, her voice left an on-going echoing in his ears... his eyes bigger than his eyelids while his mind wanted to inhabit hers.

"Oh, Agnola was right," she went back to her girlish giggle. "In this light you really have such similarities with Giuliano. May I ask you not to look in the stars at tonight's dinner, nor to predict anyone's death even if your history books may say it will happen?" Fiammetta asked. "We haven't written our own history yet. We have told the de Medici about our foreign guest from England and that he came via Flanders and France. No doubt you have enough time to invent an even more convincing story." Her voice was sound, decisive and he liked her humour and sense of improvisation. He approached to kiss her hands gently when Andrea walked through the open door.

"*Fratello, gli ho parlato* (Brother, I spoke to him)," she told him while GianLuca withdrew. "Perfect dear friend, I am glad Fiammetta informed you. It is a bit unexpected and we hope you do not mind dining with us all; Giuliano de Medici will be in attendance. Please feel free to tell a different travel story," he said in a gleeful chortle. "I am sure you will not wear your bracelet – 'watch' you called it?"

For the first time, GianLuca realized the seriousness of the whole matter. He nearly blamed himself for thoughts and wishes he had fancied on his native timeline such as *'what would it be like if I would travel back to Renaissance Florence?' Oops... but here I am.*

His wish had materialized and now his logical mind wanted an answer as to how in the world(s) he got there and, of course, how he was going to get back home. He sat down on the heavily decorated bed and reflected on the period in his earth-bound life when he had lived in Australia; a time where answers had always come easily. An aboriginal guide had explained how the human ancestors had come from the Pleiades, a star system, a gate to travel to planet Earth.

He claimed that giant beings had brought the 'dreamtime' and that the star collective was a gate to move in and out from other dimensions, into other worlds, back and forth and back and forth again throughout time, without beginning or end. It had left a disturbing effect on his understanding of the world he knew. While visiting the legendary Uluru (Ayer's Rock), one of the oldest plateaus on planet Earth, in the centre of the Australian desert, butterflies had landed on his hands, as if to tell him that dreams, just like those butterflies, were outlived by the cycles of the moon, as the indigenous claimed.

"*Nient'altro Signore* (Nothing else, sir)?" And there was Giovannino's big smile presenting what resembled a costume. There was music in the courtyard and GianLuca wondered if the de Medici brothers had already arrived. Andrea's page explained enthusiastically that the music came from a musician who was none other but his master, Lapo. It dawned on him that Lapo might expect some possible interest and future engagement for his younger daughter. He smiled at the new outfit left on his bed. At least the young boy understood now that he didn't have to wait and GianLuca took all the time in the world to get dressed.

Haha, now this really seems like a ballet performance in which I now may not have to point those feet but . . . hold this busy tongue.

On the same floor, Agnola too was getting dressed. A transparent restlessness caused her black-lace fan to take an unusual speed, like a windmill victimized by some turbulent storm. Fiammetta had chosen the necklace her mother would have wanted her sister to wear at such an occasion. She closed the chain and took her sister in her arms. "*Tranquillo* (Easy)," she encouraged her.

"He always liked you. Remember, from the days when we were all playing together as children," she smooched away the tiny fear cloud bubbling beside Agnola's head. "And the way he looked at you the last time at that dinner; that should say enough, no? Like papa always told mama; stop the doubting and the worrying, for it attracts the opposite of what you may hope for!"

"How lucky can I be?" Agnola now intercepted with her own lack of trust. "You, papa, Andrea . . . I must indeed accept life as it comes along, at times with its many surprises, even though like most of us, I like to know in advance what will occur. And yes sister, I know, and you are right, like Andrea always says; be like the river Arno and flow along effortlessly. I will do my best to behave tonight."

She sighed and turned around briskly. "I hope that your future lover will do the same!" she giggled. Fiammetta nodded dramatically. She hoped that GianLuca wasn't going to delve in too deeply in the conversations the Medici brothers might inspire. But above all she was a bit concerned as to how the brothers would react when they would see the likeness of this foreigner, who seemed to be only just a slightly older version of Giuliano di Piero de Medici.

Indeed, GianLuca resembled a mature version of Giuliano, like the one Botticelli painted. Fiammetta had picked out a more formal attire for GianLuca: dark green silk doublets her brother had outgrown but they would make her 'chosen one' look like an Italian Prince.

17. FIORENZA, 1473 GIULIANO DE MEDICI

I've closed my eyes and a tear slouched my cheek
with the beat of your music,
chilling in the simplicity of its vivid accords,
a frying fremitus of glorious syncopations
that batter on my skin to fully raising hair
on the inside of my mask and … (Music from a Past)

Giuliano de Medici walked in with a lively step. His manner was noble, and he had left his horse in care of his page. First greeting Lapo and then Andrea with equal conviviality; his eyes were scanning the inner court. The Medici nose was prominent yet not disturbing a well-balanced face. Lean and tall, with his prince-like allure, and family lineage written all over, however any physical comparison with his illustrious brother was but slight. He liked the colour green and his hat and long cape were of a heavy thread, a very deep emerald green.

While GianLuca took his time to walk down the balcony ramp, a 1950's Robin Hood movie came to mind. It put him in a really good mood. Who wouldn't like to meet with those fascinating legendary brothers? Giuliano was observing the foreign visitor. GianLuca entered while Andrea was shaking Giuliano's hand and both the sisters were impatiently smiling for more than a princely attention. Andrea approached from behind and laid his arm around GianLuca's shoulder, about to introduce their houseguest while Agnola offered her hand to be kissed by Giuliano.

Fine-tuned and sophisticated a person that he was, Giuliano, slightly hesitant, now intuitively turned his head. Something, or someone, seemed to call him from the other side of the room. And then, while the entire family was held suspended in the most unfamiliar of airs, like a wave of misty slow-motion in softly lit particles of light, Giuliano's longish fingers slipped from Agnola's hand. To Fiammetta's utter surprise, he lurched back almost squashing her … she whirled to avoid the freshly lit fireplace and landed right into her father's lap. The euphoric stillness of the next moment lasted beyond all human comprehension and while Giuliano's eyes met GianLuca's, the whole room was wedded in a golden glow.

Hidden behind the largest chair, a stunned Giovannino covered his head with his hands. Speechless, Lapo felt as in a trance for an unmeasurable pause, locked in time. The picture had frozen, and all motion had stopped.

The big wooden logs were still burning as bright and large as they had been that last hour. Time never consumed the fire, and the only ashes were the remnants of the night foregone. Two right arms in olive-green cloth had hooked like fearless knights of past times and a matrix of profound recognition connected a quivering, a trembling in both their chests; their faces shining as in an oil-painted portrait of a Templar or a stoic family portrait hung from a museum wall.

If this ritual seemed solemn to their audience, a spark plug vigour both knights had ignited brought an electrical energy blowing all fuses.

"GianLuca."

He introduced himself with his genuine smiling face. Not one whispering voice intervened.

"*Sono Giuliano* (I am Giuliano)," he stated solemnly adding, "*Che piacere ritrovarti dopo tanti anni* (What a pleasure finding you back after all those years)."

Giuliano answered, "*Anch'io, ma dove ci siamo conosciuti* (So, me too, but where do we know us from)?"

Muteness kept all other faces glued to their ears. The two men's court dance of sublime and unaffected gallantry persisted. When they turned profile, strikingly mellow as two mature twins, they embraced in all graciousness, forgetful of the house that hosted their welcome. Lapo's family outlived the living frescos on the ancient walls of their own distinct Palazzo. In their consciousness they perceived this encounter as the most unusual and extraordinary event they had ever witnessed. They couldn't express their enthusiasm and friendship while floating in a helpless cloud of non-participation.

When GianLuca suddenly caressed Giuliano's black hair adorning these Botticelli-like features, his corneas uncovered the irises sliding into the centre point of each retina, daring an avalanche of long forgotten stories. Four hands translated centuries of mystery in strange telepathy and, as in an outer space time-lapse, this moment engraved itself through a cryptic vista of perfect harmony. A painless sigh from both men whirled as fresh air and it brought back the house from the mystic incandescence. By then, the only fire left was that of the torches at the entrance door from where Andrea hadn't moved, while the shadowy patio behind him dimmed in the dusk of the evening.

In their next move all seven players evaporated, as if in the same shaded area of an X-ray screen, unframed and trailed only by unattached souls in the delight of a recognizable and agelessly mirrored alliance.

18. FIORENZA, 1473 GIANLUCA & GIULIANO

Beliefs: of beauty
staggering lack of wordings
in an ocean of untold wealth
of forgone feelings,
undefined, hidden away in a star assembly
around the beaming fire,
off the porch, behind the shaman's sweat lodge
at the apex of trees of old. (Of Untold Wealth)

Had it not been for the absence of small talk and a silence that a stomach could only momentarily bear, the supper would have been truly impressive. The diversity of the meats and vegetables, the fruits and the most amazing wines were all on display in the midst of cherry blossoms and white gardenias on an enormous table. Indeed, to any hidden spectator, a Renaissance painting had come to life. A lute player swanning gently around the culinary seductions entertained the host family and their friends with songs of tales long forgotten, yet to lend him an ear meant maybe missing a word, if any word was to be spoken at all.

Whenever GianLuca or Giuliano paused all heads would turn towards them. It was almost funny to see how one single event could change the course of an evening and maybe their entire lives. The sisters especially were well-behaved, calm and composed as if someone had passed away. They both felt as if they had been removed from the bigger picture and at least one of the ladies was truly annoyed.

Giuliano was the first one to praise the meal, after all cooked as an homage to both the guests. He had apologized for his brother's last-minute withdrawal and they had all nodded accordingly with respect and understanding; their disappointment sank with the next glass of wine. Lapo strongly affirmed how he agreed with Giuliano's brother for his strong position taken regarding the pope's latest decisions at the Vatican. Small talk had sneaked in yet again.

Little by little their own more familiar subjects, politics and religion hooked the male conversations into a vivid duality while the two sisters feared and quietly discussed a possible new presentation of another miraculous display of light. Fiammetta had been truly impressed and she looked differently at GianLuca. As a woman who knew her power, attracted to a real male, she now felt reluctant inside, as if she was about to lose the most precious of gems, and there was nothing she was going to be able to do about it; nor could her sister Agnola.

She fought hard to hide a permanent pout and her father had to give her more attention than he could handle that evening. Slowly, small talk became smaller and the musician left under a partly grateful yet polite applause and a generous financial token of respect. Andrea took GianLuca by the arm and picked up the mood. The patio looked a size bigger in this very clear blue night.

"We were excluded. Please . . . no blame to anyone, but we were excluded." Andrea's voice slightly quivered and he almost looked annoyed. "I wish to understand what really happened when you both met. It appears that for a moment time stood still."

GianLuca swallowed and he cleared his throat in absence of a convincing answer he had wished he could offer to his generous hosts. He nodded.

"You both stopped the time and I think, no I'm convinced, you did it together," Marco intervened while joining them. "This is a very strong full moon."

"I have no words," GianLuca said doubtfully, "no phrases lingering in my mind and yet . . ."

"And then again, that may well be it; somehow both your minds connected because you both may be a part of the same Alma," Marco continued with an almost childlike honesty.

"Your souls are so connected!" Andrea now commented.

GianLuca smiled quietly at their discovery. His friends had tipped the veil just a little more and he confirmed to them that he did not consider himself a specialist on the matter. He did his best to explain and he told them stories about how on his timeline, he had studied with a formidable psychologist.

"This man was not your regular mentor and he had understood the function of the mind within its greater context." GianLuca caught their attention easily. "The multi-dimensionality of the soul within parallel worlds and throughout more than one Universe ... indeed that was quite a meal to digest. It wasn't just imagined by science fiction novelists." While they all looked bemused, he quickly explained what science fiction was.

He continued, "Such theories had conquered me effortlessly since my youth. Among my colleagues, only a few had subscribed somewhat to such a far-out theory ... even in our twenty-first century." He explained to the two attentive men how he had searched and researched. Weekend-retreats galore, he had been networking like an eternal student in so many workshops, reading books through sleepless nights till he had ended up just waiting for it to happen. And here he was; reality was now only a few thoughts away. They all laughed.

How could he share the little experience he had with those gentle people while developing a new, sincere friendship and maybe even a timeless courtship? Andrea's eyes were begging for an explanation and GianLuca felt the strength of his arm around his shoulder strongly. It was Marco once again, sensitive at each single moment it seemed, who suggested that someone who had just experienced such a rare event might need some time to himself. Upon that last note, Agnola finally introduced the pout that had been waiting for hours and demanded to know who was going to withdraw after so much esoteric dessert. After all, they were all still standing around looking at an actual very handsome fruit pie.

"I am afraid Giuliano is taking his leave," Lapo's slightly saddened voice announced causing further disappointment, especially to his daughters.

All steps were now directed towards the door leading to the courtyard. While Giuliano draped his cape and his page prepared the horse, hugs were exchanged. He expressed how priceless the evening had been. Giuliano again nearly froze when GianLuca presented his *auguri* (best wishes) and tears were about to run from the eyes of both.

"We must meet soon," Giuliano said smiling. The foreigner nodded and Giuliano continued, "Why not tomorrow; that is if you are free. I will make time for you. How about a ride early morning? I will come, at dawn, with two horses, when the roosters crow. Is that too early?"

His startling flow of words left GianLuca surprised. He nodded a second time. His hesitation didn't fit his thinking process nor did the ungodly time of wake-up call required. But once again slow motion entered their space and the frequency of thought-related communication seemed out of place and out of time in this Renaissance home.

"Thank you, I will," GianLuca answered, "I will gladly await you at dawn and join you".

Giulano's gratitude equalled Andrea's genuine friendship. Hooked once again in an amicable conspiracy, they released their two arms. Quicker than a Vespa, an Arabian stallion took his master through the narrow streets of Florence while Lapo's family gathered around Marco, who was awaiting more explanations that GianLuca might have kept in the shadows. They were all quite disappointed when GianLuca showed a kind but firm reluctance to any further conversation and he gracefully bid good night to all, in an almost distant way.

Marco would explain ... at least some of it.

And indeed, Marco did explain, and that night only their time traveling guest lost himself quickly, in a very deep, timeless sleep.

19. FIESOLE, 2018 PING, PONG, PANG

You may truly like to know how we did it all in such masterful ways
as only the Gods could
till the waking up of some of you,
to some of us, great content. (Lost Flavours)

Dark clouds were sliding back and forth on the Fiesole hillside veiling a full moon where the Medici villa proudly overlooked the Italian Renaissance's most famous city, Fiorenza. At the front gate two agile figures toyed with a small device dismantling the alarm that only guarded the park and gardens.

"*Questi magnifici giardini erano meravigliosamente disposti nell'oscurità lunare* (These magnificent gardens were beautifully arranged in the lunar darkness)," a raunchy sounding voice declared while smoking a last cigarette. Admirably laid out along the long alley leading to the first ramp, these incredible gardens had taken on a haunted appearance.

The first figure took off his hood. "Izquierdo, it is really stupid to even wear this. We were told that the whole family is off to the mountains so nothing will happen. Somehow they're all away from Tuscany."

"Rightly so Derecho, she knows this place well. It's here where the 'trio' Jean-Luc Médecin, Florian and Isabel met on one of their vacations. It almost sounds like you had one of your psychic readings. Are you still into witchcraft; have your dabbles proven right?"

"Really, and you still call this witchcraft? Hadn't I intercepted her email message regarding the codes of this place, hello, we could well be at any of the many other Medici Villas, like the one far away, in Cafaggolio?" He had raised his voice while speaking and his friend looked at him with question marks in his eyes.

"And are you also familiar with the one in the Mugello above Florence and the one in Careggi where Lorenzo's grandfather, Cosimo lived? Both are big and dark residences and in great need of renovations."

"Well, at least you did your homework; but I want to move out of this ancient library and get this job done quickly so we can open a good bottle of Chianti!" Derecho joked.

"Yeah, yeah, I know you're only a historian when you're watching a Hollywood farce with mega sets and wild costumes and oh … lots of undressed women," Izquierdo ping-ponged back to Derecho who lifted his shoulders close to his ears to match their stupid cartoon faces. "Wadda ya want me ta say," he punched in a familiar, silly New Jersey slang.

"If it wasn't for the money, I would certainly not be doing this; but remember Izquierdo, I'm good at it and nobody can break a code nor a lock like me! Right?" he cried out too loud.

"OK, we all have our qualities. Together the two of you can hack any PC to keep America away from a National League game!"

"What are we actually looking for?" Derecho requested in a loud whisper.

Izquierdo looked at him while his eyebrows made him resemble a mad genius. "You mean, Frau von Weitweg didn't tell you?" his mimicking voice slightly sarcastic.

"Well, I'm not her confidante like, obviously, you have become." Derecho coughed back.

"Oh, OK we're all going for a little trip apparently, very soon. Elizabeth has found out that there's more than one way to time travel and here they've apparently installed a very unusual device, a highly expensive one! You know, you're in your chair with big headphones and bang, there you go off to another century … 'live VR'! You see, this villa and a few others may have hidden treasures to take her company, DoWell Inc., to the top of the pharmaceutical chart. That is, if she can get some of the original coded documents and manuscripts, apparently from a Renaissance past!"

And Eliza, the smart little lizard she is, hasn't told me any details yet, but she promised it'll be like stepping into a Star Trek episode!

"Great, that's what I always wanted; to be a guest star with pointy ears! Maybe the busty android will come along too?"

"Oh boy, typical Derecho," the others laughed. "At least in your case, you can say that she does pay well and who else offers you a fancy first class hotel like DoWell does?"

"True," Derecho answered, "so let's get to the damn room and stop in the kitchen on the way; I'm getting hungry and very thirsty!"

They carefully opened and closed the doors after decoding the next alarm system. In seconds they admired the renovated Renaissance home's high ceilings and the high-tech kitchen. They walked into a spacious and elegant room, over-furnished with antiques. Their pencil thin flashlight beams suddenly disappeared into a shower of venetian chandeliers lighting up the entire place. They both staggered back and hesitated as to what to do next and in total surprise; they could only think that someone had beaten them to the bait!

"Welcome gentlemen," a very ladylike voice announced, fully in power of the situation. "Where is the third party in your comic strip trio?"

"If it isn't the latest Latino-version of Ping, Pong, Pang?" a male voice joined. "We only need the opera Puccini wrote, remember *Turandot*? Ha! Yes, so where is Pang?" No first act to the Italian opera could add more ambiance to the James Bond-like scene.

"Florian!" Izquierdo screamed in total disbelief. "What in the hell are you doing here? My god, so it must be true. There were so many rumours: I heard you were never there on that boat when the newspapers reported that you drowned... what the fuck happened? Did you take a plane to the Bermuda triangle and run away with hidden treasures from Atlantis?"

"You know about this dude?" Derecho whispered.

"And who's the dame you're dating, Ian Fleming's twin sister?" Izquierdo dared to ask Florian, who had adopted a recognisable 'Bond' posture.

But a return shot came from that same dame. "I don't believe you have answered our question."

"Whose question gets answered first?" Derecho repeated in his silly slang.

"Shut the fuck up!" his pal stuttered.

"You two are an uproarious joke," the lady stepped forward into the light.

Like a chorus, they agreed in thought; *yes, she was stunning.* She pointed a long arm in a movie star manner, all silent screen glamor.

"I suppose if you are Izquierdo your friend must be Derecho. How appropriate; like Laurel and Hardy. This has got to be *Saturday Night Live* from

NYC right in Florence," and both the man who answered to the name Florian and the vixen laughed out loudly.

The new players held very small weapons in both their hands and the comic strip duo lifted their arms above their heads rather quickly.

"We've come unarmed. Nobody was supposed to be in the house. You're not the proprietors, so why are you here?" Izquierdo dared to ask.

"Why is it that I believe you're not in any position to ask questions since you both do look like a pair of stupid burglars?" Rather swiftly and before they could react any further, Florian had their hands clipped behind their backs.

"Handcuffs? You must be kidding," Derecho screamed out nearly crying, "I thought you knew the guy?"

"Oh, come on Florian, give us a break. We were once classmates," Izquierdo called out.

"A break, you're asking for a break? A prison-break perhaps? Ouch, you know that hurts!" Imitating that New Jersey slang, Florian joked and he continued, "If I were you, I would avoid that expression; words do sometimes create very odd realities ... especially 'breaking'!"

Derecho's eyes nearly popped behind his glamorous frames ... *Schmugucci Occiali* (of course), *fumé contre le soleil* (dark glasses against the sun), as the latest fashion commanded on the billboards.

"You were what ... students together?" Isabel interrupted. "Yeah," Izquierdo replied, "we studied together for a secret service entrance exam; obviously not very successfully. It's a long story."

"You didn't make it and you remember I quit after my first apprentice year?" Florian smiled. "Let's cut the small talk, OK? What do we owe such a late-night visit to?"

"I would answer, if I were you," she insisted, "He can get nasty after midnight and I think he had too much to drink at dinner". And with an epic giggle she proceeded to slide comfortably into a late Louis XV armchair.

With a small tremble in his voice, Izquierdo replied, "We came to look for a time travel code, for documents or any proof of the existence of such a code. We didn't expect to find anybody here. I mean, are you like ... living here?"

The words didn't come that easily and he felt embarrassed while thinking of his former college-time friendship with Florian, ages ago.

"Well, we don't mean bad and I am really hungry. I am willing to get out and never come back and... even for a burger, I'll do anything," Derecho continued in a funny melodramatic way.

"You are a real one-man show, aren't you?" Izquierdo shook his head.

"Is he really as talented at anything he tackles as you were?" Florian asked Izquierdo.

Meanwhile, the only woman in the room was about to lose all patience. "Well, they're obviously of no use to us. Just get rid of them and Florian, why don't you take them to the basement. There's that old medieval dungeon, hardly any air, no light, no food; like in the good old Roman days, although they often just cut them up or threw them to the lions." Now Izquierdo's stomach was about to go to pieces.

While Florian pushed the two invaders towards a small staircase, his smiling companion drew an imaginary épée from a very ineffective *Zorro* move.

"Keep moving forward and no tricks, I know how to use these even better than laser beams!" she twittered around. "Laser beams? What's next on the menu," Izquierdo mumbled, all worried.

By the time they approached the smallish basement, Florian was close to cracking up with laughter. The two prisoners, scared by a possible death by rats in an old cellar, lost to humanity and never to be found again, stumbled down in the dark.

"No light?" they cried out in a tight unison.

"We told you so. Prefer the local *Polizia* (Police)? Well, they're not so bad in Italy you know," Florian joked. "You just think about it. We'll be back later to check on you." While they stepped down the dark staircase the jailers had a laugh.

"You know Isabel, that was really funny, but even crazier is the fact that both of them may be priceless, yes even indispensable helpers! For one, I know Izquierdo and he is totally brilliant. I'm sure that he doesn't work with a dummy, even if they both look as if they stepped out of a cartoon."

"Je sais très bien, mon cher, je ne suis pas bête tu sais. Mais il faut laisser froidir un peu cette viande avant de la cuisiner (Dear, I know very well, I'm no fool. Let them cool off a bit before we cook them)!"

"Bien sûr, c'est une excellente manière de les préparer lentement pour notre prochain voyage. (Of course, an excellent way to prepare them for our next trip)."

20. FIESOLE, 1473 LORENZO DE MEDICI

On the highway of multiple thoughts,
through your veins and tumultuous canals,
like mushrooms drugging my brain with flashes of a nonsensical world,
I wish you no pain if your core won't deny
that this strangling is from a primitive heart. (Your Lips)

This Renaissance palace felt cold with its walls humid, sliding around his head, closer and closer. *A madman's dream, running naked through the Palazzo he reached his room and found her lying on his bed like one of the Three Graces in Botticelli's 'Primavera'. Under the translucent veils, her hands slowly fondling her inner thighs, provoking a slow arousal and he wanted to dive into her fountain at once. He started kissing every finger of her hands and she gave in without a single word, drawing his hips tightly to hers and the follow-up was predictable. While his hands softly pressed her breast towards his lips, she gently curved her back and her feet hooked his ankles. Their tongues entangled deeper and deeper as his pelvis pressed with a passion she had dreamed into being. His lips suckled her virgin nipples and her hands grabbed the silk pillows behind her when he kissed his way down to her awakening vulva, to him the sweetest of all fruit. In the arching of her tender loins, he lost all consciousness till she abruptly stopped him and took his head into her hands.*

'Do you just want me, or do you also love me?" she now demanded to know.

He crawled back briefly, looking at her. He lowered his eyes, surprised by her change of mood.

'Umm' wasn't a convincing start but he quickly resigned any doubt about being honest.

"Fiammetta, I must admit that in my world, we don't always enter a relationship because one has a one-night affair and then some guilt sets in. At least that is what I have experienced. You are indeed very beautiful Fiammetta, most desirable and as you

can tell I am more than attracted to you. But please, I have yet to figure out where I am. As for your family, no doubt I feel at home and I have recognized feelings of love like family members have…'

She injected the expected, "Family! You feel we could be like family – and that's all you can feel?"

But he had caught the ball graciously.

'How could I possibly get involved with anyone here in Florence when I have to return to my world; I would not know how to take you there.'

She laughed at him and he took her hands gently before she pulled them away. Her exit remained dramatic as she ran to the door and then, ever so slowly, she turned her head towards him, her chin upward and in her eyes, he read a silence that translated all the sadness of the lover she feared would, at any moment, disappear in a tumultuous squall, as if all light particles had been swallowed by a black hole in a far Universe. And he remembered nothing, and yet all.

A shuffle had him jump up straight on the edge of his bed.

That was not a fun wake-up call, he thought. What an annoying, romantically twisted nightmare that had been. Please help me with another dream I can finish.

This time traveler didn't want to step out of a realm he had hoped to orchestrate his way, but his hosts had made sure their new friend wasn't going to miss his appointment with Giuliano. The always-trustworthy Giovannino had sneaked into his room to make sure he got up before the crowing cock calls the 'peasants to the land'.

The promised horse accompanied by one of the Medici pageboys waited in the courtyard to lead him to a meeting spot, approximately a half hour ride. GianLuca recognized several of the houses and Palazzos on their way up to Maiano… or was it Fiesole? The young rider took a different road than the one from his last ride with Andrea. He wasn't expecting an early breakfast at some pleasant outdoor café or at one of the twenty-first century coffee shop chains. He smiled at the thought. To his surprise, he was taken to a kind of a mansion. At first it seemed smaller than Lapo's residence, but it had a large garden laid out in several terraces in the front and on both sides of the house. Lorenzo de Medici's brother was standing in the doorway and he welcomed him warmly.

"I am so happy that you have accepted my invitation and excited that we can have this meeting." For a moment he sounded formal and GianLuca wondered if this encounter would lead to anything as profound as the night before. They walked into an impressively decorated, big room that appeared to be some kind of a study for both the Medici brothers. He explained that they often wanted to get away from the city and their crowded family's ambitions. They just rode uphill to their hideout.

The room owed its golden glow to the fully lit fire ... the whole ambiance was amiable. A young woman brought a ceramic jar and poured two mugs full of what Giuliano explained, was to be a mixture of milk, honey and herbs. Chai came to mind.

"A recipe our friend Lapo brought from one of his foreign trips; the honey is from an abbey outside Volterra where my family likes to spend time, especially my mother and brother. And we'll also have some freshly baked bread with olives and goat cheese with grapes, figs, nuts and apples."

Sounds like we're only missing Swiss Muesli and the joke did not surface.

Giuliano relaxed in his big leather chair; there were two. GianLuca joined him, but his host mentioned that this was Lorenzo 'grand chair'. He gracefully bowed with a smile.

"This is how much I hold you in esteem and that only after last night's meeting. I could hardly sleep, and I had to send my mistress back to her husband." He laughed out loudly in youthful pride and GianLuca was startled at his very personal comment, irrelevant to the moment.

He's only twenty; I guess he wanted to show off a bit.

"Do you have a mistress GianLuca, or several?" he bluntly asked, his eyes twinkling with that youthful malice as if he was looking for a comrade to play with, to be in cahoots.

GianLuca wasn't sure what to answer and he almost stuttered. "Well at present, I am a single man, however..."

"However, you too have been charmed by the diamond in the crown of all Tuscan beauty, our glorious Fiammetta," the Florentine prince continued with a disarming brashness. "We have all been and she has been very reluctant towards her suitors though word goes that, well, she may have been plucked! She is quite a resistant young lady, privileged and with an important dowry."

GianLuca remained surprised at the way the conversation started off, at least at the approach this man seemed to have to women.

Of course, I mustn't forget we're over five hundred years back, and again Giuliano is hardly coming of age.

For a moment he wanted to leave the room, but that was too easy (or too difficult). After all, like his host, he wanted to know more; more about their encounter, the common destiny factor and especially how in the world he could get back to his own century.

"Andrea told me how impressed he was with your knowledge. You are well read in the art of metaphysics?" Giuliano broke the silence.

"So last night, did you sense what I felt last: an amazing, foreign energy invading us when we first shook hands as if we had entered another world. Can you talk about your experience?" he asked GianLuca in a very direct way.

"You are indeed right," the foreigner answered. "For we briefly were in another world, maybe ours alone. You see it is my understanding we exist in different realities... you can call them 'worlds' if you like... and last night our 'worlds' merged because we have something unique in common, hard to explain in words..." But Giuliano had literally bounced up from his chair and interrupted with a total lack of grace yet an astounding power of speech.

"I get it; I am twenty and your age must be between Andrea and his father's age, no? Maybe at first, we may have nothing in common, though you do look like a fine nobleman. You are not French nor Italian but you could be either." His breath had stopped, his heartbeat quickened as if he was about to reveal some big secret. With a sense of urgency and impatience, he continued, "Please tell me who you are and why do I feel I know you with a kind of complicity we share, one I only have with my own blood brother, Lorenzo?"

GianLuca uncrossed his legs and looked into the fire. How could he tell the truth? Such a truth would still be based upon his own experience of his own journey. This was all based upon his own very personal understanding of life on earth, gained after decades of research of the worlds around him after first having judged (often harshly) all others, including himself. He felt as if he was suffocating slowly. He had landed on another timeline; that didn't make it easier either. Imagine if he would be able to explain what he now believed had happened, they might just hang him from the windows of the Signoria like they did with opponents of the local law.

He had enough doubts about everything that had happened to him. After all, he didn't step out of a time machine like in a Jules Verne novel, nor did he really know any of these young Medici other than from the limited information in the history books. Usually (and strangely enough) there was little material on Lorenzo, aside from the politically correct pages in schoolbooks and even less on his younger brother. Thanks to a lot of research that he had done when working as an assistant on *The Medici and the Italian Renaissance,* a TV documentary about Lorenzo, he had found out that Giuliano de Medici was immensely popular and loved by many, especially by the women from Tuscany.

What he had now discovered was a whole other ballgame. Their mutual magnetism came from a very much deeper part within their mutual soul story. Were they looking at an inexplicable, incomprehensible truth? It all seemed rather confusing. He saw where his young host was leading him. Indeed, GianLuca was closer to the age of Piero, their father who had passed away a few years earlier. He smiled as he remembered the history, their Medici story.

Piero de Medici, the second son to Cosimo the Elder, the one they called *Pater Patria* (Father of the Land), crippled with hereditary gout (and therefore nicknamed *Il Gottoso*) had been entrusted at a very early age with tremendous responsibilities and his frail shoulders had carried the affairs of state unusually well. In the midst of a conspiracy to kill their father, his sons assisted him bravely in catching the villains. In his oldest son, Piero had recognized a future leader who could keep the family together and develop their commercial and political power. For his youngest, he desired a cardinal's hat at the Vatican. Before Lorenzo turned eighteen, he was sent off to Milan and Rome to prepare the political ground.

His mother Lucrezia Tornabuoni had been advising her husband. A noted writer herself, she gained instant recognition and respect. She had contributed by finding the perfect bride for her oldest son. He would marry Clarice Orsini, an elegant and pious young woman from a well-connected, rather wealthy family. This was no obstacle to him, and just like his younger brother, he was a natural charmer and a precocious casanova ... *though the real Casanova had to wait a few more centuries before making his entrance into history, and a rather twisted one apparently, he thought.*

For years this illustrious family had wished for at least one member to be ordained at the Vatican. Even though it seemed a great honour to have a representative of such an important family in Rome, no one assumed that

Giuliano would have given up a life of pleasure (and an inherited fascination with the higher mind) for he enjoyed his native city's beauties far too much.

In politics as in the arts, the brothers shared a similar taste and not unlike their ally, the Duke of Milano, they loved big festivities at great expense. In any case, Giuliano didn't appear superficial in his approach. From their first encounter the previous night, GianLuca felt Giuliano was unaffected. He also recognized their peculiar attraction was on both sides.

"If you change your hair colour, you will look like an older brother, you do know that?" He joked in a playful way. "You're less athletic than Lorenzo," Giuliano said, "yet stronger built then me. I'm being childish comparing us." He felt vulnerable and slightly apprehensive.

GianLuca grinned at the eagerness and the ardour emanating from this future young leader.

"Angelo," Giuliano suddenly called out, "I must call upon Angelo. He's from Montepulciano and he's a scribe, fluent in Latin and Greek, almost my age. We all love him, and he is like family. A student of Ficino, we have spent countless hours discussing Plato, Aristotle and especially Socrates. You will like him."

GianLuca looked at him quietly, for he had read the poet's work. "I know, he's a pupil of Ficino, the great Ficino who was so generously sponsored by your grandfather and taken into his household in Careggi," GianLuca continued while observing that his princely host was slightly impressed by his guest's latest remark. "Yes, you are indeed well informed, as few know this given!" he replied, not without pride.

"Ficino was your grandfather Cosimo's personal translator and advisor.," GianLuca continued to surprise, "... an ardent student of Greek and Latin culture and language, he had helped with the founding of your own incomparable library. Your grandfather created an oasis of the most amazing artists and architects, as if the entire galaxy had waved a magic wand of higher intelligence united in his academy and a school where you both studied."

He smiled at the silence that confirmed he had prevailed, he then continued.

"To think that after Brunelleschi and Michelozzo, you now have Verrocchio's students, Leonardo da Vinci and Sandro Botticelli to grace your homes with their unique artistry . . . no doubt a humbling experience. They are considered to be of true genius, even in my century!"

GianLuca continued witnessing more bewilderment, and he smiled an inner smile.

"I'm grateful that I have been able to meet you even though the circumstances are as astonishing as they are a mystery."

Below the surface there may well be more of a philosopher than a future politician, something that will serve Lorenzo in establishing his own uncrowned kingdom in a very different manner. After all, here is a future ruler who cherishes, no, who houses philosophy in his own home as a born ally. His closest friends included Ficino, Pico della Mirandola and of course there is Angelo Poliziano who since his teens is more than family!

Two inventive minds evolved in a now rapidly developing conversation while they agreed on several subject matters diving back and forth between themes where their fascination was mutual. How the soul progressed and what was their connection and passion for ancient knowledge and wisdom; all these were welcoming cards in a playful deck of surprises.

"I see you are smiling and I bet you'll even agree." Giuliano kept the ball rolling asking more questions. "You're not a Christian, are you?" Giuliano's eyes slightly tightened.

Oops, you better give the right answer.

"Does it mean I get convicted if I say no?" he answered.

"Oh no, not here, never at our home; this isn't Rome. Plenty of Christians do not live the word of their messiah, especially not at the Vatican where intrigue and money rules, corrupting the very essence of all spirituality."

"Well then, my young friend, you have already well deduced that my belief system may not fit this century, an era I wasn't born into either. Even on my own timeline I often feel I don't belong."

A lingering question on Giuliano's mind since their first meeting got him thinking. For the first time while searching to find the right words, he got nervous. Opposite Giuliano sat a foreigner, a man he hardly knew and yet so familiar. Had his parents hidden any information about other siblings? He gathered his courage and in the midst of all sudden inner turmoil, the facial differences with his brother, and the resemblance to his mother and not so much likeness to his father Piero . . . these thoughts had him walking in circles around the table. What if GianLuca was ... ugh ... well, he could well be his older brother or maybe an older self. It all became too much so he nearly spat out the words while his temperature went sky-high. Nearly hammering his fists on the table, he looked his guest straight in the eyes.

"You'll have to admit that ... should I be your son and not Piero's, I mean ... I love my mother and I will not denounce you ... if you were to be my real father ..."

GianLuca's eyes opened wide and the suggestion he would have miraculously fathered someone in another century was rather funny to him. But even before the end of the next phrase there was no time for a reaction as a new breeze invaded the room, and a perfume of history caught the moment in a web of kindness, yet maybe, historical power.

In the freshness of confusion sprang a new, yet similar, voice, "*Fratello e vero (Brother, it's true),* there's a striking resemblance," a generous yet highly unbalanced voice commanded loudly.

"*Ti presento Lorenzo* (I introduce to you, Lorenzo,)" Giuliano resumed in a less comfortable way. And with a grin under his strangely built nose, two vivid eyes looked right through their guest. GianLuca swallowed as he faced maybe Italy's most illustrious ruler (to be), the astute art collector, the shrewd promoter and cunning politician. The man who would initiate and search for a greater refinement in whatever milieu and, of course, also the artist himself, the poet who would influence and promote literature beyond Tuscan borders.

This meeting alone was worth the trip from any century back and forth ...

"You must indeed be a very exceptional man for I see, my brother, that you have assigned our guest to my chair ... *Ti prego non alzarti sei nostro ospite* (please don't move, you're our guest)," he declared in a more authoritative and heavier voice than expected from a young adult under twenty-five. While shaking GianLuca's hand vigorously he proceeded in a gentle yet firm manner. GianLuca could not have foreseen such an encounter. GianLuca looked up admiring the majesty in the young Medici, the otherworldly weight of a ruler if he ever saw one.

"I trust Giuliano's nose more than mine ... his is also a lot better shaped," Lorenzo laughed out loud. "And yes, we both know and we trust Lapo Buontalenti's family, so you too must be a very fine man." His charming game was very convincing.

"Now, are you on a foreign mission, maybe a secret one?" His smile showed the wit of a joker. "We have met more than once with a representative of the English crown on a strange or clandestine mission, on their way to meet with the black nobility in Venezia".

Both brothers looked at GianLuca and they remained silent; maybe they were waiting for a more informative session. But as he approached, Lorenzo di Piero de' Medici grew more and more intrigued at the likeness between the foreigner and his brother. An extra armchair was pulled closer as a young man by the name of Bruno came in with fresh bread, figs and nuts and more of the warm milk and honey replacing ... a tempting, yet untouched breakfast.

No small talk here and GianLuca pondered what subject he would choose and how to lecture those rather brilliant scholars of live Renaissance life. For a moment his mind dwelt on his last visit to their Via Larga residence when he actually looked at the Medici's tombs! Only weeks ago, he had visited the chapel behind the San Lorenzo church where both brothers were buried. It had become just like the house where they used to live, a museum called the Palazzo Medici Riccardi, well visited in a Florence overwhelmed by tourists. GianLuca thought it wise to make a very slow account of their family history, paying much attention to their immediate future.

Recounting details of the way their mother had chosen Lorenzo's then future spouse from one of Rome's best-connected families, his own well-hidden discontent, the efforts to get his brother to the Vatican and even Lorenzo's diplomatic relationship with the Duke of Milano, all this very personal and unpublished information left them stunned. The knowledge this foreigner brought to the table left the brothers mind-boggled.

He avoided mentioning the upcoming Pazzi conspiracy, but he thought of pointing out at least something about the political power Lorenzo would develop. A dramatically staged scene it seemed while Lorenzo dropped an elegant embroidered cape, walking around his armchair towards the imposing marble mantelpiece, looking at the absence of a blazing fire making the whole encounter worthy of a Hollywood production. How in the world did this foreigner know so much and *O mio Dio, chi è quest' uomo* (Oh my god, who is this man)?

The final blow on local history seemed to be this foreigner's knowledge of the local Night Watch's story and their affinity with Lorenzo who had protected many artists and friends from jail sentences, mostly due to their not so orthodox sexual preferences, their gay preferences, and deeper explanations that GianLuca refrained from. *That might have just been one too many arrows, GianLuca contemplated, even though it's written up in the history books, and the public records he had read in twentieth century Florence were pretty accurate.*

"Now tell me," Lorenzo suddenly responded in a cool manner, with that grin GianLuca remembered from at least one sculpture somewhere in a Florentine museum, "Are you at all from our world?" The silence was layered with doubts and there was a sadness that GianLuca could not cover up.

Lorenzo quickly answered his own question, "Of course not! How would you otherwise know of details of our daily doings that none outside of this room are familiar with?" And Lorenzo laughed at his own remark. But this time the tone in his voice carried a not-so-friendly tune. GianLuca noticed that a very different Lorenzo had spoken, and such dual personalities had never been foreign to him.

"What was that French monk's name again; the one from Montfroid?" Lorenzo asked his brother hesitatingly.

"We met him at Lapo Buontalenti's home last year. He came from the Montfroid Abbey in a province above Narbonne, in the south of France. He was an astrologer of sorts, was he not? Living in Rome?" Both brothers turned to each other. "He predicted a few important events to us, like when our father decided to work on the alliance with Milano. Do you know of him?" he asked turning to GianLuca in a slightly arrogant manner, which drew eyebrows from Giuliano's handsome face.

GianLuca shook his head ever so slightly, so Lorenzo continued, "He predicted that both of us, we would take a mistress, though that isn't difficult since it's kind of a tradition. He also told us that ... Giuliano would have a son and that very young, he ...'

GianLuca shrugged and now vividly interrupted, "He will become like your own son, Lorenzo, and he will sit on Saint Peter's Throne."

Both brothers jumped up looking at each other, smiling yet stunned, shaking their heads ... not in discontentment. They then sat down again while GianLuca continued.

"Yes, a pope, finally, after a very long quest! After quite some intrigues too, I can promise you," he added with a tainted smile, "and I warn you. You need to watch out for more than one of the most ancient families in the city! But eventually, swimming through tempests of great pain, your family will prevail with even greater power."

All three men now took a deep breath, but the two brothers were ready to choke.

"The rule of Lorenzo de Medici will bring about a golden age. If only you knew how much you will accomplish for the better of the entire Tuscan society and the example you will set for the entire country!"

They had listened attentively like students, almost erect statues eager to know more. Yet they didn't seem to expect anything less than the foreign 'oracle' visiting their home. For a moment they both turned into the happy adolescents they never had time to be, slapping each other's shoulders. GianLuca's mood had darkened while thinking of the many daggers that would one day violently stab Giuliano's back, and his potential warning would come either far too soon or too late. Would he turn a key for a change in history? He was getting uncomfortable while watching their boyish play and did they believe a foreigner's tale? After all, why would they?

He decided to bid farewell. It threw them back into the moment – somehow a bit abruptly but GianLuca felt this was the right time to pay his respects and leave. He lifted a hand respectfully. "I have plenty of reasons to excuse myself…"

"Yes, a beautiful lady is definitely the most convincing one," Giuliano laughed out, still punching his brother. "Indeed, it is!" GianLuca lied, mirroring Giuliano's grin.

But something was retaining them. Spry chills on their backs dressed all three bodies with a prickly feeling like an invasion of freckles of light, titillating the back of their heads, stimulating areas these brothers didn't know existed. Before they could think further, Giuliano was once again overwhelmed by that ardent glow that had united him with GianLuca the night before.

Lorenzo was now bathed in the amazement of watching them as if caught in a hurdle of thin interlacing twigs of gold and amber whirling about the vastness of this room and wrapping him into a muzzle of what could only be love. The light was blinding his eyes and the ruler of Tuscany kept, flabbergasted, all of his astute awareness alive while witnessing that this part of the house didn't usually invite the sun till the early afternoon. It reminded him of the moment his father passed away and he felt something bigger than life had come over him, something much higher than he could previously have wished for. When the waves had settled back into a present that felt like total happiness, Giuliano embraced GianLuca, hugging and thanking him sincerely. Though moved, Lorenzo's speech was calibrated to engender sympathy.

"Please be our guest any time and do return soon. We would like you to meet our cherished Angelo Poliziano. Like you, he's also quite an unusual man and an outstanding artist and human being. We must discuss all these symbols, the energies like you call them, all that was released today, the feelings we share, what we have now discovered and perceived to be of a higher kind." And so they parted and all three men had projected a following encounter . . . two days later or did they hope it to be sooner?

21. GENEVA, 2018 ELIZABETH

Close to your mum, close to your dad,
facing their truth even when sad.
So letting go isn't that bad,
it just takes time and may get you mad. (The Cabinet)

Elizabeth von Weitweg was humming a Chopin waltz while gazing through the open window overlooking the Lake below the DoWell building. She preferred the old office at the Quai Gustav Ador, next to the handsome park situated around a landmark hotel. Her favourite dining was at that very place, far left of the Rue du Pont Noir (Street of the Black Bridge). This neighbourhood was far superior to the more commercial district where the new main stores in Geneva had been opened recently. She missed the elegance from past traditions.

Seemingly untouched by time, Elizabeth gracefully became a mature woman impeccably dressed and faithful to Coco Chanel of the late 1950s, she had been one of the founding members of a major pharmaceutical company, DoWell Inc. From 1987 on, she had climbed the international ladder at staggering speed. With an impeccable reputation and having an amazing social list, Elizabeth had developed the aura of one of the toughest women in the business to deal with. A cum laude graduate from universities on the European and American continents, it was clear to her it was all in the genes. On her mother's side of her family many of the men had died quite young. Her Austrian-born mother, Gertrude, had been forced to marry very young.

Her husband, an aristocrat about thirty years her senior, would also be making her an extremely young and wealthy widow within the last year of World War II. Gertrude had loved her husband like the father she had lost when only a child. Baron von Weitweg knew he had a health problem, one he never mentioned to his family. He also knew that his wife was enamoured with Joseph, their younger friend and a scientist. Joseph, a frequent dinner guest, who had the strange habit of imposed adulation for classical music by always carrying around a Stradivarius, a violin that had outlived several generations in his own eclectic family.

While the von Weitweg family refused to leave Vienna, Gertrude's feelings for Joseph had grown even stronger. Unexpectedly pregnant with his baby, right before her first husband's equally unexpected passing, she moved to their opulent villa near Linz. As soon as Elizabeth was born, her beloved Joseph admitted to her that his own mother was Jewish. Joseph's father, once a prominent politician and university psychology professor had been forewarned about a scary future for all those who were not of the Arian race. For a while a 'hide and seek' with the local authorities paid off. But his son refused a job at the National Agency in Berlin that his father had asked him to accept urgently.

A sadness swept Gertrude away when she looked into Joseph's deep blue eyes, knowing this now represented a long-distance relationship. The Nazi regime would eventually threaten their lives, so she had a new passport made for him, paid from the sale of an antique necklace she had inherited from her grandmother. There was no shred of doubt that she was the daughter of a noble family and that she would have a title, as her father had been an aristocrat whose own lineage went back to dukes and counts as early as the Habsburg period.

So, thanks to her first marriage, nobody would find out that Joseph was the father of her daughter. Joseph had left for London, silently promising to bring his beloved and their child as soon as it was safe to do so.

Gertrude was brave and pretended nothing was going on. She blossomed as her belly stretched and then the birth of a daughter by 'her late husband' added some joy to the sadness that came with his passing. From the beginning of her liaison, her lover's name remained out of public knowledge. To protect their daughter, Joseph had suggested avoiding a 'public' mourning to cover up whatever might be discovered and especially her own aristocratic background. In the spring of 1944, Gertrude proceeded to move to Belgium. Gaby, one of her husband's aunts, a widow with a big heart, ran a small but elegant hotel and a highly praised restaurant close to the seaport of Ostend.

Yet only eleven months later she received devastating news from the British authorities. Joseph had been registered in the Royal Air Force. On a top-secret mission, his plane had crashed somewhere on the coast of North Africa and, even though his body wasn't found, they officially declared him dead. Nevertheless, the Air Force had left a very substantial pension in her name and another surprise was a fund to protect his daughter. Gaby, by then Gertrude's best friend and confidante, had arranged for new documents to show that Gertrude had married Joseph before he left for England.

As such, Elizabeth was now Joseph's legal daughter. Gaby, social and popular as she was, had all the right connections and she got Gertrude onto the first boat to Dover with much good food for the long trip. Eventually Gaby, more than just a heroic figure, led the Flemish resistance till the end of World War II and she often traveled to and from England. Either in Brighton (on business) and then again in London, she would spend time with Gertrude and her very precocious and lively little great niece, Elizabeth.

And so, it came to be as with many little girls, this tiny but very active little Elizabeth started taking ballet classes. The violin, the instrument her father had adored, even at her young age, was yet another hidden passion. Indeed, Gertrude made great efforts to keep her unusual child busy. She called her 'my toothpick-tornado,' for no matter how slender her build was, her energy often struck like a lightning bolt. Like her good-looking father, Elizabeth showed the inherited noble features of the old aristocracy.

Elizabeth had been handpicked by Edris Stannus, an Irish lady better known as *Madame,* who would soon find fame under the name of Ninette de Valois. Madame would go on to dance with the Ballets Russes de Monte Carlo and form what would become the Royal Ballet School. On one of her 'talent search' workshops, Madame discovered more than a handful of talent and a handful of future 'baby-ballerinas'. Those young dancers eventually would inspire her to create the Sadler's Wells Royal Ballet, maybe Europe's most exciting post-war ballet company, later celebrated as the Royal Ballet.

By then, little Elizabeth was taking ballet class almost daily. Her teacher called her Eliza – but not Dolittle, for like the *Pygmalion* heroine, she worked hard. But Gertrude had also looked carefully for the best violin teacher while taking advice from a Mrs Hookham, a very well-traveled woman who was married to a diplomat. It was her daughter and professionally trained dancer

Peggy, who had noticed Elizabeth's frail figure and had suggested that taking a dance class would help her build some muscles. Little Elizabeth admired Peggy so much that Gertrude and daughter assisted at almost every performance. The future prima ballerina would one day convince Gertrude, Eliza's mother to take her to do more than just watch the professional ballet class.

One day Gertrude received a letter from Madame De Valois, proposing little Eliza to be one of the children in the Waltz of the Flowers, Act I of *The Sleeping Beauty.* The leading role of Princess Aurora was to be danced by Mrs Hookham's daughter, who no longer went by her own name Peggy, but was about to gain worldwide recognition as Margot Fonteyn. Ballet training demanded much discipline and though Eliza loved dancing around the house improvising fairies and princesses, she didn't seem totally right for the profession. At least her mother thought so. Gaby had encouraged her, and at each monthly visit, with that box of Belgian chocolates, she promised wealth and glory. Eliza would dance, but one day would be forced into an early swansong.

Before graduating from the Royal Ballet School, she was asked to join the touring company and to perform in a popular mixed bill of one of the masters of Sergei de Diaghilev's *Ballet Russes, Mikhail Fokine.* His *Chopiniana* was a hit with the ballet public wherever performed. With a figure like a fashion model, one of her first assignments was to understudy the 'prelude and waltz' solos from this legendary ballet known in the West as *Les Sylphides.* Peggy Hookham, or Miss Margot as Eliza now respectfully called her, would coach her on every detail. She was now safe under her fairy wings. But next to this ballerina, the young protégée felt like a gawky bird. She grew quickly, tall like her father, and by her sixteenth birthday, she had reached a height of six-feet and *sur les pointes* (toe shoes) she felt disproportionately tall.

Whenever given a chance to dance a solo part such as a fairy in the prologue of *The Sleeping Beauty*, she cried for hours, feeling totally out of place in a short tutu amongst her much smaller colleagues. But nobody took notice of her fear and a command performance for the Royal Family was soon the next challenge to be met. When announced, the entire company was ecstatic at the long-awaited visit of their monarch, Her Royal Highness, Queen Elisabeth II.

22. FIESOLE, 1473 ANGELO POLIZIANO

Can you grab in my eyes,
the depth of my soul?
I am no Saint, not at all. (Moment)

When Angelo walked into the room, both brothers remained strangely silent. Within less than four years with the Medici family, Angelo Ambrogini, affectionately known as Poliziano, had become well regarded and now he was treated like a member of this illustrious family. Whilst his two best friends were usually involved in discussing politics or the arts, Angelo found that he would avoid voicing an opinion at those moments when they hit the lowest notes; discussing intimate encounters with the graceful young women they so fancied and yes, sometimes had shared.

And to his surprise, Lorenzo excelled in the art of gossip. This morning though, while Angelo made his way in, ever so slowly scanning the vast space, he could have cut an invisible smoke thicker than all the fumes their fireplace could ever produce. He stopped and stared at the tempting breakfast table; most cups and saucers seemed untouched ... three cups, hmm, how odd.

"I don't recall confirming my visit ... a mistake?" he shrugged.

He picked up a beaker, kind of lukewarm and remarked jokingly that, "... you'll both get even skinnier since you don't eat." That remark didn't entice even the slightest smile. Both brothers were athletes of the arduous kind, trained like young warriors ready to endure weather conditions of the worst kind and they wouldn't even notice missing a meal. Giuliano slowly straightened out of this daze, while Lorenzo continued contemplating a life-changing meeting that had finished only minutes ago.

"*Caro Angelo ti prego, vieni* (Dear Angelo, please come in)."

Lorenzo pulled in closer to his faithful Angelo. Poliziano, now obliged to listen to their account of the unconsumed breakfast with their foreign guest, smoothly moved towards the vacant chair. He scanned Giuliano. Only a few months older, Angelo admired Giuliano's olive complexion and dark wavy hair. What a beautiful frame around this prince-like face, he thought. Only yesterday, one of the many who aspired to his love and attention and one of Florence's finest daughters, had expressed her adulation in a delicate and sensitive poem.

With the innocence of a child, she had entrusted it to Angelo hoping it would reach Giuliano. Not yet twenty-one years of age and with less responsibilities to carry than his brother, Giuliano was Tuscany's most eligible bachelor who gladly confessed to more than one worldly pleasure while being surrounded by raucous courtiers fawning on him, as he was technically the future king's brother. Yes, to him, this philanderer's life seemed only one big game.

Upon request, Angelo had often carried back de Medici poetry to the more desirable young ladies. In those moments, Angelo despised his own weakness, instants where he felt as if born in the wrong body. What if he had been one of the local beauties? He knew he could never truly please not even one of these desirable brothers. He contemplated his feelings; was it jealousy, a lusty desire sprung from too many past nightmares about illusionary relations beyond the regular friendships with both brothers? He rested his head onto his right hand and he didn't smile.

Giuliano seemed to have a great liking, yes, almost a preference for a certain Simonetta, the wife of Marco Vespucci. So, whatever Angelo suppressed, would, on the surface, gain no value. In the beginning, the young man had entered into the privileged position as a literary assistant. Then very slowly he grew closer to both brothers, somehow like their own personal confidant. And then, thanks to them, he became a popular guest in literary circles and his profound knowledge of Latin and Greek, his brave, polytheistic approach to life made him almost as popular as those he served. His own mentor, Marsilio Ficino, considered a philosopher exhuming the soul's essence, had inspired the trio by spiralling different versions of reality.

One of Plato's most faithful adepts, Ficino had received more than one major commission from Lorenzo's grandfather, the great Cosimo. When he dedicated years to translating from Latin the *Corpus Hermeticum* (Hermes Trismegistus), his own Universe had changed. Plato claimed his knowledge came from Hermes. The experience of a union with the supreme divinity would become the goal and magic rituals were among the keys.

The Cosmos being central to the entire process (as in Cosimo's name), the many astrological, magical and alchemical texts formed the journey, where the power of the planets showed their immediate influence on the soul of man. Angelo and his sponsors' friends were, as was their grandfather, convinced their destiny was linked to the Universal laws where astrology could offer insights.

Being subject to such wealth of Universal magic, man became a reflection of those powers and the unique characteristics of those sublime stars and planets that would be found in the incarnations of man and woman, as to the image of their god. If the clergy didn't agree, Ficino, an ordained priest, would proclaim Plato's findings as if it was the Bible itself. Angelo had been marked for life, from his early days, he sat at the philosopher's feet, initiated to the theories of the winged god Hermes.

The idea that man could recover his and her memory of the authentic undivided divinity, while the soul would be guided towards that personal divinity, had left the youngster in total awe. He had then formed his own mind in that direction and it became cumbersome to listen to uninteresting stories that he would hear around the house of his 'foster family'. There ought to be no space nor time for gossip at the Medici residence, where wisdom and wealth were synonymous with happiness.

In Fiesole, the ceremonies and the studies were therefore not open to those who would never understand any of these theories. And not one woman had been admitted, not even Lorenzo's future spouse or his mother. Cosimo had dictated a law for all to obey. But Lorenzo's future wife would get annoyed more than once because of the intellectual gatherings at the Fiesole residence.

Clarice quickly developed a deep dislike for all of the Platonic theories, the absence of women at the gatherings and in due time she detested the young sage from Montepulciano. Throughout the years she would feel offended more than once that Lorenzo would entrust Angelo to mentor their son Piero. But just like his father and uncle, the boy was intellectually a very precocious child and in a permanent need of attention.

The first Lady of Tuscany also judged Angelo for his extreme hero worship of her husband and dedication to her brother-in-law. She wanted to vomit when Socrates or Plato's names were mentioned. Clarice Orsini blamed them all; the Greeks, the Romans and all those who approved the physical love men might experience together away from their spouses, especially the kind where the younger got trapped. She violently refused the local traditions of male friendships, though not as public in Rome as in her newly made home, Florence.

She was born and raised a true Christian and one day when her husband returned from Hanover, she framed Lorenzo with a phrase she had overheard in her own kitchen "... in Germania, Florentines are called sodomites for more than one reason, if you hadn't heard it yet, my husband!" and her voice had been snapping more strings than Lorenzo was willing to count, in that same week alone.

Yet Lorenzo would never feel threatened by men who chose their own sex over women. If anything, he had covered up some of his own close, mostly married friends, used to such extramarital affairs. After all his society was a male society. Giuliano paid little attention to the subject and he regretted greatly his sister-in-law's obstinacy in declining to invite to their home, some of those gorgeous women both brothers were so willing to seduce. Till that day, the Medici brothers' lives had been, to a certain extent truly idyllic, self-centred and often decadent.

As they were gathered around the breakfast table, they reflected that the previous night had proven a meeting with destiny and from that foreigner they had learned there was a place where none of them had ever set foot. Enthusiastic as Angelo always appeared to be, his voice bounced back from the walls... or did he try to reinforce the old complicity with the Medici brothers?

"We must invite your friend to next Friday's gathering and with him the entire Buontalenti family. He sounds like a lively guest to have at one's table."

The brothers smilingly nodded their heads simultaneously. Lorenzo stretched his neck and just as he got up, he kicked his brother's legs provoking an instant response from Giuliano. Caught between both of Lorenzo's legs, Giuliano started frantically pushing off, till he flipped his older brother onto his back as in some Roman wrestling match. Both lads tumbled on the carpet, playful kids like the teenagers they never had been. *"Condotta ridicula* (ridiculous behaviour)," Angelo screamed in a high-pitched voice.

By trying to imitate Lorenzo's spouse with his fake terror he did everything to be a humble but complicit confidante. They loved the jesting around because they didn't have to worry about affairs of state and Giuliano, well, he always reminded his brother that 'worrying gets you sick' so it's better to have a good time.

Meanwhile, GianLuca had returned to the Buontalenti residence where he found the house pretty much alive. A jovial Lapo greeted him as he crossed the courtyard.

"Ah, there you are, back from Fiesole!" Lapo's voice sounded joyful. "Did you meet our uncrowned ruler," he asked, anxious for an immediate response, "and did you have an inspiring conversation about politics and the arts?"

"I did," Giuliano smiled, "and we had quite a talk; their breakfast seemed a continuation of that great meal you served last night, only this time we talked so much that we didn't get to touch the food!"

"Well, then I will have some prepared for you immediately," he exclaimed in his usual generous manner. "Will you have it in the garden? I'll join you. My daughters left the house early; to them the market is an attractive venue. You know women love to buy presents for those they are enamoured with!"

He laughed out happily with a conspicuous twinkle in his eye. GianLuca chortled at the thought of some cold lemonade that he knew would not show up on the table, but he was grateful for the late breakfast; the ride had indeed stirred his stomach.

"What do *you* think happened, Lapo? Last night, I mean that light within the whole outer worldly ambiance?" GianLuca asked.

"I thought *you* of all people might explain that to us. I never had the same experience but this one time we attended a ceremony, an equally odd event occurred in the north of Africa, outside of Alexandria, in Egypt if I recall." He took a breath.

"There, it was an elaborate ritual though, like a coming-of-age of a young man and a young woman." He lifted his shoulders in disbelief that he even remembered it all. "It is very long ago, even the great Cosimo was in attendance."

He had GianLuca's full attention. *"Oh, Cosimo de Medici, il nonno di Giuliano* (Giuliano's grandfather)?"

"Ah, yes it was an invocation for ancient Egyptian Royalty. It's all coming back. They were on some kind of a checkerboard with lots of garments, smoking and singing. Well, it all seemed very much like an illumination rite. But there was magic and it was impressive. Last night was similar, yet different, because more personal, more intimate."

"You know,' GianLuca intervened, "some phenomena cannot be explained, I think they just happen. I can only say that when it happens more than once within less than twelve hours there's got to be a bigger hand in the game, wouldn't you say so? And Lapo, let me tell you that after meeting Lorenzo, a slightly different but similar repeat happening took place when I was about to leave the Fiesole Villa."

GianLuca continued with a mouth full of too much good food. He swallowed too rapidly and nearly spat out his words. He coughed and laughed at the same time.

"It happened once again, today, while approaching Giuliano".

"Well, you two certainly had an unusual contact; it left us all frozen. My daughters insisted that you two have to be brothers on one plane or another."

GianLuca shrugged when hearing the word 'plane'. "Hmmm, what story to tell you now? Or should I start inventing some explanations?" he laughed, "Ha-ha, maybe a confession to you and Andrea. Yes well, Friday evening all three of us, we will all be the guests of the Medici brothers at their weekly philosophical gathering in Fiesole. It was Angelo Poliziano's idea. I still can't believe I got to meet him. I read the book he's about to start writing." And that sounded funny, even to GianLuca.

"He has such a different physique, so different than I could have possibly imagined him to be. It was all very exciting."

Lapo nodded approvingly and the bright twinkling in his eyes showed nothing less than equal excitement. He instantly called out loud to his son before Andrea was near enough to shake GianLuca's hand.

"Do we have to wait for Friday? Have you really come from ... out there, from another dimension?" Lapo pointed towards the sky. "We are very anxious to find out more about it. But do we have to wait till Friday?" he repeated.

"Won't you give us a few more clues?" Andrea pleaded, "or must we remain frozen in front of a riddle even Medea or Ulysses couldn't untangle?"

"Why... do you think I have more information to offer? A few ordinary predictions of what appears to be your future simply because I might have been displaced or misplaced from one point in time to another? Ever so mysteriously, I do agree," and Andrea and his father severely straightened their backs.

"Let's look at it this way. What if I inform you of Lorenzo's endgame, maybe it is the reason why I landed on your timeline?" he asked gently looking into their eyes.

"Yes, all our history books have taught us that this period in Florence is of major importance. The way Italy and its politics will develop is formed right now. I could describe the many power wars, the invasions from other foreign monarchies, etc. But would any of you change your ways of living or the ways of looking at your everyday life? In my own century, very few do and most people do not care."

GianLuca paused in a serious way. "As of late, the probabilities I have seen, through our own recorded and often manipulated historical evidence and the way our world, mine that is, has emerged from the worst of natural disasters and inhuman experiments, all this is unlikely to be changed if people do not dare to believe in the simple fact that we are all creating our own reality! No?"

He again paused as this new monologue stirred curious minds.

"You, dear friends, you have grown close to my heart in such a short time and from an emotional point of view, far quicker than I could have expected. It confuses me as much as it does you, and I can understand how eager you are to enter the bigger game with a greater consciousness." He paused.

"In this lifetime, in 1473, you have no doubt acquired much knowledge already and you want to practice that kind of higher knowledge, and not only lessons taught by your tutors you understood as a child. In later centuries, governments will create schools, places of study where the books are mostly dictated material and very often the truth has been manipulated." His eyes met Andrea's and both nodded. "But if I am a teacher, I am full of imperfections. I am still searching and looking for my own path of empowerment. I am questioning every minute of what I am experiencing here in your epoch." He shrugged.

"Till now my life has been lived ... shall we say more in 'the moment' than in the 'expectancy of the future' ... of course, a future of another century! But to be in the presence of those who have studied with the great Ficino, that alone was worth the trip."

Sighing, he broke out in loud laughter which left everyone stunned. He sat down on one of the marble benches and in no time father and son joined him, their body language showing the keen desire to know more ... much more, and they weren't about to give up that easily.

In an avalanche of questions ... more and more questions, GianLuca blamed himself for his lack of precision and he truly doubted any answer he gave proved convincing. But Lapo was all ears and trusting in that moment, and his son remained equally thrilled at every new direction and any new information their guest would reveal. Regarding the women, GianLuca had his doubts. Fiammetta and Agnola were used to their father's traveling nuggets of wisdom. His daughters would invariably judge his pearls of knowledge amusingly, find them highly entertaining as both girls had grown up in a mainly male environment ... an environment they were both sheltered by and protected from.

These last days had been full of unexpected events; his arrival, the many conversations, last night's magic. GianLuca tried to read their bamboozled minds as he sat back wishing to help resolve this entire puzzle. He returned briefly to that one event, just a few days back when he fell into both sisters' arms.

Have I slipped into an abyss and no words can give away the reason why I have landed in the year 1473?

23. GENEVA 2018; LONDON 1959
THE QUEEN

And yes, healing is dealing,
while peeling stop schmealing. You may need some humble kneeling
and for whose sake stop trying, don't think of dying,
... just go for real feeling. (The Cabinet)

Elizabeth closed the terrace doors after her afternoon cigarette. It seemed her mind had traveled far back while the radio's rendering of some Tchaikovsky ballet's medley had distracted her. Her eyes remained fixed on a photo in a Florentine silver frame, of herself and Prima Ballerina, Dame Margot Fonteyn. As she plunged down in the dark red, velvet sofa, kicking off her shoes in a delicate and gentle way while pointing her feet like ... in the old days, she looked at her high arches and she found herself right back in her ballet past. Queen Elizabeth II and her entourage appeared at the theatre where she would dance her final performance. She trembled and slumbered into an unplanned nap to a visit to fame she almost found in London.

London, sometime in the year 1959

The young dancers at the company's ballet studio were in shock when one of their leading soloists fell badly ill with the 'flu and was taken to the hospital right before the afternoon dress rehearsal for the evening's gala performance. All eyes went to Eliza, who never would have hoped for such an honour and frankly, she wasn't ambitious enough to think of herself as 'the understudy that went on to save the show'. Greatly appreciated by all the professionals in the group, she was the artist they counted on simply because she was simply 'that dancer all about feeling; feeling the music, feeling the style, feeling the space' and still creating a unique ambiance all of her own. She was a rare breed indeed and the ballet mistress knew she could always count on her.

And so it came to be that this one night at a Royal Command Performance, Eliza stepped in for that leading dancer. Fortunately, it was that waltz solo in '*Chopiniana*,' a part she always felt comfortable with. The ankle-length white tutu dressed up her confidence. Elizabeth was still only eighteen, so Miss Fonteyn and her partner kept Eliza's morale from sinking. These great professionals were convinced that one day Eliza would make a truly fine ballerina. Yet then it happened, 'the great misfortune' as her mother would call it for years to come.

Walking down a dark and narrow stairway towards the stage, she slipped. A scary cracking noise caught her attention and pain pinched her lower calf. But there was no time to check, she rubbed and rubbed her muscle and, after all, the curtain was about to rise. The national anthem announced that Queen Elizabeth II was ready to be seated. Miss de Valois was hurrying all the dancers to take their places and there she was in pain, statuesque in the middle of the stage. She promised herself that if she got through this gala performance, she would never dance again. The waltz solo felt light and easy, and for a moment she disappeared in Chopin's notes. Thundering applause accompanied her exit and she caught her breath in the wings. While watching the duet that Margot Fonteyn had made into one of her signature pieces, Eliza quietly wiped her tears. To her surprise she forgot all about her painful calf and the next series of lyrical jumps once again invited a huge applause. The young woman excelled in the jumping section, called '*Grands Jetés*' and her height made her look even more impressive … one of her colleagues compared her to a Greek Goddess. The performance was an unprecedented success and while the audience remained in the lobby discussing the performance, her Majesty entered the back stage.

"Her Majesty, the Queen," and an entire line of tutus bowed before the restrained grandeur the monarch displayed while congratulating the company. Accompanied by the director Dame Ninette De Valois, her Majesty made brief stops greeting each of the soloists, sometimes addressing them with a few words of appreciation. She spoke to Eliza, ready to faint from pain, and also from awe for the 'Eliza with the crown'!

"You young lady, have been remarkable," she smiled at her, though the clear blue eyes seemed devoid of all warmth. "I understand you actually jumped into the role this very night and what a jump you command! Bravo!" she declared with a kind of controlled humour in her voice. In an almost permanent curtsy to make her look smaller, Eliza had just nodded, "thank you, Ma'am."

"Well, I do hope we will hear more of you in the future young lady. Britain can pride herself to have such talented artists as you. British ballet is truly gaining international 'Renaissance' thanks to the tremendous dedication of your director and the Royal Ballet. The Monarch then held Peggy Hookham's slightly trembling hands, announcing that their leading ballerina would be soon known as Dame Margot Fonteyn!

The surprising promotions, the encouraging speeches and the entire company applauding left droopy black mascara lines on Eliza's cheeks. With genuine excitement the dancers continued to congratulate first the future Dame and then a strangely sad-looking newcomer. Eliza looked inside herself for answers; she couldn't hide the devastating pain any longer. When she slipped out of her skirts, the dressing lady, a humble yet down-to-earth woman, screamed. Fonteyn's colleague Alexander Grant, who had just triumphed as the Bluebird in *Aurora's Wedding,* burst into the room heroically, immediately calling out for a doctor. First annoyed by all the noise, Margot, herself barely dressed in a long silk gown, opened her door, while a small crowd was blocking the front of the hallway to the soloists' dressing rooms. When she finally made her way through, she found her young friend in tears, both hands holding a rather swollen lower leg.

"Oh Margot, it's all over! All this because of a stumble on the stairs and now I cannot even move."

"My poor child, no. It's probably only a bad twist, a stressed ligament. But when did it happen? The variation was the best you ever danced; the jumps were faultless, goodness, just beautiful." She wanted to comfort her. "And only moments ago, I convinced Miss de Valois to give you the role of Mirtha, the Queen of the Willis to my next *Giselle*. Sir Fred was mentioning the ballerina role in Pas de Dix in his new *Raymonda* next fall. There you are: an entire future in front of you and you allow yourself to be discouraged by a small, you said, 'tumble on the stairs'?"

Her voice twinkled in a light-hearted manner, but Eliza slowly tuned herself to silence. "Don't be silly. We all fear the worst, but before you know it, you'll be flying over the horizons with your magnificent leaps just as you did tonight!"

"And you weren't even drinking," Alexander added in his usually funny rough voice while holding up an open champagne bottle. By then, the entire company had gathered around her and there was plenty of laughter to make her believe it would all be all right.

Dame Margot's husband Tito, alias Roberto Arias, a charming diplomat from a prominent Panamanian political family, offered to drive Elizabeth to the hospital. But Margot's mother, Mrs Hookham, had decided it was safer if she accompanied Elizabeth. She mistrusted her son-in-law with young women as she had bluntly told her friend.

At the hospital, the nurse insisted that a gallon of awful tasting pills would 'help diminish the pain'. But the young dancer suffered like hell and the injury was much deeper than the calf showed. Elizabeth alone could feel the future outcome. And she wept, for no fairy wings would ever adorn her dresses ever again. The next day, no surprise, she was unable to walk and the diagnosis of a calf injury seemed about right. Yet the worst was still to come for no ligaments had stayed intact.

Her plaster cast was decorated with plenty of good luck messages. Flowers and many boxes of bonbons flooded into her hospital room. Back home and three weeks later, the x-rays showed that this wasn't only a twisted ankle and pulled calf-muscle, but alarmingly a tibia hairline fracture of the rarest kind. The unusual way this was healing, added a dreadful, almost permanent cutting pressure on her Achilles. When another unexpected bone spur showed up, the doctor decided to operate immediately. At that very moment Elizabeth was convinced there was no more hope. The season would finish without her and she dared not think how long she would have to spend in therapy before re-joining the company. And what if it would happen again ... where to go, what to do and would she even walk again?

She was still young and if she made the right moves while she could, she could still enter university, get a degree and become a doctor and help dancers with similar injuries. At least this solution popped up in all her present dreams, or was she simply daydreaming to escape the reality that swept over her like the Niagara Falls?

Tears ran down her cheeks while Margot sat with her through one of the saddest afternoons of her life. Eliza discussed how she would strive to find better methods than they had used on her when they put her in that depressing plaster. She had kept it all to herself and Margot couldn't smile her tears away. They just sat there holding hands.

A day later the doctor told her that the operation had been a success, but she needed to stay off her feet as long as possible. Not only that but she was not to wear 'those tight shoe-boxes' for at least a full year; no *pointes* were allowed. Instantly, Elizabeth decided to make a new move.

Her mother drove her to the university in Cambridge. The following month they packed their bags, and Gertrude cried even more than her daughter had through all those dancing years. But both women knew it was the right decision.

The night before their departure, Margot and Tito insisted on giving her a dinner at his embassy. Margot presented her with a gorgeous twenty-four carat gold antique chain. It was right after the premiere of the new love scenes from *Raymonda* at the end of November 1959. Margot had been through a rough time herself, as that year she traveled back and forth between Britain and Panama. Her husband had disappeared for a while due to his suspected involvement in a failed Panamanian *coup d'état*.

"I know that whatever you choose in life Eliza dear, you will be victorious. You're one of the most talented young women I have ever met." Margot had been holding both Eliza's hands in a rather unexpected moment of deep emotion and genuine friendship. Tito's personal photographer had been called in to take pictures of that evening dinner.

"You know, I have been lucky," Margot said. "I'm pushing forty and, well I can really feel it in my bones; that long war period and those years right after when we performed in mainly awful conditions! It's a glorious art and I will dance as long as I possibly can." She smiled as they walked out of the 'powder your nose session', "… yes, it is a daily addiction I share with Sir Fred! What comes after, I have no idea. You though, you may well become a great doctor and help us all, for our profession certainly needs a few serious pioneers.

Maybe you'll be one of them. I can see *The Times* headlines; 'Former Royal Ballet ballerina saves dancer's feet and legs!"

They had laughed a lot and the entire evening ended with a surprise visit by Dame Ninette. The director handed a document to Elizabeth, a written offer that if she wanted to change her mind and return to the company in a year, once she was fully cured, she would still be the youngest soloist since Dame Margot herself.

More tears were shed and the next morning the train took Gertrude and her now very pensive daughter to Cambridge. Eventually graduating with first class honours in medicine, she remained in the historic university for her PhD. Her natural curiosity led her abroad for additional study in kinesiology and osteopathy with some of the best in the profession. After all, as in dance she showed more than just promise; she excelled with a passion coupled to an innate wisdom. Her teachers loved her and her co-students admired her greatly. Margot and Elizabeth remained close friends and they would visit each other between Margot's many performances, haunting world travels and a jet-set life that followed her like an imposed phantom. Eliza could help her with minor pains, though Margot knew she might have to give up her career as she had reached her early forties.

By then a new Russian star had emerged, his name as glamorous and magnetic as the man himself. Rudolph Nureyev would become the first ballet mega star. Together with Dame Margot they would create a legendary partnership, perhaps the most celebrated in ballet history.

Whenever Elizabeth was in London, or Margot was touring the USA, she made an effort to catch a performance and have a Sunday lunch with her old friend, who by then had joined the pantheon of world stars, giving up a conventional 'life of her own'. It was a life Eliza did not want to lead, not ever. She would never compromise her freedom and her strategy was planned to live a peaceful life, where cultural events were but a *divertimento.*

Her university years made her discover an America she would really love, one where seemingly a different freedom led to a new, maybe lesser British understanding of life. Later, an astrologer explained to her and her mother that once you move timelines, so the influence of the exterior worlds becomes different. In London, she had befriended many immigrants from the colonies, especially from India; and on the East Coast, she made friends with many African American students. Like her mother who thrived in the arts societies, she became a part of both New York and Boston elite society, and eventually she dated an African American Professor of Philosophy. With him, Karl Jung and colleagues brought inspiring topics to their weekend tea parties, where they thrilled mother, daughter and their many friends.

24. FIESOLE, 1473 FLORIAN'S TRIO

Absent of the wisdom I bought for no display
and away, far away from the pressing messages
others have invented
to involve me in their daily schemes,
only a slight image of my own mirroring
their lives, oh no, not futile
for their lives are theirs
not mine. (Answers)

The dark was not a place Derecho liked. The humidity and a possible invasion by Renaissance rats looking for a twenty-first century dessert was indeed an unattractive prospect. His partner in 'limited crime' remained silent. It was now time to activate at least one person's mind, after all he was an ace in cracking computer codes and playing with little techno devices ... but in a dungeon, he really was at a loss. Why didn't Izquierdo react?

"I hope you have a plan C, because B we can forget ... we've got no hands," Derecho said, shaking the handcuffs.

"Patience was never your forté now, was it?" was a dry answer.

"Oh, this is the right place for patience; like prison is a better place to be than this one," Derecho continued complaining.

"Derecho, be quiet. I'm convinced it's just a trick they are playing on us. I bet they were even expecting us and we fell into their trap. There's something they want from us and we'll soon find out." Izquierdo somehow saw through the whole scheme.

At least some comfort, Derecho thought; please want us, want us, want us now ... I'm too hungry! He was ready to cry out loud.

"I remember Florian," Izquierdo said. "He was a real smart kid and he knew very well how to handle people, and he was also a master at playing games. He knew how far he could go to get you ..."

"Well, that was clear," the other one mumbled ... a mumbling that went on for another half an hour and the noises they heard weren't mice. More talk was no longer needed as Florian had descended the stairway, overly lit by plenty of gaudy neons, and so totally out of tune with the building.

"I wonder why we didn't see those," Florian said, pointing at the neon wall lights. "Ugly! But useful when one has to take a look at one's prisoners, no?" He pretended seriousness, but Izquierdo surprised his companion with his quick answer.

"OK Florian, you are on the winning side. If this were a contest, well, let's close this chapter right now, OK? We have got something you want, and I have no doubt that you actually were expecting us, right?" Izquierdo stepped back and hit the wet wall; Florian too had a quick answer on his lips.

"Indeed, we are in the strong position, aren't we? And yes, we anticipated your coming. Only your arrival was a bit sooner than we hoped for. It did disturb our dinner!"

He grinned. "OK, yes we do have a job for you both. We'll have to all play it cool and be reasonable because actually we could also continue our adventure – with you both left in the peaceful company of nibbling mice. I'll admit though, that your talents might make the next steps a bit easier, and who knows? Maybe you can simply resign from your company and drop the DoWell job, and continue life without visiting a real jail once the whole adventure is finished."

"In jail; an official one or this one?" Derecho screeched out.

"We are protected you know and ..."

"Oh, just shut up ... Doh!" Izquierdo insisted. "Like I mentioned before, Doh is really good at his job but only at his job! As for the rest – forget it; no heroes here, just a crack in his pants as big as the egg he carries up his arse!"

"Well, you really are a cartoon pair!" Florian said.

"No," Derecho interrupted, "we would say the Three Stooges, because we have an accomplice outside sitting in the car, waiting for far too long. Yeah, and his name, (hold your breath) ... is Dritto"

Florian laughed, asking: "Is he the one parked off Via Beato Angelico? You'll have to call him on his cell phone because the house here is under full surveillance and anyone walking in the garden now will get caught by a very unpleasant dark animal!"

Izquierdo said, "Really Doh? Have we made that kind of a mess?"

Isabel's pinching voice sang down the stairs, asking if things were about to move because, "We have certainly lost enough precious time."

"Strong lady, isn't she? You're involved? Fiancée or just..." Izquierdo teased.

But the strong lady answered while descending mid-stairs. "How lucky can we get with this clever *duetto?*" she ousted with clarity.

"I'm afraid you'll have to strip right now. No, I do not have a twisted mind so don't worry. You can shower and change; your new suits are on the beds on the first floor. I won't look!" She flinched off.

Doh got the chills while she spoke and immediately said, "*Yes mam'selle,*" to the new boss.

"Good," she replied. "So that's all set, one by one. Laurel goes first, then take Doh; and here's your laser B, Flo."

"Laser B? Flo?" Izquierdo whispered. "She's got you in her hand, hasn't she – *Flo*? Well, she's stunning, almost a Halle Berry lookalike" Izquierdo teased. My turn, he thought.

"Iz, shut the fuck up!" Florian turned around and he pulled down Izquierdo's pants from his hairy legs. Derecho choked. "Lift your arms, I'm cutting the vest"

"Oh, please don't, man," Iz yelled," This one is brand new. Just open the damn cuffs; you remember me? I'm no hero type either, nor is Doh and you got that Star Trek weapon." He swallowed.

"OK, you Chewbacca – upstairs and leave your belongings on the kitchen table." Florian said while he unlocked the handcuffs. They walked upstairs in their undies and a summer breeze wasn't unwelcome when they entered the rooms.

"Hey this is still first class," Derecho smiled, "You know, these guys are a class act, a bit 'à la DoWell'."

"OK smart arses... you in the next room, Iz. You have about half an hour to wash up and change. We'll leave no later than in an hour."

"Leave for . . . any place we know?" Derecho hesitantly inquired, "and what about our third party?"

"Surprises aren't surprises if you know them before dinner!" Florian said as he closed the first door, leaving Doh behind in another restored fifteenth century room. When he closed off Izquierdo's quarters, he smiled and walked down to meet his own Halle Berry.

25. FIESOLE, 1473 FRATELLI MEDICI

Am I the drug to myself,
devoid of any higher vision tweaking
while compelled by my despairing disbelief,
my senses poked by breathing streams of unfolding perceptions
I forgot to feel in this unleashed nothingness
or is it otherness? (Unleashed Otherness)

Angelo Poliziano remained in a pensive mood as he slouched through the gardens to play one of his many roles. He didn't care much for being that occasional go-between to his secretive masters. These were small services that were a part of his spoken gratitude to the legendary family. How could he not? Shortly after his father was murdered, he had been sent to live with Italy's most famous family. A permanent sense of indebtedness had grown like a second skin and feelings of obligation almost suffocated him. The moment he returned to their villa, he was accustomed to that sombre mood he was always ready to give into. Contemplating his worst fears, he admitted them to nobody; no revelations, not even to his closest friends, his new family and yes, personal Maecenas! He dragged his heels.

Meanwhile, Giuliano stared at the patterns in the windowpanes. Intricately woven circles or triangles in a mesh of startling colours, contrasted with the window's main character, possibly a knight. He broke a long silence with a feisty cough. Lorenzo thought that the breakfast, seemingly stewed for hours, had disturbed their stomachs, stomachs used to a different drill. He pounded Giuliano on the back but the last slice of bread refused to surface so more loud laughter penetrated the walls. Lorenzo truly loved his brother who since their father's early passing had been under his mentorship. These last few months they had grown closer than ever before; like having a son and a brother all at once. He stroked Giuliano's big mop of long hair and kissed his forehead like their father used to.

"You know you'd make a great pope, Giuliano. Look at all your quiet wisdom; honest and fair, as God's ways truly must be. You fit that perfect papal profile, and this pope would be a very handsome one and hidden mistresses aside, you'd have a little time for God, as politics reign supreme in the Vatican!" Giuliano cringed.

"Honest you say; I'm not that honest. The moment I leave *una bella fanciulla* (a beautiful young woman), I think of the next one who may walk into my bed. You know that only too well, brother. Oh no, me in the Vatican? I'd be grieving all women on earth, daily. I don't think the cardinals would appreciate a married pope with more than one official mistress, or will our history book prove differently?"

He shrugged away the idea, jokingly, bowing over and over again till his humour nearly brought him to his knees.

"And dear Lorenzo, you only wanted to carry out all of father's predictions and political ambitions. Would you like to be in the holy seat yourself reading Mass for the leisure of those overdressed hypocrites who carry themselves like huge snails in gold and diamonds, over-weighed by hypocritical importance?"

Lorenzo's eyebrows took a stretch and Giuliano remained merciless.

"You, my brother, you may have the stature of a soon-to-be king, yet I have none of St Peter's obedient and wilful 'rock' in me. You know only too well I love life and for now, each woman is the most precious gift, for in any unpredictable moment, I may embrace the perfume of her beauty and hide myself in her veils… I care not, at least not yet, to follow a godlike path." He chuckled as he took his brother's arm. They walked onto the lengthy balcony overlooking the city, admiring a view so spectacular they couldn't have ever dreamed up anything like it!

"Ah Fiorenza," Lorenzo suddenly changed the subject, *"avete visto la nostra madre ieri* (did you see our mother yesterday)? These days her bones are hurting nearly as much as our father's. I had sent him off once again to the Thermae near Volterra to take some herbal hot baths. I could use one myself but the council at the Signoria has called for another gathering to discuss the financial future of the treasury. Yes, you can guess; they want to raise taxes and they know I'll oppose it," he sighed heavily.

"Run off Giuliano, let me not burden you any longer with any of this and do not play the guilty Christian … be the saviour of your horse only! Run off like Tuscany's Alexander the Great, all of Olympus is too small a playground!"

Giuliano escaped his brother's dramatic embrace and his equally histrionic and rhetorical speech. His page had brought his horse. Like a true horseman, he mounted his Arabian stallion swiftly, strangely pulled by some unknown force towards the city. There was more to his life than he had ever dared to think, and he wanted to know why he was so excited.

26. GENEVA, 2018 SIEGFRIED FREUNDREICH

You pulled me into your cave.
I felt lost for years.
Roaming around this world, endlessly eloping labyrinths
till I remembered my own amygdala. (Smiling Voices)

For quite some years, the ballet and those days of glamor and ruthless hours of hard work had stuck with her. Now Eliza had grown into Elizabeth, a strong-willed woman who had made different choices for a life of purpose. Her daily regime included a yoga-like workout, a personal training once a month and a healthy love life. Siegfried, her last boyfriend was a high-achieving doctor, born from a stunning African American mother and a German nobleman. His grandparents had witnessed the budding NSDAP, where their 1921 party head, twelve years later, would lead the official nationalist, totalitarian Nazi regime. They spent their family savings to travel, via Dresden and London to the United States, building their family a whole new life.

His grandfather, Edelhart had become friendly with composer Gustav Mahler, whom he had advised during a painful period, when the celebrated composer returned from New York to try and rescue his marriage. Gustav had introduced Edelhart to Sigmund Freud and they had a few amazing *soirées de discussion* discussing of course 'the higher mind and the lower abdomen,' that didn't make always the best match.

Edelhart's grandson had a passion for biology and biochemical research since his early days. A wall full of diplomas could have proven why he rose to be one of the country's youngest professors. But to also have such a position as an African American at a major university kept many in disbelief. It didn't to Elizabeth. She thought that all higher education had to be available for anyone, no matter the colour or the gender of the person. So, it was no surprise that she met her future husband at one of her mum's 'higher mind with tea and cake' afternoons. Outspoken young woman as she was, her first approach had slightly scared away the young professor.

"I am Elizabeth and you must be Harry Belafonte's younger brother." She had no idea of his background and he had inherited his family's more aristocratic approach when kissing the hand of a woman for the first time.

"I am Siegfried," he had answered in a somehow reserved but proud manner. "Siegfried Freundreich and as you may know, I'm a university professor in biochemistry." Not only that, he was also a high-ranking doctor in a pharmaceutical company that he co-founded.

He then had turned his back to her but continued an enjoyable conversation about Freud and Jung with Gertrude, Elizabeth's mum. "Well, the old aristocracy always attract," she had told her best friend, but "this man is hot!"

Both graduates had agreed. Calling him the "party's Swan Prince" did help this first encounter and Prince Siegfried didn't appear till a few weeks later, when Gertrude had matched them at a ballet performance of *Swan Lake*.

He was so impressed when he met the legendary ballerina, Margot Fonteyn and her partner, Rudolph Nureyev. During the dinner that followed, the Russian-escaped ballet superman sat extremely close to Siegfried and jokingly announced that he would gladly 'teachink you prrrivate class.' Interestingly, Siegfried sympathized with Rudolph and eventually showed his empathy to the gay liberation.

Both had become quite animated about it and at that moment Elizabeth understood she wanted to spend her life with just that man. She made the first move during dinner as she had put her hand on his knee searching for his hand and Siegfried nearly pulled down the tablecloth! For a moment she had thought, *"What if he's gay"*, but he had read her and surprised her, *"I'm really ticklish at the knees,"* causing a major laughter so loud that Dame Margot joined them and raised glasses to her old friend Eliza, the ballerina who had retired too soon, but would very soon find the most happy of lives! How right she was and it would be a life Elizabeth and Siegfried could not have foreseen.

Eliza was shocked when within months of their relationship he put the ring on the table. Siegfried Freundreich's scientific mind possibly calculated the alchemical value of the diamonds, and his almost unromantic apologizing for requesting Elizabeth to be his wife had the charm of a college graduate.

She, on the other hand, had interpreted the relationship as rather entertaining, growing ever so slowly into a loving one and even when he was a workaholic, she cherished every hour they could spend together. The day her mother was diagnosed with an advanced stage of bone cancer, he decided to take off for the most progressive hospital in Switzerland. Elizabeth's husband was the leading doctor for a company he had co-founded with another former doctor turned entrepreneur, the wildly ambitious Simon Averardo, grandson of a South-American industrial magnate.

Elizabeth had seen her mother Gertrude wither away, drugged most of the time. There was nothing more she could have done. Before the final departure, she gave away a secret. She held her daughter's hand and said: "One day you may like to reach out for a young African American woman by the name of Isabel." Gertrude could not stop crying but finally on her last breathing moment told Eliza the truth about her father Joseph. It left her flabbergasted and angry and by the time her mother finished out of breath, Elizabeth was in tears with her head in Gertrude's hands.

"Don't blame your father. I loved him and my heart stopped when we were told that he had died in an airplane crash, but that was never the truth. In the war he had shown a great courage and sense of self-sacrifice. He had joined MI6 and to protect us during the Cold War, he preferred we didn't know where he was living and working. He was allowed one phone call and in those days you couldn't read the number on the cell phone!" Both women had laughed through their wet cheeks and her mother continued.

"Joseph asked that we would never meet because he would never leave me again. He had promised to fight for the UK and help destroy the Berlin Wall and that took till 1989. Our mutual pain could not be described. He had created a college fund for you and I would have a home to my name as long as I never ever told anyone. He said he would one day retire and he would marry again so he could forget he had chosen country over love and family." Eliza had remained equally breathless while her mother stared at the ceiling.

"Somehow deep inside you knew, my sweet Eliza. That's why you chose my first husband's name, Von Weitweg because Joseph left Austria before I gave birth to you and that war kept us from ever getting married. So, the name Lieverkussen only remains with Isabel, your half-sister. When she entered Princeton, Joseph had sent me a photo of his beautiful wife and their daughter. Please keep it and one day reach out for her because I never had the courage to do so. I was too afraid I would die seeing, after half a century, the only man I ever loved."

That same day Gertrude found her long-awaited peace and she slept in quietly while her daughter and her son-in-law, sat beside her bed. Eliza now blamed herself for having given up far too early her first love, ballet and then again later, what she called 'the art of osteopathy'. Elizabeth had been convinced she could help many through the healing arts; but one day unexpectedly, her passion was dropped on the back burner.

Like her mother she had preferred dreaming about spirituality and like most of her circle of high society friends, she liked being a magnet for the arts and an intense spiritual tourist.

Cambridge and later Princeton Universities had introduced both mother and daughter to powerful business people who put financial ambitions before health. Elizabeth became hooked. When power befriends you, is there a way out?

27. FIORENZA, 1473 A MEDICI'S PAST

How magical when I let all past fears
return to their home station,
recycled waste for cosmic tourists
all lined up with sharpened lenses aiming Earth. (Your Chair)

At their Villa, Giuliano de Medici stared into the void. His thoughts on what happened these last few weeks seemed warped and the simple meaning of his own Tuscan daily life went topsy-turvy. Change was in the air, whatever airborne feeling he had about the foreigner; nothing was any longer what it appeared to be. He also saw less and less of his own family and he felt more and more guilty. GianLuca, a man with a kind of energy similar to Giuliano's, his own brother's, yet so different, the morning visitor with that peculiar Italian accent: who was he really?

Giuliano de Medici and GianLuca (or Jean-Luc Médecin), even the name was a translation of his own 'Medici'. He felt as if GianLuca had left him stripped of all superficial intent, from those typically superior family airs and their own often miscalculated actions. It was rather disturbing that right after meeting with GianLuca, women weren't even on his mind. Suddenly he felt incapable of thinking of any of his familiar manners of seduction, the wrinkling of the skirts of that young poetess whose verses, unfit for her own youth, had not so long ago stirred his loins and whose virgin fruit he would gladly peel. Her unread poetry awaited his shameless lewd ears, though he cared about her verses as much as putting his hands of lesser chastity on her hips.

Now he had this man on his mind and it utterly muddled his views. He grew annoyed and impatient. His mind skimmed another chessboard where he dreaded an unexpected novelty in the game of seduction. That would bring him back to the hidden mystery of his alter ego, one he hadn't learned to control, not yet.

He laughed at all the drama that caught him off guard. He might as well pick up Lorenzo's preferred pastime and write his own poems. Maybe Angelo would know what to do with this new dilemma, or was he just waking up altogether? New challenges introduced another colour on the chessboard of his life. Was he no longer in command as he thought he used to be?

While riding to the top of the hill, right below the cavern where local architects looked for the *pietra serena* (excellent gray sandstone), he smiled. Many sculptors like Mino da Fiesole (who sculpted his father Pietro's bust) dug there for the rock that would bring them their glory. The view remained familiar to him for in his early childhood his mother would take him for a walk or an occasional ride. It reminded him of the great fortune he was born into. She had promised him one day he would share these lands with his brother.

Florence, founded on the river Arno, was Tuscany's unequalled pride and beauty. He lingered at his horse's strong neck and felt his own thigh muscles tense. Indeed, he felt fit like a horse himself, yet a different muse now rang in his ears. There he was, the brother to the man who soon would become the next ruler and maybe, as GianLuca predicted, Italy's most powerful leader. He knew instinctively that it was an unwritten truth. Both he and Lorenzo were magnets for the most beautiful women and their heritage of power shone at each instant of the day and at each public appearance. It all seemed conspicuously easy.

With the mind of a spy, Giuliano liked to question all reality, so one day he paid a visit to a woman from the mountains near Siena. Locals called her *la strega bianca* (the white witch), for she could foretell and even explain your dreams. Slightly obese, with hypnotic eyes that could rival a rainbow, she had warned him of a growing jealousy amongst some of the other noble families in Florence and especially of a figure cloaked in religious power. She also had told him he could learn much from a mercurial traveler who was to appear unexpectedly at a friend's dinner table, and this man would be like a mirror to Giuliano. That riddle had stayed with him; a mirror to himself and what this could be like. She had pierced him with that complex question of destiny and our goal to incarnate on planet Earth.

An intricate labyrinth that now trapped his brain as much as the power that might soon twist his brother's mind, Giuliano had prayed it would never happen to any of their siblings. He found peace climbing mountains or bathing in the river, running around naked behind one of the young women he loved to conquer and playing in the voluptuousness of nature. From '*La strega*', he retained that every moment of the day, each thought and each action would result in an inevitable reaction. And since that last dinner at Lapo's, the *strega's* prediction had again returned to haunt him.

As a very young boy, theories from the masters of Greek philosophy had enthralled him while he sat almost hidden in a corner behind his older brother and sisters, who discussed the hereafter passionately with their all-knowing grandfather, Cosimo, who had animated such eventful evenings with plenty of educational subjects. As all the children grew up, Giuliano noticed quickly, how their own development would rarely marry with the authentic truth they strived for. Yet he had watched through all those years the lies unfold into a web of politics in which his family had long conquered their lasting, rightful place. And then sadly, he admitted stepping into that same network of manipulation, following closely in his brother Lorenzo's footsteps.

Only recently, Lorenzo had returned from a trip a full day earlier than expected. He had found Giuliano happily positioned underneath a totally naked woman who Lorenzo had expected to be his exclusive and secret mistress during those times when his wife was visiting her family in Rome. Neither words nor looks helped to cover up the pain Lorenzo felt as he inaudibly shut the door. Giuliano rarely felt remorse, but tears had sprung from his eyes when he briefly noticed Lorenzo's ring finger in the doorway. The brothers rarely discussed their conquests, some of the games yes, but nothing in depth regarding any feelings for the women sharing their beds. And now Lorenzo carried enough culpability for both of them, especially when he succumbed to his late-night activities in the absence of a spouse with whom he rarely shared the same chambers. He never had wanted to be married but *noblesse obligé* – or was it, politics obliges?

Neither Giuliano nor Lorenzo ever questioned their parent's decisions, yet the latter's marriage wasn't called for, at least so they both thought. Yes, their mother, Lucrezia Tornabuoni, had picked one of the better-looking young women from a mostly politically corrupt Roman society, not without *un ventaglio di pettegolezzi* (harmful gossip) from the local Florentine families. They concluded none of their local daughters was good enough for the next ruler of Florence. Lucrezia insured the next leader of this Tuscan republic would have all the right connections to the Vatican and beyond. Happiness had not been an issue; we serve the family cause and what other kind of happiness could one count on?

Lorenzo could have only imagined that puberty would inspire the discovery of a future passion, but as a young boy he was already overwhelmed with responsibilities and there was no time to play. His siblings grew up, side-lined by the fame of Tuscany's first son. So, Lorenzo kept a distance at all times, even when he tried to be friendly. With this weighty destiny, he knew he could only count on his brother Giuliano. The elderly clan would politically prepare him and then a private life of secrecy would create itself.

From the moment Lorenzo was able to act the part of the heir to the throne, his family used him for that purpose, excluding any distractions. There were more and more important travels, meetings for reasons of State, as his grandfather had taught him. Cosimo convinced him these would prepare him to change the political landscape of the country, as Italy could not remain the same. Later, Lorenzo would be representing his ailing father in the important banking business deals. By then, all of fifteen, he was accompanied by Bruno, a pageboy at his service day and night. Lorenzo, still very much of a pure and noble mind had begged his father to be left alone; after all there was always at least one guard present. But the page wasn't excused. A shadow, even at dusk, the young lad followed him everywhere. Lorenzo even refused to speak to him and the boy had wept daily for his genuine admiration had turned into a love beyond all poetry.

Lorenzo remained stubborn and silent. The kid had yearned for him and would kiss his feet if needed. Well one morning he did... no poetry here. Lorenzo woke up with the boy naked next to him, fondling him, his lips on Lorenzo's genitals. He threw Bruno out and he was banished to the stalls, feeding the horses for the year to come. His parents knew that there would be more similar attempts to entice their firstborn and this future young leader was stubborn. Sometimes he lacked all humour when a relationship involved more than friendship. One day, Machiavelli would call him, 'the Prince.' A cunning Lorenzo presumed he was being tested just like his grandfather had warned him.

Lucrezia, his mother made sure that a marriage would take care of all nature's needs and desires. A spouse would serve him well and as Lorenzo was destined to rule, everything else must become secondary to the family's destiny. Cosimo's approach to preparing his next of kin had consisted of sculpting his grandson rapidly into a life of kingship. Before his own precocious manhood secretly broke all rules, Lorenzo gained respect and admiration from many, even outside the Medici family. He had been an excellent listener to both his father and grandfather and he was well aware of the existence of the many Florentine brotherhoods that, like a vicious spider, had spun an intricate web, socially and politically.

Cosimo the Elder, not without a certain disgust, had warned him that many powerful men had sexual interactions with boys and that it was considered expressive of the brotherhoods' noble values of protective love. One day Lorenzo would glance through judiciary records that omitted some of his own political friends. Under his grandfather, the Institution of the Officers of the Night had been created to protect the city from crimes, especially related to sodomy and male prostitution. In Lorenzo's time, same sex activities weren't arousing great concern to either the community or the authorities.

In Tuscan societies, as was the case in Rome or Venice, homoerotic bonds played an important role and Lorenzo quickly learned the importance of discretion. The Medici supporters would eventually dominate that Office for a long period and their young leader had well understood that in politics, youth played a crucial role. Lorenzo would have to cover up their unlawful and hidden actions through an intricate and secretive labyrinth.

But Lorenzo really loved youth and in his own poetry he bestowed his admiration and openness to all forms of beauty. For years now, he had slipped into the comportment that could befit a mature ruler of forty after having made such a premature debut in politics. He forgave himself that permanent grin on his less than handsome face, as he judged himself. Bearing the weight of being 'twenty going on fifty' and having no childhood trauma to express, tolerating happiness for all others, seemed an acceptable challenge.

His own life emphasized the liberal lifestyle idealized by Plato whose philosophy he so admired. He and his brother had followed Ficino's teachings since childhood and felt perfectly aligned in a male oriented society. He aspired to be a new kind of ruler creating a different kind of freedom; the freedom of thought and the choices one made in the privacy of one's home.

Giuliano had given him some other ideas. He said that if 'God' gave as much creative power to his female counterpart, the 'goddess', why would the clergy be so against this? He needed time to figure out how to create that middle way and to give women the power of freedom of speech, though that wasn't cast in the traditional Platonic school. Certainly, very few women, mainly of royal descent, had proved powerful. And then there was the fact that those gods that Plato's school was so enthralled with, well they were always playing games, disguising and seducing … if not raping.

Lorenzo knew he just had too much on his plate. His studies went on forever; he had been reading books since he could decipher man's language, listening to his father and grandparents since age five. His youth hadn't been drawn on a playground with friends. His mind went blank when he thought of the games he played as a child. Did he ever get to be creative like other children and was that what compelled him to support so many artists?

His own grandfather had been a friend to the great sculptor Donatello, a man of the most ghastly taste in clothing yet unwavering in his love for men. But Cosimo showed no objections. So Lorenzo, who found beauty in all things, wondered if he were being groomed into a kind of new Alexander – a conqueror of continents, women and … even men? Silently, he ignored most laws. Though in awe of the many extraordinary artists and philosophers his forefathers had employed, and with whom he was now raising this republic to an unseen level, the future rulers of Florence would meet their own challenges. Friendship wasn't one of them and the way the brothers had been brought up made it natural to Lorenzo and Giuliano to be really close to their friend Angelo, a closeness that would develop in a most unusual manner.

28. GENEVA, 2018 ELIZABETH & DOWELL, INC.

Sluggish has become your touch,
Flushed from a whacking sea
To shores on bubbles of tiny pebbles
Little mouths of secrecy . . . (Masterminding Minds)

Elizabeth was slowly sipping her green tea on the terrace of the Café Rivoire on the Piazza de la Signoria. The last month's stress had been too much and she decided to kidnap her own husband for a last-minute weekend to Florence. She was clever at finding an online deal and the five star hotel included their flight. Geneva was so close that Siegfried didn't even have time to take a nap. She had business friends in Fiesole who had bought the Medici Villa decades ago, but she didn't want to stay there. She smiled at the coincidence of her meeting with Izquierdo who would have arrived there at her organised request and that of her boss, Simon. She just hoped that there wouldn't be any problem with getting into the villa in Fiesole since she had given them all the necessary codes.

All I wanted was time with Siegfried.

She contemplated on the last decades of their relationship. Her marriage changed everything, even the old family pattern of women marrying a father figure. She had fallen for Siegfried from that first dinner when he had seduced her with his calm composure and witty knees. Handsome and slim, he hardly looked the few years her junior. He habitually overworked and behind his glasses the deep-blue eyes gazed at hers with a sense of love and care.

He would have made a towering long-legged partner, a gem as the few African American dancers had become in leading companies like the New York City Ballet. But Siegfried's two left feet made even a waltz a dangerous adventure. He wasn't like one of those strongly muscled ballet dancers, whose thighs could press her into a quick orgasm between rehearsals ... as some of her colleagues were familiar with on the company's exhausting tours, perhaps hidden in the back of the company bus.

Oh no, Siegfried took an entire night of sensuous lovemaking and swept her fully away into another realm. With him, a single night made up for the many years while she had avoided the most handsome of millionaires lining up. He was often absent, and his workload was overwhelming. It did annoy her not to have him beside her every day of the week. At least so she thought. The first years of her marriage left her with luxurious time for reading and socializing. And then, little by little, she witnessed the change. The more he became successful, the more he traveled. He grew his waistline and dark circles surrounded his eyes.

At first, she wouldn't admit to the loneliness that haunted her, as if caught in a cage of unawareness. The active jet-set life, the parties, the concerts and the opera, had her befriending the rich and famous more and more by the day. She wore designers' labels of fake happiness. Well-read as she was, and then only in her mid-thirties, she was a very beautiful and elegant woman. Admired by plenty of other married men, including Simon, Siegfried's business partner in all crimes, she smiled away all their attention. If any of them would make an effort to get closer, she called upon Siegfried.

Simon, their president and CEO, had been born into a wealthy South-American diamond family that had produced leaders, bankers and plenty of politicians. Their influence was vast and with a hand in everything that went on in the Swiss business world – it sometimes confused her. Did Simon have some special hold over Siegfried who had enthralled him into co-founding DoWell Inc? When Simon was out of town the other one was right there in Geneva, so either one could attend important business events.

Professionally, Elizabeth evolved, creating an entourage of excellently trained business associates. She handpicked the best doctors, a staff of Indian and Chinese researchers and her presence as an advisor in international business transactions had propelled her internationally as a key-player in the field of scientific research and pharmaceutical development. She did so with the gusto of a seasoned crook, even though she felt like a traitor to everything she had stood for in the past. Now Simon and Siegfried had involved her in a scheme she started to dislike more and more every day. She searched for a way out, even at this late stage. Then the unforeseen gift came.

One of their oriental doctors discovered how to extract and modify the protoplasmic disk in the yolk of an egg from which the embryo develops. The yolk containing the fat and the protein, needed from the female germ cell to nourish the embryo in its growing process – carried some unusual genetic codes. At least, and according to Doctor Zhiang, this amazing find proved to function like a reading device for general health, longevity and survival. Although it seemed unclear to her, she heard talk that even space travel could benefit greatly from this breakthrough.

Then suddenly, Simon decided to take Siegfried and Elizabeth to the United States to lecture at a major convention regarding the amazing possibilities this research would bring about. Wall Street and the government as well as the mega pharmaceutical corporations saw their investment rise in prominence daily beyond the millions. Elizabeth was dancing on a dangerous chessboard and unsure if she was pleased about this sudden ascension into a global elite market where politics and power inevitably cohabited.

Months later, while attending another jet-set party in a former Medici Palazzo in Florence, she was introduced to a former minister of state who knew just a little too much about her! Harry Khope declared himself to be not just a politician, but a close friend and mentor to Simon and that he had done a great deal for the company. Loathing politicians altogether, she surveyed his predatory charms. Trying for a one-night stand, as she assumed he was, would be wasted on her. She looked upon most politicians as vicious, and if they weren't already, they'd eventually grow into some kind of power gremlin.

Over drinks he had introduced her to a smaller man he jokingly called *Iz dottore* (Iz doctor). She found out his name was Izquierdo and as fluent in Spanish as she was, she giggled at the irony of meeting a man called 'left' while standing with such a right-wing politician.

The next week she received Iz on short notice after a typically pressing email from Simon Averardo, the president of DoWell Inc. The latter referred to her brief meeting with Harry Khope, whose future influence could be significant regarding the Wall Street value of DoWell. The politician had asked him for what seemed a 'small favour', of great importance to the present project.

Elizabeth didn't understand why Simon, a natural micro-manager, had to send her so many emails, when he could simply call her. But that wasn't enough – he had to exert power, an obviously compulsive trait. He insisted she must meet Iz at a restaurant and not at the office. Time and place were set. His driver took her to Annecy, just over the French and Swiss border, a gentle little town where she had dined countless times with her mother in her last year before she had passed. Iz proved to be a wealth of information. He explained that the codes Doctor Zhiang was researching also had an esoteric sounding past, an Atlantean-like history with a theme that had become popular in the New Age community. He called him brilliant and that his discoveries were vital.

"The survival capacity ingrained in the human DNA had been largely underestimated," Iz had confirmed. Suspicious enough, Elizabeth wanted to listen to his explanation. This was to remain a secret and frankly, neither the world press nor their readers would ever believe anything like it. She knew better.

Elizabeth never drank at lunch but this time she ordered the best bottle of Cabernet Sauvignon. She was stunned at Iz's stories. Iz, something of a scientist himself, told her of several of his own 'brief encounters' with Harry Khope, leading to more unexpected discoveries. He said he had to exclude some of the details because most of the information wasn't to be disclosed.

She had been surprised at the whole 'club scene' he seemed to be involved in and for a moment she imagined it as a stereotypical lair of 'Bond villains' with a vast entourage of seductive, busty women in tiny bikinis and macho guys in black suits; world domination being their sole life-purpose. She had laughed, but Iz hadn't. He said he was glad he hadn't come to her office because it probably would be bugged.

She sat back and coughed. She grew slightly tight in her posture, although the wine got rid of her inhibitions; she hadn't had fun like this in years. Then suddenly, he got up and looked at her straight in the eyes. "This isn't a funny game, Miss Elizabeth. And I'm going to have to play it by the rules and leave right now. You have no idea what this can lead to and frankly we all prefer not to know!"

He took a breath and reconsidered, sitting down. He relaxed and finished his meal while she ordered a pack of 'Agitate Light'. She hadn't smoked for weeks! When they finally parted after a long conversation, she gave him a phone number. She asked him if he could handle the task on his own and he told her he needed two more guys.

"Contact them," she said, "but only if you can fully trust these men ... fully trust them!" she repeated.

"I will investigate the place you were told you will find these missing codes, maybe Italy. I was just in Florence and I know people there. I'll need some time to find out, though I have an idea where to go and visit."

The next day, after a morning of phone calls, she knew where this adventure would lead. She was confident that there would be no problems getting into this former Medici Villa in Fiesole, on the hills of Florence, because the family presently living there would be away. She spoke to them before she decided to make the weekend trip. The easy access for Iz and his team was secure. From Iz and his team, Elizabeth requested an update every eight hours, and even though she detested cell phones, she agreed he could send her a text message at any appropriate moment.

The 48-hours with Siegfried had been pleasant, if not over-excited. He had shown her that there was a caring that had replaced the passion. She wasn't sure how to act upon this when he fell asleep on the way home before the plane took off from the Leonardo da Vinci airport, back to Geneva.

Florence, the Medici Villa in Fiesole, that same day

The quintet had walked down the historical, reproduced gardens and they entered a villa built on a lower terrace downhill.

"There's enough food," Isabel anticipated. "Just one more thing, let's not stretch dinner time, Florian. We want to get on with it. You're convinced they're the right guys to plan this?"

"You trust me?" he replied.

"Yes. I guess I'm getting impatient. The entire ritual seems a bit too long and what do we do when the third party shows up?"

"Dritto, hum, maybe I ought to invite him to come along," Florian figured out with a smile.

"And may I ask, what is his speciality? Riding cosmic or comic waves?" She shook her head and continued, "Well, we were lucky we got these theatre costumes from Franco's storage and at least they're pretty authentic looking."

She walked into the dining room and the chandeliers winked at the visitors in a real de Medici villa ambiance. Florian laughed at the two time travelers in mock Renaissance attire.

"You have a masked ball in mind?" Iz asked them.

"Well, whatever costume you want me in, I'll oblige as long as dinner is on!" Doh smiled through his yellow teeth.

"Please help yourself, it's a long trip to the old town."

Isabel thought they did look a bit ridiculous.

"Wait," Florian raised his voice, tongue in cheek. "There's someone out there. Just who could it be?" and he stormed out through the balcony doors and came back in no time with the third party. Dritto couldn't believe his eyes.

"Yes, we're all going to join a big carnival and you're right in time for dinner! Have a seat!" Florian pushed his new victim into a chair. "Gentlemen, bon appetite! We're not waiting for the lady; we'll take turns watching you," he said while picking up a piece of roasted chicken.

"Yummy, really tasty ... lots of rosemary and those new potatoes! Go slow on the wine; I mean we have a long trip ahead of us."

"What is this all about?" the surprised newcomer asked.

Izquierdo said, "Listen we've been rotting in a dungeon, undressed, washed, dressed up and now we're eating and that's the first good thing, so let's continue to act like the Three Stooges, OK?"

Iz refrained from any further questions and he looked at Doh hoping he too could shut up his thoughts.

"Excellent gentlemen; enjoy your meal. While Florian changes, I'll have a bite myself. So, Monsieur Dritto, and ... yes, I'm Isabel. I am the TTP Director: Time Travel Program Inc., and you're the third Stooge?"

She smiled to make him feel a bit more comfortable. "Let me tell you that whatever may happen tonight, remember one thing; we will meet at Piazza Santa Croce where now the famous Dante statue stands, right there. I promise you, you can't miss the cathedral, but I make no promises about Dante.... you'll see what I mean."

"Oh *Dio*," exclaimed Doh, "I cannot stand the tension any longer. Are we really going to a party Mademoiselle Isabel ...?"

Dritto slurred "Mademoiselle Isabel".

While Florian hastily took Dritto upstairs to change, a deadly stillness took over the room. Isabel seemed to enjoy her meal and the *boys*, well they appreciated it equally even with their worried faces. As he walked back into the dining room, Dritto felt ridiculous in tights and he fumbled his first words. "I, what ... you think that, this is ... ugh, serious?" he whined.

Isabel's straightforward voice brought up the Italian speciality: "Gentlemen, if you have no *problemas* with your prostate, there is a real café espresso waiting for you because, ha-ha, in the old centre there won't be anyone who's going to serve you coffee. You'll literally have to wait centuries for an espresso," she sighed dramatically while Florian put five small cups on the table.

"Are we going to die?" Doh begged, "Is this like one of those American TV series?"

"Yeah," Florian replied, "die laughing, though not before we are close to or over a hundred!"

Isabel picked up her skirts and assigned capes to match everybody's attire and gestured to them to follow her. "This trip will not end like one of these *Manchurian Candidate*-like scenarios we are accustomed to, scaring us away from using technology to advance humankind. What we want to bring back from that timeline is information to avoid a future of *Hunger Games*."

Familiar with the film series, they now became very serious. She swept around as if ancient knowledge needed dusting while tearing open one of the heavy curtains.

'Firenze by night', she smiled at their planned adventure.

"That's where we're going," she giggled, pointing at the lit up Renaissance wonder.

"So why don't we take our own van," Dritto interrupted, "There's enough room for twice as many."

"Stupid Stooge," Izquierdo said smilingly. "Aren't any of you getting it? The costumes, the secrecy, the hidden room, a trip? We're going to leave this century! Aren't we Miss Isabel?"

"Well, that is very good of you Iz to use those brain cells; glad you brought them along," she giggled.

"Florian was right after all; you are a lot smarter than you look and act. Soon you will be 'in the play', no longer as pitiful victims and you'll see yourselves as three technical wizards. You are going to enjoy this ..."

She got up and with a magisterial gesture she indeed performed a magic trick as within centuries-old walls, bricks started to turn and slide in different directions. The floors shifted under the prisoners' feet, disorienting them, and after seconds that felt like minutes, they all found themselves aghast, surveying a transformed room. About seven small desks, all with a kind of large, polyester-looking hood, above comfortable looking fake-leather armchairs, made this look like a futuristic hair salon.

"Please, before we take our seats, I'd like to give you all a bit of historical background unless, like Florian, you majored in Italian Renaissance and you know the Medici Family story intimately." Isabel's voice had taken on a sweet velvety softness.

Florian picked up the thread, "Now we don't have to play silly any longer. Where we land, we might have to pretend a lot, I promise you. Only when we land, it will be like Le Grand Theatre."

The trio dropped down, helpless in a large modern, wine red sofa. Their timing was impeccable ... they even bounced back on the same note, "When do we land?" they all asked in perfect unison. *Cute, Isabel thought.*

Geneva, the Freundreich Residence

They landed at the Geneva International Airport and their flight had been effortless and short, even with Siegfried's light snore next to her ear. While getting off the runway, Eliza had opened her cell phone, but there was no message from anyone. She was pleased that she was back home. A cigarette and a glass of Bordeaux; Izquierdo's team had entered the Villa Medici more than ten hours ago. *That appropriate moment for a call ought to be any moment now, she thought while putting out a nervous cigarette. My goodness ...* she was laughing at her own *Englishness.*

She walked down from the four-bedroom apartment right above the stylish offices her husband had redesigned about a decade ago. The company contract included their home in the same building where they initially had started their offices. But on the international market, DoWell had suddenly done so well that Simon wanted to expand and move all of their administration to a huge Manhattan-like skyscraper, with floor-to-ceiling windows and marble everywhere.

All necessary research could then take place under the control of an international board of directors. DoWell's president pulled all possible strings, yet politicians were unable to convince the city of Geneva for such a building to be constructed. The Lake's fountain and the celebrated Jet d'Eau were as high as the city of Geneva would go; no skyscrapers would ever break their clean horizon. The Swiss government wouldn't allow it. Instead, DoWell moved to a vast estate close to a magnificent Park, La Grange, off the Chemin du Port Noir (Black Port Road). They had a superb view of the Lake and the site was big enough for this new five-storey building, designed like a snake that could hide itself like a Loch Ness monster, behind plenty of recently planted olive trees.

The couple still appreciated the luxury of living on the top floor of their own former office, close to the private UN beach at La Perle. They occasionally would join a close friend, Judith, a wealthy heiress and sister of the renowned high society portrait artist Harold Mannowsky, for a little *diner sur le bateau* (a gourmet dinner) on the lake. Well, mainly only Elizabeth would accompany her, because Siegfried didn't have time for entertainment let alone social gatherings. Judith, also a glamorous local patron of the arts, always joked how 'Siegfried', the name of the original male protagonist of the ballet *Swan Lake,* was absent, when so many swans were around. Elizabeth was fond of Judith, who remained aloof and discreet in all their private escapades and their *petits voyages secrets aux boutiques de-luxe* (little secret trips to the luxury shops).

Siegfried's work often took him abroad but when in Geneva, he chose to work out of the new building while Elizabeth preferred the older world, only visiting sporadically the company's new premises. After all, the technology, even at long distances, would bring everyone closer. But to Elizabeth this digital era of informatics and superhero technology would lead to artificial intelligence and suppress true human contact. Why did we have to remain more and more absent, have longer business trips, even if long distances were bridged by laptop screens offering temporary happiness when seeing one's beloved across an ocean, so far away? Yes ... you can look, not touch!

She smiled as she took to an old Lenko record player with a black vinyl record taking her back to the days when she lived in London. *My unusual debut at Sadler's Wells with the Royal Ballet.* She hummed that Chopin Waltz, or was it a Mazurka?

29. FIESOLE, 1473 ANGELO

I was so very young to know it was all right
when I hid the girlish swaying of my left hip
behind my cousins' broader shoulders.
We were only twelve. (Speaker for the dead)

Angelo Poliziano had designed his life like a true Plato scholar and like this grand master, he didn't cover up his preference for male energy. He developed a penchant for late night promenades through the private parks of some of the wealthy who had been seduced by his precocious literary talents, and yes, utterly charming persona. He was only too aware of his own darker sides and he did not resonate with power games. Most of his lovers had been men in their early thirties, married and Christian, while he remained far from the Vatican's religion. The Medici brothers had taken on an equally disrespectful attitude towards the church and God, and they preferred their own private ceremonies imploring the Roman Goddess, Venus.

Both Angelo and Lorenzo loved competing in luscious erotic poetry. Amongst all this, Lorenzo had carefully watched over his brother. Giuliano didn't have even the slightest interest in their homoerotic games even when plenty of opportunities were offered. No one could touch Giuliano, because Lorenzo would grow into the ultimate impenetrable family-protecting patriarch. And Lorenzo was shrewd, and he could read his closest friends to the core.

Giuliano wondered if, the genius he detected in his beloved brother was as much family heritage, as it seemed a miracle. Once, alone with Poliziano, Giuliano asked the young philosopher, who smiled at him almost cynically.

"Giuliano," he answered, with that little tilt of his head and the smile that smirked from his thick lips, commanding the subject, "your brother is not some regular human being from this daily world, but then neither are you. I always thought families like yours belong to the Pantheon of the Gods, like the Greek and the Romans used to venerate every day of their lives. You know very well what I mean. Just the other day you had your white magic ritual for the goddess. I had suggested this for obtaining the attention of that, hum … married woman you're obviously so fond of."

Angelo smiled, his eyebrows drawing a strangely convincing angle. "Now about your brother, you might say that his realities are only a 'thought' away," Angelo mused, diving deeper into Giuliano's eyes.

"He has tremendous powers of manifestation in him and I predict that more than any other ruler in the history of this country, he will want to honour that power and truly use it to bring happiness *per il popolo* (for the people), and not only for his own goals or friends or family. He will of course have to play a very long and tiring game, one even more intricate than the game of chess your grandfather taught you."

"And I was born into that same divine family," Giuliano sighed heavily, "Only I have no desire to wear any crown or cardinal's hat! How ridiculous I may appear next to Lorenzo's inflamed ambition! Well, the least I can do is give him a hand; one day he may well need someone to cover his back. As for my ancestors, I will have to disappoint them. I will never move to Rome." His voice translated the willpower so typical in his family.

When their father Piero had died at the Villa in Careggi, just like his grandfather Cosimo, Lorenzo had taken special care of his younger brother. His wife would purposefully and gladly receive her joyful and handsome brother-in-law. Giuliano had brought her from Rome to her future husband at the time of their wedding because Lorenzo was then looking after more urgent affairs of state due to Piero's ill health and also because of his spoken lack of interest in this arranged marriage.

Contrary to the more angelic looking Giuliano, and like his father, Lorenzo had inherited a few of nature's flaws; his face featuring a long and strangely-built nose unable to smell the difference between the scent of a flower and the smells of a pigpen. Some described him as strikingly ugly, but there was more than one contradictory opinion pointing to a striking duality in the face and an endowed body showing an accomplished, athletic warrior. He had told one of his mistresses that he wasn't born to pose for great painters draped in fancy royal capes nor to look in the mirror for the Adonis he could never be, but the young woman had been impressed by more than just his muscle tone when he coaxed her hips to unknown heights.

Lorenzo had been careful in his intimate escapades and after hawking or a bold game of *calcio* (a football-like game), he might often disappear for hours. He so adored competing with his siblings *a la caccia* (hunt) and on such an occasion, this hunter would forget his own pregnant wife and all basic respect he owed to any other 'matter of state'.

The arts in general were dear to Lorenzo, but like his brother, the exquisite faces of the lovely women masterly painted by Filippo Lippi, enchanted him. The latter sent one of his favourite pupils, Alessandro, to live with the Medici family who welcomed another nimble youngster as one of their own. That precociously promising young artist had enhanced the Medici house with many of his works before he would become known as the legendary Sandro Botticelli. Besides his talents, Sandro was handsome and his host did not leave him indifferent.

Subsequently Lorenzo, not only the cunning diplomat but also the lover, promoter and great Maecenas to all art forms, would be well known and remembered throughout Europe as Lorenzo, *Il Magnifico* (The Magnificent). As one of Botticelli's most important patrons, he helped the exceptional draughtsman and painter (yet not so much a clever businessman himself) survive financial disasters more than once. Sandro was indeed another lover of male beauty, and he honoured the family by including brothers, their father and grandfather in prominent positions in his masterpiece – *The Adoration of the Magi* – indeed *un capolavoro* (masterpiece) still admired in the Palazzo Medici Ricccardi. *Pensieri, pensieri (*More thoughts).

Lost in too many thoughts, Giuliano's eyes were closing when he realized he was about to doze off in the shade of a handsome cypress tree. His horse shook its head with a big question mark between his eyes. Briefly indecisive, Giuliano started walking with his horse right beside him till he got on, directing the horse to the road to the residence of the Buontalenti family. He wanted firstly to address some serious questions and only GianLuca could answer them. He galloped at death-defying speed downhill on his way to the Santa Croce district leaving Maiano beaming in the tender rays of the Tuscan sun.

Meanwhile two sisters, their father and brother were staring in total disbelief and utter fascination at their foreign guest. They were confused yet captivated by the story GianLuca had just disclosed. Twenty-first century international politics, wars with intricate weaponry, the word 'technology', including the conquest of space, the internet, television, landings on other planets ... and international lies projected through the media; none of which the people in Renaissance Italy could have possibly had any idea about. When GianLuca talked about men in black and secret societies, Lapo agreed he had heard about plenty of similarities within the black arts.

Now on the table between four elegant, burgundy *bicchiere* (glasses) and lots of paper notes with the strangest of designs, GianLuca's waterproof wrist watch and his turned off cell phone had found pride of place as representatives of a world they couldn't dream of touching. As for the cell phone, even though he suspected the battery was still full, where would he be calling in an unwired 1473?

Morello, for years Lorenzo's favourite horse, was steaming, but a horse that doesn't run isn't a happy one. Giuliano didn't want to make his appearance too obvious and he preferred walking down to Lapo's house through a few of the smaller side alleys off Santa Croce. He felt a thrill and his own breath followed a quicker heartbeat as he approached the big wooden doorway. A restless Giovannino, who hadn't been sitting for long, let Giuliano in and immediately took care of his thirsty horse.

It seemed that there was nothing else to do or to say to this gallant man who had hardly uttered a word while simply making his way through the garden like only a born prince would. Surprised, Andrea instantly jumped up. Lapo smiled at the 'non-coincidence' and both young women were ready to greet and embrace him as much as to run off in the middle of all the perplexity; what else but to change dresses.

GianLuca slowly stretched his right arm and slipped his cell phone in the lower left pocket of his own now freshly washed pants that he wouldn't dare to wear anywhere but in his hosts' residence. But that wristwatch on the other side of the table had instantly caught Giuliano's eagle eye. This man wanted immediate answers yet no words, nor even greetings came from his lips. GianLuca instantly noticed his confusion.

The young de Medici suddenly stepped back; an armchair wobbling. His eyes captured GianLuca as if returning to a long-lost lover. In his next move, Giuliano tripped on Andrea's foot and he stumbled slightly in an existing spell that belonged solely to two players in a timeless realm they couldn't rule.

"Anything we can offer you to drink, *caro Giuliano*?" Lapo politely asked noticing the present bewilderment in his unexpected guest.

Andrea moved back and said, "Would you like us to leave you two gentlemen alone?"

Agnola grabbed her sister's hand and Fiammetta squeezed back in despair. Now, nobody wanted to leave this moment. GianLuca blew invisible stardust in all five faces, for he knew what had happened.

"Please, my generous hosts, please sit down, all of you." But Giuliano didn't take notice of GianLuca's pleading. Giovannino had put an extra glass, water pitcher and a chair out for their new guest. Wanting to be part of this scene, the kid sadly retired to the nearest oak tree far off in the splendour of the garden.

With tears welling from his eyes, Giuliano only saw GianLuca's face in front of him; all others seemed to have disappeared.

"Why do I need to talk to you so badly? I have asked myself since our first meeting; why is there such closeness; I find no explanation for, similar to my beloved brother. There is a kind of inexplicable calling and I rush to see you as if it were Lorenzo."

Sweat was running from his sideburns while his youthful body was nearly shaking.

"GianLuca, you have been on my mind permanently, almost like matters of state are to Lorenzo. I fear I cannot let you out of my sight for a minute longer."

Fiammetta's eyelids popped open as if waking up from a bad dream. She didn't remember any man ever saying such a thing to her. If it weren't for a reputation both Medici brothers had with the women in Tuscany, and even abroad, both sisters would have mistaken this for a wedding proposal. Andrea imagined that in a few weeks GianLuca's hair would be longer; some dye and a change of dress and they would almost look identical. *They so look so alike,* Andrea contemplated, and once again, several heads in the same family nodded in total agreement as if their thoughts aligned.

Amused, Lapo sat down and quiet wisdom brought his speech back to their present moment of unexpected shared happiness. "You are both extraordinary".

He inclined his body to the side of his armchair and finished his thoughts. "And we are truly privileged to be witnessing such unusual movements where time has no impact on the remembrance of two souls, meant to meet just once more."

While both visiting men read each other's thoughts, Agnola hurried to her father, taking his hand, begging for an explanation. "Father, you have actually understood what is going on here? Then you must tell me," she insisted in a childish manner and Lapo's eyes twinkled like little blue stars. "I mean you must tell us all. I'm scared; this isn't, well a normal way of behaving for two men who have never met or gotten to know each other, I mean for men of..."

"Sister," Andrea softly whispered, loud enough for Giuliano to lower his eyes, briefly remembering the presence of an entire family. "Tonight, it may occur to all four of us that after having listened to GianLuca's story, and let this not be repeated outside these walls, that indeed in his century GianLuca actually is no one else but Giuliano de Medici, like a future version, reborn and therefore, only he may know the outcome of this happening, one confusing us all."

GianLuca and Giuliano stared at one another and a mysterious veil had finally dropped.

30. FIESOLE, 2018 IZ'S CONFESSION

What is the madness
but a brilliantly dressed-up party in gowns of failure others won't admit to wear.
A daily prêt-à-porter,
a ready to wear hidden, repressed excellence
on an avenue to escape the purple road, (Mad)

"Naturally we are taking a risk expanding our team by three more travelers." Isabel sounded almost solemn. "Florian though, feels you will benefit the mission and he was very confident about all of you gentlemen," Isabel said as she scanned their discomfort and looked upon them *comme des petits voyoux* (like little thieves), after stealing a few wallets, right out of a Charles Dickens novel.

Florian continued, "You know when DoWell offered you this contract they never considered to keep you on after this job. You do realize this, don't you?" Two were now grinding their teeth and Dritto acted a little more nervously. Isabel's mouth adopted a self-indulgent grin typical for a model strolling down a catwalk.

"*C'est plutôt drôle tout ca* (it's rather funny, all this)," she laughed

"Look Izquierdo," Florian said. "I knew you well. But I am no longer the same guy you remember. Much has changed of course, and I'm not even sure you know anything at all about what happened after you left the campus. I can tell you quickly that it wasn't fun and you were lucky to have been released from the university. I can tell you now that it was for your own protection that I didn't stay in touch." He grinned at his friend.

"One day I'll tell you a very long story," Florian said. "For now, you'll have to trust me. I did a lot of checking up on you and your talent is wasted playing on the crook's team, especially since you don't have a clue what's going on. Yet, it'll be your choice, and I won't lock you in a dungeon for it."

"True, it is your own choice!" a feisty Isabel giggled, "We won't keep you from it, even if I'd love to put you away for a while longer. Have some water; please help yourself. I know it's a kind of situation that can get heated!" she continued with a broad smile.

"Thanks," Derecho smiled. She is quite *simpatico* after all, he contemplated.

"I understand the situation better now!" Dritto said.

Izquierdo picked up his friends' thoughts, "I had no idea we'd ever get into anything really dishonest ... ugh. I had actually only agreed to check the device we would be discovering and the same goes for Dritto and Derecho. We all have compatible technical skills needed for this operation. We were going to look at a ... well what do you think? When I signed up for this ..." Izquierdo looked Isabel straight in the eyes, then he continued, "... and since you know so much about us all, you do know we also did some terrific work for two other companies. If anything, we are over-qualified for breaking into an old villa." It took him a moment to find the right words. "The idea was that, well we wouldn't exactly steal anything. We'd reproduce whatever we'd find. We were given three months to finish the job."

"So now," Dritto picked up the thread, "we'd be working for a few months and for a very high salary. In our profession, we do not really get those opportunities very easily if we don't work for a government."

"Of course, gentlemen," Isabel said, "you were impressed by DoWell's offer and you had no reason whatsoever to question your employer, to look any further, or, shall we say 'look lower' into why such a company has made over two hundred and seventy billion dollars from the last wars in the Middle East."

Three pairs of eyebrows looked in disbelief at her cynical reply but Izquierdo dropped his chin fast enough. "So, tell us Iz, why did you drop out of your membership with *Le Club* after three months?" Florian was pressuring the annoyed-looking Izquierdo while his bemused colleagues murmured, "Le Club, le Club, le Club ... Iz, hello, le Club ... *s'il vous plait, expliques* (please explain)!"

Annoyed, Izquierdo had to answer. "Le Club is a private organisation, kind of a fraternity, *mes amis* (my friends), which is heavily supported by big firms and their CEOs, men like Simon Averardo."

"Right," Florian interrupted, "you cannot quit. That's why you walked out after their so-called trial period. You had to promise you would finish that one job for them and then they would leave it at that. They said later on that if you changed your mind, they would welcome you back, *mon cher* (my dear) Izquierdo."

Iz shrugged.

"Ha, you guessed well. To them it was obvious I would never find better protection than under their wings", Iz unburdened himself.

"*Biensûr mon cher* (of course, my dear), that's French haha," Derecho joked. "You probably wouldn't, because there isn't really a way out after you have committed a crime, *amigo* (friend) or you might just run like *Speedy Gonzalez* and that only works on the television! Ha-ha." Iz was all sweaty, and he stood up. He threw down his mock Renaissance jacket and picked a cigarette from a pack that he had left on the desk behind him. His eyes were teary and Dritto got up and shook him by the shoulders.

"*Hombre, no te preocupes de nada. Todo bien. Esta gente son correcto. Hombre* (Man don't worry about anything. All is well. These are honest people)... OK, you made a mistake and you got scared, but hey, there's another chance right here to make up, and this one sounds a lot better to me."

"You know, my friends," Iz said "maybe I always dreamed of such an opportunity, you know, to use technology for a far-out purpose like your travel program into other worlds. Well you know, do something good... that is what we're doing, right? Something good, no?" Iz asked, wide-eyed like a twelve-year old.

Isabel addressed the trio. "Well, you can join our own little club; it isn't a social one. We have a plan to find solutions for some disturbing worldly situations, harmful causes due to political decisions in these last decades where power abuse has brought in a very dark force. We want and hope to correct a few major mistakes from centuries back, and those of today's manipulating political leaders."

The trio looked at her and repeated, "... and by some of us?"

"Reincarnation?" Derecho joked while his two colleagues turned their eyes to the ornate ceiling. Florian jumped right in. "OK, evil is a big promotion machine and our present reality blossoms and spreads more seeds of change. We can, and we will, change it. We will experiment and see if we go back in time and well, with some magic," he said "we need to succeed and make the difference! Worldwide, the governments and their leaders... they all play with magic! Remember Stalin? Like Hitler, he was a master in black magic."

Florian took a breath in his long monologue. "Did you know that Stalin slept in a different room every night or hid away in a huge hidden library devoted to his favourite subject, black magic? When humans remember that we are an experiment of creator gods, 'in their own image' we can use the same or similar tricks. That is how the human race tries to survive. Everybody in power wants to play god, history repeats itself tediously."

Florian had sounded rather serious and all three men looked at him in awe and in doubt.

"There's some really ugly stuff out there," he continued, "and Iz, your eyes tell me you saw some because you suddenly look a little scared. Did Le Club show you a few examples of their power games?" No sound came from Iz's mouth and his friends walked him back to the couch and gave him a glass of water. He looked down at the black and white tiles. The floor reminded him of the first 'session' when he had joined Le Club. He shrank once again and trembled at the same time. He took a deep breath and felt undressed by Florian's piercing eyes. His confession was genuine, and Florian knew he wasn't about to lie. Silence waited to be cut.

"There were a few political heavyweights at the first meeting, and I guess Simon Averardo, the CEO thought I'd be impressed. But how Averardo knew so many details of my entire life, was a mystery to me. I didn't like his grin when he told me that I had joined the 'right' society and that I would help the 'right' cause – and that those stupid bastards who keep fornicating the Third World countries into an overpopulated whirlpool, would never have to worry about poverty again. I took it first like, 'Wow, he's going to help them'. Of course, I was dumb, as I would find out within the first minutes, "Izquierdo explained while he requested some more water

"We had a few drinks, and the more the man talked the more it became clear the plan was not exactly humanitarian. For some strange reason he was extra nice to me. I mean I'm not your cute kind of boyish type, so I wasn't worried he was after my arse! He said he did like me and if I worked well with the DoWell project, he would be offering me a very successful life. He could even get me connected to the White House! Imagine, me in the White House with that President?"

Isabel shook her head and unleashed a gorgeous head of dark auburn hair, flowing down to her shoulders.

The White House, but not a similar job she thought. Let's have the confession now. then we have to get going.

"Yes, there were a few lunches. I always got picked up by a limousine, we would have a tête à tête either at a very private restaurant... I could never have remembered the locations... or we would simply meet at the DoWell headquarters where some of the offices have their own kitchen and even bedrooms! One afternoon he took me to a private bank on Wall Street; cocktails and a glamorous preview of an exhibition of several paintings from a huge collection especially flown in from Florence. When we finished our discussion on the Renaissance's most famous family (the Medici family portraits were on display), and he seemed to know their story well..."

He smiled nervously and continued, "He wanted all technical details regarding the possible making of a time traveling device to get into *their* world; a world he called 'parallel'... I must admit for a man in his late eighties, during all our discussions, he showed brilliance and tremendous clarity of mind. Of course, from a historical point of view, and in his own darker hierarchy, he'll go down in the annals of time as one of the men whose veins stretched into pure evil."

He sighed feeling somehow a bit relieved and continued his lugubrious story.

"That day I first met the Minister of State, Harry Khope, he gave me a phone number. He said I should enjoy myself and not just work late hours and that they would do anything I wanted, he had said with a smile. They're trained for the job and they too are well paid. He added that 'they're pretty brainless', but that will never happen to you, at least not if you make the right choices!" He sighed and continued.

"The man's eyes had turned icy, and while I froze, he grinned convincingly before an intense hugging ended the meeting. On my way out, I noticed a very handsome young man in his twenties, with wavy black hair embracing Harry in a rather more intimate manner. When he took off his stylish sunglasses, I nearly dropped my jaw to the floor. I couldn't figure out his name right then. He was one of those new faces, another movie star; one of those young kids you've never heard of, and then after some action movie trilogy, they join the best-paid actors in the business. I always thought that was a bit weird, but that night it became clear why!"

"Right indeed. One of the many!" Florian commented.

"At least that's what the public is told to believe," Iz continued, "overnight career or a television academy discovery! The media are very deceiving, and those actors aren't making the millions of dollars their agents publicize. Remember they are actors, so that's what they do for a living and they are always on stage! The money isn't even real because those digital millions have no gold to cover the paper! The bank mob and the government in one bag – creating digital currency that may have no value!"

His friends all zoned out for a moment and each one got a drink.

"So that's what their real job is," Isabel interjected, "and few actors can escape the web. Their priority isn't the making of great art; it's to be the masters of distraction. But there are a few exceptions and they live usually well hidden away."

"Right, and they often marry a movie director, or producer," Iz continued... "They pay them off eventually for good behaviour and pass them on, sometimes to a new colleague of their choice."

Florian laughed out loud, "But that's for the big award-winning stars!"

Izquierdo wanted to hide his head in his hands and after his last words Derecho had jumped up, walking back and forth in the room.

"Iz, my... Jeez... Iz, are you gay now? You mean you went out with..."

"No, no..." Florian now intercepted laughingly. "He didn't even try to sleep with Iz, but.... with what was her name again, Penny...?"

Dritto now got his five cents in, "The singer, wow... you had a chance to..."

Isabel shook her head in disbelief. "Oh, you men," she smirked, while Iz still looked very sad. "How do you know so much about my life?" he stared into Florian's eyes.

"Later Iz. It all has to do with my own past. But for now, let us return to yours. Please proceed with your fascinating story, you wizard of Iz. We have a flight to catch," Florian replied gently while Isabel looked at the clock.

Iz continued, "Don't get me wrong. I didn't call the phone number he gave me; oh no, they called me. It was to be a simple party; drinks and talks with the big man, arriving this time accompanied by yes, Penny."

Florian nodded.

"At that time, she was on every magazine's cover because of her divorce and her ex-husband's affair with his new on-screen partner. She wore a see-through dress clearly showing a diamond-decorated G-string and no bra! I couldn't believe it. It was obvious she was his slave, and maybe soon to be mine. He didn't even say a word. As he walked over, a giant Latino-looking guy, all muscles, joined them. I forgot what movie he had been in, maybe one of those warrior types. Penny had an intense conversation with another blond beauty in an equally revealing dress. She also had been on one of the international fashion magazine covers. I never remember their names because I never go to the movies."

His glass was now empty and while Dritto immediately gave him a refill, Izquierdo continued his story.

"At first, I thought Penny was high. She's got to be on drugs and to a certain extent she was. While I studied her, I noticed there was a lack of balance in her eyes. She looked scared. I suddenly remembered that her godfather had been a famous television star and she had been in the business since her childhood. Before I knew if I wanted to meet her, she stood in front of me while 'the boss' smiled and watched over us with an approving paternal smile. I must say she was disarming and her approach was so sweet, almost childish. She obviously was a natural at charming men, not as much a talented actress on the screen as in life. But this was a social scene she had mastered ... for a long time it seemed. She addressed herself to me and I was nearly shaking. "*What would you like?*" she asked, and I was so stupefied that I answered, "a *cappuccino with only the foam.*"

"Of course you would! You always preferred cinnamon to cacao;" Derecho joked, remembering his friend's habits.

"Little did I know this was a code for some kind of sadomasochist ritual; you know, whipped milk on a black espresso coffee?"

She swallowed briefly, and her nostrils tightened. Fortunately, I didn't mess up any further and the mood relaxed until I felt I could ask her if we could just leave the place and go to a real coffee place in town. She answered she thought a hotel would be the best. I was very confused; she took me by the hand and waved back at 'the boss', who seemed more than pleased at our rapidly improvised engagement."

"Oh my, oh my, with the dream girl Penny," Dritto's breathing was more like a moaning!

Isabel looked up at the ceiling and shook her head more than once.

Derecho insisted; "And … go on, go on *mon ami*."

"We went to a very fancy hotel, you know, on Fifth Avenue and 60th."

"Yeah, never go there, sneezing costs a dollar!" Dritto commented with a subtly sarcastic expression of a grand dame waving a little finger.

"She had her own key and the doorman greeted her very politely," Iz continued with more details. "When we got into the elevator, I told her I got the story and I wasn't interested. She froze and started shaking as she put her index finger on her lips and then on mine, with some pressure. I shut up. The elevator took us to a suite and she insisted I'd carry her in, like in a movie. Really, like that stupid wedding movie she had been in. I am surprised people go and see that garbage."

Iz took a moment and continued. "Anyhow, we sat there for at least ten minutes in silence. I looked for water in the fridge and got some ice and faked a gin and tonic. She started to look a bit better. I was holding her hand for a while. She suddenly got up as if she had changed totally, a different mood, like she had flipped. She walked to the door and once again she put her finger in front of her lips."

He took a breath and continued. "She ran into the bedroom with an open door and, while I froze, she took off her dress, and, to my relief, put on jeans and a sweater. She took my hand, and out the door we went … this time the back door. Soon, we were on Madison Avenue and under a big floppy hat and sunglasses you couldn't have recognized her. A few blocks further, we jumped on a cross-town bus … imagine with her on a bus.

She even had a bus card. We sat in the back, her back to the driver … a nearly empty vehicle. 'I know a little place, on Amsterdam Avenue … I hope you don't mind we're not having Italian … ' I remember smiling. The very simple looking macrobiotic food-bar was empty. She ordered a soup, brown rice and veggies. I just had green tea. And then came the full story and it was long. It seemed we stayed there for hours but she spoke quickly … I had a hard time following it as a headache invaded my temples. We stood outside, a few times, the time of a cigarette.

"You're not one of them," she said sounding less nervous now. Despite thinking she couldn't light a cigarette without her designer lighter – she found matches did the job. "I noticed it from the first moment, but after I tell you more about myself, you'll understand why I'm so often in doubt, I'm always in fear something terrible is about to happen." Her smile was as captivating as the persona she was known for in the television series that had launched her to front cover fame for more than a decade. "They all think we're just bimbos. You know anything about MK Ultra?"

I nodded, not in favour of discussing the subject. I had studied this mind control program the government had started with post-war scientists. I swallowed painfully as I felt burned by the countless victims I had first heard about in my late teens, later reading their tiresome and awful stories.

She then continued: "Well, my mother was one of their favourite subjects," she explained eagerly, "and I was born in a Satanic ritual while my father was sacrificed. I'll spare you the details; it is mind-blowing and that's of course the effect ... they want to blow your mind. I was brought up, partly by my uncle, yeah, a sugar daddy, an eternal hugger. He was big on TV and it all started before I was five. Afterwards, I was trained to serve that type of man. I turned twelve and as promised, 'the man' came to fetch me, just as my uncle had said."

She took a breath, "He was a really important politician and very powerful and one day he promised he would make me a big movie star and the whole world would know and love me. As a little girl, I liked that idea because I thought that way I could disappear into another world where no older men had to be serviced any longer. Then, when I turned a rather tall fourteen, I was shown pictures of the man I was going to marry. It was a big surprise because he was all over the news and engaged to a very pretty English actress. A year later, I made my debut in a new television series and soon after I met my future husband on the set. The rest I guess, you know from the press. What they don't print is that he went through the same story as I did. All of our stories are planned years ahead. We are in a Holy Wood, Lalalanding distraction territory; our lives are totally programmed!"

"You know what Hollywood really means?" she asked me next.

"The wood of a holly tree. Shamans used it for their so-called magic wands to create different realities or enter them like a wizard, like Merlin. In other words, Hollywood is a metaphor for throwing stardust in people's eyes. We, the actors, are supposed to be multi-millionaires but we rarely ever see a dime; we're living in huge mansions picked for us and loaded with cameras. Our lives are never ours, if we're not on a set making a new film, we're at a party or put to bed, rarely our own! When I saw you this afternoon, I thought there's something about this man that's different. You know, to the public I may look like a stupid blond who can't even act – even when the agency makes it sound like I make millions of dollars and I have new roles whenever I want – but I can tell you if you want to survive, you better be a really good actress – especially when playing a dumb one – and I have become one hell of a specialist at playing stupid!" she exclaimed cynically.

"I faked our exit from that hotel where they bring their clients, or those people they want to blackmail, and that's about ninety-nine per cent of all those invited to meet 'Teddy, the Bear'. That's his nickname." She bit her lip.

"I'm telling you now – Izquid, your name was? Get out, if you still can get out. I'll help you fake an affair for a few days only, because without sex they'll be suspicious or think you're a closet queen and instead they'll send you a cute slave boy. I've seen it all. I'll tell them you're a classical romantic with wedding plans, largely stuck in your computer stuff and the kinda guy who takes time to get to know. Next Friday at 3:00 pm, let's say we'll meet here, and if I'm trapped, I'll call you here from a phone booth; don't ever call me! You have a cell phone. I'll call you and you must delete immediately whatever message you get from me; maybe get an extra chip or better still, a burner-phone. Anybody who has been in touch with them is usually checked daily even though you may not be of a major importance to them ... yet. The secret service has an amazing satellite system and once you get caught, they'll count the toilet paper you use! Now don't tremble, I doubt they'll really bother you, not that soon in the game and never if you have something they want. Are you a scientist?" I had nodded hesitantly.

"I thought so," she said, "Play nervous; make them believe that you cannot function if you're not left to work by yourself. They'll check you anyhow, or at least in the beginning. Make them believe you're the type that needs to finish up before taking a vacation, a control freak and that you really like me a lot and you'd love to go to the Bahamas with me. Yes, send me flowers, chocolates. I'll give you some money. I have a big enough expense account. Just win time, and again, get out. You may be lucky."

She left me, and she jumped into a cab. But that next Friday, she didn't show up. She called from a movie set in California and that same day I told the 'Bear' I was quitting because I couldn't handle the pressure and I needed to concentrate on my work.

Next, I was called into DoWell and the big boss Averardo told me he felt really worried about me and that I ought to take a few days off and he would gift me a free flight to the Bahamas. I turned down the offer afraid another slave exchange would be waiting for me and told him I'd love it some other time. He asked me to make sure I told nobody about my meetings, and I assured him nobody would ever believe me anyhow and that I appreciated his job offer and I hoped for many more. Later that week he asked me to put a team together for the villa.

I agreed to the well-paid offer to close the chapter."

"And the rest is right here." Iz sighed.

The small audience had not gone to sleep, and Isabel and Florian were happy the extended story-telling had come to an end.

"That took some courage, Iz," but Florian's sincere congratulations made no impact on a tired man who for a while had thought he could have slipped through the maze of unethical international politics. "I knew you were my man, and you know Iz, like Dritto said, after this trip, everything is going to be just fine and I promise you all that the next movie you're about to step into will outlast your wildest dreams."

"I really hope so," Iz answered. "I really do!" he repeated, and he closed his eyes sinking deeper into the travel couch.

31. FIESOLE, 1473 GIULIANO

Designers sketched me into life?
and you, untouched by godlike wands
obscured by architects not from just one Universe,
a multi-verse,
in all operable codes of life
we are not versed in
those symbols dressing the sketch,
the eye has yet to draft. (Inner Voice)

For a moment, Giuliano di Piero de Medici was put off by Andrea's last remarks; as if this otherworldly visitor knew the outcome of 'his life', that even this stranger he had felt so close and familiar to – that this man might know his future. People with clairvoyant abilities had walked in and out of his family's home for generations and after all, where did GianLuca actually come from?

For heaven's sake he thought, the Vatican, the French or the English Kings always based their decisions upon studying the stars.

La nonna (grandmother) had told her grandchildren plenty of stories about magic, witches, and fairies. Yet this was so different. On each occasion he had met up with this foreigner – the attraction, the fascination had been overwhelming.

Is he only a messenger to warn me about stepping into some kind of a Greek tragedy?

He looked across the table where GianLuca quietly drank a glass of a local Tuscan wine and nibbled on some bread and goat cheese. He allowed a new and easy flow to move through his veins.

Suddenly there was no drama and... *what was a psychiatrist? Giuliano thought.*

"What is a psychic.... psychiatatatrist?" Giuliano questioned ever so shyly. "That word, I... I have never heard it before."

"Psychiatrist?" GianLuca smiled. "Excellent, my friend, I didn't speak. I didn't mention the word and you have picked up, yes, you have read my thoughts!"

Their eyes were gliding in the same horizon.

"And actually yes, the word is psychiatrist." GianLuca continued. "That's quite something; our thinking process is wide open between us and telepathy is one of man's greatest gifts and in my world, we have forgotten how to use it. We must be connected." He smiled.

It was a moment when Andrea, who was obviously quite a brilliant scholar of various languages, intervened with great pleasure. "Did any of you study the language of the ancient Greeks? For *psych* means 'soul' as in *psykhē* ; *iatry* is 'medical treatment' from *iātrikos* and *fiāsthai means* 'to heal'.

"*Bravo Andrea, Grazie tanto* (thanks a lot)," both GianLuca and Lapo called out.

"Now while you might think of magicians," GianLuca explained "in your family, at the Vatican and the French and English courts, I think in terms of psychiatry, because in the dimension I came from, the profession of the psychiatrist, well it's like a doctor who is supposed to clean up the mind when it's confused or in disorder. He is someone who analyzes and helps the other person through such a process. In my century it has become a popular profession, one not always lived with full integrity. And in my century's society, money has taken over most of daily life's ambitions."

Four people just pricked up their ears all at the same time.

"Are you such a *dottore* (doctor) in, um, your world?" Giuliano asked, still in quiet disbelief.

"No, I was a man of science and yes, I have been writing books about scientific subjects and..." he smiled.

"And that includes traveling in... time?" Giuliano asked with eyes wide open.

There was some more heavy breathing and Andrea and Lapo laughed. While the two sisters remained, like Giuliano, glued to their own beliefs, GianLuca joined them in some more laughter.

"Well, like we say in England, that is another cup of tea, isn't it my dear," GianLuca continued, while his eyes met Andrea 's penetrating look (though he wasn't sure if tea was already served at court in these days!).

"All right; imagine that tomorrow, let's say we walk into the Milan Cathedral where your brother will actually meet the Sforzas very soon, no?" More open-eyed sighs had escaped from the other four listeners.

"You sit down ... pretend to pray, and then you doze off for a moment, you know, like many visitors often do in churches. You may feel like you have left your body and you notice that those around you are no longer the same people. Their clothes look from maybe the days of Averardo detto Bicci, a century ago. You recognize your great grandfather, Giovanni di Bicci, because you knew him from the drawings and the paintings. So, you walk straight to him and tell him that his son Cosimo and his grandson Piero, your father, are all going to suffer from the terrible disease of the gout. You'd like to bring him a remedy to help them. He looks at you in disbelief, as he's a man of great financial means and full of cunning, a man trusted by the pope, a banker magician if ever there was one, and yet without any knowledge of the body."

Giuliano slightly tensed, and his huge active hands urged for this story to be carried on with the explanation GianLuca is offering in such images. GianLuca proceeded, "You are able to explain to him that you're bringing him recipes from earth's womb. Those herbs and essences will cure the pain that will otherwise invade your family for the coming centuries. Your great grandfather is a prosperous man of big business, shrewd but witty. He is surprised you know about his health because he has never met you. He looks at you with his hooded eyes figuring out if you are a charlatan, but he likes you right away. Maybe intuitively, he knew you ... well you are family after all. As you start telling him about his son Cosimo and his wife, Contessina Bardi and their son Piero, your father, Giovanni di Bicci starts to open up and truly listens. He then realizes this cannot be a coincidence. The next day he invites you to his home and you discuss many a subject including of course, your family's health. He and his wife take your advice and what do you think happens?"

"Go on, go on," Giuliano impatiently commanded, to the sisters' surprise, in an authoritative manner. GianLuca grinned almost wickedly and jumping up from his seat into a brief little tap-dance, clapped his hands as if in a

Broadway musical… all heads looked stunned once again, while some laughter lowered all tension in the room.

"And what is next? Simply, they all live longer, healthier; his rule doesn't end when your grandfather becomes *Gonfalonieri* (holder of High Office in Florence) in 1421 and your own father Piero may now have to wait to rule till much later and no, he does not get sick. Maybe his brother, your uncle Giovanni avoids his own early death. Who knows, you all may have been born a decade later!"

"We get it!" Fiammetta exploded enthusiastically. "If this is true, then you Giuliano… you will indeed live and nobody will get to kill you," she cried out joyfully.

While covering her mouth, Agnola glanced at her sibling with hope in her eyes. Slowly, Giuliano got up, pressing both his hands on the table. There was no smile any longer.

"A conspiracy, right?" he asks GianLuca in a still gracious yet quivering voice.

"The pope, I bet. They want us dead, both Lorenzo and me. I've been told before. That's why we don't appear alone often in the streets of Florence. *Bene* (alright), if your theory is right, as your own history books must have confirmed… haven't they GianLuca?" He looked rather tense now but continued while contemplating his destiny." Then you know, I guess, even the year, the month, the day and time of such a gruesome event?" His voice now trembled.

GianLuca nodded and he felt truly annoyed to have to confront this man with that kind of information. While he looked over to Agnola, she dived into her father's lap.

"Then we can all change such a destiny? Do you believe we can?" Giuliano asks.

"Well, it depends on how strong your belief system is. From our history books I remember very, very little about you and Lorenzo. The writings of Poliziano and other letters and publications speak ever so highly of both of you, though at times reluctantly of Lorenzo because he grew to be deeply involved in the power games as rulers eventually may choose to."

GianLuca appeared more serious than he wanted to.

"Your brother will equally commit to some amazing endeavours. Lorenzo will give a boost to the arts to an extent that nobody else in our world's history may have ever accomplished in such a short period."

"I will tell you all you want to know about both Lorenzo, myself and my family if it is helpful to ..." Suddenly Giuliano stopped speaking. Agnola was about to burst into tears and her sister held her tight around the shoulders, so he continued, "... to live longer than, what, my 21 years of age? Or about how many years are we talking here?"

GianLuca now faced a very much-confused Giuliano. "Maybe we can go for a ride, GianLuca, would you like to?" Andrea got up from the bench neither he nor his father had dared to move from.

"Giovannino will prepare a horse for you GianLuca, and dear Giuliano, please do not worry and just trust this man, for he may very well be the magician who will change your destiny and that of your family."

"Thank you, Andrea, I appreciate, as always, your insights and your family's warm hospitality. With GianLuca's arrival, he may have the solutions I may have otherwise prayed for. I admit being vulnerable, which is not my usual state of being."

A faint smile dressed his lips and while Andrea's page walked them to the gate, Fiammetta comforted her sister in silent tears, hidden from Giuliano's eyes.

32. FIESOLE, 2018 ISABEL'S PLAN

You challenge your life away,
for no longer do you own this Earth,
but owe it much,
a cosmic debt
far greater than all destructions can withstand. (Mea Culpa)

At Medici Villa in Fiesole, Isabel, as though fashionably trapped in a second skin, looked stunning. Loose-limbed in an uncommon rider's outfit, somewhere between an exclusive haute-couture design and a theatrical costume from a cloak and dagger movie; a Swedish, post-silent movie star came to mind. "No, I don't vant to be alloone." She giggled at her own silliness. Somehow autumn colours made her look like a Forest Queen, Florian thought.

"Gentlemen, listen well," Isabel solemnly declared, "there's a time portal right here. As Dritto, who is so well versed in esoterism knows, every country has at least one or even several."

Well, that was a good opening for a time travel speech. Partly in disbelief of Isabel's knowledge, Dritto stared at her, almost swaying lightly as if entering a trance.

"They have been installed throughout the centuries and very few can access such portals. It's sort of a matching DNA trick, if you can read the codes!" she said as she glanced at Florian with a flimsy smile. He had picked up where she had left off. All time travelers relaxed and laid down as Florian's soothing voice gave a few more directives, till Isabel jumped in.

"Florian and I will travel to that part of France called Les Cathars. That place is our landing portal, some sort of a traveling troubadours' station," she smiled. "Rennes-Le Château is known only to initiates and it's about the nearest place we can get to, because on our way to Florence we have an 'esoteric' errand to run.

She smiled mysteriously at their three future 'time-slaves', their eyes enlarging by the minute.

"I did find another portal and that's where the three of you will enter, from northern Italy, not too far north from Milan. It's somehow too long to explain; it needs about three DNA combinations and yours will fit. I've already checked".

They were impressed once again. How had she got ... their DNA? Maybe when they had cuffed them. Well, Isabel wasn't ready to give any further explanations while Florian helped them better understand how a passage through time portals in the French Cathars or the Tuscan Hills enabled their voyage. The trio remained in permanent nodding mode, and obviously, Izquierdo wasn't the only seasoned techno-nut.

Florian continued to give more examples of coding and decoding and Izquierdo had a few details to add. They all agreed that to bring the trio as a secure back-up was a good idea. After all, this was a tricky mission and they were unsure about assembling all the necessary codes. Both Isabel and Florian were to travel to Rennes-Le Chateau and in the Cathars, they would acquire the missing piece in their time travel puzzle needed for their return trip. Once they had this accomplished, they would join the others in Florence.

"You mean we are going back a few centuries without any guarantee of a return?" Derecho's voice glued to his throat, almost out of breath. "I do have a wife and children, Florian, albeit hidden away. Why don't we just stay here? I will guide you all along, long distance."

"I think you're better off with us than in an Italian jail." Florian's voice did not sound charming. "Remember how long it takes for the *Carabinieri* (law enforcers) to file papers, and of course we still have the dungeon ready for you all, right here," he joked while Doh seemed to want to cover his eyes. And Dritto, well he actually had dozed off.

"Gentlemen, it isn't as scary as it sounds," Isabel said, "I'll admit to one inconvenience; there's a person we may well be meeting and he or she is already in Tuscany ... in the year 1473, that is. Florian developed a program by which he can monitor travelers from our timeline and any European gate. There isn't just one-way. We're using a device yes, but entering parallel worlds can be done by some of us through a new PLP, or 'Past Life Program' connection we developed. We know that at least one person from our time and place has landed in 1473 Florence this last week."

She sighed. "We presume that he or she is connected to what we're looking for. You see, some of this 'technical wizardry' has been heavily researched and guarded by many secret agencies. Well, we are aware of the existence of many such organisations and their numerous sub-divisions. That's why I asked Florian. He was involved in some of the research in the past, so he knew some of the keys, yet he wasn't the only one in the lab! Well, we better get moving. Some day soon, Florian can explain to you all how those little beauty parlours will raise your hair to a cosmic ceiling."

"I'm going to prepare the stage for our big act," she teased good-naturedly.

"But ...," Dritto just opened one eye. "You want us to wait for you in the year 1473 at the Piazza Santa Croce where today, Dante's statue is standing. That's clear, and then we have to look for maybe 'your unknown friend' and then take him to you both, so he can take us all to the villa where we are right now, yet in ... 1473?"

"An Alfred Hitchcock thriller will be like a kids' tale after this movie," Doh interrupted smilingly with very wide-open eyes. "You're right on. You'll have to look out for a twenty-first century looking person," Florian agreed. "This is part virtual movie, isn't it? I'm just jealous of your opera costumes, so much lighter than ours, but we have a lot of horse riding to do in France, at night. You're lucky; you'll land right where you need to be. Just don't get in trouble and avoid speaking in any ancient rusty Italian!" he laughed.

"Oh gentlemen," Isabel turned around from her large screened desk.

"So, are we stealing the Medici gold?" Derecho asked.

"Sorry to disappoint you, but the purpose of our voyage is quite a bit different. It isn't of the material realm; it is simply – how to change an event in the past that will make a positive difference on our present timeline and of course, how to return safely with some more knowledge of how ... to alter the course of history," Isabel replied matter-of-factly.

All three swallowed and it wasn't till Doh finally got up and took a look at the chairs and devices, when the others gained some trust that this could indeed be a useful, magnificent experiment.

"This is advanced stuff," Doh said while positioning himself in one of the chairs. "I've seen a few, but hey, I have never seen anything like this. It'll light up differently to the frequency of the person who sits down so no other person can use it because it is only programmed for you and for the century you're traveling to, correct?" his breathing was getting a bit heavier.

"I told you Isabel, he's clever." Florian gladly confirmed with a wicked eyebrow.

"The anti-cloaking device on the left front arm has a 'no memory decline' program!" Izquierdo said, now thrilled. "Wow Florian, you certainly covered quite some ground since I last saw you! Congrats!"

"You have got yourself a brilliant team." Florian said. "Professor Doh's intuition is up as high as his background; he even got to his specially assigned chair. This isn't just pure telepathy!" Iz and Dritto looked at a very confused Derecho.

"OK, we are impressed;" Isabel said. "What's the next good news Doh? I see you were won over easily by the prospect of a free trip."

"What if we don't make it back?" Doh worried.

But Iz was already figuring out how the procedure would work. Isabel and Florian winked at each other and cautiously left their voice-recording pen on the smallish desk next to their seats. While they all took their seats, not without hesitation, Doh explored the small screen and understood the departure procedure, and Isabel was happy to have him on board, even if it meant she had to accept his colleagues. Florian had been right, Isabel thought. Izquierdo was an artist, and his friends knew their craft well.

"Let me congratulate you all," Isabel joked, "Though this isn't the first time such a trip is being organised, it is from our more private point of view, the first 'home team' taking a voyage this way. Of course, it really is quite different from what you may expect to happen."

"It sure will be," Doh said, "We aren't going anywhere! We're going to contact, no, even better, we will create another self in another world and make him/her do the work. Incredible; the costumes are just so we don't transfer our twenty-first century consciousness and we don't need to be concentrating on anything else but the mission, as opposed to the appearance! The scan fits the parallel bodies!"

He yelled uncontrollably. This was going to be the most exciting event he could have dreamed of. "Wow! Brilliant, brilliant!" And a huge happy face even seduced Isabel. His enthused voice brought a smile to everyone's face.

"That is just so amazing; this program is like a dragon's breath blowing you out of all our own limiting thought patterns. And who built this system?" Doh asked.

"Not that we cannot give it all away; at least not now." Isabel said, "But as you may have guessed, Maestro Doh," and Isabel softened her voice looking at Florian, "Florian's research was a lot based on Nicola T..."

"Tesla!" Doh yelled out with a childish enthusiasm, all his. "I felt it the moment I walked into this room; that guy most likely came from Mars."

"Who says he didn't?" Florian replied with an equally loud laugh and he proceeded with some extra information impressive enough to keep the trio in confined silence. They smiled but there wasn't even a whisper accompanying him.

"During our entire time traveling process our bodies will remain in a deep sleep. We're never in danger because a 'clone' version actually does all the work. We'll move like in an elevator through a space-time continuum."

"All right, gentlemen," Isabel said, "we'll be off in a moment and when you're entering this 'dream', you'll see that everything becomes clear very quickly, and the only thing we need to ask for, is that we are all participating of our own free will. If anyone wishes to leave now, then we'll postpone the event by an hour and we'll make sure that person is able to freely leave the premises."

"Anyone who wants to withdraw from the most important adventure since Jules Verne's first storybook?" Florian asked.

"OK we'll stay, but in the end what will we gain from this?" Iz asked, his eye on the financial deal he'd like to make.

"Freedom, my dear and discovering your own exceptional capabilities to travel in time," Isabel replied almost cynically. "It's like unlocking parts of the infinite, a diving into a power program we may actually have been born with, when we were told to only believe in super heroes in harmless cartoons or overpriced Hollywood productions set by digital tricksters."

Her eyes lit up while she continued, "Governments have caused countless catastrophes while disrupting the fabric of space-time. Remember the *Philadelphia Experiment*?"

"That was a great movie," Dritto intervened.

"Not just a movie; that was a true story, minus the romance," she smiled.

Florian fired back, "But it was disturbing, and it left major anomalies in our reality, even today! It's no good to play with primary forces without knowing its critical points. We don't help by collapsing the structure. After all, we're not playing with Lego!"

Isabel joined his thoughts, "Our time traveling dribbles into pockets of unstable time we can't escape. This will be very much a collective effort, that we as a team, must hold together. We have to depend on each other. We are almost playing time against itself while actually time needs us to exist."

There was a brief silence that Dritto happily broke. "If I can be free from any firm, any corporation that is abusing our planet, I'll take the ride, especially with your team." Isabel threw him a kiss.

"See Doh," Dritto said, "you've already figured it. Let's push the start key, right? That's easy; so far so good." Dritto smiled shyly.

"OK, before I forget," Isabel said, "don't forget to drink from the little glass bottle. It's a harmless multiple mushroom-based elixir, I brought from South America ... a fun story for another time. It gets you out of your busy mind; like taking liquid meditation. Haha!" She pondered how lousy a speech she just made.

"And let's not forget our language pills; ha-ha, pink for Italian, and for French, the red capsule!"

"Organic, I hope!" Dritto shouted out with a laugh.

"OK, enough talking," she said impatiently, "let's proceed; let's click on 'move' and then 'sign in'. You see the gate; the code is *medici memento*, spelled backwards *icidem otnemem*. Now please put the 'wristband' on your left arm."

Her voice turned serious. "A few deep breaths and then push on 'Lower Cap'. Don't worry, the chair will follow the shape of your back and you'll be lying down, like on a first-class flight, with your head capped by that big mushroom hovering over your brain. Abandon your thoughts as quickly as you can while breathing deeply."

She continued, "After a short while, you'll hear a soft whispering and then the sound of a mystical gong; you'll feel coiled. Just go with it. From then on you'll slowly see a new vision and by then ... you'll be in it."

The silence was golden, and Florian enjoyed every moment of it.

"We'll meet right as I mentioned before at the Piazza Santa Croce in about 72 hours from now. Remember to act in style and not in twenty-first century mode! Upon arrival you'll check the new wristwatch you are wearing. Derecho; leave it on in the reception mode; wear it from now on. Do hide it under a sleeve or move it up towards the elbow. Everything is set to unfold accordingly. You'll have a good time, I promise you and when you open your eyes it will seem you remember everything because, if you think of it, you had already imagined it! *Buon viaggio a tuti* (Safe travels to us all.)"

33. FIESOLE, 2018 FLORIAN'S STORY

Each one of you, of fame,
even as short as the moment
born with the symbols on your head or chest,
carrying sceptres in your slick hands (The Genie in Town Hall)

Golden spirals brought an unpredictable speed to the next series of astonishing moves. Though not one body on any of the chairs changed position, each one quickly felt they went through an entire dimensional shift. A turbulent play of flames, not unlike those strikingly fiery solar flares, illuminated their minds while an endless series of spirals pulled them into a vacuum of an indescribable spectrum of fluorescent colours, leaving behind their nearly scattered third-dimensional mind.

Doh remained in a state of total rapture while moaning an extra-human noise. *We're going through a black hole, was all he could think of.* Even Dritto who had pulled himself together, promising not to lose any control over his present vehicle, was flat on his back; two fists keeping him grounded. Iz was held back the longest, through his total lack of confidence. But hey, there were four other beings traveling already and bathing in such an unbelievable energy that he finally forgot where he was taking off from; maybe the little brown bottle had an effect after all.

For Isabel and Florian this wasn't a first and they were comfortable enough and confident once they knew three team members were on their way. Like Florian, Isabel had seen this more than once: it was like entering a crevice in a time continuum of vivid photographic memoirs.

While they were graduating from Pentacle University, close to New York, they used to share a ride before studies off campus with George Cygnus, an astrology specialist from the

Carolinas. Both graduates were unusually fascinated by the subject and by the teacher. He had told them that they were very compatible beings, as their composite chart reading proved.

Cygnus saw them as a couple, at least in one other life. Besides, accepting in her early teens that she preferred women, Isabel had been a bit attracted to Florian, and not only by his fine-looking classical appearance. Despite all his brilliance and success at everything he attempted, he always remained humble. He flew through his studies in physics with the ease of a future Nobel Prize laureate. Then they graduated and one day he just disappeared.

Much later she found out he had gone straight into an unusual university training camp for such exceptional students, hand-picked and under the surveillance of a legion of secret service and government officials. At that Quantico-like camp the students were given total freedom to work on inventions that would turn out like fine-tuned defence programs for this great nation and against, no, not against terrorists ... but beings from outer space.

This was the first government sponsored secret space program that grew from a series of unusual research programs made under the name, The Night Watch – which bore no resemblance to the legendary, historical painting by Rembrandt.

On premises with unlimited facilities, Florian got to work and research undisturbed. He became aware, very quickly, that he lived under total control; even his bathroom was bugged. His strategy had been to pretend developing habits like keeping the lights off, so he could work on several self-made devices that he would not declare to the university's authorities.

Using orgonite, his own energy field simply locked itself off from all disturbances around him, even from negative thinking patterns and much of the other 'wired frequencies'. Some of the students found their brain hemispheres' natural balance was disturbed, and they were trying to prove how devastating many of the imposed experiments were. As 'scientific inmates', even family visits were only allowed once a month, and the students could not leave until they finished the entire term of three years.

In that period, he had befriended another equally unusual student, later misclassified as a 'difficult subject'. Armando Izuequierdo was instantly renamed Izquierdo thanks to his loosely leftist ideas ... but Iz to his friends. The school let go of Armando/Iz before the end of the first year and it was partly thanks to him that Florian called it quits later on. Iz knew where this government program would slowly be taking them and like he said, it was "gripping all of us by the balls. No, not those: by our brains! If he decided to play the game, it would be wealth and fame with the NF price tag: Never Freedom!"

Florian would have preferred leaving the campus as quickly as possible, but his own brilliant mind would never go unnoticed. So, he made up an intricate plan and Armando was his first key. The day Izquierdo left the university premises, he walked to a public phone booth as promised, and called Florian's family. About a month later, Florian's father faked a heart attack. Armando knew the right clinic to set a well calculated scenario and Florian's mother came to beg her son to take leave from the campus. He pretended to refuse, saying, "My father never had time for me when I was a kid." So his mother had a meeting with the board president, acting up an academy award worthy performance.

She had checked into a local hotel close to the premises and within a day the president, Mr Allmight, who had been a scholar and colleague to several Nobel Prize laureates, received her. The president of the university proceeded to tell Florian that his duty to his country included his family, and that one day the world and the media would judge him, especially on the way to Oslo!

But Florian didn't have to act; he was deeply shocked because he never considered working to get any award, certainly not a deep state sponsored Nobel Prize. It was clear to him that such honours were mostly given to other kinds of 'beautiful minds', those who, in his understanding, had also been manipulated since the very beginning of their careers. The board had looked upon him in a strange way when he had refused to carry a cell phone. Eventually, they only cared for the result of his work and after the second year of their 'well-invested' working relationship, they knew they had grown to admire and trust this brilliant new mind in their midst.

When his mother picked him up at the highly guarded gates of the mansion where they hid more 'dazzling minds', he finally could breathe again. Beside the USB sticks in his left boot's heel, Florian didn't take any belongings. For months he had worked his own magic, projecting and visualizing the clear outcome of what he really aspired to; making sure the 'multiverse' as he liked to call it, was his first and only real accomplice... and that the multiverse seemed to have sent his mother.

Till then, the plan had worked and now the whole family conspired to hide the prodigal son. He was barely twenty when his father convincingly survived his physical traumas and to celebrate this, the whole family took a long cruise before anyone could stop them from leaving their home. The moment their ship reached a first harbour, one of his older cousins with an astonishing likeness, took Florian's place. The man mostly stayed in the cabin with a 'not feeling great on the ocean' syndrome. A fortnight later the 'accident that never happened' was written up in the local newspapers of his Florida hometown, Saint Augustine. The papers reported how he had drowned after a dinner, a few drinks and yet another dispute with his father. The body was never to be found.

At the university, the controllers behind the board of directors had their doubts, but Florian had made sure there were plenty of witnesses to the event. Even the police at the French port of Marseille saw no mystery and convincingly declared that there really had been an accident. A young, slender woman by the name of Isabel Lieverkussen had testified she had seen him fall overboard and several guests at dinner had noticed the family had a rather violent argument. Their son had abruptly left, as witnessed by the bartender, taking a bottle of vodka from the bar.

After this well-executed plan, his parents flew to Paris and then back home. His mother's encounter with a lovely stewardess resulted in a small box of Belgian chocolates, that had immediately confirmed Florian's safety. Nobody but Florian knew where to get her favourite pralines; in Brussels' best-kept secret, *Chocolate Passion.* In the last layer she found a cell phone number and a date to call, stamped in black and white chocolates. It all melted away in her mouth before she landed. Once home, her weekly shopping was an easy cover for a temporary burner phone call. This way, she kept updated on all his travels.

In public they grieved and at home they had a sad smile for he was alive and well, but far away. The life insurance for the passing of, 'a brilliant mind' now permitted them to move to a comfortable house sheltered within the woodlands of North Carolina; a house that wouldn't need to be bugged any longer. And as they had taught their son, worrying was no longer necessary.

The moment he was born, his parents had made sure their child knew the best conditions in which to grow up. As such, a precocious five-year old, he would stun the family by pointing out the secret codes of a cult film called *The Matrix* and how to read them.

His father Jules had been warned that Hollywood and television were just similar weapons of mass distraction; negative energies of deception and thanks to the internet and cell phones, the world would easily and inevitably become trapped. 'The little Martian' (a regular joke to his macho uncles) had his aunts on their toes. Both of his uncles and their wives that they had to stick together – all of them – to protect this unusual boy. The women were without children and they were the best babysitters. They didn't have to worry about baby showers, church and christening. Those rituals the family had refused since the late seventies when Europe opened chapters on scandals of paedophilia linked to the church in general, the Vatican and their Opus Dei, all investigated under an international looking glass.

By age six, Florian's mind had traveled far beyond anything the school system was teaching. With homeschooling, nobody would notice this remarkable child until he finished junior high school earlier than anyone else, while preparing for senior studies at the age of twelve. When he entered university with a dispensation at fourteen, his uncle, a successful lawyer, had intervened obtaining a written promise from Pentacle University that there would be no press. The boy would not be part of a circus act.

As a gangly six feet tall teenager, Florian had a belief system stronger than any genius at any university, yet never in need for fame or wealth. At that time one of his uncles, a professional health specialist and shaman, had taught him much about the existence of other worlds. He got to beat his dad and uncles at a triple chess game and that was cool enough, especially with his aunt's chocolate raspberry sorbet on a homemade brownie cake as his coveted award.

A friend of the family had warned them against governmental programs set up like reality shows, but the hidden truth of what was really going on behind the scenes, an obsessive TV-oriented public would never understand. Jules and Emily de Trèsloin were fully aware of this kind of program during a time when mind-control scientists had launched their 'Indigo Children' set-up. This was another New Age scam program that enticed parents to give up their own children, believing that they might be the future's brightest, maybe slated for world fame. Worldwide television and other public contests convinced millions to offer their kids on the public entertainment grill. The child trafficking had a field day. Local food stores' national gossip papers narrated the strangest stories about these mini-Marilyn Monroe acting songbirds with a Judy Garland vocal talent or even a guitarist clone – like Elvis Presley. But few researched about the lives of their 'show heroes,' infested by drugs, alcohol or sex addictions.

From Florian's parent's past, way before they got engaged, his dad's friend Nick, one of his old study mates came into the picture as 'Nick Skul' (or at least that's how he was called before his personal *NoScales* website bewildered more than one politician). Nick was a colourful and truly unusual soul; a man who had done major research and thought he had found the truth about the way this planet was run. Seats of governments were left with an embarrassing dilemma. He had published intricate details about MK Ultra and other mind controlling programs pushed by one of their own, a Swiss born secretary of state who had changed the course of the national and international political scene and who had been linked to ... the CIA. All these disturbing stories shocked Jules, and Nick had warned him that he needed to protect a son with such precariously exposed gifts. "They'll be after him, sooner or later," Jules told Emily, and for weeks, fear took a hold of both parents.

After an evening of bickering back and forth they decided to risk it and invite Nick Skul for a weekend at a nature hideout. Jules knew Nick appreciated down-to-earth people – people not addicted to media and entertainment; people like Jules, Emily and Nick. He was a man in touch with his own authentic self and he loathed meaningless relationships or trivial conversations. A real shaman like him would feel welcome in a special weekend under the guise of a sweat lodge workshop. Emily's half-brother, part Hopi Indian had it all organized, and they took off to the New Mexico-Colorado border close to a natural warm spring.

After the sweat lodge, they had never felt clearer in their heads while their physical health got a real boost. That Saturday evening, after a tasty bowl of Quinoa and veggies, and a surprise box of Belgian chocolates, Nick gave them what they had waited for: a very long and informative story that took them to the place of their deepest fears. Nick knew his material well and they all hung on his every word, even if they hated it.

"You know," he began while he lit an ancient looking pipe, "originally the brainwashing started way back, centuries ago." He puffed. "Think of the infamous Spanish Inquisition; there are plenty of examples in the past centuries, but you could say that today's 'secret agencies' flourished while the two great wars were fought. Formed in 1947, the CIA created masterful programs based on experiments that seized control over the individual."

"No worries", he smiled, "all the data is now online! Within less than five years they had gathered exceptional talent from a cluster of some mad geniuses formerly on Hitler's Third Reich scientific and medical staff. Nick was convinced that the German Führer was one of those first mind-controlled leaders. Remember Stalin, with everyone around him living in fear? Not so normal." he exclaimed. "What you do to others, someone has done to you before in whatever life-time that may have been." Emily listened well, not always agreeing with his theories, but her own life had never been a hell and it scared her that her son's future might become one.

Many years later, Nick's many websites attempted to prove all of the above but who would believe it? And yet some online information helped to wake up many, inspiring plenty of new, daring and revelatory sites.

"Let's remember in 1953, I believe the year that television made a big splash at family dinner time, that same year MK Ultra got officially baptized … well-hidden of course." He continued, "Considered by the CIA as an 'umbrella-project,' it played with a variety of methods. From an extensive use of all sorts of mind-altering drugs and psychedelics to the most advanced electronics, the project created human robots, pre-programmed to be 'kill and forget' assassins; couriers and high-level spies were a top target. The Cold War hadn't seen anything yet and neither had America." He spoke in a very conspicuous way and Emily held on to Jules's hand all during Nick's startling monologue. When he mentioned chips and implants, she stopped him.

"But Nick, we had read this in several of the 1950's Philip Dick books. We have seen it in movies like *The Manchurian Candidate. Minority Report* or *Artificial Intelligence.* Why would they reveal their own methods? It makes no sense," she exclaimed.

But Nick answered her unemotionally. "That's exactly it. That's the best way, to scare the people on their visits to their subconscious, with your movie *ET* calling home, few will believe you; you'll be called a complete nut!" His mad story was about to end.

"Those with extrasensory perception were the chosen ones; sensitive actors, musicians, singers, painters. In whatever profession, members of the controlling group, the powers that be, would find you. Many had claimed that genius stems from a dissociation of the mind, or even a traumatic pre-birth experience or at least one trauma at a very young age. Artists often are highly creative, emphatic beings yet with a tendency to dissociate easily." He sounded uncomfortably exact. "They may well believe the roles they play. In one of the famous universities, a scientist discovered that while using certain radio waves he could influence brainwaves. A doctor at an army-based institute, figured out that electromagnetic waves would provoke a kind of sleeping state on his patients. Soon he was able to channel unusual noises, sounds and eventually, through pulsating microwaves, was able to transmit 'the spoken words' into their heads. The amazing thing was that the subjects knew of nothing, remembered nothing; at least for quite a while."

During this entire storytelling, Emily's Hopi brother had remained very tranquil. He had only chosen to become a shaman after having suffered from traumatic initiations imposed by his grandfather Thunder Rock. While still a child on his first Vision Quest, he had slipped down into a cave, losing consciousness for seventy-two hours. The cold and the isolation had taken him to another level; his own antennae had sharpened tremendously, but to what cost? And had he fought the demons that seemed to have attacked him violently. Emily had been stunned at her brother's alarming confession.

"Well, for quite a while I was under cover, connected to certain organizations," Nick continued, "for years, private organizations had recruited – even kidnapped – foreigners, offering highly paid positions to develop programs beyond even George Orwell's craziest ideas. A chessboard of wargames had changed patterns, and subliminal messages now joined the daily soft drinks' commercials influencing millions of people in their living rooms, thanks to their TV addiction; a television with a multi-layer of programs! Major fast-food chains developed at the speed of light with enticing burgers like a slow death framed by fries." All in attendance shook their heads.

"*Tel-a-vision* quickly 'told a vision' of life to the world, supporting pharmaceutical companies and a petrol-based industry, eagerly sponsoring them in return." Nick chuckled. "Most of the highly classified documents I watched being destroyed, and several staff changes, were making it difficult to recover written proof. Yet all evil thrives in brief forgetfulness when thrilled by its arrogant glory. Eventually it slips into a temporary state of dim-wittedness, so some of these former collaborators and mind control survivors were able to eventually be released from their handlers. Later on, some went public."

Too many unsettling details had left them in shock and Jules's arm around his wife couldn't reassure her. They wanted nothing more than for this informative session to end. Nick finished a very tiring rant, which Emily felt would fuel nightmares for the rest of her days.

"Soon these tools will grow sophisticated beyond human comprehension simply because the ruling forces and corporate-linked superpower madmen will do anything to have the command of our world and outer space . . . a place they should write off their agenda. Study movies like, *The Manchurian Candidate* as a document, a revealing proof of the methods! And I won't talk about artificial intelligence, not now," he added cynically, much to Emily's dismay

From that day, she refused to have anything to do with Nick and she blasted Jules for his friendship with such a crazy man. She considered him dangerous because he might just wrap her family in a veil of negativity, even unwanted publicity.

So, through his puberty, she had kept her son at home so she could quietly nurture the inherited Hopi heritage and his rare talent. His shaman uncle eventually would marry a French woman. To his son alone, Jules would occasionally mention a few more details from Uncle Nick. But his wife refused to listen any longer to more tales of Templars, Freemasons and other secret societies.

Emily admitted to some very unpleasant, but necessary homework because she wasn't about to allow an opportunity for anyone to kidnap their son and his 'brilliant mind'. On one of their yearly trips to Paris they had agreed to a brief meeting with Nick, the man who had become a plague to corrupt politicians (as are most of them). At a typical French Bistro near Saint Sulpice, Nick and Jules hit the well-trodden roads once again. The next day Nick took the whole de Trèsloin family to visit a few amazing sites. He called them the hidden power spots of *La Ville de Lumière* (the City of Light) that Paris feigned to be. Lunch and dinner were accompanied by a series of stories that demolished all the history books and the young couple didn't even seem a bit surprised.

As a matter a fact, they were relieved because the way the world economy was going someone had to connect the dots. Florian's upbringing had nothing to do with the regular society, but his family had him well prepared. They took him to the mall, showed him the hamburger joints, and explained why they never ate that kind of food though they had a weakness for fries ... whether Belgian or French. It all gelled with Florian except one thing; he was fascinated by the movies and now and then, he got to see one right there at the Mall, or on the large computer screen at his uncle's.

In the years following his alleged accident, Florian was traveling a lot and on a weekend layover in Brussels, he had become friends with the daughter of a local chocolate shop, where he had left enough credit so that they could send his parents messages printed in pralines. During a very controversial presidential election he had sent them black and white chocolates in the shape of 'skull and bones', the secret fraternity where many heads of state had been trained.

The first years after Florian's so-called 'deadly accident', his parents saw their son only briefly when dining in the same restaurant, seated back-to-back. He would meet his dad in the restrooms, and mum would meet him in the cabin of a major clothing store, trying on a designer shirt or sweater.

But then, little by little, when Emily and Jules vacationed on a small Spanish or Greek island, the Croatian seaside or even in the Belgian Ardennes at the end of the summer holidays when crowds were much smaller ... and all three would go unnoticed. Florian would rent a small apartment right next door to theirs. If they would book a hotel room, they'd look for small, innocuous places mostly with conjoining rooms. When in the United States, he could meet his mother in one place, his father possibly in yet another city and then both of them somewhere at a big lake or in a forest, camping out in tents like when he was a child. At least he was alive, healthy and happy, doing a great job helping to create new programs without ever endangering his family.

During those student days, and on a more regular basis, he really had enjoyed his friend Isabel's company. Even though she had a few girlfriends, she remained his sole confidante and she was always around when needed.

Yes, Izquierdo's return, had also made Florian really happy. He knew he had made the right decision to invite him into joining this adventure; and once this was over, the 'Three Stooges' wouldn't have to be under contract with DoWell ever again, and the pharma-giant might no longer be *doing that well*!

34. PISTOIA, 1473 TUSCANY TRIO TRAVELS

> *Form the terrace smiling cypress,*
> *Fusing canvas on Tuscan hills*
> *Of autumn's springtime carnauba*
> *Deferring to the sunlight on my beaming polished back.* (On the Wax of the moment)

Right outside of Pistoia, a very different trio landed like rather unusual intergalactic tourists on a laughing gig. After their first arrival up north, they got totally trapped in what appeared at first to be some sightseeing tour till they found an easy way to Genoa. Eventually, happily recognizing a famous, but very much unfinished tower in a rather empty postcard piazza in ... Pisa, they were enjoying this trip immensely. While discussing how such a monumental building could even stand up straight, Derecho remembered that throughout the many wars the cities of Florence and Lucca had halted the tower's construction for almost a century.

There were neither tourist pizza joints nor espresso coffee shops anywhere and even though Isabel had mentioned there were plenty of places, they wondered where to get new horses. Pleasantly playing time tourists, they admired the unobstructed nature. Their tempo picked up slowly and they finally reached a charming old town by the name of Pistoia. Derecho had given a more in-depth explanation about their travel program, set in such a way that they would have the time to adapt to the new timeline. Well, they didn't really exit 2018; they just remained safe in their chairs!

They were just like puppets in a comic strip. Even if they felt jet-time-lagged, they were in those seats in twenty-first century Fiesole. They strolled through a few smaller villages where houses were scarce and once again no *bistro* (small restaurant) in sight. They decided to take a ride through and simply enjoy the Tuscan landscape. Night surprised them and the houses faded away in the horses' dust. The friendly trio didn't waste time trampling through any city gates.

While Derecho's restless companions were hoping to find a nice warm bed, only a mile behind them a strange and obscure figure handed a small purse containing an ample amount of gold coins to an equally obscure, dark clad figure surrounded by a small group of similarly cloaked horsemen. The night finished in the glow of a startling spell and seven hooded capes wasted no time to race against the light, with the promise of disposing of the three foreigners as higher forces had ordered, on a very different timeline.

Not yet a full Moon, the clear-lit sky made the dirt road quite safe. An open landscape welcomed the riders galloping past a few smaller *villagi* (villages) between Lucca and Pistoia. Derecho was still disturbed by last night's happenings in the villa. But it didn't concern Izquierdo. Although excited about their visit to a 1473 Florence, his mind was still in Geneva. He had forgotten to call Elizabeth with news, as promised. Of course, they got trapped into this strange adventure and now he really was concerned. Dritto was as anxious about where they might be going and especially sleeping. Right now, this trio would have preferred an old carriage to these hard saddles, but ... they had bought into the game and being tired was a real illusion!

Iz's thoughts wandered off into nature. He had such trust in Derecho, the most brilliant of his trio, that he gave little attention to the roads they now journeyed. An occasional halt and his eyes sparkled at the beauty of the woods, the fields ... Elysian-like as in eighteenth century poetry, making contentment a rapturous delight. In the midst of his happiness and truly grateful for such an exceptional moment, he counted his blessings. In the simplicity of such peace, he smoothly hugged his horse, bending forward toward its right ear, and in a caress of a gentle whisper he uttered a few Italian words he so loved.

At that exact moment, an arrow violently missed Iz's head by a hair. A second one whizzed by and then a third pierced Izquierdo's shoulder, the next threw horse and rider to the ground. Having jumped clear, he tried to push his stallion into the meagre-looking woods off the road they traveled. Dritto and Derecho acted with a similar move and they both caught their friend and dragged him behind a humongous oak tree. More arrows seemed to indicate an army, yet sooner than expected only seven horses made up the apocalyptic vision of fear. All of them but their leader had jumped from their horses and long, unusual-looking sabres were drawn.

But Derecho's fury was bigger than the evil force ready to be unleashed by the heartless, strange-looking creatures surrounding them. He walked steadily towards them and in an unexpected blow, two heads dropped to the floor and their bodies crumbled in front of the horses' hoofs. A cold-blooded screech preceded an equally violent move as three of the capes revealed faces from an underworld of horror. Dritto thrust a small dagger straight to the centre of the throat of one of the demonic attackers about to bury his own. With three out of seven floored, Derecho challenged their leader, who with fiendish confidence, showed a shining blade, much finer than he'd ever seen ... all movies left aside. In the next instance, without a weapon being lifted, all action was brought to a standstill. An animal-like groan, right out of some hellish inferno, boosted Derecho forward from the ground. Izquierdo's attempt to get up lost in the dust of a trio beating him right down.

"No more," Derecho screamed, with drama worthy of a famous movie trilogy he remembered. "No more killing, you aren't human! You poor evil creatures move back miserable scum of the earth. Whoever brought you to the world of the living, couldn't join the Light; it must be Beelzebub himself and I curse you all! Lose your powers in this dimension, right now and forever, you miserable vid-game characters!" And he spiralled up as if some Japanese ninja warrior popped up from his being.

His own cape shone as a transient light. It made Derecho's body grow bigger and elevated as his closed eyes, burning the hearts of the invaders one after the other. Iz stumbled up, as in a virtual dream, grabbed the first sword he found and beheaded one of their last opponents. In the same panic as their horses, three evil flames retreated and while the howling became unbearable, the last cloak burned away in the ashes leaving nothing behind. Screeching Izquierdo and Derecho, perspiring heavily, were left dumbfounded at their victory. It all seemed like a virtual world, some odd video game. It dawned on them there were very few alternatives.

"Let us take a moment, attend to his wound," Dritto looked up. "Here, use some of our red-headed witch's potion we have in our backpack. It'll work," he suggested. "He will heal quickly."

The damage to Iz's right shoulder was minimal. To their surprise the wound didn't run deep and the medallion he wore, seemingly a part of his 'costume', had stopped the arrow from penetrating deeper. He couldn't move his arm too well and the potion tasted like year-old soup, but he didn't doubt his friends. His tendons felt raw, but he was much more upset that he hadn't participated more in the battle, especially after all those years of video games.

"I would have hashed them to pieces," Iz said. "That first blow, Derecho, I've never seen anything like it. It was so impressive in strength and you were so in control."

"Indeed, I felt fearless and with an unknown force behind me. It wasn't exactly me doing the moves. This really wasn't anything but a virtual trap... something very much like a video game. Yet someone's willpower set this in motion and whoever that was, it was strong." Iz's eyes fired pain and solitude, for a moment losing all awareness.

"That's how my Tai Chi & Martial Arts master conquered his attackers and that's what he taught me. He knew he dealt with immortal men and so I fought them that way. True evil you cannot overcome with just a sword."

"Bravo Derecho," Iz said still resting against the oak. "But how did you stop them?' he asked eagerly.

"Well, when spirits who don't belong to the living use a body in our dimension, they are working solely under an exterior higher command; not exactly of a higher order. They can create an unreal image, like demons. Yet it's all simply like another computer program, a virtual trip."

Dritto's eyeballs nearly popped out of his head.

"You mean like a phantom?" he asked

"Like a phantom, only the tools will seem real – a horse, a weapon, a cloak, and so, one would naturally use a human self-defence system to which the spirit is impervious." Derecho clarified, "You can only vanquish them with that understanding, by sheer willpower they are powerless in front of any fearless energy, based on love and peaceful intent." He chuckled.

"Anyway, I didn't need to fear for my life, because my soul doesn't die, and my real body isn't on this timeline." He sounded convincing. "We are still talking about programs here, we mustn't forget. Fear has no place in this realm! The drive to protect you both had enough of that energy, like a magic potion to defeat this, it is like the frequency of love and friendship! So, learning this unique lesson was enough to fight any dark force, especially the one from a video format."

He put his right hand on Iz's shoulder and Iz could feel the heat. Derecho sadly looked at the horse that had died so quickly. Dritto caressed the dead animal, his friends read his thoughts, and he smiled at yet another illusion. He wondered.

"Yet Derecho," he said, "the arrows were poisoned. That must have been why Isabel insisted on putting this little container in our backpacks, because it clears the poison away. Iz, you'll be fine by tomorrow when we meet Florian and Isabel, it will be only a scratch."

"Tell me Derecho, where did you learn all this? It all sounds like ... magic," Dritto asked curiously. "Remember I worked for the military," Derecho smiled, "for a while we were developing programs to, um ... initially to protect their digital system. You wouldn't believe how far we had come with the technology. What we have today is, Dritto, is so utterly advanced and, my friend, make no mistake, not to be understood by most of us."

Many conspiracy theorists claim it is connected to an outer space program; an exchange with the extra-terrestrial world. Great warriors, armies led by legendary generals like Alexander the Great, they know how to access and use a higher knowledge, and the magic. They checked the way the planets were moving and how this would be beneficial or not, sacrificing animals to favour their Gods when they attacked the enemy or when conquering other lands, and you know what? It hasn't changed. The tools have become, let's say somewhat more sophisticated by the century. Why do you think Generals, Commanders, the whole army hierarchy wear little stars on their collars, jacket or kepi: it translates very simply that 'we are from the stars'!"

Izquierdo shrugged while Dritto added loud sneezes. They helped Iz onto Derecho's horse and decided to walk a few miles as they approached a small village. Maybe they would find housing for the night ... another *Albergo* (hostel). Derecho closed his eyes and thought of Santa Croce! But he was truly concerned because those Tolkienesque creatures that had attacked them ... they didn't exactly belong to this particular world. In other words, there were some more players at work, and they weren't about to reveal themselves, not in this dimension.

He prayed that all was well in Fiesole, Anno 2018. Like in some advanced virtual war video – this battle reminded him of his early scientist days when he was propelled to work for the department of defense and he turned down their offer!

35. CAREGGI, FIORENZA 1473 THE PAZZI CONSPIRACY REVEALED

Of ages of torturing innocent souls,
Stealing their land,
Snatching their spouses,
raping their siblings and selling their offspring. (Mea Culpa)

At Cosimo de Medici's Villa, Giuliano had lost all appetite. The velvety red wine hadn't comforted his nostalgic mood either. Before dinner, while finishing their conversation on the *loggia* (a covert open gallery), GianLuca realized how much healing this Renaissance family really needed... and wasn't it also somehow 'his' family? Years ago, he had worked with youngsters from broken families. His own twenty-first century had plenty of those and these experiences were indeed as intense. On this timeline, Lorenzo Il Magnifico had a younger brother who sat right in front of him. And Lorenzo, one of the most illustrious Italian rulers who would influence majorly the world of arts and politics, had question marks in his eyes. GianLuca was as flabbergasted as he could have been, and he knew he had to give the brothers some answers. He listened carefully to some issues that his family certainly had never even considered talking about.

GianLuca had read the pain in this damaged soul. He felt that just like his brother, Giuliano had been brought up with the sole focus of the family's political power. Lorenzo might have dreamed of promoting art and education, but those early dreams had faded slightly, becoming eventually the sole outlet for his inner travels to the depth of his soul. He would assume the many contradictions of falsehood – the puppet show required while safekeeping his sincerity and love for the arts, his sole escape from the menace of power struggles.

But he remembered that the grains of pain are conflicting and when you are born a thief, it's hard to give without expecting something in return.

And usually that is love, the theme for our planet, GianLuca contemplated. It's always about love and recognition. Sadly, most behaviour isn't about a spiritual approach, but a material way of living supported by the illusion of the 'appearance', the presentation and not the inner frequency: there is no authentic Self!

The Renaissance would eventually propose thinking out of that box while till today, politicians rule countries worldwide by selfish purposes and lies. Then the arts would secretly help to develop hidden weapons, mostly encrypted and someone like Leonardo da Vinci used such symbols frequently. He would also open the doors for others to find the courage to express them and to go beyond their own fears about survival, the suppressing elite and monarchy, and also their own hidden sexual preferences.

Giuliano hadn't given it that much thought. It was now the time to do it. Whatever he had understood and liked from the teachers like Ficino or young, almost fanatical disciples like Poliziano, he couldn't understand why one would not share it with the masses. GianLuca would tell Lorenzo how their proud family tree initially joined Charlemagne, when one of their forefathers had been a courageous knight in the army of the great emperor. The heroic man had fought and conquered a giant at the Mugello Valley to protect the local peasants.

The legend told of the emperor bestowing a rare honour upon him by allowing him to create his own personal coat of arms that included an undefined number of red balls on a golden shield. These balls were maybe representative of the 'pills' the doctor had brought to the local community. In the early days, it seemed that the Medici intended to heal the society, at least economically. The stories of bravery and great endeavours were numerous and there had been a time where one would be proud to be compared to such a prosperous and successful family. Yet tonight, Giuliano felt none of that pride, not even the desire to be a Medici.

GianLuca had enjoyed his meal very much and he remained surprised at the quantities of meat he had been devouring during those days. All in the absence of his enzymes, vitamins and supplements, he chuckled while smiling thoughts about his own vegetarian habits. He had no funny story at hand, nor any joke would change his host's mood in his present ambiance of sad inner echo. He got up and did the simplest thing he could offer. He hugged Giuliano candidly and the young man felt relieved, releasing his sadness in a tempered heart-stream, deeper than he had had with anyone in his own exclusive inner circle. So, this man from whatever planet he came from, he knew he could truly trust.

"So, it matters little if I die. My brother will create an empire that will last, won't he?"

GianLuca nodded and lowered his eyes. "There is no reason to accept being sacrificed for one's family," he answered.

"What do you mean being sacrificed?" Giuliano returned the question.

"Well, there will be a conspiracy to kill both of you. Yes, your pope will be behind it all. He will have made some powerful allies between now and 1478; the Pazzi family for one will be eager to participate in this abomination." He seemed shocked, "You have seen how in these last years, your impetuous brother has handled the countless attacks on him. Not only Tuscany, but history may have condemned him, especially at the uprising in Volterra, where riots could have been prevented."

He continued to watch a very attentive Giuliano, slightly nervous at his knowledge of facts. "Giuliano, there have been records of all these events, and as usual, just like the Officers of the Night have kept their own written accounts of all crimes, many books have been written about what will be known, world-wide, as the Pazzi Conspiracy."

An anxious young Medici stared in the open fire and his hands nervously ran through his long hair while his guest continued.

"What you don't know is that some of those records show how your brother is protecting many men of power. A few of the privileged have escaped the law thanks to his influence. They may have paid a small fine for seducing and sodomizing young men at night either in brothels or public places. Some of those men belong to your own circle of close friends, even your own entourage! The records I'm talking about are 'official records' and even your friend Angelo Poliziano's name was written up amongst them. This, I read myself!"

Giuliano looked straight into GianLuca's eyes, no longer sure if he should love or hate the man. But of course, from the beginning he knew that he was speaking the truth. Could he continue to look away as he had done in the past?

"Again, the official records mention Lorenzo favouring a certain freedom and protection to the elite, many of his personal friends, as his position allows him to. Of course, when young men or children get into trouble or are jailed for 'being passive in sex acts' (a phrase used by the Night Watch in the city files) well, that doesn't mean that they are selling themselves on every street corner. There is a market, but a very secretive one and this awful truth has continued throughout all centuries and on my timeline, while governments know the child trafficking is a real problem! Your brother has known about it all along. Somehow within the fraternities who support and will defend him as a future ruler, secrecy covered up the inevitable bribes. What you sow, of course, you will reap! My suggestion is to discuss this with Lorenzo."

There was a scared look in Giuliano's eyes and this fearless athlete suddenly turned into a frightened child, plagued by doubts.

"We never were taught about 'fear'; it's not really in our vernacular you know," Giuliano said. But he almost wept at the thought that his brother lived by a set of lies.

"Lorenzo was always true to his family, protecting us all," he said in a concerned manner. "He is a good man, GianLuca. What you have told me hurts me and yet it makes me think. But all that secrecy, I won't be a part of it and that my brother knows. After our last meeting at the Fiesole Villa, I made a point to always withdraw to my quarters. A few of the guests stayed on late, often drinking till the early morning." He shrugged.

"There's also this; I never question him when they have their little monthly ceremonies in the grotto at the back of the park. Lorenzo had told me once if I ever wished to join them, it couldn't just be one time only. Once initiated you became bound to secrecy and you have to return regularly to their meetings."

He took a deep breath. "GianLuca, you gave me a lot to think about, I'm grateful, and I know I can trust you even if this was a very uncomfortable moment to navigate. You don't make up stories, as some of those around us so frequently do, and of course, you do not expect anything from me. I fear you'll even leave before the year has ended."

But the subject had fired up some more issues and Giuliano decided to continue and explain. GianLuca followed him attentively.

"There were specified dates for their little ceremony, like on a full moon and especially on the solstices or on the eclipses. They want to invoke the spirits of the ancestors and they make offerings to the gods. I thought it to be all quite childlike. I now know it isn't." He now sounded clearly more confident. "They have some kind of a repetitive prayer, a code you might call it, and they use it to get in touch with higher forces ... the pantheon of the gods, as Angelo calls them. At those occasions they might even be able to read the future."

Giuliano took a moment to think. He got up and his energy had shifted. "I shall talk to Lorenzo about our conversation," he sounded grave. "Now to be specific; you said I have only five years to live. Can I change this? Do I go out and kill those whose names you are giving me? Or do I wait till a few weeks before the planned event and tell the criminals 'aha, I know what your plan is and now my big brother will throw you in jail and hang you for planning such evil deeds'!"

He obviously was getting upset, agitatedly walking up and down the room.

GianLuca responded quietly. "Indeed, it could be an easy play for you and Lorenzo to plan ahead. Knowing the line of events to come, you could, for example, be absent at the last moment and even have extra guards at your side at every exit you both make during church time. Or even better, have someone take your place with extra guards on top! Yet you needn't only face your genetic line, Giuliano, you need to be in peace, first with yourself and understand why you have attracted a visitor like me into this dimension right here in your home. Was it maybe to warn you and to teach you about your own power and how to use and not abuse it? We are keys to each other's healing process and that of many others, including our siblings. We may avoid that option."

Till this very moment Giuliano had never given it any thought. Life was not about fame and women, so what if it was all about healing? But now he was facing an awkward destiny; his own and that of his family, and, as his guest explained, maybe even the entire country. Uncomfortable, he continued to pay attention to what GianLuca had to say.

The latter explained and tried to comfort him. "What if this were simply a dream where someone, a lookalike, perhaps yourself in your dream state, warns you about an attempt on your life? You do not have to act upon this right at this moment. In your 1473, you still have plenty of time to plan ahead."

"What do you mean? I have called you in to come and help me, in a dream or … wait …" Giuliano sang to another tune, "I just remembered something important. Angelo once taught me a trick, like in a ceremony, he suggested I would …" And he proceeded with some excitement.

"Listen to this. About a week ago, I followed Angelo's advice and I rode to the grotto in the Fiesole Villa to make an offering to the Goddess Venus so I would be lucky in finding the right partner in my life. While I was in the cave, the same one where Lorenzo does his ceremonies, I felt drowsy for a quite a while. Maybe I lost all consciousness and actually, now I think of it, I'm sure I did. I assure you it was around midday. Yes, it was before I went horse riding, I'm sure it was right then."

"A few days before we met the first time at Lapo's?" Equally intrigued, GianLuca asked.

"Oh yes, absolutely. I can ask Angelo for he always keeps a written record of his own personal teachings. Just like Lorenzo, he's always been interested in magic. And the more I think of it, you're right. I bet my brother also did 'something' to bring us to Cafaggiolo …" the young Medici's mind wandered off again.

"Hold that thought," GianLuca said, "You may be on to something important, Giuliano! The magical part of it; 'you' might have brought me to this dimension! What were your thoughts that day and do you remember the ritual you used?"

Both men looked intense and inquisitive.

"Well, I recall it being very warm and I was alone at the villa. Angelo told me to clean up, bathe and wear perfumes and light clothing for a short ceremony. It would be like the one the Greeks did for Aphrodite when they wanted to please her and ask her to order Cupid to shoot his arrow into the heart of the one you desire. I know it sounds silly and childish, but he knew I had expressed a desire for a very beautiful woman in Florence. She is quite remarkable, and we have the same age. Unfortunately for me, she is being pushed into a … very unhappy marriage. We have met only once but our burning longings didn't end in a kiss. That's why I wanted to invoke Venus / Aphrodite to help me conquer this woman's heart, but also to understand how I could make her happy." Giuliano looked guilty and GianLuca thought of it as rather charming. His host continued.

"In the cave, sometimes there are fumes released from the walls. Angelo says he experienced these fumes more than once. He mostly accompanies Lorenzo at those secret ceremonies. I'm sure that's what took me out for a while. Yet I was not totally unconscious; it felt like leaving the planet on the back of an eagle and looking down at the earth. But right before, something else happened!"

His voice sounded excited and GianLuca paid equal attention.

"Firstly, I sat for a while with my hand covering my eyes because I felt there was some unusual energy, maybe an entity in attendance. A sudden feeling of being humbled came over me and in a brief vision there was some kind of a mirror, presented to me exactly like in the dream I've been having for months. In this dream I'm separated from Lorenzo, like being autonomous, so to say. This may well be my deepest wish." Slightly more relaxed, he smiled to his houseguest.

"Often, I feel like a bird in a golden cage. I do want my own life ... my family sometimes suffocates me. I would marry tomorrow just to escape." Giuliano's thoughts wandered back to the Fiesole cave.

"That's it, that must be it!" GianLuca exclaimed. "You said, you were out, like in another dimension? And I may have suffered something like sunstroke in an exact parallel time frame, co-creating this magical moment by which I must have crossed through a time portal that you must have opened unconsciously. Yet how in the world did I land at Santa Croce and not in your villa in Fiesole instead, when you were at the Fiesole Villa?"

But just then Giuliano made a smart remark: "Santa Croce you said? Well, that is where I have met Simonetta the first time, after mass and that's what I must have been thinking of... our first meeting on the piazza". How odd Giuliano thought, "Without any doubt, my mind must have wandered off to her as it now so often does."

GianLuca enthusiastically added, "Well then, your villa's cave is a time portal, enveloped in fumes, like in Apollo's Temple in Delphi. You know about the Oracle, right? Now we only need to find out what are the codes your brother and his friends have discovered in there, because if they were stored in stone, certainly for ages, we may have a powerful portal into other dimensions and that's why there can be no 'visitors' other than those who were initiated. Does Poliziano know anything more about any of this?" GianLuca asked and he excitedly sprung up with new hopes about his own possible return back home in the twenty-first century.

"We can ask him tomorrow," Giuliano hesitated. "He comes here once a week usually together with Lorenzo. Now that will be a stimulating gathering, though I guess we'll have to cancel dinner with our other friends. As well as I know my brother, I'm sure Lorenzo won't like to share his secrets even with a family as friendly and as close as Lapo's." He turned to his new friend and his heart smiled.

"Thank you. Thank you so much GianLuca for opening my eyes."

36. LAKE GENEVA, 2018 DÉSIRÉ LESCLAU

Answer to life when the shutters are frozen on visionless wired brains?
So, when humans,
do you wish to acquire full knowledge?
of the power you gave away
and claim it to be yours in a Universe that doesn't allow only ...
a walk through the lions' gate? (Tower of Innocence)

Désiré Lesclau looked very annoyed. He had been waiting for more than an hour at the 'Bistro du Lac' and Elizabeth hadn't shown up yet. The newspapers offered nothing interesting to read but some duller world news he chose to call 'International Flies'. This local edition offered an entire page dedicated to 'Book XV', of the popular Mary Stotter series ... fifteen altogether, he thought it a joke. Who would ever be interested in fifteen instalments of the same repetitive story? A child ingénue, and of course an orphan, whose odious magical acts with the power of her crystal wand, had her fly around like Mary Poppins, defying dragons and evil spirits. The longest decay(de) in (un)literary history with a world audience of (too young) children, and teenagers, not to mention their parents, addicted to this mind manipulating character seemingly always lovelier and of course, smarter than all the other frighteningly brilliant students at Humming Court, a gothic castle hidden in the clouds of imagination.

And of course, Mary Stotter could sustain any energy frequency, whether vampire-like wizards nibbling her toes on deserted graveyards, tasting her blood to bring back to life ancient evil or she would break out dancing to the *Carnival des Animaux* (Carnival of the animals), a waltz by French composer Camille Saint-Saens. Désiré judged it to be appalling, in bad taste and it was one big hobbyhorse he could live without. He couldn't believe that the public bought such mind-snoozers, but then, they also watched television till they faltered off married to Morpheus, a theme he always got truly distraught by. He was about to light a cigarette when he realized even in open air; restaurants didn't allow smoking on the terrace.

"Je suis tellement désolé d'être en retard (I'm so sorry to be late.)"

A voice worked herself forward through the rather crowded Terrace of the Bistrot at Lac Léman, *"Mon cher Désiré, je n'ai jamais manqué une entrée sur scène, mais des rendez-vous j'en ai loupé pas mal* (My dear, I never missed an entrance on stage, but I cannot say I didn't miss any appointments) Lunch is on me, promise!"

Elizabeth had made an obvious entrance. She slipped out of her long dark lace summer gloves ... the calculated act of a fashion model.

"Ah, *ma chère,"* Désiré said, "I was getting a bit concerned and these newspapers only publish crap these days."

"Quel discours mon ami (what a speech my friend) and are you well?" Her embrace was almost formal, he mused, like Bette Davis kissing Marilyn on the cheeks.

"I have no news, I'm really worried," she whispered in his ear before sitting down and ordering a spritzer. She raised her voice and he looked surprised.

He got up and picked up a *serviette* (napkin) that she hadn't dropped, and he whispered in return, "you'd make a lousy spy."

But she proved the contrary when she gave him the menu with a little note popping out. She insisted loudly he could choose whatever he liked, till his eyes opened to a phrase scribbled on the *plat du jour* (menu of the day) – "I have been followed by a spy!"

While his eyebrows lifted to a mountainous level, she hammed it up to the max, announcing, *"Un grand verre de vin rouge, rouge comme la robe de la dame au bar* (a large glass of red wine, red like the dress of the lady at the bar.)" Of course, as a former police investigator – a very private detective, Désiré immediately noticed the elegant 'lady in red'.

"I have an idea," he said.

"I knew you would," she answered with a big smile. "You always have."

"Two houses down the road, a friend of mine has a small boat he hardly ever uses. If we have the 'plat du jour', lunch will be over quickly and I'll take you for a little romantic moment on the lake," he joked.

"Two *Plat du Jour* (daily menus) *s'il vous plait* (please, young lady)," she ordered "And one romantic boat ride," she giggled.

"*Quelle bonne idée, mon amie* (what a good idea, my friend), no romance like the one twenty years ago, haha," Désiré shrugged.

"Did you see the latest *soirée de ballet* (ballet performance) at the Opera House, at the Grand Theatre, " he asked adding, *"un spectacle qui ne vaut rien du tout* (a performance not worth a penny.)" Small talk was not her thing but she graced him with an answer. "I am so bored by all these techno-saucy contemporary works with great bodies devoid of soul! *C'est vraiment ennuyeux* (it's really boring!)"

She continued as blasé as she possibly could. "After a while, they all look alike! No more true inventiveness, no more personalities. We've been spoiled for a few decades and now, *mon cher Désiré,* it's all over. The musicians, the singers, the dancers; too much *talent brute* (raw talent) for too few jobs and ... *l'horreur, encore pire*," she exclaimed dramatically. "*Plus du tout de Stars* but lots of television reality shows, they called them ... far from any reality at all!" *How horrible, even worse, no more stars!.* She slowly paid on her way to a narrow bathroom, to have a better look at the 'lady in red' from a tiny window.

Very pretty she thought ... an afternoon affair for any straight male. When minutes later they were rowing onto the lake, the 'lady in red' couldn't be missed, being the only person in a flashy dress, underneath a blooming willow tree, using binoculars.

"They're checking on me," Elizabeth said. "I know that's my company; DoWell has something up its sleeve, and our meeting, well, I guess there is but one thing I can do to cover up," and she drew Désiré near to her mouth and faked the best Hollywood kiss ever.

"Oh *Ma chère (*my dearest*)*, you are a remarkable actress. Why did you not pursue Hollywood instead of tutu-land?"

"At least here we're not bugged," she said in a very convinced voice.

"You were so right, the bug was under the breadbasket," he confirmed with a grin. "But you were very convincing in your 'Garbo-style' act," he continued, "OK, let's come to the point".

"No news, I hope nothing went wrong at the villa in Firenze," she said.

"In Fiesole, you mean? Your trio got into the villa safely?" Désiré asked.

"Well, I hope so. Izquierdo ... can you believe the name ... was supposed to call me every eight to ten hours and I haven't heard a thing for days. Should I worry?" And indeed, she worried.

"They may well have had an unexpected surprise and may not have found the villa empty," Désiré replied.

"What do you mean? You and I had it all checked out. Do you mean one of the proprietors returned, suddenly after having just left? Rather unlikely, I spoke to them a week ago when they invited me to stay with them on my weekend trip with Siegfried."

"*Mais non* (no), I have a feeling we're in for a much bigger surprise."

She looked above her sunglasses, nearly forgetting she was sitting in a small boat. Getting up on a wave, she nearly landed on top of Désiré.

"Well, there goes your reputation," he laughed.

"Like my husband could care. I have gone past the age of seduction and how would anyone be interested in such an old hag as me?" She sighed dramatically with a wide set of silent movie gestures. The former inspector shook his head in an equally melodramatic way.

"Well, who else could have been there, at the villa?" She teased him with her specs.

Désiré stopped rowing, or at least pretending to row.

He looked Elizabeth straight in the eyes. "When was it you saw your baby half-sister last?"

"*Mon Dieu, Isabel? As-tu vu Isabel?* (Goodness, did you see my sister Isabel?) Did you really see my sister?" She got excited.

"*Impossible, elle avait déménagé aux Etats-Unis* (Impossible, she had moved to the USA). Yes, I heard she had moved to the States and she loved it there!" she exclaimed in some southern US slang that didn't sound right.

"I mean that's what I know. It's been so long since she moved to Vancouver and then down from Canada to the US. We haven't spoken for at least a decade. Remember, she's only a half-sister and it was never even proven that we actually had the same father. Also, I never got to know our father. Isabel claimed he had been hiding after the last war and didn't go public because he was working for Interpol. He couldn't reveal his identity in order to protect his later family once he had moved to the USA."

In one breath she spat out all past information, she no doubt, had given him ages ago.

"The rest you know well enough, I'm not going to repeat old hat and it's time to kiss again. What else did you have in mind to entertain the lady in red?" she quickly pulled him towards her while the boat suddenly made some very brisk moves. He dived his head into her lap while they drifted away, leaving Geneva's stunning Jet d'Eau behind. She covered his face with her big hat while laughing frenziedly.

"We are going to have to shoot a few arrows if, by tonight at the latest, we haven't heard from them," she said.

"Do you know Florian …? Florian deTrèsloin, the American college wunderkind?" he spoke out far too loud. "Ah, you do remember him. Did you know he faked his death together with *your* half-sister as an accomplice and that they are playing a game of… time traveling?" He smiled while throwing a kiss. "Interested in joining in?"

On the other side of the Geneva Lake, the woman in red had given up waiting. A rather nervous but brief phone call and she stepped into a slick Jaguar, the DoWell signature company car.

Parking nearby the lake was hardly possible that time of year, so the loudly laughing detective couple finished their little promenade on the lake and they jumped into a taxi. Elizabeth dropped Désiré off near the park he chose to walk across before returning to his hotel. They would call each other later that night.

Odd, she thought, that a woman connected to her own company was following her. After all, Averardo was the one who had wanted her to meet with Izquierdo. And as usual, her husband's 'boss' hadn't bothered explaining any details. Elizabeth had ended up saving them from a future problem about the decoding. Yet Averardo had insisted: he 'wanted to see pictures of each code engraved in the walls, the floors or any manuscripts found in this ancient de Medici villa hidden in the Fiesole's hills'. He had claimed that if you weren't a decoding specialist or a Sherlock Holmes, you'd never notice anything linked to such a code. Secrecy remained a topic she wasn't about to fight him on. As if between some fancy looking decoration, or even strategically placed little checkers hidden between plants and flowers pots, one might just find some tablets with ancient codes in that Renaissance villa.

Odd, she thought. She was hoping this was all about discovering a new alchemy, a remedy to use in a new night-cream, marketed in an elegant shiny tube as a 'rejuvenation mir*a*cle'. She knew that would be the biggest lie. Companies were more competitive than ever and today pharmacies seem to have a cure to distract one from a wrinkle to the next crevasse. She laughed at her own stubborn and old-fashioned manners.

Her personal health program was an open book of plenty of sleep, two litres of water a day and a lot of greens to please an alkaline stomach. Not like her husband, who preferred more hours on the computer, with more coffee, alcohol and bags under his eyes from a sad liver and unhappy kidneys. And it was his choice, as she had reminded him plenty of times. Yet she loved him even if their paths weren't crossing that often, or was it just a temporary intermission, the time of a waltz, that one Chopin waltz she was so used to humming.

37. GENOA, 1473 TESLA TECHNO

Can a sage not forgive the pain,
an oversized cosmic depth genetically corrupt
from long-forgotten stars you claim do not exist. (The Genie in Town Hall)

The ambiance was light-hearted, and Florian knew that wherever they would land, their ageless friendship would conquer all. His jokes weren't always the easiest to grab, but Isabel had accepted them over the years and now she had grown used to them. "If we ever play this travel game again, I want a long weekend off to go home," he joked, remembering where his body really was, comfortably on their miracle travel couch.

"So, thanks to the research we've done since Nicola Tesla, the advanced technology has made it possible to time travel and to look even further through the veil," Florian commented.

"Yes, my dear, you sound like a commentator of some new age network", Isabel laughed, "and soon you may not even need any costume at all. But, of course, I bet you'd rather have a shopping detour to Milano? I'm sure the latest fashion has at least the da Vinci cleavage as featured on most Renaissance haute-couture."

Florian slowed down the pace his horse had taken over the last few hours. "Amazing what strength those stallions have. I'm glad we have rested a few times; parts of my body are just no longer made ... for a saddle," he joked.

"Let me guess what part that is, you old reptile," she carried on happily.

Florian replied jokingly, "Why don't we take the highway ... that'll be shorter. You're certainly in a good mood. Any weather predictions I'm not aware of?"

"Yes, our phone system is acting up! Let's see if the frequency is strong enough to reach our trio of wizards!" She moved up her sleeve and whipped out the 'holo-screen', but there was a disturbance. She couldn't figure out why, and so they stopped.

The horses were only too pleased with another halt and the stream water winding down from the mountains was fresh and cool. Isabel pulled three tiny pencil-like antennae out of the wristwatch under the long sleeve and switched the smallish front panel to an upright position as if it popped up from the rim of the jacket. *Cette chose* (that thing), as Florian called it, took on a spider look as she projected a tiny elongated hologram cone towards the earth. The small screen became activated.

"He's smart, Derecho, he's got his turned on. There he is, roaming around the Tuscan hills, aha. Now he's a Cancer Sun isn't he, intuitive and curious."

"You better call him on that time travel cell, he hates rubbing his arm," Florian giggled like a teenager. Isabel took out a hairpin and pushed a few tiny, un-numbered dots that looked like a tiny diamond collection.

"*Salvé* (greetings) Derecho, I hope you're not looking for that hotel down the road because it isn't there. How smart of you to look for us in the villa… just don't go too near, because we're not in there!" she said jokingly.

"Well, did you ever, if it isn't Signorrra Isabella," his jokingly funny voice responded. "How far away are you, because we're all three very excited about getting into the city and having a night on the town! How was your flight over… or is chit-chatting not the right thing to do?" He answered in a kind of pleasantly rude manner.

"Now, I'm sorry but we have been delayed a bit; blame it on cosmic weather conditions. I think if we get new horses on our next stop, chances are good that we'll catch up and be on time as planned." She continued. "From your voice I hear you're in a good mood and are your friends enjoying the adventure?"

"Well, apart from missing our morning cappuccino we're all fine and we found a pleasant inn at the picturesque Pistoia, although we were attacked by some very strange beings. We'll tell you more about it when we meet. The distance from there to Fiesole is still a couple of hours' riding. The road is quite different from what I had imagined. There were few horses and we paid handsomely to get them; I hope you can put this on your travel expenses, or should we open a bank account at the local Medici bank?" he now giggled.

"We just noticed a small court leaving this lovely town; everything seems to have been built in a circle, absolutely magnificent, your ladyship," he joked.

"Well, that isn't Pistoia, my friend," Florian said, "... that actually is Lucca and indeed a handsome little town mostly built on circular streets. It's quite probable you may have witnessed the magnetic presence of Lorenzo de Medici and his wife, Clarice Orsini and maybe their son, Piero. Congratulations on your first live *momento historico* (historical moment)."

Isabel interrupted, "One thing, because I won't waste our battery-packed suits, ha-ha. Please stay out of trouble because, after all, even if you could speak Italian, the vernacular is quite different! I have no way of getting you out of a Florentine jail!" she warned jokingly.

"OK, we'll be fine and skinny; no nice restaurants for dinner in sight either! In any case, thanks for the dry fruit in the travel bag, much appreciated!" he replied.

"We'll connect when we approach the city, hopefully by tomorrow afternoon. And the drink had all the necessary food for the entire trip! *Arrivederci*!" and she swiftly closed down the whole device. The trio remained stunned by the thought they needed no food and then remembered why.

"What a clever little surprise you brought along," Florian said. "I wonder who invented that little monster, some very advanced Nobel Prize winner?" he joked.

"Now don't you start looking for a compliment Mr de Trèsloin, you're not getting even one!" He kissed her cheeks.

"*Mon cher*, we promised not to get involved privately on this mission. I know what your genes can do when you ride the saddle too long, ha-ha and by the way, I still have the same Italian girlfriend."

They both had another laugh and he held her in his arms for the longest time till they got back on their horses, riding along to make it as fast as they could to the next city before dark.

38. FIORENZA, 1473 GIULIO

Farewell all winners of pre-cooked noble prizes;
Earth paid for the genius of well-planned childhoods
who will never recognize the genie your elite must venerate. (The Genie in Town Hall)

At the Medici residence at Careggi, the lights were being dimmed and Giuliano would have liked nothing more than to continue talking the whole night and find answers to all his questions about his existence. How could he survive being twenty-five and change the destiny of his family? A good night's rest seemed actually the better solution. Before showing his guest to his room, they had walked through the magnificent mansion and GianLuca had admired the splendour of Lorenzo's study, looking out on the gardens and the enormous rooms with only a few paintings and statues by the artists sponsored by Cosimo, their grandfather. It had become the family's favourite home, as it was now to Lorenzo.

"My family partly resided at the mansion in Careggi and here the meetings with the great Marsilio Ficino and his classes were set, thanks to our grandfather." Giuliano said.

"Upon our father's request I was introduced quite young to Plato's amazing philosophy. His teachings were dear to our entire male lineage, and Cosimo had decided to house Plato's Academy right there at Careggi, long before we continued at the Fiesole Villa. Ficino had become a regular guest and teacher." GianLuca nodded politely, but he knew the history of the Medici family well.

"I am indeed most grateful GianLuca that you have come to share your knowledge with me, with us all. And of course, the fact that you are here to warn me about this so-called conspiracy of the Pazzi family and then the Vatican's initial involvement, as your history books are to witness ... well, it is all a little overwhelming, as you may have noticed, and I apologize for some of my explosive demonstrations, and I . . ."

GianLuca interrupted him briefly with kind gestures, "You do not have to apologize at all. You are so alike – your brother is an unusually gifted young man and it is no easy task to be born into one of the most influential families of all time. You cannot imagine how future worlds will be influenced by what you all are about to accomplish here. Allow me a last thought for you to take to bed before you enter your own dream world. It isn't the 'act' that's important first but how it is accomplished. The quality and values you project, and of course the initial intent, they are the basis of it all, and as such you will reap."

GianLuca wanted to leave on a grateful note. "And now, it is I who wish to thank you because the experiment I have been subjected to is more than I could ever have dreamed of and 'to physically live' this moment remains beyond my own wildest dreams." He wrapped it up, "I have never been more excited about such a voyage than I am today and the reception at your home, the welcome at Lapo's, all of it has been, to say the least well beyond all possible words. It has been like coming back to my own family!" He almost blushed.

"You have called upon me in another dimension, on another timeline, and I have traveled beyond my own human understanding. Magic may have reunited two of the many versions of one soul and that event will indeed change the course of our lives and . . ." he took Giuliano by the forearm, "and that may even change the course of history."

The two embraced and bid each other goodnight. Giuliano took the candelabra to his room and stood for a while longer on the balcony lifting his eyes to a star-studded summer sky. How could he take all this new information to his pillow and fall asleep? He now doubted all former values he had prior to this last week's meeting. How would he translate this into a new life? He closed his eyes, smiling. How would his brother Lorenzo react to the latest news that had come down from such a faraway sky!

Giuliano decided to take a walk around the grandiose building and after the intense but enlightening conversation with GianLuca, he needed some time to think. The young man had wanted to explain so much more to his new friend. He wished he could call upon his grandfather, Cosimo de' Medici, the father of the fatherland, as he became known in all history books. He had spent his last days at the villa when he passed away in 1464, and Giuliano was only nine. As very often was the case for a Florentine family with acceptably high means, they had farmers on the land making this family autonomous. Cosimo's friendship with one of the great architects, Michelozzo, allowed this fortified villa to take on the character of a small castle. Like a medieval garden with gorgeous upper storey loggias, the villa's stately structure was softened by the green decoration of trees and plants.

The young Medici had not stopped talking to the foreigner about his family, his brother and his wife. He was really annoyed at a particular situation Lorenzo got himself into and he did not want to hold back about this intense tale. He was winding down in contemplation on a bench beside the little pond.

Should I tell GianLuca or not? He seems so unusually open to so many subjects. I imagine people have evolved tremendously in the centuries to come. I wonder if he is already asleep; should I disturb him?

A fully undressed GianLuca relaxed on the balcony admiring the Florentine hills bathing in the moonlight. With Fiammetta on his mind, and his nakedness against the Renaissance décor... self-pleasing came easily into action. He sank down on the cold stone bench, his eyes closed as if burying his head into Fiammetta's robes entangling him to the perfumes of her silken skin. His eyes reached for the stars when a blissful explosion released all the tension from his hips onto the oozing green plants hanging down from the balcony frame. The soft knocking on the door came as a surprise and he wasn't sure what to expect. Maybe it was the muse from his dream, but he knew Fiammetta was miles away in the safety of the Buontalenti home. As if he hadn't left this trance, he opened the door where a startled Giuliano looked down at an almost athletic nude so similar to his own morning appearance.

"*Dio Benedetto* (Oh my god), I so apologize", and hardly knowing how to react otherwise, he turned his head sideways. GianLuca turned his back and picked up a sheet to cover up and started laughing. And so did Giuliano, still slightly shocked, he repeated himself.

"*Dio Benedetto, otra volta* (Dear god, once again), I am so sorry, I do apologize. I really must leave you in peace." GianLuca continued laughing and waved away all excuses while wrapping himself in a silk cloth.

"*Prego* (please)," he said, "I was not sleeping yes, as you can tell, and I imagine you actually have some more questions and that's on me."

It embarrassed Giuliano even more but he was eager to speak.

"May I talk to you about my brother?"

"Of course," GianLuca answered signalling he could sit down if he wanted to.

"You know already so much about my family, so please call me, Giulio. Now, do you know that Lorenzo's wife Clarice disliked Angelo from the first day they met? Both Lorenzo and I are very disturbed by this even, well the fact that they are lovers doesn't help."

Giuliano was surprised that there was no reaction coming from his guest. The latter tilted his head sideways. "Proceed Giulio!"

And so, he did.

"Well Clarice has no proof of the intimate rapport of this young man with her husband. She must feel it and that's why she swore he'd never touch her children again. Lorenzo sees Angelo as a great educator and mentor to their offspring. Angelo Poliziano was brought from Montepulciano to Florence to live with our family after his father was murdered. We met when I was sixteen; he was almost a year younger." GianLuca was aware of this information and nodded in a friendly way.

Giuliano took a deep breath under an avalanche of his own thoughts, then addressed the issue.

"When Angelo came to our home, he was my age, and poorly dressed. At that time, my father had entrusted my brother with countless tasks. Lorenzo was taken by Angelo's precocious talent, seductive charm. In no time he became his patron, his personal support, on more than one level."

Somehow Giuliano seemed to enjoy the storytelling, especially when he spoke of his family.

"So, Lorenzo had clothes custom-made for the young Angelo and soon he'd be living with my family and the two of us, we all played like brothers." There were some afterthoughts and some silence till he proceeded.

"He might have felt sorry for Angelo but of course he recognized his virtuosity with both the written and spoken word instantly. We spent so much time together and there were moments when, well we would discover new things about our body. You know what I mean. Angelo was fascinated by the body and mind connection. And he loved the male beauty." Once again, Giulio became slightly nervous.

"Angelo always needy for a cuddle and lots of attention. The lack of love in his childhood was evident. The imposed discipline had made him even more vulnerable it seems. One night he came naked into my bedroom. He insisted showing me, well ... what he had learned from his own teachers, he had said. He wanted to share it with me, and I assure you it all started quite innocently."

His face wore the pearls of a Florentine mist and one day Sandro Botticcelli had captured that beauty.

"His way of seducing was unexpected, very passive, like a woman and .... after a while ... he admitted ... I just had to ... ugh .... well, he wanted me to ..."

By now a very much sweaty Giuliano, was no longer facing GianLuca. The latter insisted he didn't need any details, but Giulio continued, "Angelo said that his teachers had told him it was a gift from the gods that man could use his entire body to the heights of pleasure especially through youth and beauty. But his ways were like those of a snake merging with his victim. Well, is any of this in your history books? Do you know more?" he asked.

There was a different kind of arrogance in his voice. GianLuca replied in a softer manner, "Much has been written about your Italian *Rinacimento* (Renaissance) and your family. Maybe I have some useful information fit for the present."

Or the present version of the reality you're living now ... GianLuca chuckled to himself

While his lips drew a long smile right up to his ears, Giulio bit his nails. He didn't consider himself as talented as Lorenzo. As matter a fact he felt very different even though his brother was much on his mind and before his thoughts took over, he spoke.

"You know GianLuca, I just need to share more, if you do not mind."

Again, slightly uncomfortable, he seemed urged to start a new story. For a moment GianLuca felt tired and he could have just gone to bed. But he looked at this scholar of life and he remembered himself at that same age wanting to know more by the day.

"Only a few weeks ago, I found one of Angelo's poems in Latin, on Lorenzo's breakfast plate. Intimate details revealed a very personal and yes, 'physical relationship'. As you mentioned, even if the verses were that of a poet:

'*Quest'ultima notte il peso dei tuoi fianchi mi ha trasportato in un mondo che ormai il mio corpo e il mio spirito non potranno più afferrare.* (The weight of your hips took me to another world and from now on nor my body nor my mind will be able to forget.)'

As such it ended, with no need for further explanations. Then there was that afternoon about three years ago, just as last month Lorenzo caught me with his mistress, I discovered him on top of one of the male servants who very much seemed to enjoy the master's hips. It was in Cafaggiolo."

"Oh Cafaggiolo, what a splendid and imposing fortress you have there, another Michelozzo marvel!" GianLuca replied, rapidly remembering a visit to the woods and hills of the Mugello Valley, north of Florence and hoping to change the subject. But Giuliano was eager to tell him more about his discoveries, and not to discuss architecture.

"I had noticed that Lorenzo would sometimes stay away in Cafaggiolo and invite our 'distant cousin' Franceschino, or Luigi Pulci, one of his oldest comrades, who is also a writer. Like my brother, I love nature and one morning he had left me a note that he would only return the next day from Cafaggiolo. So, I took my favourite two horses and offered to show Angelo the fortress. He was very excited about the visit because anything related to my brother made him happy. When we arrived, I noticed several horses in the stables but proceeded to show him the garden."

He paused. "I recall asking Angelo if he never had any desires for a woman; did he at all dream about them like I did? At sixteen, I was truly surprised that he strongly refused to even look in that direction. To him the greatest gift was to have a male lover to whom he could be faithful till the end of his days. I was not offended because I knew Angelo lost his father very young, and how strongly influenced he was by all of his male teachers. Remember, I had seen how talented he was from his very first manuscripts. As I mentioned before, Lorenzo was more than fond of him. He admired his exceptional writer's skills and had declared he would become the next Virgil. Lorenzo had great intuition."

"So anyhow, I had recognized Franceschino's horse; the saddle was laid on top of a black and white checkerboard linen. So here we go. I discovered my cousin, his face covered in a young man's groin, a very muscular stable boy in his late teens! I backed up before they would notice us, but Angelo got really excited and hid behind a wall and continued watching them. Stunned and annoyed I departed to look for my brother and to report my find." Giuliano paused, to take a deep breath.

"Yet there I found my brother in one of the upstairs bedrooms in an equally honourable position. I felt lost, disappointed and angry and didn't know what to do." Giuliano sighed.

"Now he had me admit to having sodomized Angelo months earlier because the young lad had begged me to. Angelo had said I wouldn't just find any girl as willing. That was my sole reason, nothing more. It had bothered me – for after all, he was also my friend, a male friend like family and we were so inexperienced and young!"

"But my brother, I admire him so much, and on all levels, I consider him a superior being. It wasn't his nakedness, while he does look like a young god, but the way he was behaving, I promise you that he was not himself. When he noticed me, he pulled me to him in a most unexpected way with that strong grip putting a chalice in my hand, one he had been sipping from and shamelessly he forced me to drink it. He had never done anything like it."

'Giulio join me here and drink this elixir of the gods,' he commanded. I was so flabbergasted, not thinking anything of what seemed like a cup of wine. My whole body started trembling, perspiring, sweating all over."

"Within no time, I felt lustful and aroused beyond words. A dark-skinned young man about my age had undressed me with no other goal it seemed, than to swallow my genitals. He slathered my entire body in an obscure burning passion and crawled around like a reptile. It felt as if he was taken over by an animal of sorts. While little by little, I lost myself as in an erotic labyrinth driving my hips onto his, like a violent beast, my mind no longer belonged to me."

Giuliano shook his head slowly still in doubt about what had happened.

"Meanwhile, Angelo had left the stable over-stimulated, his own sexual instinct driving him upstairs. His eyes were shining with desire when he discovered Lorenzo in the nude, and he threw himself at my brother like a long-awaited lover. Lorenzo raised him, kissed him and effortlessly devoured him."

He continued his story and his face had turned burgundy red.

"By then, Angelo was his most willing victim and looking much more mature than our age, endowed with well developed, tight buttocks and his strong thighs not virginal since he was nine. When away from Florence, Angelo became Lorenzo's daily play field. The man Angelo had aspired to serve, that master took every part of his young and limber body to the fullest. My blinded eyes bathed in the total mist for an endless afternoon. I remember little more but the arrival of other men, only hours later when I lost all consciousness." He continued the lengthy adventure.

"When I woke up, Angelo was sleeping tenderly in my brother's arms and I found myself curled up between two new bodies, one a young woman seemingly of Asian descent. I will never forget Lorenzo's look on his face; he smiled to me like never before. His eyes were radiant with an otherworldly happiness. He looked glorious like a Roman emperor after an orgy. Eventually he carried Angelo in his arms to another room where he spent most of the night and the next day. In the midst of all confusion, like stumbling out of a dream that was imposed on me in the dungeon of one's deepest secrets, I got dressed only thinking how I could escape my grandfather's now corrupted residency."

"Morello, my horse was the sole key to my salvation and on his back my exasperated wearied body rode back to the city as quickly as we possibly could!"

"Well, that is quite a story my young friend," GianLuca said with an elusive smile.

"Well, you certainly were initiated the grand way and Lorenzo didn't take you into the confraternity he belongs to?"

Giuliano's eyes nearly popped. "You know about that too?" He asked, dumbfound.

"It sounds like the kind of private ceremony; the drinks, the sex, a mating ritual. He planned it well, didn't he? He knew you'd come; otherwise, he wouldn't have left you a note. Your brother is quite a magician and he didn't act alone from what you told me!" GianLuca confirmed with a certain empathy. "It will be interesting to check the names of his other guests, no doubt amongst the elite in Florence."

"That's what I had to figure out!" he answered. "Only a few days later he called on me for a talk and I didn't answer him. I was still quite irate, incensed at the whole experience. I refused to see him. He found me at our parents' home and deeply apologized. He said he would never force me to do anything I didn't want to and that he hadn't been himself that day." Giuliano looked appalled.

Furious, I hit him in the face, really hard. His nose was bleeding and then I kicked him in his iron stomach. He remained immobile until he pulled me over and held me tight by the shoulders with his enormous hands. I had stopped fighting, my eyes bolts of fire. Lorenzo couldn't stop repeating continuously that he would never hurt me nor get me into anything similar again. It was the first time he spoke to me in a very different language telling me he had been initiated when rather, yes, just like you said, about the same age. Slowly it had grown on Lorenzo, like an addiction and he had felt like someone was controlling him. He admitted he noticed the presence of someone, and he didn't know where and who. In a position of ultimate power, he claimed, there were moments where even the most powerful of men were powerless in front of the invisible. He mentioned something about a sacrifice and being the first son and his eyes just turned ice cold."

"We never touched the subject again; he did ask for a vow of secrecy on the subject, one I just broke. He confides in me a lot more now and Angelo remains his protégé. Of course, he is still a maturing artist in our house. He hardly leaves the enormous library and the moment Lorenzo is free, the three of us go to the Fiesole Villa where a couple of nights a month we have great discussions like the one we are having right now. Sadly enough, women aren't allowed. Nobody else knows that Lorenzo shares his bed with Angelo. I'm sure though his wife Clarice must feel something, for her husband doesn't visit her chambers too frequently. Women know; my goodness they birth us. Isn't their womb our heavenly gate?"

He spoke up with a passion all his own.

"I'm always around, so I become a perfect cover. After all, our grandfather had promoted the academy. I must tell you that Lorenzo's wife Clarice, had taken a real liking to me since the first day we met. Some say she would have rather married the younger brother. Now that I've turned twenty and since that afternoon in Cafaggiolo, I lost all interest in other women – except for one."

"That whole past experience felt like it was a part of… a heritage I wasn't comfortable with anyhow. Hopefully you haven't misunderstood my feelings for you," he finally smiled. "The more I look at you, I do feel like I'm talking to a mirror-self".

GianLuca thought of a genuinely productive response to the long discourse the young Medici had given.

"There's a lot to be said about possessions," he said. "When you recognized this physical attraction, it may well be one of the entities, maybe even a family genie playing with you. Your brother was not using you, but the entities do for their own needs, like an invisible vampire traveling alongside."

Giuliano looked at him almost absent-mindedly.

"I know how you feel," GianLuca said, "I have had similar experiences when I was about your age. I was, let's say as wild as you and Lorenzo together, but I had a very unusual upbringing, one that brimmed with spirituality." He shrugged.

"When I became aware of how to make my own future choices, I searched to understand the complexity of the soul. You see, our cosmic genes haven't changed. We are all connected yet our own personal demons are uniquely our own!" said GianLuca.

"Do you mean one can influence a healing process to an entire family lineage? Lease explain," said Giuliano, reacting quickly and in a demanding tone.

"You know Giuliano, whatever our parents have lived, whatever they have been able to accomplish on an emotional level, if they were able to address the issues between them and heal their families, for generations, chances are that their children will not have to repeat the same story. If not, one will continue to live the same patterns. We may discover why and how to get in touch with our own soul in its most complex of labyrinths!"

"Piero di Cosimo, your father, must have loved his children and yet how much time did he have to play with you all; have evening meals together; share quality time of love and uncomplicated exchanges? Where was the complicity between the father and his sons?"

GianLuca noticed how his host tried to straighten his back and his eyes delved into a cloud of sadness.

"While your brother took on the role of a young ruler; while he represented his father at official visits; while he proved he could handle family and affairs of state so grand, he indeed was hoping his father would not just appreciate or praise and trust him ... but that Piero would simply show that he loved his son! Centuries will pass, dear friend before such simple and noble gestures will know an easier flow from our human hearts," he smiled.

"Those who are so impressed by power; those to whom love is foreign; those who repress the simplicity of life by obstructing nature ... and keep us from living happily in the present moment, free of expecting a traditional outcome of life ... those beings are but a reflection of our own lack of self-confidence and higher trust. Of course, we all have a need for healing. Indeed, we can heal past wounds because healing is nothing more than reinterpreting what we believe happened to us."

"Can you repeat that last phrase?" Giuliano asked, his eyes sparkling with renewed interest. GianLuca gladly obliged. "Healing is nothing more than reinterpreting what you believe happened to you."

"Doesn't one have to understand though, what really happened in the primary event before 'reinterpreting'?" Giuliano asked in a humble but clever way.

"The mind does not know the difference between a real and an imagined event; they are one and the same. Yet you chose the colours you like to paint your own picture, to make it solely your own!" GianLuca continued in a quiet voice. "Yet, if you do find out the original cause, that specific moment within your family's history, of course the conscious action you add to it will ripple on the lines of time and indeed affect your families! Somewhere in the field of existence that place where all is connected beyond human comprehension and judgement, right there we can find the unlimited possibilities to pick the tools, to pluck the symbols we need to recreate that moment of our choice."

GianLuca continued. "That moment of choice was right before you went into Lorenzo's room at Cafagollio, and at that very moment you may have been 'pulled in' by the entities that govern your brother. These entities manipulated all who attended and sucked you into an old family possession, easily activated by copulating – especially when it is devoid of an intimate, deeper love energy between two people in search for a heart connection."

GianLuca gave a hug to a slightly agitated Giuliano and closed off the conversation.

"It is yet to be seen if between your brother and your friend Angelo, there is a loving energy! Life's lessons Giuliano, every moment of our lives, more lessons and challenges to make us grow, wouldn't you agree?"

Giuliano closed the guest room door and slouched back to his own quarters. He thought of the last classes he had enjoyed at the Fiesole Villa where Ficino had taught his privileged audience some of Plato's deeper thoughts about life itself. Though he didn't agree with the great philosopher that 'love was a serious mental disease', he had experienced himself a similar pain when he did not act with integrity and honesy. Indeed, Plato had claimed that 'the human behaviour flows from desire, emotion and knowledge' and the young Medici now contemplated how to manage such a source of infinite wealth.

The measure of a man is what he does with power and he wondered what Lorenzo would create with all his sovereignty. Could he transform his inner wars into an everlasting peace in Tuscany and even Europe, or would his family become a Trojan Horse?

39. FIORENZA, 1473 PRATO TO CAREGGI

How wrongful is it then while hankering for the simplicity
as destined was to me away from backbiting bitterness,
I have become jealous of anyone who can,
from all ardent discontent, send you free. (Envy)

Three very tired men with conspicuously foreign behaviour had arrived really late at night at the city gates of Florence. The Porta al Prato wasn't closed yet and walking their horses, they made their way towards a small inn recommended not by the local tourist office, but a few Florentine people they had met in Pistoia.

The place seems foreigner-friendly; whatever that means, Iz thought.

When they asked for three rooms, the innkeeper laughed out loud assuring them that this wasn't the Palazzo Vecchio. They could have *una stanza* (one room) and that there was enough room for three. Izquierdo, who wasn't exactly excited at the prospect of sharing one bed with his companions, announced that he was going to take a walk.

"I wouldn't go cruising on the first night in the town now, Iz. Not with that little wound still healing, I heard Tuscan beauties are fierce in the summer!" Derecho made a joke, long over-due. "Right Derecho, shall I bring three of them over here and we'll have a party?"

"That's a bright remark Mr. Know-it-all," Dritto put in his five cents.

"Somehow I don't think it's a good idea," Derecho said. "I really mustn't let you go off on your own like this. I'll come along as long as we don't make it a late drinking night." That closed off the subject.

Dritto was happy at the prospect of resting and the other two went off with the innkeeper's grin and grim warning. "You gentlemen watch it. The Office of the Night is currently very active," he insisted. "As we were told,"

Derecho replied with a clever wink in his eyes. "We won't be late; we are just having a nice glass of your local wine."

"There isn't exactly a mini bar in the room now is there?" Iz remarked. The man gave him an annoying look and wondered what a mini-bar was . . .

"Let's go towards the Medici family's district," Iz continued, "I read somewhere that was the more vivid, yes, the livelier part of town. Cosimo the Elder, you know, the very respected Medici and a bit of the father-of – the-nation-like figure, he built a house in Via Larga, one that is a prototype for Renaissance civic architecture. He has left it to his sons and now his grandsons, Lorenzo and Giuliano. Of course, Via Larga is the present name . . . we know it as Via Cavour!"

"Well, well, you are a history buff!" Derecho joked.

Minutes later the two men looked up at a rather impressive two-storey building. Italians called it a Palazzo; this one was austere and solid.

"You should see the chapel inside; gilded ceilings framing amazing frescoes," Iz continued as they strolled toward Via dei Servi.

"Oh, also an art-connoisseur?" Derecho giggled

"We should open a store, *Arte Magia* (Art Magic). This would go over big in Manhattan, especially in the Village," Iz replied.

"I know what will go over even bigger in the Village, downtown New York," Derecho pointed out towards the two men behind a large column engaged in some deep throat moves. While they looked for something like a pub, they followed a few other men and landed at La Caccia.

"La Caccia, well that speaks for itself," Derecho said. "The hunt is indeed the right translation; I bet we'll get more than just a good meal!"

They walked in and all heads turned. So much for going unnoticed. Derecho almost nodded to the crowd and found a table in the back. They sat down and a few women, all smiles, immediately approached. One of them took their order and two more made it clear they wanted to sit with them at the same table.

Iz reminded them not to get into their vernacular. A rain of questions came down on them: who were they, where were they from, what did they do? And then the one answering to the unusual name of Galessa, clutched herself to Iz. She slowly put her hand on Izquierdo's knee moving slowly up his inner thigh. He swallowed and admired her busty approach but gently pushed her hand away.

Galessa whispered in his left ear that instead, *'she could fetch him a nice young lad if that was what he was after.'*

He violently shook his head, but an angelic looking youth had already squeezed in right opposite them and Derecho now felt an equally warm hand on his knee. Izquierdo broke the silence in plain English. "I think we'll get out of here before the night watch catches us and thinks we're an ideal example of a Renaissance style gay couple!"

But the woman gave a loud lioness's roar and bumped in with a very heavy Welsh accent. "You are English? Well, have you ever!"

Her grin had turned sincere. She nearly crushed Iz with her expansive voluptuousness, while claiming her name *Galessa*, translated as 'from Wales'.

"I have worked in the Pub for years; it belongs to the family!" she proudly continued. "I also make more money with, well you know…" and her hand slipped a bit further than Izquierdo's inner leg. He jumped up like a marionette.

"Well, you indeed look like a gay pair of lads," they both looked at each other with a large grin and big eyes.

"Heavy accent you've got here and a very different one, eh? Another cup? It'll be on me. I guess you're not interested in my younger brother. He is cute, isn't he, and he's got an ass like his father, who's not my father… but that's a long story. That one has got some noble fluids dripping in his veins. Admittedly, he's the perfect breed of male and female nobility, but his father cannot have him at home. The worst is that he doesn't speak, he's dumb… but he can open his mouth real wide…"

"Please," Derecho interrupted; more vulgar words were about to bounce onto the oak table. "We only came here to have a drink. We had a long trip. We have a friend waiting at the Albergo and we're tired."

He put money on that table and got up, gently asking them to let them through, when suddenly several guards took him by the arm and Iz had no time to even move sideways, thanks to their natural corpulence. Before they knew why, they were dragged from the pub by five men – and everybody else had a laugh.

"How much money were you planning on spending on the young lad, mister?" the first one howled out to Izquierdo while he was being pushed against the wall.

"Wait a minute," both foreigners screamed out simultaneously.

"Well, where do you both come from?" a second one joined in.

"Picking up our local boys ... aren't we horny foreign bastards. A night at the *bargello* will be appreciated and we can fill those records with some more details."

"Great, we can serve on a panel for gay rights in the Italian Renaissance," Izquierdo said, squirming, but he didn't attempt any Italian slang while cracking a few more jokes to cover his nervousness.

The slightly broken, wooden door slammed open. And Galessa broke up the current street scene with the operatic entrance of an acclaimed opera singer's *prima donna con gusto* attack. She screamed at the guards that these two men were friends from England and that they were her guests, and this was all a misunderstanding. It made no impression on the five expressionless faces.

"A misunderstanding you say, when I saw him lay out the money on the table?" one of them shouted back.

"And young lady, we see more and more of your young brother in the tavern and on street corners, and less time at home now, haven't we? Training him to make hay when the sun isshining?" He laughed through a mouth of filthy teeth, while an unwashed finger pointed in a vague direction.

While the five Officers of the Night were pulling the two so-called Englishmen steadily by their arms, Galessa bawled they would hear from her tomorrow.

"What about tonight?" Derecho called out in desperation.

Politeness and good manners got them no further than a visit to the spectacular inner court of the *bargello*, not the twentieth century museum but that original impenetrable Florentine jail.

The guards quickly disposed of them and they were left in a small underground cell.

"No papers, no investigation?" Izquierdo looked at Derecho in surprise. "Sounds familiar?"

"And no light but my watch. At least we weren't asked to strip and drop all accoutrements," Derecho answered.

"I bet they went back on their nightly tour to bring in some more dangerous species like us. Here we are make a mistake in one world and you are punished in a another ... centuries back!" And they both cracked up laughing, which really worried the guards making their way out.

"We have to get a message to Dritto," Iz stood in front the heavy cell door sounding annoyed. "You better start working that watch, Derecho," he insisted. And in no time, Derecho took the bracelet off his arm, finally using the laser pencil lamp. He directed the light towards the walls and stopped at the door.

"At least we have a few hours of light," he shrugged, "but through these walls it'll be a miracle if I get this device working as a communication tool."

"We are about one floor below ground, right?" Doh asked.

"Can't get the layout of this building, the stupid device doesn't do it here," Iz said and he didn't get much more than a widening pocket lamp effect to admire the inside structure of this Florentine dungeon.

"Iz, you don't think we can get stuck in time, do you? That little incident on the road has nothing to do with part II of *Mala Fortuna in Toscana* (Bad luck in Tuscany), has it? I hate to tell you but we're going to have to do some visualizing and meditation trickery. You actually look a bit oriental in this light."

And both of them sat down after checking out the absence of skulls and bones, mice or rats, chairs or benches – and hoped they could change their present reality rapidly. "At least, this cell in a hot summer keeps us cool," Derecho smiled.

"Jeez, you're even smarter in the dark, Iz." Ancient bricks had no impact on Derecho's good mood.

Careggi, the Medici Villa

At only two miles distance from the main city, the Careggi Palace slumbered in its walls, restored by one of the geniuses of that period, Michelozzo. This architect and sculptor, a student of Donatello and an intimate and most faithful friend of Cosimo the Elder, had also designed the Medici Palazzo in the Mugello, in the shape of a fortress ... and another villa in the Fiesole district, Cosimo's gift to Piero's brother, Giovanni, also of outstanding taste. Its foundations were sunk into the hillside and in each of the commodious living spaces, architectural marvels abounded. The villa overlooked the magnificent valley that gave birth to one of Italy's marvels, Firenze.

Of all three constructions, Lorenzo favoured Careggi and called it the jewel in the Medici crown. The vastness, the high ceilings and the spacious rooms, made you feel as if you were still in Florence, while actually being in the country. So even past midnight, when in the mood, and depending on his many functions and very active private life, Lorenzo would secretly ride out to Careggi, the castle that wasn't one. He had done so last night, and he was pleased to notice his brother's horse and one he recognised to be the Buontalenti's, presumably for their foreign guest. Before going to catch his customary five hours of sleep, he had peeked into Giuliano's room and was relieved to find him fast asleep.

Better so ... no late-night conversations.

He had much work to do for the following day's midday meeting with the bankers from Flanders. Before his father's passing, Lorenzo had often represented the family. His grandfather had taught him well, and he could handle the monetary business with the same flair that made his family unequalled in all of Europe. He sat down in his own quarters, elaborately decorated full of magnificent works of artists his family had supported in the last decades. At a smouldering fireplace, Lorenzo's eyes were about to close when Giuliano came sliding in from behind his leather armchair.

"I heard you, little brother; you know I have terrible sight but like you, I inherited a pair of pointy ears."

"One couldn't just sneak up to the great Lorenzo, could one?" Giuliano mocked his brother in a series of courteous bows. "With hidden daggers?" Giuliano laughed.

A minute later, like kids, they were wrestling on the Persian carpet till they screamed so loudly that Lorenzo put his hand over Giuliano's face and finally kicked him away. Giuliano flipped on his back and stared at the ceiling. Lorenzo said, "We really must get into some Roman wrestling again like we did that year we traveled with father, down south. It seems we've been stuck in our minds instead of taking care of our bodies."

Giuliano got up, dusted off and put a large towel-like cloth around his hips. Lorenzo smiled at his tight abdominal section that had grown stronger than his own. It seemed he needed to aspire to a more athletic life like those of his Olympic heroes.

"Well speak for yourself," Giuliano said. "You haven't heard anything if you haven't heard what our guest had to tell me! It's enough to make you want to leave Florence forever, thinking we may house traitors amongst us, and with our sister married to one of those horrible families who may want us all dead!"

"What? More treason ... and the foreigner knew the outcome?" Lorenzo stared, disturbed by the statement of his younger brother.

"Let us have a walk in the park. We can certainly use some fresh air with this story".

Lorenzo paid close attention to everything Giuliano reported to him. If anything, like a future conspiracy was to take place, the seeds had already been planted long ago.

I'm not surprised at all, Lorenzo thought. His father and grandfather had survived in the midst of all conspiracies and controversies. They had never chosen victimhood. Better not to speak to their mother, for she would lose more sleep over this.

He accepted it all very calmly, apprehensive of his brother's attitude; Giuliano wasn't too keen on giving up his own private life. Lorenzo had given his brother much attention since their father died. Indeed, they both were quite young when their mother Lucrezia became a widow with two daughters and two sons – Lorenzo, then an unusually mature twenty years of age, and his even more popular brother, simply the most handsome youth in Florence. Lorenzo felt responsible for him and wanted nothing for him but the best education. The Holy See had seemed a great solution especially from a political point of view. He had it discussed within the family and his grandfather had been very articulate; the Medici needed a foot in Rome, with at best, a handsome young cardinal, popular enough to become pope. That wouldn't happen, at least not right now and both brothers had agreed.

Now at almost twenty-one, Giuliano had developed a huge gain with this attractive reputation with the female elite, though not only women. Many rich families fancied this striking and athletic bachelor to entice their daughters. He was also his brother's most trusted ear though everybody thought Angelo Poliziano seemed to have housed himself into Lorenzo's earlobes.

Lorenzo was a born master in manoeuvring in the world of commerce and politics. He knew exactly how to throw the dice for his family's and in his own interest. Sometime soon, he wanted to place his brother in a high position, maybe as an ambassador to the French King, with whom the Medici had enjoyed a good rapport through their grandparents.

Maybe a Medici could seduce one of the French Royal family members; an option they had all hoped for, for decades.

But it would take another century until another member of the illustrious family, Maria de Medici, would marry Henry IV and give birth to *le dauphin* (the eldest son of the king of France), Louis XIII. This meant Maria de Medici would become the first Italian royal grandmother to France and to the illustrious Sun King, Louis XIV.

"It will be another exciting breakfast if I understand well, Giuliano. Our foreigner certainly must have some suggestions other than praying for our salvation, with plenty of historical details too? I can hardly imagine that, as you said, he actually 'studied our family background in his timeline'. I still cannot believe the future brought us such an emissary! Amazing it all is; here he comes in on a cloud from that unknown future to warn us about a murderous plot against us and now we'll be able to stop it before it's even planned? Amazing, amazing!" Lorenzo boasted in a joyous exaltation.

"Do you think I ought to go abroad for a while?" Giuliano asked. "Maybe we must start planning way ahead of time; there will always be someone ready to kill us or throw us into exile. The stronger you are politically, the more steadfast into your saddle, the more jealousy it will breed." Giuliano's voice took on an almost irritable tone. "You will be the sole ruler, *tu fratello Io no (You brother, not me)!"*

"Goodness that's the last thing you would want to do! Rule!" Lorenzo swayed away the argument. "Giuliano, I need you by my side for a few more years. Remember that from the second day after our father's death, the city requested me to be in charge! I didn't go fishing for a crown! Just married and barely twenty-one, nobody even thought for a moment about the life I wanted to lead. The family imposing it to be my duty to proceed where father and grandfather came to a stalemate! Oh, I had not only sworn to protect our mother, you and our sisters, but to make Florence the central focus of all Italian business, then in art and education in Europe."

He sighed heavily. "I have to think every day as to how I can keep the city and the counsel on our side. Few will understand the plans I have made and not undermine them. I just know that it's all about slowly building it up. It's like I'm working for a greater architect, the one on top of Olympus, pointing at me!" Giuliano had never heard him talk about an architect and he wondered why.

Lorenzo continued, "We must soon offer another *giostra* next year, one that will leave you victorious and that will win you the hand the lady of your choice! A grand festivity will show our generous spirit and bring many visitors to the republic and the people of Florence will see with their own eyes that you are amongst the brave and great athletes of our day, and not just the most handsome, *caro Fratello* (dear brother)."

He grinned. "The audiences always like the games and they will recognize the turf you come from. This will honour our family and our forefathers!"

Giuliano exclaimed, "Mercury, Hermes, you have indeed become him, my dear Lorenzo; thinking of making me a favourite item on your Italian political market?" Giuliano sounded sardonic with a seriousness Lorenzo did not expect.

"It's been already four years since you won your *giostra* (joust), an almost deadly event, remember? You went out there like a true conqueror, reckless in strength and courage; Federigo the only victim ... I was sorry that he lost an eye. Those games mustn't exceed in savagery and turn into a painful and bloody spectacle. I admit I hate that, and I won't have a part in it! I tell you right now that I'm not interested." Giuliano sounded angry.

"Of course, that's not what I want for you. I'd like you to become the most popular man in the republic; the crown prince of our family!" Lorenzo smiled as he tried to hug his brother, as always with great gentleness, pinching his butt.

Giuliano grabbed his hand and in no time, they were kicking each other till they both took a deep breath. Lorenzo was no longer sure that making his brother 'an object of outlandish desire and international aspiration' was what would change their family's destiny. It felt more like being trapped within one's own castle of illusions.

"Tell me, is Angelo coming over this morning?" Giuliano brusquely changed the theme.

"No, I believe this afternoon; why?" Lorenzo asked while picking up a few books from their family's extensive library.

"But if Angelo arrives late, you'll be gone," Giuliano said, "because you have the scholars coming from Pisa to discuss the plans for the education and arts exchanges in Puglia. If Angelo is late, he won't even see you. Remember you asked me last week to preside the meeting, so I won't be here either."

"What a pity you're my brother, you'd make an excellent *segretario* (secretary) with a head as big as the bible!" he laughed. "As for our dear Angelo, we're running into some problems with my dear Clarice," Lorenzo continued.

"Not 'we', but 'you,' brother!" Giuliano answered. "You've accepted to marry into a wealthy family and bed the future mentor of your children. I didn't!"

"Thank you, brother, I wasn't expecting a payback reaction from anyone, especially not from you after you enjoyed at least a few of my former mistresses!"

"Lorenzo, no dramatic speech ... just wake up!" Giuliano sharpened his tongue.

"You know only too well that I consented in marrying for the benefit of our family. As for Angelo, I beg you to never say anything like this ever again. The walls in Florence have ears. We are both fond of him and ..."

"Fond, you say? Both of us are fond of him? Lorenzo, besides our mutual fondness, Angelo has changed. He is not in his mid-teens any longer, and he is more than ever looking up at you like his saviour, his substitute father. He will do anything to get your attention."

If I can believe GianLuca even his silent thoughts are guiding Lorenzo's words, Giuliano thought.

"You're soon to be Italy's most powerful lord, my goodness, have you grown blind, Lorenzo? You *are* his god! And even with his talent, and no doubt he has much wisdom in store and knowledge to offer, but you are like Jupiter to a willing nymph!"

"Please, Giuliano, what are you saying?" Lorenzo pretended to dismiss his brother's reasoning.

"What I mean Lorenzo, is that you have bought into his game. You have invaded his youthful life and accepted his intimacy, yet you will not regain your own lost youth, while Angelo searches for the father in each of the men he will seduce!" Giuliano took a breath before proceeding and he picked up a chalice filling it up with a deep dark red wine.

"He will never like women, and frankly, he sometimes acts like one. It doesn't disturb me, but his intent does. His tastes are just different. To me this is not a problem, yet to our society, it will be! And you are not in the position to be, um ... or brought to the *Uffizi della Notte* (Office of the Night police) because of your children's mentor's nightly escapades! Not that they will ever question you. Anyway, I know you are feeling some innate benevolence towards him since the first day you met, but even there, your feelings have grown in an unacceptable direction and I feel your mind has been twisted." He sighed.

Giuliano continued, "You remember he trapped me when I was just a horny kid and now, he has totally enticed you, my brother, or what else will you call this manipulation? At times I feel he's possessed, I can see him change into another being, no longer himself. I will ask GianLuca what he thinks of this. You know that in his world he has studied the art of the psyche and he's quite a stunning guide as I have witnessed."

"My brother, what are you saying?"

"Lorenzo quit it! We all know that you have a brilliant mind and that your intuition is optimal. Remember Lapo's friend, the astrologer? He gave us some very convincing information – and warnings! The planet Mars is in your twelfth house of secrecy, in the sign of Pisces. There is a conjunction with your moon in that same house and in Aries. Watch out for your emotions being burned!"

Lorenzo stared at him; eyes wide open.

And Giuliano continued, "He had warned you about getting lost in your feelings; remember? How did he put it ... swimming in an ocean of emotion and then drowning at any instant? And he didn't, my third eye reads you quickly, brother. Your new friend has indeed developed a strong influence on you, and for the better, I would say," Lorenzo now confirmed in a surprising manner.

"Since when did you get so interested in this subject? It seems to me that GianLuca has a very strong influence on you. Fortunately, my Cyclopean eye sees that he rapidly has developed an excellent influence on you and ..." Lorenzo tried to joke.

"Lorenzo, you really are wonderfully adept at changing the subject. I told you a while ago that I didn't think your relationship with Angelo is a positive note in your family life. Can you understand this?" He walked up and down at a now quicker pace, aggravated and frustrated. Both brothers got equally annoyed.

"You have to talk to Angelo, or must I speak with him? You're also having an affair with that other woman, right?" Giuliano said, fully passionate, not only about his brother's wellbeing but a far deeper subject. Lorenzo knew that it was true, and it left him exasperated.

"Look who is clairvoyant," Lorenzo smiled hopelessly covering up his old heavily coated pain.

"This isn't clairvoyance. Remember what happened in Cafaggolio; you were under the influence of that potion your friends gave you. So, was it Franceschino who brought it?" Giuliano stared at him. "Old, old magic and you just weren't yourself; or better, another version of you danced around naked, not the best example for the Florentine society! As for Angelo ... he was only sixteen and he didn't even need to drink at all. He lives the Greek and Roman days as if he were an emperor's slave. I am not sure I can accept this kind of attitude or lifestyle. Not within my family's home."

Giuliano didn't feel very comfortable at his own speech, but it had taken years to get to this point and now was the time to speak up. His right fist hit a brick wall. He bit his lip and Lorenzo grew incensed at his past and all of his compulsions. He felt guilty involving even his own brother in such schemes.

"Sorry to sound judgemental, but it just isn't healthy, Lorenzo. It isn't healthy and you're getting caught in this dangerous web more and more. I can tell from the look in your eyes; there's an obsession!"

"Did Clarice speak to you ...?" Lorenzo deepened his voice, looking down in a strangely pensive mood.

"No, Clarice hasn't spoken to me about what she may have already guessed," Giuliano's higher voice chirruped, "... you share her bed a lot less than she'd like you to and she is birthing your children, Lorenzo. She is connected to you and she feels a lack of clarity in your relationship to her as her husband. Have you given this any thought? If you need to be with Neptune, do not forget to get out of his ocean of illusions. Stop the dreaming in mid travels!"

Giuliano bawled out too strongly as he proceeded with an unexpected discourse; explosive, as only a tempest could be.

"How I love you brother and even if our father is sadly missed, and after all, we saw very little of him, but I'm not looking for a substitute in you nor anyone else. But the challenges and traps are many. We'll have to be strong together. You have the leader in you, I don't. Yet I clearly see what's happening to you." And with this he finished his monologue, noticing suddenly how hungry he felt.

Lorenzo's face cleared up and his eyes pierced his brother's, but there was truth, and there was anger, and yet there was love.

"Shall we attend to our guest and have a hearty breakfast?" he asked, lightening up the room. "An excellent idea," Giuliano replied.

They walked slowly back to the house and Lorenzo had his arm around him like he used to after the death of their father Piero, *Il Gottoso* (with the gout).

"Thank you," he uttered in all honesty. "You're quite right. I've been closing my eyes. I do not love Clarice, a woman who sees Christ in every corner of the room, but reasons of state have made her my wife and I will respect and treat her better. I owe it to her for she's a fine human being seeking solace in her prayers only. As for Poliziano, you are asking me to keep him out of my bed and you have good reasons to believe I'm trapped because once he's under the sheets you cannot get him out. He has found a way to make me feel good about myself. It's true – with him I feel beautiful, like a god! It's true and you know how I think about my own appearance, the gods gifted you with a classical attractiveness as in the days of old."

Above that crooked nose, his eyes cleared up. With his strong sense of time, he felt that the bells of the campanile were to announce breakfast, and a minute later those bells confirmed that he was never really alone. He did have a surprisingly bright younger brother.

40. TUSCANY, 1473 BUONTALENTI, NEW FRIENDS

... into an unknown gut of un-earthy sponges,
of absent faces in extraneous dimensions
reading our keys locked in the symbols
we reveal with eyes wide shut. (www.Lostcodes)

That same morning, they felt that they had won the lottery! The day before, as they were about to leave Genoa, Isabel had helped an old man. Crippled with gout, he was on his carriage making his way back from a cure resort somewhere close to the beautiful town of Volterra, known since the Etruscan civilization for the healing springs.

Vincenzo di Luca di Pistoia was his awfully long name, as most citizens carried the name of the father and their birthplace. Isabel's elegant moves reminded him of the dancers he had seen in his youth, when Domenico da Piacenza (a distant cousin) was one of the first composers to also write treatises, including their own choreographies.

Isabel told him that when she was a child, she had taken ballet (influenced by a half-sister who had lost all contact with her). Instead of pursuing dance, she chose higher studies which led her into a world of healing. Vincenzo nodded, having felt she possessed great healing powers – especially with that 'magic tool' she wore around her neck.

He was referring of course to how the massage Isabel gave him with the orgonite, left him feeling much better than the whole time he spent at the cure resort! Isabel gently corrected him, explaining that orgonite was a man-made jewel including rosin, crystal gems, copper or gold spirals ... and other metals. All through the trip Florian and Isabel explained more about health than the man had ever heard. He found out how to get sulphur, the main healing factor for the gout problem and Florian gave him the formula. Once they arrived at his home, his driver took them to Florence, and they were given fresh horses.

Early for their meeting, they entered a 1473 Renaissance Florence from the west. Very quickly, they were reminded how vastly different this city was. Once they went through the gates, they were even more admiring of the architecture of the houses, many even half a mile away from the city walls. There was the majestic church of Santa Maria del Fiore, as well as the one built for San Lorenzo, and, of course, Santa Croce rising amongst very few, but impressive enough residences of the rich families making up the city of Fiorenza.

"No cappuccino or cheesecake in my classy coffee bar, right opposite the Palazzo Vecchio?" Florian joked.

"Rivoire, oh yes a splendid place," Isabel remarked smilingly, "deluxe and over-priced, in an atmosphere from an Italian fifties movie. You pay for the historic view of the square!"

"So, no gelato either?" Florian replied.

"Let's hope for some fresh bread and cheese. There must surely be a market close to the cathedral and there are certainly plenty of piazzas we can visit".

"Piazzas, yes and finding a pizza? No?" he joked, and she ignored his silliness.

He was amazed at the ambiance that governed this old city. No stores, no cars, no parking lots or pharmacies or fast food chains; this was indeed marvellous. After crossing *the Ponte alla Carraia* they walked by the River Arno. This time the water was clear. They both smiled while checking out the quality of the stream: clean waters.

How it has all changed, they both reflected, watching a slow rower taking a small boat into peaceful magnificence. What did we do to our planet?

They found food at a market growing increasingly full by the minute. It was a colourful scene. The women were covered from the neck to the feet, so Isabel's disguise fitted right in. A lot less men around; some salesmen really looked Orthodox Jewish and were very animated in the way they used their charm, showing off the gorgeous, dutifully made clothing, the wealth of the *stoffa;* mixtures of rare silks, rough threaded cottons and linen and plenty of carpets from Persia, even diamonds were on display. Florian enjoyed this visit tremendously. He felt so privileged. They left the horses with Gentile, Vincenzo di Luca di Pistoia's servant, and his equally petite spouse. The couple made their way slowly towards Santa Croce, where, at another market even bigger than the first, one saw an impressive crowd floating in and out of the church and onto the square. Florian noted quickly the absence of Dante's statue. There was a tiny scrawny kid and a few more fourteen or fifteen-year-olds, pointing at them, playing something that resembled 'hide and seek'.

A bit further, they saw two strikingly charismatic men, perhaps father and son, who had a way of carrying themselves; they were accompanied by a robust boy. They nodded and smiled as if they knew Isabel and Florian. The older man spoke.

"You foreigners look very similar to someone we know. Allow us to introduce ourselves, I am Lapo and this is my son, Andrea Buontalenti, and this is our page, Giovannino." The man offered his hand and Florian shook it without any hesitation. Isabel looked him in the eyes and there was an instant attraction from Andrea that couldn't escape Florian's attention. They were feeling at odds speaking Italian and Florian broke the silence in a Cockney voice that nearly had Isabel crack up. Oh goodness, she thought mockingly ... whatever you choose, no Shakespeare; he wasn't born yet; watch it 'oh my noble knight'. So – French it was.

"Nous venons des Cathars, le sud-ouest de la France. Je suis Florian et voilà mon amie, Isabel. (We came from the French Cathars. I am Florian and this is my friend Isabel)."

His presentation was quick and slick.

He must have taken his French pill before leaving. Isabel covered her thoughts with a move whipping the summer heat from her long hair.

The Buontalenti family greeted them and immediately invited Florian and Isabel to join them for some food and a pleasant surprise at their home nearby. Both had studied Latin and Andrea had taken some French from a friend of his mother's who had resided at the French court.

*"J'ai l'impression de vous connaître cher Monsieur (*You seem familiar, dear sir)*." Andrea* replied in a friendly manner emphatically rolling the 'r's.

Isabel responded, *"Nous aimerions passer un moment ensemble pour partager votre repas du soir. Je suis désolé, mais en ce moment, nous cherchons des amis. On vous remercie, peut-être une autre fois* (We would love to have a moment together for dinner tonight. We're sorry but right now, we're looking to meet some of our friends. Thank you, maybe another time)."

Isabel had interrupted the beginning of a pleasant conversation they had no time for. But Florian didn't agree. There were plenty of reasons to have a local contact and he immediately said they would try to at least visit them before leaving the city. Shrewd as he was, Giovannino had noticed a strange looking bracelet on Isabel's right arm. He had noticed it while her sleeve moved as she fixed her braids. He addressed Lapo about his discovery in a soft voice while the latter continued the conversation in very broken, but charming, English.

"Please feel free to join us tonight. We have a foreign house-guest who resembles you very much; maybe from the same place, with similar kind of jewellery and who knows, maybe even from the same century?" He smiled with a charm of the father everyone would dream of having. For a moment both Isabel and Florian were taken aback. Isabel avoided any further continuation of their meeting, but Florian took out a small notebook to write down the name of the street with a brief description that Andrea gave of their house, pointing at the side street of the cathedral. Before they parted, Andrea whispered something in Latin into Florian's ear about a great physical similarity between 'their guest' and him. They nodded again and left.

"Well, what was that all about and in Latin?" Isabel asked him.

"He spoke of a similarity between their house guest and me. Now that couldn't be Iz or Derecho or Dritto, because we don't look anything alike. If someone else arrived here in Florence, 'from the same century' as Mr Buontalenti mentioned, that means he may know where we are from and from the look, he gave us, I'm convinced that this trio does know. They both looked like very bright, very educated men. Both of them, don't you think so?"

Isabel said she liked the way they had introduced their servant as a page; they indeed seemed humanists, definitely men of certain wealth, for she had noticed the fine quality of their clothing. "Who else but our trio and the two of us could be visiting this timeline?" he wondered.

"Weren't we aware of another possible traveler before we took off?"

"Well, if that person doesn't have a similar device to the one you have created, then he or she has to be connected to another person or an event in this same year, and it remains to be seen if that traveler has come through the same gate as we did. Probably not, I would say," Isabel contemplated, convinced; and then again, not so convinced.

"Why am I thinking of you, Jean-Luc Médecin," Florian thought out loud and Isabel agreed. "I kind of thought of him too, even if we haven't heard from him for ages."

Both Florian and Isabel looked at each other as if they had lost all reason.

"We need to get back to our mission," she said, "and concentrate."

"Well, for now let's get to our trio." Florian said eagerly.

The market had changed into a massive gathering of eager consumers. It wasn't too difficult to get by unnoticed, but it was hard to find anyone specific in this happy sea of Florentines. Isabel hoped they would be waiting where 'Dante' would be absent. She smiled at the silliness of it all. They continued to make their way into the small courtyard of a sturdy house right on the first street opposite the Church of Santa Croce, *Borgo dei Greci* (Greek district). She nervously opened the device while Florian looked out for any unexpected intruders. Just when she was about to get an image, he wrapped her in his arms and pretended to kiss her passionately.

"It's OK now. There were two 'wall flowers' that had followed me with their eyes since we talked to the Buontalenti."

Isabel took a big breath, questioning him, until two women with cleavages too obvious to charm any 'real male', appeared. Isabel returned Florian's kiss with equally played passion ... the women almost got embarrassed when she threw her leg around his waist as ready to get onto a tango flight. Florian overheard them and their remarks about 'competing and losing' clients, seemed rather funny.

Thanks for the comic interlude, he thought.

The scene finally evaporated like the midday heat dripping down their backs and the bell tower confirmed it was 2:00 pm. While their eyes were still hooked, Isabel's restraint took her back to where she had left off and her annoyance at the image she didn't get from her inter-dimensional toy.

Derecho didn't pick up and the screen remained dark. She waited a minute and launched the mini-search program one more time, once again without any luck.

"That's all we need. Losing them on this timeline. Hopefully, I'm wrong, but we might look around the Fiesole Villa. With the horses and no traffic jam," she said facetiously, "we'll be there in under half an hour."

Still a real commander, Florian thought. She hasn't changed a bit since the first time we met at the university.

Making their way back, he took her by the hand.

"How come you know the way?" she asked while they walked.

"The map," he answered dryly.

"Oh yes, how come I didn't get one before we got to Fiesole?" she joked.

"Because it was programmed into the PC program so I would never lose my way and I just remembered from a former visit." He laughed and by then they were almost running.

"There, this way we'll get to the Porta Romana." He pointed in the direction as they crossed the Ponte Rubaconte towards Boboli Gardens.

"Giardino di Boboli, the gardens behind the Palazzo Pitti?" she asked.

"Absolutely, not yet the property of the Medici family, it will be though, later next century!"

"A history wiz needs a quiz," she joked. "Glad you've remained so mentally athletic."

"There are the horses," Florian noted as they approached Vincenzo's friendly assistant and they bid him farewell. They gave him a thank-you note for his master, explaining they would do their best to get back to him when they had finished their business in the city.

"There's no bridge to the right of the Rubaconte we just crossed," Florian said, "so we must go back the way we came and then we can ride along the Arno towards the Gate of Justice and move on from there towards the other gate at La Croce. From there we can ride towards Maiano, neighbouring Fiesole within a mile."

She felt like teasing him. "You've become my favourite tour guide."

"Yeah… join our 'Time Traveling Troubadours', the agency that will take you beyond the lines of time!"

At the market, Andrea and Lapo picked up a beautiful hand-woven cloth, a gift for GianLuca. They had no idea that he would not be able to ever take any memorabilia to… his world. To them it still seemed only the future. Soon after, they arrived at their residence right off the Via dei Malcontenti. Though smaller than the Via Larga's Palazzo Medici, the similarities between the two were manifold. Cosimo's friend, Michelozzo, the architect of the Duomo, had also done quite some work for Lapo's family home. Those walls of rusticated stone, made of the renowned *pietra serena*, divided the three-story building. A golden fleur-de-lys emblem on the windows of the first floor reminded the visitor of the similar style used for both the Palazzo Vecchio and the one in Via Larga.

In that period, Benedetto da Maiano had been working at the Palazzo Vecchio to enlarge some of the rooms and he had promised Lapo that after he finished the commission for the *Gonfalonieri* (holder of a highly prestigious communal office), he would continue at his residence. But Lapo did not call his house a Palazzo, because he didn't consider himself royalty as many of the Florentine families of wealth pretended to be. Envy was something he had never befriended and he had taught his son and daughters accordingly. Giovannino opened the gates and while he and Andrea walked through, Lapo told Andrea of a note he had found on the table that morning. It had been written by GianLuca, and it contained a poem dedicated to their family.

"What a rare being he is, this GianLuca, and now also a poet?" Andrea said to his father.

They stood still for a moment as Lapo unfolded the page made of an unusual paper.

He noticed the paper had perforations on the side, and had been written with a different kind of blue ink.

How unusual he thought and also it wasn't easy to figure out the vernacular of such a different Italian, obviously from another period than their own. The note read that this poem was probably a bit modern. And Lapo pondered what 'modern' could mean, maybe just strange or unusual, or perhaps new as in a future ... something. Andrea noted that 'modernus' from 'modo' or 'just now' was late Latin, a word they really never used. His father smiled, and Andrea liked the sound of it. This Italian was different to his own. The style too was so very unlike anything in poetry he had ever encountered. Like the title, this poem was all about envy and Andrea read it out aloud:

You didn't stop by to charm me with a jaundiced eye begrudging all other's fortune
I may have missed this time around,
green as I was, not of envy though.
Why is the thirst for your fame
absent from the frame of my mind
like the malice I knew not
to bequeath all my desires
invidiously comparing those deadly seven sins
No saint I was born
nor free of longing I have been
yet you shot others with cupidity
and in spite of all venomous animosity
their hunger lessened not.
How wrongful is it then
while hankering for the simplicity
as destined was to me
away from backbiting bitterness,
I, have become jealous of anyone who can,
from all ardent discontent, send you free.

An excited voice shouted from the mezzanine while Andrea and his father strolled through the fortified main entrance with its gilded copper pendant, the shape of a sun and a moon topped by seven stars. He looked up and Fiammetta waved hilariously while Agnola wrapped her sister in a red and purple shawl, a giggling little girl awaiting her imaginary prince. Their brother had already gone to the study and both Lapo's daughters caught father around the waist just enough to remind him he would always be ticklish.

"Papa, papa you know what?" Agnola fired off with that enticing smile fathers never resist, while her sister sought to pull her back.

"Don't you dare, don't you dare, sister," Fiammetta repeated. "Papa, tell her to stop babbling and please don't listen to what she'll make up next . . . she's making it all up, papa!" she unconvincingly proclaimed.

"So, what is it you are making up, Agnola. You're stirring a burning curiosity within me. It isn't about our house guest is it now?" Lapo guessed in an amused way.

Agnola nodded vigorously. "Papa, like me my sister is in love, but with the foreigner. You guessed?" Her voice raced with every word while she looked over her left shoulder, knowing her sister was right there. Andrea appeared within a minute and as usual he picked her up, playfully threatening that she'd land in the fountain. They all scrambled their laughs into an explosive omelet of childish fun except Fiammetta who was pouting on the bench.

"Papa do not worry ... it is impossible, I know. He isn't from our world and I cannot imagine even living somewhere, like ... the land where Marco Polo found his fame," she uttered in despair. "At least through Marco Polo we found out about the Orient, their produce, the jewels and fine clothing. What a culture this amazing adventurer had brought us. About GianLuca's world we know nothing, only that it is far into the future and for any of us to exist in it, we may have to wear these strange bracelets," she declared, fully confused, though smirking while covering her own sad reflections.

"Well, maybe he has some kind of a carriage to travel across time and he can invite us," Agnola persisted. "I'll be fine with my Giuliano right here!"

"Ladies," Andrea interrupted," it is fine to dream, but you'll see that neither one of you will be the brides to these unusual men."

"Brother, these are the rudest words I have ever heard from you." Fiammetta raised herself, displeased, her hands defining an even thinner waistline.

"Unfortunately, that is the truth my child," and Lapo joined his son. "We've been fortunate to have shared in small portions of some of GianLuca's knowledge and experiences. He is indeed a fine man. He told me at home his family name is *Médecin*, French for Medici. Interesting, no?" he added. "I would have been delighted that my two daughters married cosmic twins and we'd all have a universal party inviting the gods at our table!"

"Why don't we simply enjoy the moment," Andrea said, "and while we continue learning about the future, have a pleasurable moment while sharing all this new information? Only this morning, father and I ran into two very similar foreigners. They didn't realize that Giovannino's quick eye noticed that the woman had a similar armband to the one GianLuca has!"

"A handsome pair they made up, didn't they?" Lapo said.

"We have invited them to join us for the evening meal and I'm hoping that GianLuca will have returned from Careggi," Andrea continued.

"How exciting," Fiammetta said, while crossing her arms in a pouting departure.

"Sister wait for me. We must get dressed in our best robes and show these foreigners what a Florentine family really looks like!" Agnola ran behind Fiammetta, as usual ... giggling.

Lapo and Andrea's eyes met in a smile. "Wait till they see the 'new couple'... what were their names again, Andrea?" Lapo asked.

"Isabel and Florian, they came from the land of the Cathars. I think I'll look into a few books to know more about that part of France, maybe their origins too! Papa, I'm going to the library now, will you join me?" he solicited.

Of course, they may have traveled from afar, much further than the Cathars, he pondered.

But first, Lapo checked in the kitchen and decided what surprises tonight's meal was bringing to honour the new guests. As they got to the centre of the town, Florian slowed down his horse. The hills weren't very steep, and they reached Maiano quicker than they had expected. Isabel knew that road well, though inevitably, it wasn't exactly the same.

"There it is, the Villa Medici," she said. "It seemed like a detour at first, but we cannot reach it from here, I made a mistake" she admitted.

"Right now, Via Beato Angelico doesn't exist ... we've got to take that narrow road below the villa," Florian replied, tightening up his horse. Isabel loved her companion's precision, but she worried and took the bracelet from her arm to open the device again.

"Why don't they answer?" she questioned impatiently.

"They could just be stuck somewhere. Maybe lost, it's not like Iz not to answer a call especially after yesterday's call," he gently answered. "Something went wrong, Isabel," and it dawned on him they got in trouble when entering the city walls.

"They must have arrived two nights ago," Isabel said, "but where did they go? A tavern? We must search the taverns and see if they know of any foreign-looking strangers. One cannot miss a strange looking trio like theirs and whatever will they think of the two of us!"

Their thoughts embraced, and they knew that accepting dinner at the Buontalenti family was as perfect a foil to get some more adequate information. They might really need some local help to find a solution to the present situation, and why not? A really good meal was most welcome, even in this reality. Leaving the Fiesole area, they looked down at the villa they knew so well and yet they were in 1473, not in their own century! It seemed weird indeed. They also guessed that they weren't the only ones to possess that kind of knowledge and doubtlessly other similar technology was around to play with. But the trio was a priority.

"We'll let go of the worry," Florian said, "we'll find them." And they made their way back down from the other side of the hill.

Fiorenza, Via San Egidio.

Voluptuous, entertaining and very serviceable, Gallesa's patience was far from endless. The queen of the tavern had spent an entire morning running around to find her brother's father. He was an influential man with an important position in the Signoria. Surely, he would be able to help 'a few friends of his son, accidentally visiting the *bargello*'. A real mercurial saleswoman, she could make up a story in an instant, if only she knew more about the two guys she had sympathized with. But she felt good about them and they were earnest men. Her gut told her so. The third man in the party that they had mentioned before their abduction by the local authorities, had to be found in an *Albergo* (inn). There weren't that many guesthouses able to house foreigners, because usually they were really picky! So decisively, she knew exactly where to go. When she reached Beppe's Inn and looked through the window, she noticed an unusually dressed figure with decidedly different eating habits than any of the locals. She figured out quickly he was the man she was looking for and pushed the door open. It almost slapped into a customer's angry face. Beppe, surprised, looked at her.

"You're looking smart these days, young lady and how is…" But she greeted him too quickly and there was no time for stories, scanning a foreigner alone at the table finishing his late breakfast. With an insolent charm all of her own she stood in front of him and asked:

"Sir, are you a friend of the two gentlemen who speak English?" She cleaned the table before he finished the meal. Dritto nearly spat out his oat-meal and looked at the woman with a big mouthful of food. She didn't look in his mouth but fixed his eyes with approaching eyelashes.

"I, ugh, yes, well… where are they…" he stuttered in surprise.

"They were jailed, by mistake! Come with me right now." She continued.

"We have to find my brother's real father; he knows the right people." She pulled him by the sleeve leaving breakfast for another hungry stomach. Beppe would no doubt take care of it. As they were quickening their pace, she introduced herself explaining to him the improbable tale of last night's goings-on.

While Galessa and Dritto ran through narrow streets, Beppe on the doorstep of his Albergo watched a handsome couple in a slow gallop, riding by and he wondered if there was some festivity planned, for only then, foreigners visited Florence. Once close to Santa Croce, Florian and Isabel preferred to walk, not to command more attention. After reaching Via dei Malcontenti, they easily found the Buontalenti Palazzo. Giovannino's big smile welcomed them and while he took their horses by their reigns, Andrea entered the open courtyard to greet them. Isabel and Florian were surprised to find such a fine residence.

"Your home is absolutely magnificent," they exclaimed enthusiastically like a friendly chorus. "The architecture is splendid; have we seen anything like it?"

"I know," Andrea answered while shaking both of his guests' hands. "Father has gone through much trouble since our Medici friends were using the same architect."

"Ah, Michelozzo, what an architect he was," Florian replied gladly, to his host's surprise. Isabel's eyes widened: "Did you say: he *was*?" Florian corrected his last statement: "Yes, what an architect, I meant he is!". He grinned to his companion and he continued.

"Of course, Isabel, that's what it is; the style of the house and this courtyard are similar to the Medici Riccardi and…" and while she faked being attentive, she quickly interrupted the start of another historical description that she knew Florian loved to bestow on his audience.

"I'm sure Sr Buontalenti will be able to give the right information himself, after all, this is his home". Florian got the message too late. He had just mentioned the name of the family to whom the Medici family would eventually sell their Palazzo.

"Did you say Riccardi?" Andrea asked. "Did you visit the Medici residence? Then you must be on a commercial mission if you know the… de' Medici?"

"Well, no," Isabel quickly took over. "We actually just went through Via Larga and we admired the building."

Andrea smiled, *"Je pense que Florian connut la cour intérieure* (I think Florian knows the inner court)," And he turned around to welcome his two sisters, surprised at his perfect French.

"Puis-je introduire Agnola et Fiammetta (May I introduce Agnola and Fiammetta)?"

Florian instantly took a bow to their beauty, especially Agnola, who looked strangely similar to Isabel who was equally enraptured by her youthful exquisiteness. While they were all introduced to one other, Lapo joined them and Andrea insisted in a few whispers that their new visitors had to know GianLuca. They took their guests to their special spot in the garden where something similar to traditional refreshments were served. Isabel started to suspect something was amiss, but for now small talk and polite, pleasant conversation kept everybody interested in each other.

And just then, as Agnola offered to refill the cups with some more of the delicious juice made of mixed fresh grapes, she noticed that this face was also familiar. She looked at Florian, who silently turned his head and continued discussing Michelozzo architecture. Then Lapo stood up, and, as was the family tradition he proposed a formal toast to everybody present.

"These last days, dear friends have been amongst my most precious. Since last week we have been fortunate to meet three unusual human beings, each one so unique. I can see that our new visitors are an equally accomplished pair. We are awaiting GianLuca tonight. He has become, let's say, like family to us. Even Giuliano de Medici appreciates him tremendously. He will return soon from the Medici Villa in Careggi to join us."

Careggi, Florian thought, that's where the hospital had its administration when we visited Florence two summers ago. How curious, and who's GianLuca?

"We are very curious indeed. Does this gentleman speak your language or ours?" Isabel asked, enticed by their statements. "Oh, he's a man of many languages and he does speak yours too and ..."

At that very moment Giovannino answered knocking on the back door. He took the horse's reigns from GianLuca, who walked right behind him, unleashing the thin leather gloves Giuliano had given him that afternoon. GianLuca noticed two new people with their backs to him and four other smiling faces. Fiammetta arranged her dress and her eyes twinkled with excitement. She got up, stretching out her arms and hands to him. Isabel watched her every move and wondered. When their eyes met, there was magic in the air and nobody in attendance could deny this.

Well, this young lady must be in love, Isabel thought, while watching Fiammetta closely.

"There you are, dear GianLuca," Lapo said. "We are so pleased you made it back. Please meet tonight's new guests."

Everyone got up. Isabel turned around almost stumbling back. Florian held her up, both astonished, as if looking at a ghost from perhaps an infinite past. As frozen to the patio as they were, they both wanted to move forward and embrace a man they hadn't ever expected to meet again. The Buontalenti family was by now getting used to these new phenomenally surprising events, and they all stepped back. Isabel felt as if she was about to faint and Florian seated her then shifted towards GianLuca, who was truly moved.

"You? You indeed are alive and in this century? This cannot be true. Were you caught in a time loop or did you return from the death?"

41. GENEVA, 2018 SIMON & DOWELL

When I gave up TV, I owned my mind a little,
just a little more, I hoped.
Then a satellite called me up
so, I could be found wherever, whenever, forever. (People who own their Mind)

"While Elizabeth waited for the private elevator to the top floor office overlooking the entire city, she felt strange indeed. Why did he call her to a meeting this late in the evening? She wouldn't have even considered accepting had it not been that her husband Siegfried was, as usual, working late and he (obviously wanting her to intervene) had promised to take her back home. For Siegfried, that didn't really mean he would stay home. No, he probably would return to the office regardless. She stepped out confident this matter would be resolved quickly. All the secretaries had left (Simon Averardo made them work overtime more than once) and the doors to his very high-tech office were wide open. He waved in his usual distant royal manner and to her surprise, she noticed her husband walking towards her. He took her in his arms as if he had missed her for years.

*"Eh bien mon très Cher, qu'est ce qui te prend, tu vas bien (*Well darling, what's happening to you? Are you well?)" Elizabeth answered his romantic call rather coolly. She greeted their boss in a similar distant manner, somehow like a queen to Simon's kingly approach.

"OK, Simon, this better be worth millions. After eleven, I don't leave the house ever and it's now almost midnight. If it's about the three guys in Florence, I have no news otherwise I would have answered your excessive emailing of the last 24 hours! You know how I loathe repeat emails."

Wow, how about that for starters, Siegfried thought.

"Darling you mustn't be so hard on Simon, he's worked like a maniac on this project and a lot of money, indeed hundreds of millions, has been invested and . . ."

Simon poked in with a very annoyed look on his face. *"Ma chère,"* he said sarcastically, "my dear, the company will save a lot of money by cutting the executive staff by half. I have given it a lot of consideration. Do you realize that Siegfried is almost killing himself for this work?"

She couldn't stand his sleazy fake friendly voice.

"I know, I never see him but just switch the words slightly and you'll say: 'that the work is killing him', Simon, – you worm. And who looks old in this room, you or Siegfried?" She lit a cigarette in a Bette Davis pose.

"Elizabeth, we can fight the rest of the night and neither of us will win. I know you don't care and that I have nobody of your capacities . . . yet! I'm well aware you're still strong in your saddle. But do not play my game of chess!" he threatened. "I repeat, do not make any mistakes like this afternoon," and by now he sounded rather angry.

"Excusez-moi, cet après-midi (excuse me, this afternoon?)" she was now leaning over Simon's desk rapidly blowing a lot of smoke in his face.

"Come on darling," Siegfried intervened, unexpectedly worked up and restless, "you weren't boat-lifted on the Lake I presume, or kidnapped by a terrorist?"

"Aha, right, 'the woman in red'! She was your spy after all." She faked vomiting on the director's desk as she planted both gloved hands on the antique mahogany

"Simon, tu es un être dégoutant. Tu sais ce que je devrai faire? Démissionner à l'instant! (You are disgusting; you know what I should do? Resign right now!)"

Both men jumped up from their seats, flabbergasted at her Wonder Woman display.

"Well, who do you both think I am? A late blooming Mata Hari of the international pharmaceutical stage? My goodness – and you too? *Siegfried tu n'as donc plus de couilles? C'est vrai comme je ne les vois plus, peut-être tu les as également vendues à ton patron* (You have no balls either. True, since I don't get to see them any more you must have sold them to your boss!)"

Siegfried replied in an angry way: "Elizabeth, this is one offense totally uncalled for. Yes, I'm dedicated to my work and to this company and yes, sorry I have neglected you and again, I am sorry, but if this is your way of getting back at me and in front of Simon ... let's rather talk in private, maybe at home, OK?" he whispered in an embarrassed way. Siegfried's boss got more and more twitchy whenever they spoke French too quickly. It wasn't 'his' language and not mastering it made him even more annoyed.

"Home? We'll talk at home. When do you ever get home?" Elizabeth snarled.

Siegfried fired back, "and anyway, who is that man who you seemed to be involved with, so ... *tendrement* (gently) ... to be lying in his arms on a small boat on Lac Léman?" He finally sprang forth, angrily showing her the pictures from that same afternoon.

Elizabeth shrieked. *Oh goodness, he cares and he's jealous. Haha, that's good news, she thought.*

Then she exploded laughing. "Wow, we were convincing after all? *Mon cher, je ne couche pas avec mes employés*, get it?" She turned her head towards Simon, translating with a grin, "My love, I don't sleep with the people I pay. He's our private investigator who was actually doing us a favour and we had a big laughing session as I fell over in the small boat ... nothing more. And if that's it for your inquisition act, I think I'll take a taxi instead of continuing this nonsense of a cross examination."

Simon turned his back to her. He had enough of the circus and wanted answers. But Siegfried wasn't convinced this talk was over. He held her left arm vigorously as he continued.

"And kissing you was a must on his behalf, or did you proceed to seduce him?"

"Cela fait mal, espèce de brute. Let me go. Lâches-moi espèce de bête stupide. Vraiment je ne te reconnais plus (You brute! That hurts! Let me go, you stupid beast. Really, I don't recognize you anymore)."

She lifted her eyes to the immaculate ceiling, an overwhelming copy of an entrance hall in a Medici Palazzo, and pushed him away with the same ardour, as she dropped down in an antique armchair.

"Je ne savais pas que j'avais marié un mec si con, si bête qu'il ne peut pas voire la vérité (I didn't know I married such a jackass, too stupid that he can't see the truth.)" But she wasn't ready to indulge in any of this. In a steaming mood she lifted herself from the Louis XV chair and spoke in a deep kind of voice that could have landed her a Marlene Dietrich part in any movie.

"You are both pitiful. You my husband, soon to be impotent from carrying a cell phone right next to your unused genitals and aging quicker every month from living with a computer as a mistress." She was vengeful and all the knives were out.

"And Simon, I won't discuss your case at all, look at your own broken family and you'll find all the answers you need. Money does not replace family!" She now despised both men as she lit another cigarette.

Goodness, I'm chain-smoking; I better get out quickly. Seems the act is a success.

She proceeded with her dramatic speech.

"Just remember that it is I who made it possible for this company to get off the floor. I've introduced you to the jet-set and the big money. Since last year, all you want is more and more until you drive your own car into a brick wall!"

She took a long inhale and killed the cigarette on a Napoleon III plate, infuriating the man behind the desk even more. At last, she was almost finished, and she just needed to drop her last dagger in his lap.

"After I have heard from *Le Trio* we had to hire, as your former minister had ordered (a man possibly wanted for war crimes and more), you believe he has all solutions?" With her voice clearly injected with venom, she continued, "... after you get the information you, oh so badly need, to make sure you can '*retarder par une dizaine d'années* (to slow down the aging process by a few years)', the 'aging process in the human being' or any other hidden programs, I will, oh yes, I am resigning instantly ... '*espèce de petit Mussolini* (you little dictator')*!*"

She turned her back and took off while Siegfried's face remained frozen. He ran behind her, kicking his foot between the elevator doors just in time. Elizabeth said, "You're not choosing him over me now? Well darling, that is no longer amazing. Love over millions of Euros, *bien sur* (*of course!*) ... Sorry too late. You know I like younger men and you are in deterioration mode it seems, and quicker by the day. Divorcing should become really easy now, for us both."

She squeezed her lips and eyes and her nostrils flared like a dragon. But he pressed his whole weight against her and started kissing her, almost wildly. She pushed against the far wall and the elevator shuddered to an immediate halt.

"Parfait (perfect), a scene from a Hollywood movie. I'm sorry I'm not wearing a mini-skirt; we could recreate 'Bossy Instinct' or whatever that ridiculous movie is that you guys watched over and over."

Siegfried couldn't step back because there wasn't that much room.

"You cannot light a cigarette in an elevator" he said, startled in his scared little boy-like manner. "No, but I will as soon as I get out," and she pulled out the stop button that was stuck. The elevator dropped shakily while her next weapon, a classy lighter magically appeared in her long fingers. A few moments later smoke came from between her teeth while her high heels clicked like clockwork on the marble tiles of that ostentatious entrance hall.

Siegfried looked silly in his summer shorts, open shirt over a tank top, unmatched socks and a pair of 1950's sandals.

"Look at yourself Siegfried, the name of a hero, yet dressed like a teenager in his seventies with bags under your eyes. *Ma parole, des cheveux gras, non lavés* (my word, greasy hair, unwashed ...)." Her nostrils were funnelling tobacco.

"Et ta jeune maîtresse, elle aime ça (And your young mistress, she likes you that way?)"

"That's why you took a detective?" he said, hardly convinced he could now state his case. She thought that was rather smart to shoot an arrow that low. Siegfried said, "That story is too long to explain right now, but I can assure you that it is ..."

"Over? It's over? Oohlala, *Jacqueline t'abandonne pour le patron peut-être* (Jacqueline is maybe leaving you for the boss*?),"* she now chortled like a happy piglet and stepped outside. *Checkmate, she thought.*

Siegfried looked desperate and at the same time he realized how much he still loved his wife. He tried with a renewed passion. "That has been over, yes, for over a month. I wanted to get back to you, explain and start all over. Yet every night I had to fret over this huge project and Simon threatened to tell you about Jacqueline. So, he did tell you? Of course not, your private eye did, right? And you didn't care. I was desperate and then this happened three nights ago during the full moon ..."

Elizabeth had stopped at one of the benches around a monumental metal fountain she always thought incompatible to the stark architecture of the DoWell building. She sat down and while lighting yet another cigarette, she paid attention to his story for the first time in a very, very long time, because even fighting, this was more of a conversation than they had had in months. Siegfried too stopped and there was a glimmer of hope in his eyes that she might listen to his story and so he went on.

"I am glad this has happened, because if I get killed tomorrow, I want you to remember me for loving you, even if I did a terrible job this whole last year."

Somewhat in a pensive mood, she blew the smoke away from her husband as he started his tale of destruction and redemption. "*D'accord, je t'ecoute* (OK, I'm listening to you)." She looked even more pensive.

"It all started about thirteen months ago when we were at the Benderberg meeting in Oslo. Last minute, Simon insisted I would come along. I told him you should go because you're excellent at public relations and you know how I hate these social events. Oh no, I had to meet one of his political friends, one of the great politicians of this last half a century, a man always in the wings. He was acting like a patron to the new project. He explained he was big buddies with the most powerful people in the world and after Oslo, he claimed that everything connected to the project would become easy. For Simon, it did turn out that way because I continued to work like an animal, the real DoWell slave." He stiffened up and she felt sorry … and this time it was real.

"H.K, yes? Harry Khope, one of the worlds' highest-ranked politicians, made Simon feel so important, as if he was to become the new president of a new world government that was being built since the fifties. That man, Harry K, had actually orchestrated some of the greatest hoaxes of our last century. Pharmaceutical wonders would be supported by a new world order where our Simon …" Elizabeth instantly pointed a finger at Siegfried reminding him it wasn't her Simon! "… would head what I'd call the 'the pills and sleepers department'. Billions of sales, a pill for every possible disease you fear you won't get. As we know, the media have been instilling the worst fears for our health. Fear is programmed through more than just the satellites".

Elizabeth briefly hesitated but decided to take his left hand into hers and he put his head briefly on her shoulder before continuing. He was thrilled and felt encouraged while she looked at the cameras installed at the front of the office building.

"In Norway, we got trapped in an unplanned scheme. Yet had I reflected earlier about the trip, it would have been clear that the underlying goal was quite different. It seemed at first a simple luxury snow retreat where the meetings were to be held and where we could ski, snowboard ... you name it and ... relax in the arms of whoever we imagined."

He coughed his way through, embarrassed. "At night that place turned into true pandemonium. I won't describe to you the men and women who were at our disposal. And can you imagine most of them appeared in major motion pictures or glamor magazines! Each one looked like a model some definitely not even sixteen. You know that I have no time to watch television or even look at the newspapers."

He sat back still amazed that he was actually telling the story. She moved a bit closer and there was a light breeze flirting with the sultry summer night.

"Couples came to meet us for after-dinner drinks. I've never seen anything like it. The strangest crowd of either quacks or clones. In any case, they were unreal and yes, they were celebrities straight out of the movies."

He paused. "I tell you Eliza, stars and models like you see on the Academy Awards. The couple that Simon introduced me to, and he was so excited, well they were on that television soap my nieces are addicted to. You know the one where a bunch of graduates all live in the same building. Simon was getting their autographs for his kids. That actor was getting a divorce like a month later and you see him on all the covers with that other brunette with the big lips." He sighed in disbelief of his own story.

"Well, that night, he was in bed with guess who? Simon! Can you believe this, Simon sleeping with that actor? And he isn't even gay ... at least not that I would have ever expected him to be. Before the cocktail party, I had felt rather strange and with my allergy to certain spicy drinks, you may remember ... that night oddly enough, I didn't even touch a glass of wine."

"Oh, how saintly of you," Elizabeth said, trying to break up the tension while she saw his nostrils where catching her cigarette smoke, something he didn't like but was still fine to put up with.

"Well, there I was the only person on water! Water I had to get from the fountain because they didn't serve any. Fortunately, I had taken Apis, the one homeopathic remedy I always carry for my many allergies, thanks to you!" He smiled at her like a teenager on a first date. "And within no time, there was an orgy in every room complete with porn films on walls melting into big life-size screens. Some of the older guys didn't show up at the after-dinner business drinks and we saw none of the teenagers."

By now Siegfried had started perspiring.

"I was so out of touch with the whole scene, and I would not have a part of it, so I walked, like in a daze, through the hotel, finally taking some air in the surrounding park. The next moment I discovered where the big politicians were housed, yes, in private cabins! I walked around and ended up curiously enough, watching while hidden in the bushes. Guess what? Young kids, maybe fourteen, fifteen or younger, like totally drugged, dropped out of the small, yet very de-luxe apartments, I tell you – I was dumbfounded." He continued, "I recognized one of world's greatest conductors, heavy as he was, his head full of boyish curls, buried underneath a small group of real kids!"

He sounded frightened. He was now sweating out the truth in vivid details and Elizabeth watched his every move. She admired him for his almost childish innocence. He hasn't lost it, after all these years, some of him hasn't changed, she thought with a caring smile and let him continue his story.

"Who else was in one of those cabins, you think?" He composed himself, with an air of a long-time hidden detective. "No one less than Harry K. Well, I was so disgusted, and I couldn't get away from the premises … I had no car as we had all been brought by private deluxe buses.

The next afternoon when we finally left, I sat in the back of the company bus and I pulled my hat over my ears even though I wasn't that cold. I didn't speak to Simon till we sat in the sponsored private jet back to Geneva. Well Simon, he claimed he didn't remember anything … just a real bad hangover."

Simon was really convinced of nothing less. He said he had taken that great 'stomach cleaner' they brought us with our breakfasts in bed … everybody seemed to have taken that pill but me, and strangely enough there was no breakfast being served except in the rooms! I was the only one who had chosen the skis over food, grabbing a croissant and coffee at the ski cabin! To play it safe, not trusting the provided meals, I again used plenty of homeopathy and that fulvic acid which does miracles." He now relaxed a bit. "Whatever they all ate or drank, they all had forgotten what had happened!"

"And poor Simon has no idea? … Aha". Elizabeth said while taking out a new pack of 'Organic American Spirit'.

"Do you think they bugged the office you work from? You know that's what they always do in the movies and you never have a private moment.

At the Bistro du Lac this afternoon, *Le Panier au Pain* (the breadbasket), was bugged!"

Siegfried said, "Why would they be watching you and not me. Do you think I'm under suspicion too?" A cold chill ran down his spine.

"Possibly on both of us darling, yes quite possibly," she replied. "He set you up with Jacqueline. Of course he did, that pig. He probably obeys his political friend at all times, and he'll be doing anything to just please him, no? That's Simon's style."

She sighed almost angrily, but satisfied by confirmation from her own husband, Elizabeth continued maliciously; "It was so well planned."

"Everyone now has an 'Oslo story' and the pictures will keep any possible confessions or affirmations regarding the 'work' out of the public media. The newspapers have always been in the hands of the most powerful. Well, they do fight each other, that political elite; jealousy is an old snake even amongst the willing wealthy."

She dropped her silver cigarette lighter and he caught it before it hit the grass. He looked at her and couldn't believe how youthful and beautiful she still looked and he, the younger one, felt worn out by his job and older than his own wife!

Elizabeth said, "They must have been confused not finding anything in their Oslo records on you. And right after that, Jacqueline showed up. I'm now more than ever convinced I will resign, but I cannot act upon my decision right now. It will be too suspicious." She took his hand and he was convinced it was real. Their love hadn't changed.

42. FIORENZA, 1473 LIKE FAMILY

Arouse the unfathomable myriad of universes
deeply hidden in each tiny particle . . .
of my magnificent body (The Void)

While Renaissance minds were buzzing quicker than ever, at the Buontalenti Residence, Florian and GianLuca had very slowly approached one other. The two old friends finally hugged. The electricity in the courtyard was unaccounted for as if a semi-darkness drew in, making them aware of the absence of flashing neon lights. Isabel stood up and swallowed all pride as she softly touched GianLuca.

"Jean-Luc Médecin, tu es vivant. Comment-tu as fait pour arriver ici (You are alive ? How did you manage to get here?)"

All three were clasped tightly in each other's arms. Andrea and Agnola whispered in each other's ears that their house had to be a meeting place for beings from other worlds. Lapo observed his own inner world without judging the world or anyone around him. He held his daughter Fiammetta in his arms, her teary eyes desperate at not belonging to the scene. All through this new and surprising encounter, GianLuca's eyes had hardly left hers as he looked at this fifteenth century family, he felt sad that Fiammetta would never see her dream come true, no matter how deep her feelings for the foreigner, and she wept on her father's ever-present shoulder. When both father and daughter hesitantly started making their way out, GianLuca, in a gentle manner called them back.

"Oh, please my friends do not go away; please allow me to at least explain a few facts. You see I haven't seen this man, Florian, since we were fifteen. We were the closest of friends, actually much more . . . we are family." GianLuca took a deep breath and he continued.

"He would stay with his uncle, a native-American shaman, that is a man who comes from an original tribe where people live in harmony with nature and by nature's laws." He explained in an excited voice, "He knew nature's alchemy well and he taught us a lot of this ancient knowledge. Maybe magic, as you might call it. One day, Isabel came into our home. Both Florian and I befriended her instantly."

Isabel blushed and looked down thinking it all sounded like a historical novel, ready for the big screen staring Dame Judi Dench as the mother and a young Meryl Streep in full historical dress. At least one woman shuffled her robes. GianLuca glanced briefly at Fiammetta as she took a deep breath while Agnola held hers. A cloud of nostalgia invaded his space.

He had softened his voice on the last phrase and smiled freely to Florian, who chuckled. "You don't know but much later I picked up arts studies in Florence and when I majored, my thesis was about de' Medici family and their influence in the world from the Renaissance until the beginning of the twenty-first century."

Andrea, who was now sitting down watching Isabel's reactions with a quickening heartbeat, wondered what it would be like if he could join her in that other world. He admired her as if he had never seen any other striking woman before.

GianLuca had finished rapidly telling his story to his old friends. "I met Giuliano de Medici these past days, and during our conversations we were able to discuss our lives in great depth. These last days, I started to realize that this voyage in time to 1473, brought me a lot of healing for myself and all of our families."

Isabel was startled while Florian felt he could read his thoughts. "You're him, aren't you, Jean-Luc," he asked, as flabbergasted as he was clear. "Giuliano de Medici. He looks just like you too, doesn't he?" Now Isabel sniggered away.

"And your name, Jean-Luc Médecin, or 'de Medici'. When you were almost sixteen there was a picture in the local newspaper of the boy who wanted to live in the mountains away from society. You were looking down, dark hair down to your shoulders just like that Bronzino painting of *Giuliano di Piero de Medici*."

A silence had conquered the room and the effect was cosmic. Lapo and his family had their eyes nervously glued to their celestial houseguests.

"Well, this is truly remarkable because you all came to the year 1473, just to find each other again." Lapo allowed words to escape thoughts that rushed through the history of his own family and those of his children. He admitted though, that his mind remained as confused as his daughter's, but his voice had a festive tone. "I believe this does call for a great meal. I have ordered my finest wines to be served. Of course, GianLuca, your friends are welcome to stay here too. We have plenty of rooms!"

"Thank you dearest Lapo, you have been so good to us all. How can I ever thank you enough, in this life-time?" Lapo dragged his feet towards GianLuca and in a soft-toned voice he asked, "If you could, would you take Fiammetta with you? It would be precious to have you as a son-in-law, although in my heart, I feel that this time around it isn't possible."

"I would like nothing better than to either stay here forever or take your daughter with me," he answered in a kind but diplomatic way.

"Thank you. You would make the finest son-in-law."

And while they all moved towards the dining room, Isabel and Florian were still under the spell of what had just taken place. How did Jean-Luc even get here? There were so many questions and yet so little time.

Isabel said, "We mustn't forget our trio, Florian." She pinched herself in the butt and reminded herself of three human beings they had taken along.

"No, we won't," Florian replied, "and of course, all will end well, you'll see. With Jean-Luc here, and his friendship to the most powerful family in Italian Renaissance history, we will find our trio before dawn. That's for sure!"

Agnola gently took Isabel by the arm and while they proceeded towards the kitchen, Florian wondered if anyone had noticed how striking the resemblance between the two women really was, even if one was much younger and a very sheltered Renaissance woman and Isabel, a bold and a seasoned twenty-first century commander!

43. GENEVA, 2018 SIEGFRIED, ELIZA & SIMON

Peeled away is all of your myth,
your male exuberance that flew me off to other planes.
Where cruel gods resign and reign no piece but only game (Endings)

You know what's going on in that villa in Florence, Elizabeth wondered as she looked at Siegfried. He was staring but his eyes were itching, and he felt ready to fall asleep. She kicked him in the leg and jumped abruptly from the bench. With her hands on her hips, she lifted her voice. "Well, you dump, are you driving me home or must I get a cab!" she called out loudly.

Now that wasn't necessary, Siegfried thought.

At the same time, she muttered in French, *"Joues! Lèves-toi* (Act! Get up). Please act up a storm, fight, follow me and drag me to the car! He's watching you from the camera hidden in the insignia above the entrance door. I always wondered why they had to have the lights on, day and night, especially at that door frame." And she walked away from him, screaming something obscene, so whoever watched their movie, got to hear it loud and clear.

Heading towards the taxi stand further up the road, she briefly looked over her right shoulder and fixed a shoe jammed in a drain. He waited a moment with his head in his hands and then ran behind her. He tried to take her by the arm which she at first, very lady-like, rejected. He opened the car door for her, always the gentleman. A few moments later when he hit the red lights and went through, she laughed.

"Voilà mon héros (there you are my hero)," and she was about to grab him and kiss him on the neck when his cell phone rang. She had turned off her own and the ringing stopped. The car radio popped open and on a little screen it

read; please *pick up now!* Sig, as she called him in emergency cases, pulled over and pushed the answering button. Promptly Simon appeared on the screen.

"So, buddy, still fighting Artemis? I guess you will not be coming back here tonight, except for early divorce papers?" The mocking contempt in his voice was clear. "I'll close your room. See you at the luncheon tomorrow, wear a nice tie for a change and wash that hair and tell your goddess we don't want her to quit! Or alternatively, I'll get you a hot lawyer for the divorce," he laughed. His sarcasm had Elizabeth open the window to let out some more steam. She had nearly swallowed her chewing gum and spat it out imagining it was hitting Simon's face.

The bastard, she thought, a total control freak. The screen turned itself off and Siegfried restarted the car. He put his finger to his mouth. She nodded and made a sign to turn to the left. He was briefly confused and by then she had written on her notebook; Annecy! They picked up their act where they had left off. *"Merde alors, tu ne comprends plus rien, imbécile, arrêtes la voiture* (Shit, you don't understand a thing, you imbecile, stop the car!)," she screamed and tilted her head to the right.

She got out, slammed the door while Sig did the same and when about twenty feet away from the car, she took him in her arms and the kiss that followed had the taste of raw passion.

"You need a good night's sleep, *mon amour*," she said. "We're going to Annecy, to a little hotel. If they haven't bugged all hotels around Geneva, we should be fine right there. He had you sleeping at the office, right, didn't he? Nicely controlled. At his disposal any time of day and night; big money at stake here."

Siegfried nodded. He was really getting tired. He said, "He arranged the back office into a 'studio deluxe'. I just walk into my office … the balcony has a view of the city. He said it was his present, but it's poison. I never leave. Three days ago, I had tried telling you, Simon took me to one of the offices in the basement! Of all places, I didn't even know we had a basement. He told me this was totally confidential.

I joked that I didn't have anybody to even speak to anymore. We walked through a long corridor and I couldn't believe it. We arrived at a door and Simon pressed his palm and brought his left eye close to a lens and the very heavy door opened. We entered a massive open, oval-shaped space. This had been divided into plenty of small compact cubicle offices. At least a hundred people working at PC's and on phones! He took me to a more private vaulted office, like a high-tech crypt."

"Oh *oui*, high-tech, that's him all right!" she relaxed on his arm and while they walked on, he continued telling his tale.

"A very skinny, oriental and sneaky-looking guy sat us down and two screens lit up while the private studio dimmed itself. I was expecting some more pornographic content like in Oslo, but a Renaissance setting on the screen made me doubt it. The scene was similar to one of those majestically costumed ballet productions … remember the *Romeo and Juliet* we had loved with your friend Margot and that Russian dancer?"

She smiled fondly remembering that night's gala performance.

"Simon called the little creep, the Mouse because his political friend had brought him to the project, and he had to live in the basement and work non-stop! So, Mouse pushed a series of buttons … and mine!"

Elizabeth went cross-eyed. *I'm ready for another cigarette she thought, this story sounds endless.* "Mouse belonged to a team that worked on a program to cross the lines of time. He had an impressive background of years in the USA. Montauk was one of the places, he had confirmed, ever so proudly! They were sending some of their own people into … imagine, into other dimensions, other worlds … can you believe it? Have you ever read or heard about the Montauk project?"

"Oui, bien sûr (Yes, of course)," she responded dryly. Years earlier, Simon had her research all possible information about this New York State based *'secret d'état* (State secret)' and how and why master magician Alistair Crowley got involved.

"Remember that amazing movie; *The Philadelphia Experiment?*" Siegfried asked.

"Mr Khope's government has apparently been at it since WWII. In other words, we've been aware of parallel worlds, crossing timelines and how to move back and forth for quite a bit longer than the last century. We know shamans and magicians had such knowledge without electronic devices. And that's what they are after, not this cover-up operation of pharmaceuticals. Even if they want to make billions selling unnecessary product, in the end it's all a hoax. Simon wanted me to lead one of the missions! Like I'm the heroic type!"

He said he was sending off a trio to look for some ancient codes of primary importance in that Medici Villa in Fiesole."

"As I already knew," she answered. "We'll talk more tomorrow! Here's tonight's scenario; we'll check into the hotel and while we're driving, we'll finish our scene in case your car's also bugged. After all, it's a DoWell car so it probably is! If he asks you tomorrow, tell him you dropped me off at a friend's place, like at Françoise des Farouches, we see her for lunch anyway and you can tell Simon you were so tired after our fight you fell asleep in the car... it's certainly big enough. I wonder what he thought of when he got you this expensive Japanese car. Oh right, another present from Khope?"

"Yeah! You know what he thought of?" he replied. He held her close to him and he was hoping he was up to it, because for the first time in ages, he really wanted her, and it excited them both despite being tired. He felt happy like he hadn't for years.

"*Je t'aime Elizabeth* (I love you)." And she finally looked him straight in the eyes with more empathy than she had felt for him since, well, she couldn't remember. When they got in the car, the front and back leather seats melted into one and so did, in all silence, the couple.

At the DoWell office

Simon Averardo checked the audio systems connected to Siegfried Freundreich's residence. He loved having all of the control at his fingertips. At least HT (high-tech) was still his best friend. He knew Elizabeth always left on some classical music for the plants and the cats. Whenever he thought of her, he shrugged, and he pondered about her resigning. Maybe it was better; after all she was always resisting and questioning his decisions, and just like his own mother had been, she was far too strong.

Oh, he loathed women telling him what to do. He hated altogether that anyone resisted his beliefs and contradicted them. Just like that man in the White House who claimed he had no collusions with foreign powers. He had admired him as a perfect example of dictatorial power. He didn't have any ambitions to be in any government and why would he? With Dr Khope, he was having the best chances ever. Privately unhappy yes, for he seemed to have married someone just like his own mother! And this wife gave him only daughters – not even a son he could teach and groom to be just like him, in total control.

He looked in the only mirror in the office, always annoyed at his own mediocre appearance. Once again, he could blame his mother. Indeed, a pretty woman she had been, but hardly five feet two; it left him with a smallish and un-impressive size. Although his father was a handsome six feet two, he still ended up way too small, just five eight. It made him look younger and he had hated being treated like an infant in his late teens. Sometimes he really, really disliked women, but he didn't like sleeping with men. He just wanted to be as athletic and handsome as a movie star. At the gym every morning, he worked like a maniac; his abdominals a washboard, his pectorals dry muscle. When Jacqueline came to the office, she surprised him with a new inventive seduction number at each visit, as delicate as in his favourite TV soap, and his youthful looking body would turn her on. At least so she told him, and he liked to believe her.

At home, he hardly showed up and his wife called him a cold fish. In a way it was true. One day he would be one of the most powerful leaders in pharmaceuticals, thanks to his friend HK or Uncle Harry as he had been allowed and honoured to call the great man. He giggled at all the abbreviations or nicknames he had made up for those people who were but pawns on his own chessboard. Uncle Harry was the king, and in his game, Simon knew he was but a runner. It scared him, but he felt confident that he was cut of his preferred wood.

Uncle Harry had even gifted him with a unique present: Jacqueline. He told him she was there for him only and to 'inspire' him while working on the project. What a gift ... full of imaginative moves. But then again who else could afford to offer this office building as a cover-up for one of the greatest operations of this new century: time travel research and not just the virtual version!

Different screens were blinking, images popping up, others fading away erratically but still, there was nobody at the Freundreich's residency. He grew a bit annoyed. They must be home by now. He worried while attentively watching one of the screens light up. But only Siegfried's Persian cat, 'Dragon', stared into the camera hidden in the smoke alarm where the claws didn't reach the eye. Harry K certainly had the most up-to-date techno gems installed and Simon loved it.

"Damn! Where are they? It's almost 2:00 am and they should be home by now," he screamed to an imaginary audience. He checked the radio control system, but all seemed silent. Had he imagined a click of a door being opened? He looked at the other screen where 'Dragon' was still delightedly licking his feet. Next, a seductive voice, not from any screen, meowed its way in.

"Is that what you'd like me to do, Simon, lick your feet?" Jacqueline said, slithering slowly out of the dark entrance and adding a bit of frisson to Simon's high-tech investigations.

"That's a creepy intrusion, Jacky. How did you get past security? Even if you came from the basement the monitors are on and ..." and his blood started boiling.

"Simon, I'm not alone and famous people always make a surprise arrival. *En plus, mon cher*, Robert at the security desk does know me. After all, I'm the woman everybody talks about in this building. Rumours are we're lovers Simon ... is that so?" she teased.

By then a strangely handsome man appeared from behind her and took off his sweater while she slipped out of her tiny dress. It revealed her gorgeous body, dressed in black stockings ending at a classic garter belt. She stepped in a spotlight meant for one of the original Egon Schiele paintings Simon had collected during his years as CEO. He sat back in his office chair and admired her guts and the unparalleled surprises only she was able to invent. She had all his attention and he forgot momentarily he had been spying on his own staff.

But as in some jazzy Broadway show, two hands firmly grabbed her breasts, then circled her waist, holding her up while she slid down on the abstract Picasso-inspired carpet. Simon's heart sped up. He couldn't see the man's face, but he seemed familiar; his Oslo-visit came to mind.

"Wanna watch us, Simon? I'll let you know when it's your turn. Just let Bill show you, he has so much experience!" And she moaned, purred and purred. The athletic man called Bill, had buried her head in his unzipped pants; they dropped to the floor. Her eager hands slowly caressed an impressive manhood. Then in a split second she thrust this between her lips while Simon failed to get a grip on his own, envious desire ... she then crawled towards a red and white checkerboard carpet, while Simon found himself flustered by that entirely staged seduction scene. Two perfect bodies were dancing in front of him.

Oh my goddess, Simon thought. Of all places in my office; this is like the beginning of . . . what?

During the last year, his secret liaisons with this woman had made his wildest dreams come true. In dreamscapes of some of his craziest new addictions, Jacky had grabbed Simon's hidden truth from his loins since their first lakeside dinner. Her well-thought-out set-up was a success and Simon had walked straight into the mouth of the lioness. With some of the money made on some fishy deals, he had bought a luxury two-bedroom apartment, a rooftop hideout in a classy building close by the Lac Léman.

Month to month, he moved into her newly created wor ld as if starring in a permanent porn-movie version of his own life. Forgotten scenes would re-emerge in his mind, layering himself over his daily reality. His latent fear of being controlled faded away in these highly charged encounters. Each one jolted him to alertness as some of the memories, buried for decades, resurfaced. Anything that re-emerged from his youth was a complex reminder of a painful family history of scary experiments of an early slavehood. His father had sold his son to the highest bidder and for the first fifteen years of his life, more than one member of his male elite had abused young Simon, while his mother was sent off on luxury shopping sprees.

At each inflicted adventure, he escaped into one of his many personalities until an early marriage with his teenage sweetheart, arranged by Simon's family with an eye to appearances, altered his track. With a loving young spouse under the age of twenty-one, he found the therapy he needed to balance his life. From the many years of dissociation, he had flipped the coin into a brilliant career in business and management, following a university PhD. During the time his two children were growing-up, life seemed easy and traditionally oriented with holidays in expensive ski resorts and Mediterranean boat cruises. But then his relations with the 'rich and famous' took him to their lifestyle and so he accepted to become one of them, just like his father had wanted him to be. He met Jacqueline at one of her movie's premieres, surrounded by her glamorous co-stars, including a strangely handsome man described as her half-brother.

Yes, Jacqueline was stunning, and she had been well trained in the grand art of seduction. Seduction was a craft and she had only learned from the best. First her father had trained her, apparently encouraged by his brother, uncle Harry Khope himself. Eventually her own private teacher, Harry took her from Disneyland up to his own sheets, wrapped like a brave twelve-year – old girl in a magician's hands. Tonight, Jacqueline's eyes shone with startling complicity as if she had brought her favourite child more toys to play a game, he soon wouldn't be able to control. Just like her uncle had gently insisted for her to proceed tonight. She would never refuse any of his demands.

Tonight, behind his desk, Simon had quickly turned off the computer. His pants off, he grabbed some poppers out of the bottom drawer. The Apollo-like figure pulled back from Jacky's mouth and Simon's eyes jumped out of his head. He screamed for her to finish Bill off and get on her knees, like a dog. But in a barefooted sprint Bill had reached Simon, pushing him violently against the wall. Between the huge windows, right under the illuminated painting of a vibrant Hercules, Bill asked his willing victim, "Simon, where do you want me to start? You have a cute butt!"

The entire scene took him back to some locker room orgy, nothing Greek nor Olympic to win a medal! Simon looked at Jacqueline who lit a cigarette, slowly sagging into the dark red cotton couch, selecting snow-white lines of the most expensive coke. The new game-player got Simon more bewildered by the second, ripping off Simon's shirt, his huge hands crawling upwards pressing all his fingers deep in the eager flesh.

A legion of little hairs on Simon's neck stood up in hopeless self-defence as Bill's lips softly closed onto Simon's open mouth. He abandoned all logical thinking as all three swiftly sniffed the two remaining white lines from the table. Jacky sank further into the couch.

Simon imagined a rattle that didn't come from a snake; perhaps an unanticipated tail wrapping itself around the easy prey he had become? Jacky pushed his face into the cocaine, got up and then opened the huge glass door behind them. Nothing could keep Simon from merging with this unknown god-like figure as he got pushed down on both his knees. He shuffled, ending up on the balcony. He was breathing in all of that male odour, feeling weaker within Bill's muscular forearms just strangling him. He was ready to abandon all resistance when a familiar longish nail flirted with the inside of his right nostril and while she closed off the left, he inhaled so strongly that it seemed to have entered his brain.

Jacky was again beside him, shining, dreamy, her breasts grimacing to his absence of comprehension. Below, in his belly a new flickering painting came to life. Her fingers disappeared in her own heavenly port. He pinched her nipples, his mouth begging for hers. Simon nearly collapsed with his face down while Bill penetrated him violently. He cried out in pleasure and pain while Jacqueline's nails drew red lines from his shoulders to his hips and her small auburn curls rubbed his nose. The curve in his back shaped the way for Apollo's next arrow. A white snow avalanche came down on him from ethereal skies while her hands covered his ears and her tongue whispered, he could now let go of the denial, ... that he too was reduced to being a sex slave.

His groaning proved his deepest bliss. The perfume of a long-suppressed quest warmed all his senses. He gazed in the over-sized Roman mirror and just then, he recognized the picture he wanted to see one day could only manifest like an Oscar Wilde hero. It had Dorian Gray written all over it.

Below the balcony window, Jacqueline watched Bill. She had venerated her timeless partner in crime from the day she found out they were half-siblings. She now slipped into the warmth of the river that ran down his back as in a long-foregone caress. Bill smiled as he gently laid her head on his lap and she crawled up and wrapped herself around him. Simon had passed out and little did he know this night might never end.

Bill put a pillow under her head and while Jacqueline fell asleep, he turned on the computer to check if the security cameras had captured the last hour. The images were harsh, and he made sure they were saved in the system. He sent them off before he closed off the PC. He slouched to a hidden door that led to a private bathroom. Moments later he was covered with lavender foam and he relaxed in the huge bathtub.

Nearby, his cell phone rang, and a happy smile came to his face. "Uncle H, yes, all went really well, she's resting," he said in an upbeat voice, "and the footage is very convincing. Simon could well become a coke-head, but I think I will easily become his prime addiction." They both laughed. He bathed in congratulations and nearly dozed off till the magic of the bubble bath endorsed no higher consciousness.

44. FIORENZA, 1473 BARGELLO

Turning pages on the story that called for love,
Fairly recent, before more viruses
made their home in your belly,
in your heart and now your brain
as you can lose yourself in the full passion
of the ninety-nine messages in your multi-coloured cell. (Turning Pages)

There was no way to describe a dinner as luscious as the one they just had been presented. The time traveling troubadours had forgotten their own more vegetarian twentieth-first century approach to food ... the abundance of meat, fresh from yesterday's hunted boar, roasted for a nearly a full day with herbs and a wealth of vegetables, served with that unique fruit *composta* (mashed fruit) and then the local wine; a delight, Isabel and Florian both agreed.

"At home, nobody will ever believe we drank a 1472 Chianti Classico," Florian told the lovely Agnola sitting to his right. The joke was not understood. The other travelers at the table heard the remark and smiled. They exchanged silly stories that took them back to their high school days, unwittingly forgetting the actual timeline. Their hosts were once again fascinated. Florian was briefly lost in Agnola's big eyes and for a moment he didn't want to leave this Italian Renaissance.

"We have a rather useless but very popular tradition on our timeline," Florian said out loud. "For entertainment, we go to theatres, sometimes these are beautiful old buildings the size of your Signoria or even your palaces. We may see big performances of dancers, singers, musicians but more and more our families like to watch 'television'." They all looked puzzled when hearing the word 'television'. Florian continued, "It's a device that produces images as if you would look at a painting come alive, or you would see the story from a book materialize 'live' in front of you. We actually sit in front of a simple metal-framed box and inside all the actors are alive and talking, on a smaller scale that is."

"I'm not sure what you mean... maybe like a painting come to life?" Fiammetta asked, "Is it like a play with actors in costumes from another time similar to a Greek tragedy?"

"Yes, in a way it is; how very clever of you," GianLuca answered and Fiammetta shyly smiled.

"It is almost as if you would be a part of it," Florian continued," From this active device where you can also see what has happened yesterday in another part of the world!" She looked confused. "But a painting that has come to life is indeed a close description, I could not have found a better description," he confirmed avoiding more intricate details she wouldn't understand. "Only in our world people are reading less and less and are addicted to this kind of *'divertimento'*; they may watch a different 'play' or 'story' sometimes day and night and they end up living as in a permanent sleep," Florian said.

Isabel added, "and of course they have such tools" as both GianLuca and Isabel put down their cell phones and watches on the table. Lapo and Andrea wanted to know more and almost grabbed them to check them out, but they put them back down immediately.

"These are, well they seem to have a titillating feeling to them," Lapo said in a childish way that made his daughters smile.

"Oh yes they do," Florian intercepted, "and they tickle your brain so strongly you can go mad if you're not well-protected. In this dimension these have no effect."

GianLuca showed his phone devoid of sound and he briefly explained the necessity of a network based on 'electricity', another unfamiliar word in their century.

"Yet, our watch," Isabel said picking up her bracelet, "does have some magic to it because it is actually set for 1473 and let's say if you, Andrea would have the same one, we could talk to each other from another city or country!"

They had stunned the entire Buontalenti family, and Lapo mentioned that he regretted that their friend Marco Farini wasn't with them to experience these rarities.

"Our friend Marco, whom you met," Lapo pointed at GianLuca, "former astrologer to the Vatican, told us last year that our own Leonardo was secretly inventing tools for the pope's highest office and for the monarchy, with the sole goal of conquering other countries. He is an inventor you know, not just a gifted artist or painter. No doubt in the future many talents like 'da Vinci' will appear."

"Well, that was very well said, *caro Lapo*, and you are so right," GianLuca interrupted.

"Indeed, da Vinci will become one of the greatest engineers, and century after century man will develop techniques that will lead to the most amazing discoveries and we are now close to forgetting the original human being's reason for this voyage on planet earth."

"Now we are getting somehow to a subject I do respect highly," Fiammetta challenged in a very convincing voice and a most dignified way.

"For what reason have we come to this 'Terra'?" She smiled at GianLuca, a smile that would forever entice. "And the answer to the un-asked question is 'love' isn't it my dearest GianLuca?" she said with a flirtatious look in her eyes.

"It is indeed and maybe that's why we are all here. Today, we can certainly feel such a beautiful frequency, one of love and friendship," he answered as he turned his head towards Isabel and Florian, who could only nod.

"Was it that way in Careggi yesterday?" Andrea asked, shyly regretting he hadn't been asked to attend.

"Yes, it was, *caro Andrea*. I can only confirm that between those brothers there's an exceptional rapport. We had some wonderful exchanges. I will help them during the time I'm here." GianLuca smiled.

"You told him, didn't you?" Agnola feared. "Giuliano knows that chances are he may die very young, I dreaded it all along," and tears popped from her young eyes. Isabel approached her with sweet and motherly gestures.

"Yes," GianLuca continued, "I explained the course of history as we have come to know it from our history books. Yet also, how it could be reversed if we chose to? Of course, when you offer life instead of death there's a price to pay and the heart is a major player!"

Florian and Isabel had followed the conversation, slightly unsure what was actually being discussed, but as GianLuca spoke about the 'brothers', they guessed it was about the Medici.

"So, you know them well, Lorenzo and Giuliano?" Florian asked his old friend.

"Probably a little better than they would like me to, although they do not really understand that. But yes, Giuliano especially has confided in me in a very profoundly intimate way," he confirmed. Then Florian continued, "We were just wondering if you could ..."

"Get an autograph?" GianLuca joked and they all laughed, though again, the Buontalenti didn't know exactly why they laughed.

"Oh yes, I'd like to forge a check from one of their banks and make a deposit in my Renaissance savings account" Florian joked.

"Well, actually we need some help because we have three characters who are working with us and they're lost somewhere around the city," Isabel said as she opened her device while everybody at the table paid close attention and even Giovannino had drawn closer with big open eyes. When she had it ready and the little screen lit up, they all backed up breathless.

"A piece of devilish magic, isn't it?" Andrea now laughed.

"No nothing like that at all," Isabel answered while showing him the device. Andrea didn't know what to think when he saw that his own image was frozen like a painting, hardly bigger than a medallion. His father and siblings all rushed around him, equally stunned.

"You see the image is now you, and if don't store it, it disappears." She showed him how and her photo gallery caused equal admiration. "This is one of the many functions because its capacities are manifold, like to call people up and speak to them or leave *un messagio (*a message) on their own device."

They were all stunned at Isabel's explanations and mini voyage into these foreigners' world. "We can see ourselves over a long distance and have a conversation!" Florian took Andrea by the arm and he called Isabel from the other side of the courtyard. Andrea remained frozen as he saw her wave from afar, and on the little screen. His sisters ran over and back and forth and laughed and joked like little schoolgirls.

She understood why they were all speechless at a possible future technology 540 years ahead. The sisters were voicing their surprise so loudly and remarks about Kublai Kahn, Marco Polo, inventors from Far East, boats, travels in time and Venice, were all mentioned in one long breath. Lapo joined them and tried to calm them down.

Isabel continued her explanations and her male friends looked each other in the eyes, thinking that they would soon be having a workshop on inter-dimensional traveling. But she continued. "Now let us say Florian has a similar device ... we call it a phone ... and he's at the market-place and he has forgotten his shopping list; well imagine that I can communicate and actually speak to him and remind him to buy the right vegetables!"

"Oh, don't do that," Agnola exclaimed "if somebody sees or hears this, they'll report you and you'll be thrown into the bargello, in a dark cell with walls so thick and people often even die in there ... " While Isabel laughed affectionately, Agnola's remarks rang a bell.

"Oh, my goddess! That must be it," Isabel said laughingly. "Maybe that's where our trio have landed. You called it what? The Bordhello?"

The whole table shook with laughter. "Hell no," GianLuca joined the giggling.

"No, no," Andrea explained. "The *bargello* is a complex building where they jail dangerous individuals or those who may threaten the society."

"Yes indeed," Florian intervened, "and in our century, it has become a fabulous museum full of Michelangelo works."

"Oh really?" Andrea looked surprised once again

I remember Lorenzo talking about someone of his own age by that name. A sculptor or was he a painter? Andrea contemplated silently.

"Why do you expect your friends may have been recognized? Foreign travelers with dubious intent thrown in jail?" his father said.

"You see," Isabel continued, "they are supposed to answer with this, ugh little box, well, the 'phone', this kind of 'speaking tool' and I haven't been able to contact them. Maybe because they are locked up." All eyes remained attentive and stunned. The sisters looked at each other with big question marks in their eyes.

"They remain silent and they may well be closed up between heavy walls. There the walls are quite a bit thicker at the *bargello*, so no, you cannot hear a thing and you won't get any connection at all," GianLuca said.

"GianLuca?" Giovannino suddenly spoke up.

"Questo edificio ha pareti molto spesse. Una volta ho dovuto fare visita ad uno zio molto lontano. Era orribile. Una volta che sei dentro in non puoi più uscire. (Yes,

this building has very thick walls; I once had to visit a distant uncle. It was horrifying. Once you're in, there's no way out)."

His teary eyes caught everyone's attention. So Lapo intervened, "I will do one thing immediately, because we're not very far from the *bargello*, I will send our Giovannino to find out if any foreigner was picked up by accident." Before he turned around to look for his page, the teenager closed into his master. He affirmed having understood the matter with few words and off he went through the backdoor into the garden and into the street.

"Before nightfall we will know!" Lapo confirmed. "And no doubt through Giuliano and Lorenzo we'll be able to free them easily, that is if that's where they are!"

Isabel felt relieved.

"See how easy? It's like dining at Fisherman's Wharf; you can see the island of Alcatraz," Florian said. Lapo graciously got up after a final Vino Santo and GianLuca toasted once again their generous hospitality.

"My dearest friends," he said to Andrea and his father. "How I would love for you to join us in 2018! At present, it will be impossible to invite you to come along. I'm confident that Florian, who on our timeline is a bit of a genius, will maybe be able to get me back home." A sudden sadness had invaded the two faces in front of him and a long silence followed. "But it doesn't exclude that we will be able to communicate in our dreams."

"When do you think this will happen? Is your return that imminent?" Andrea asked while glancing at Fiammetta who had turned her back to them.

"Well, it will depend if we can get their friends back to our world, for if they're in prison it may take a few days. I read in our history books that to get out of *bargello* isn't easy, although no doubt Lorenzo . . ."

"That will be the least of your problems, I promise you. Even if you weren't linked so closely to Giuliano, I can promise you that papa or I will get a foreigner out of jail especially when based upon a mistake, which no doubt it is."

GianLuca wanted to continue but Giovannino had rushed in and the kid, (out of breath) showed both thumbs up!

"Due uomini, arrivati proprio ieri sera (Two men only arrived last night)." the kid shouted out with a proud, big smile.

Andrea told the three foreigners not to worry as he quickly drafted a note explaining in few words that two friends of their houseguests were briefly visiting and had been admitted by mistake to the *bargello* and they needed to be released immediately.

"GianLuca, you mentioned the brothers were staying at Careggi tonight?" Andrea said as he rolled the paper and put it in a thin container.

"Yes, Poliziano was joining them this afternoon," GianLuca confirmed while he noticed a tall young man being called by Lapo. He and his son spoke to him in a quiet voice and within minutes he was riding one of their horses and on his way to the Careggi residence of the illustrious brothers.

"Thank you, Isabel and Florian will really appreciate this," GianLuca said as he came up to Lapo and they fell into each other's arms without any inhibition. The older man especially felt moved to tears.

"Would you say there isn't any way at all... any way at all, a chance you may see us again? You said the other night that you knew our souls leave this body behind and then the game goes on and continues? How long? Can we actually foresee our next life?"

"*Caro Lapo* (dearest Lapo), you can plan the next life ever so carefully by taking care of this one in full confidence and honesty, as you are doing daily. You are a truly good man, so just be healthy as you have the great fortune of living in this amazing Tuscany, and you are inspired by your highest guides who sit on your shoulder day and night!"

They all smiled as GianLuca gazed at them. It was as if this was now truly a long lost and found family. So GianLuca proceeded, "When you know the time has come to leave this world and you can be with your family, tell them your deepest hidden story." He stopped and looked at Andrea who listened with his usual scholar-like attention. And GianLuca continued, "The day you leave, you gather your loved ones close to you and you remind them of all the good times you had together.

"You remind them that you will only leave this body behind and you will join other worlds, the field of existence if you will, and maybe even choose to return to this world or play another role in the ethers, say, maybe in a parallel world. You'll see the exit towards that light is magnificent and once you have moved on without fears and worries into a higher dimension, you will see how easy it all will be!"

"Can we join him later on?" Andrea insisted immediately while turning to his father.

"You know Lapo," GianLuca said, "it has been known that there have been a wide variety of contacts. This life is only a passage and we are like actors in a grand comedy or tragedy that unfolds, depending upon our beliefs! The continent called Africa where you just visited, I believe you traveled to Egypt?"

Lapo nodded, still attentive. "Well, when you travel south, deep inside Central Africa, way below the place where the Nile is born, you will come across an indigenous race. Like those on many other continents (not yet discovered), their elders live with the knowledge that these gods came from a star system known as the Pleiades, a kind of universal university ... and a gateway for many of the souls who would come to earth to play ... The Game."

"Well now, bravo *Monsieur le Professeur* (Sir, Professor)," Isabel interrupted with a broad smile as she stepped into the courtyard. "He's right, *gentile uomini* (gentlemen)."

She hooked GianLuca's arm while holding onto Florian's, "and before we leave, we'll make sure you have a lot more information to digest, for now," Isabel warned, "you only need to cope with the Officers of the Night!"

And GianLuca brought more information on: "In less than a century the Vatican will create more horrors ... like the Inquisition. You'd rather be absent from those decades, for all the beliefs from our lives that we have shared with you will be called diabolic!"

Isabel added, "Those 'holy' accusers are actually living in the seat of all evil. It's like they are fed by it, yet this is another very long story and an intricate one!"

"Oh goodness, Isabel what are you saying?" Agnola asked in a very scared voice.

Florian gently interrupted, "Do not worry dear friends, we will give you some more revealing facts from your near future before we leave this home and thank you, once again, for your hospitality."

"We really would like to give you three some space, for you have much to talk about, no doubt?" Agnola said, with a joking pout on her lips as her brother took her by the hand.

"We will all see you for the morning meal and you'll have more answers, no doubt," Andrea said. "*Amici,* please do not thank us, for once again we are truly happy and honoured by your enlightening visit."

Fiammetta smiled, and after a short series of emotional embraces, she joined her family, leaving their new friends, the time travelers to their own stories. With the stunning neckline of a supermodel, she glanced over her shoulder and at least one man's eyes were meeting hers, while another female time traveler admirably looked upon her beauty.

45. ANNECY & GENEVA 2018 GERMAINE, JACKY & BILL

The grace of grazing rumination
of my absent pensive mind,
wistful muse to your yearning heart, you child aghast. (Worded Scent)

'*I say a little prayer for you*' Aretha Franklin sang out boisterously. It was a recording made with the Royal Philharmonic and Elizabeth loved it enough to have the whole album on her cell phone. At the French border, in this fine but smallish hotel in Annecy, hardly beyond the French border, Elizabeth and Siegfried had not slept much. After a year of living like strangers they had found their old passion and she pondered if sex would continue to get better with age. She covered her mouth wanting to laugh out loud when she detected the shorts and the sandals in the corner of the room.

She knew the best thing to do was to buy him a new shirt and a pair of slacks of the same size. He certainly had lost weight, she thought. Eliza didn't need heroic muscle tone and she liked her man just as he was. Her hand reached for the cigarette case; but instead, she stopped, tenderly caressing his thick mop of hair.

She drew the sheet to cover his body spread out on the bed and wrapped herself in his free left arm. When the Annecy church bells woke her up too few hours later, he hadn't moved. She slipped into a lukewarm bath and started planning a summer's day that would not exclude loving her husband again and again.

Geneva, The DoWell Office

But on the top floor of the DoWell offices, there wasn't just one body spread out. That tempestuous night had created chaos where three bodies had landed in some very odd positions. The place looked like an island afte a tsunami where the CEO had somehow finished his nightly adventures wrapped in a very pricey carpet at the front door. With the arrival of the company's official cleaning woman, *Directrice du Sanitaire* (Director of Sanitary department) as Germaine had demanded to be called, punctually at 7:00 am as always, she stood in front of a closed door. Slightly annoyed that she couldn't get in, she tried a few numbers from her company cell phone database, but nobody answered. As the alarm system in the apartment was still on, she had to go back down to the main entrance and demand that the doorman call up.

"I swear I didn't see Mr Averardo come in. This last week he's been out late and in around 10, not like Mr Freundreich who doesn't seem to leave the offices anymore, apart from last night when his wife came around," the doorman said, before continuing in a secretive mode, "Mr Freundreich has had a visitor over, at times and she..."

"I know, I know, that woman most of the time dressed in red with a figure like a night club dancer, right? He has the studio apartment and I always see him working!" She already had a half-used cigarette between her lips. "I think Mr Averardo is the one working on her, *la salope* (the bitch), if you ask me. Haven't you heard the CEO doesn't see his wife anymore?"

She did enjoy the gossip. "So why don't you call up and check who's doing who?"

She pounded on the grey metal desk, "You never know... someone's up there and I haven't got all day!" The doorman called and after several rings... a female voice answered that the doors would open in an hour. Not to the doorman's surprise, the cleaning woman threw a fit and went straight back into the elevator, continuously pushing the top floor button.

Germaine banging the front door made not a penny of difference to a Jacky not yet awake, who simply continued to clean her face in the bathroom with the most expensive miracle cream. She picked a stretchy dress hidden in Simon's closet for unexpected events... well like this one, she laughed.

"Williaaaaam," she cried out loud. No, she wasn't sure what to do with her William (ah Bill, I do love your original name, so much better) and then called out something nasty to the other extra body, Simon. But Simon hadn't moved. By now Germaine had started a full attack on the fortress and Jacky found nothing better than to push Simon sideways from the carpet, his naked butt hitting the cold marble. "Ouch," he moaned.

"Sorry Simon, about this funny wake-up call, but your cleaning woman is in front of your door and you're just going to have to answer from a different position than your top ten from last night!" she giggled. Germaine had her ear glued to the door. She got it and it was obvious there was more than one voice. She was so furious and ready to break into the entrance hall like a tornado when Jacqueline finally unlatched the lock and Germaine violently pushed her way in just as Mr Averardo, her employer, held up the 'Full Monty'! From behind her thick glasses, the director of upkeep's eyes bounced back and forth.

"Well, have you ever ..." and she ran out disgusted.

"Who was that?" the voice on the other carpet behind the authentic Louis XVI sofa, squeaked.

"Oh, my head, it hurts so badly!" Simon complained, slouching to the bathroom and returning wearing a beach towel around his hips. "She saw me, didn't she? And what about him; did she see him? Germaine is the biggest gossip bitch you'll ever meet." And he pointed at Bill while he desperately looked for more of what Bill had given him the night before.

"No, our Apollo was still on his carpet, brave as he is, he didn't fly off. Don't panic Simon, he can have you again and again, ha-ha! My cherries!"

Neither of the men was in the mood for a joke. They both looked at her in a more or less disapproving way ... no sunny humour on the horizon, not yet.

"Coffee, of course. That will do it and we have that smug little NosPresso machine in that adorable little kitchen of yours." She smiled and went to make a triple espresso ... hers a decaf.

Not good ... all that acid in my stomach, she thought. I soon have got to get back to my green drinks.

When she opened the bathroom door, she shut it immediately. Simon was in another deep embrace and Bill didn't do anything halfway, especially not on a hip level. After about fifteen minutes she heard the shower run. Her cell phone sang its usual tune and she picked it up. 'The Rose' was a song programmed in her head like in a Manchurian answering mode. Her voice turned slightly robotic, a bit like a tiny Barbie doll in Disneyland.

"Hello Uncle Harry, yes all is well, and it was wonderful as usual. Yes, it's all on tape and Bill was amazing. Yes, he is now in the shower with Simon. I think they've fallen in love. It is so funny. Oh, I'm so glad you're pleased".

The voice congratulated her on a job well done. The 'uncle' also confirmed, that she was still his number one little girl and that he would soon have another assignment for her with Siegfried, since she had prepared the terrain well. She thanked him in a childish and very polite voice, and he ended the conversation.

She rubbed her eyes and took a deep breath. For a moment she felt totally at a loss. Still with the phone in her hands, she looked around the room. She felt ditsy and it took her a while to get back to earth. She opened the balcony door and shook her hair in the morning breeze. And how very strange, she thought looking at the cell phone in her hand. Still slightly warm, she saw the last incoming number and yes, she had answered. But now she didn't remember a thing. The air felt good and the open sky was a clear blue ocean smiling at her. The bathroom door opened with a fanfare and with Bill's deep voice requesting food.

"Sorry, we got stuck in the shower; anything to eat except Simon?" he popped up with Mickey Mouse vocals. Simon toddled behind him like a little duck and got onto Bill's lap. She didn't recognize the man. Loud and macho as he usually was, he now behaved like some sixteen-year-old.

"Hand me the phone will you Jacky, I'm going to cancel all my appointments today. I've worked too hard these last months," Simon almost begged Jacky.

"You mean while Siegfried worked like a maniac and you sat behind your desk watching him on your screen?" she grunted, imitating the way Simon judged everybody else all day long.

"Did you both have any clothes on when you walked in last night?" Simon asked.

"Don't be stupid," Bill joked, "we're just really good at taking them off."

"Do you do a lot of these trio numbers because I could help you make a fortune?" she laughed, "Although, I will be very jealous if I'm not that third party. That was the best sex I have ever had." He took Bill's head in his hands and Bill kissed his palms.

Jacqueline reminded Simon the cleaning woman was about to come back any second and she threw Bill pants and shirt from the couch.

"Let me show him Siegfried's studio. Sig wasn't in last night," Simon told Jacky.

But Jacky unexpectedly opened a door, well hidden in plain sight. She dangled the remote control in front of Simon's startled eyes. How did she even know about the door, let alone the remote? Simon was stunned but her sexy posture took him to another level, right below her waistline.

"Well now, it's all very '007' isn't it?" Bill threw a last kiss at his new lover, and as in a magic act he disappeared.

The sliding door looked like a stunning David Hockney painting of a swimming pool as it closed behind him in a very soft way. Digital of course ... well, with Simon you never know, he loved technology. With cameras in every corner, Simon was able to control it all. On the other side of the Hockney, a stunning Kenneth Nolan, a triple-coloured painting was equally arresting. Bill took a look up close. Damn, he said, another original! He took a not so little golden gadget out of his pocket, ready to check his messages.

Meanwhile, in the main office, Jacky had closed the balcony door and lowered the venetian blinds. She was curious as to what her William was up to and she peeked in. For a moment she watched him in that familiar posture where he straightened up and answered the phone call, in a dry, very polite voice. She knew it was the 'uncle of all uncles' – and she had befriended many – checking up on his nest ... *he cares for us like his own children; we're so lucky.* When the monologue stopped, Bill turned around and acted like the Bill everyone knew, a real hot Aries with a Leo ascendant, ready for all action, entrances and exits. He saw Jacky smiling while she slowly moved herself into the room.

"Look at me ... the boss was most pleased. He said I could take a month off and even stay with Simon if I liked him. He told me that Simon was an old friend. He added jokingly that he had been waiting for him, like forever, to get out of the closet. He did ask not to make it obvious in public, so we may go to the Caribbean for a while ... no date has been set."

He laughed. "Boy, I'll admit Simon has a tight hot little butt; you were so right. He does look like that Mercury statue uncle had at home at the entrance of his study. It was that Giambologna copy he had bought in the village when we all were in New York."

William threw himself into a yoga position that resembled that of a dog stretching and she smacked his butt. "How lucky we both are to have Harry taking care of us both." They smiled at each other in the familiar complicity classmates develop over years of cavorting together.

This time around, Germaine had knocked carefully before entering. The boss seemed to have left, so she made her way in ever so slowly. Goodness, what a mess.

An orgy they must have had those two, she thought. Scandalous! One day I'll go to the press and get a lot of money for that story. This is, after all, sacrilegious. For heaven's sake he has three children. She judged in a ferocious mistreated lover's mode.

Simon stormed out of the bathroom, impeccably dressed in a designer suit, and walked straight by her. He didn't pay any attention to his 'garbage director' at all. *'Director,' he thought it a bit pretentious, but she had always taken care of every building, including Simon's private home.* He got into the elevator, then into the underground parking garage and called Jacqueline's cell phone. She picked up immediately.

"I'm in my car . . . coming down?" he ordered in his traditional arrogant manner.

"Well, that was good old Simon, his old bossy self again. He ordered us down!" She copied his attitude as she hung up.

"I'll order him down all right," Bill laughed.

"Thank you. After last night I believe I've had enough. I have no doubts you can handle this late bloomer beautifully on your own, dear William." She watched him seriously and at the same time she dismissed any further thoughts incompatible to her state of mind.

"William, you called me William." His voice soothed his whole attitude. "Nobody has called me that for years, little sister. That's what our mother used to call me till father made it into triple 'B', inspired by my testicles and we both landed on that island with him. Do you remember sex breakfast-lunch-dinner?"

"It's long ago now," she replied not really making a happy face. "We have forgotten most of it, have we not? I was twelve and you were seven when Uncle Harry saved us from him and took us to that wonderful private school on the amazing Hawaiian island of Maui. You became a surfboard wonder by age twelve and…"

"And you, Miss Hawaii, right before your eighteenth birthday. Those four years away from you, that separation was so hard. We're always in the business, aren't we? Do you not feel we're getting abused a bit even if we get to see each other more?"

"But look what you've become sweetheart; a Hollywood star, acclaimed 'the sexiest man alive' by all top magazines!" She laughed out happily.

They got out of the elevator just when her cell phone rang again. She checked the message from Uncle Harry; they got in Simon's sleek car and drove off.

"Ah, there you both are; what took you so long, I called hours ago." Simon sounded slightly hysterical in his accustomed exaggerations. Bill said, "My sister wanted me to avoid an encounter with a certain Germaine, your cleaning director, right? It would have resulted in an autograph and next we'll all be in the local news or the popular *Miroir de Genève,* a free newspaper. He nearly sneezed and his voice took an angry tone.

"I have a new movie out in a few months, not a good idea!" He gestured mischievously and then left Simon speechless when his hand cruised down his belly. Jacqueline shook her head and proceeded to take out her eyelash curler and mascara.

"You are gorgeous you know, little man," Jacky teased Simon. "Working out every day, getting those abs so tight, right Simon?" Jacky followed up in a somewhat ordinary slang she knew he hated while now painting her lips.

"Where are you taking us? Not to a bistro, I hope. Let's go to Bill's hotel. There's a restaurant with a terrace and at this time, nobody will be there. They have valet parking. Just follow our lead. I promise the staff will bow to the floor when Bill arrives!" She enjoyed ordering him around a bit and she could feel Simon was clearly annoyed but her brother's hand on his knee and then up his crotch had taken all the attention away.

She wasn't as lucky as she had hoped for because when the car approached the hotel front entrance, she noticed a handful of photographers. She shrieked at Simon, "Don't stop. Drop him at the back door and we'll leave the car right in the back of the hotel, one street over. Bill, we'll meet at *La Terrace* – run up there," she urged while he looked annoyed at being ordered where to go. "Just tell the front desk they must keep the reporters away, *à tout prix* (at all costs)."

It was all a bit much for Simon, not used at all to being ordered around, but Bill was the lover he had dreamed of since his teens, wrapped up in Oscar Wilde's 'Dorian Gray'. He had waited forty years for this god-like being to show up and he would do whatever it took to keep him; even becoming his driver! Well, for one day, he chuckled. Bill jumped out quickly. Simon found a parking spot a block away.

Jacky took his arm and for a moment he was going to push her away, but he saw the reporters pushing to get in the hotel and one of them had recognized him – after all he was somewhat of a local star himself, he liked to think. He put his arm around Jacqueline's thin waist and whispered something stupid in her ear, followed by a kiss. A pretend Marilyn Monroe fake smile sang, 'are diamonds really a girl's best friend'?

"There's the DoWell CEO!" one journalist screamed.

What a show man; is there ever anything real about him, she wondered.

"Mr Averardo, your business is still booming and the young lady? You are still married? A divorce, a new ring?"

Simon smiled eagerly, hoping at least one photo would get him into a newspaper or an international magazine, as long as there was no text to decorate his own stupidity.

Puke, that ridiculous macho image; a pity you missed him this morning rolled up on a floor mat, Jacqueline thought.

"Please don't have them ask anything more about me," she whispered in Simon's ear in an angry manner. She hadn't made a movie for two years and for a moment she had enjoyed being anonymous. But one journalist from *Le Journal du Future* had called her out. She gently waved, and she put her fingers in front of her lips and, with that tilt of the head, a trademark of the stars, she smiled graciously. One of the reporters called out loud enough asking if she wore any underwear these days. She lowered her dark glasses ever so slightly and smirked in a most decadent way. Her lips read to 'go and fuck yourself, bitch'. But no Swiss reporter could ever read anybody's lips. They hastened towards the restaurant.

Angelo, a handsome bell boy-turned-concierge and some staff members stopped the press from getting in. Minutes later they found Bill, partly hidden behind a few palm trees on the terrace with a dry Martini in his hand and with Angelo grinning beside him, all sexy arrogance dressed in large fig leaves! When they took their chairs, the latter got up and remained calmly in front of the door.

"Personne passera, Monsieur Lawless (Sir, nobody will get by)," he said, repeating in English for the new guests, "Nobody will get in." He spoke with a charming English accent, his eyes turning to Simon, who was still in awe of the fine and beautifully framed face of the waiter.

"He is very cute, isn't he?" Bill said, "I always invite him to keep me entertained – that is when I visit Geneva."

Simon looked most uncomfortable at the sight of an extra Adonis on the scene, but Bill lifted his right shoulder in a coy way.

"You know that Bill was a junior surfing champ before Hollywood fell for his chest?" Jacqueline amused herself greatly. Simon was now second violin to both of them, and he bit his upper lip.

"Bill, I'm not used to being ping-ponged around," Simon broke in almost violently and in a very annoying voice. "We're teasing you," Bill said. "Listen, next week I have to attend a voice editing for my last movie. In London that is, wanna come? Then I get three weeks off. There's a beach house in the Caribbean waiting for me ... so I thought I'd have Angelo and you over ... as my guests and playmates. Like the idea of days of sex under the palm trees, in the ocean, on the hot sands?"

Simon's nostrils were breathing fire and he took off his dark glasses, his jacket and sat back in surprise when the very well-endowed Angelo filled his glass with some very expensive spumante.

"Don't worry, I'm not going on that trip!" Jacqueline grinned while coasting down Angelo's perfect abs. "And yes, Angelo is a model and a few years over the age of consent," she giggled. "He's already twenty-three and well, like you macho guys like to call it, Bill's 'fuck buddy', get it?" Simon didn't feel too comfortable, but he couldn't help slipping his hand onto the model's very tight buttocks. There was no fig leaf untouched and when Angelo bent over to pick them up, Simon lost all patience in little clouds of lusty thoughts.

"Let's have an early 'meaty brunch'; Angelo, I've ordered your favourite champagne waiter and he dropped his Dorian Gray disguise just for you," Bill announced, laughing outrageously.

Simon was feeling slightly off-balance; phantoms were around him triggering him into an unaddressed past. After a few lines of white magic, they toasted to life and more great sex and the butterflies in Simon's head were flying around till Angelo sat down on his bossy guest; his athletic arching and back bending brought Simon's eager hands on the hustler's rather voluminous genitals. Simon wondered if they were custom-made from Silicon Valley.

Bill didn't wait any longer and French kissing followed a shower of more champagne dripping down from both naked men. They caressed their nostrils with more white powder and taking off Simon's shirt and pants in a slow manner while the host saw every drop of his hidden fears disappear.

Jacqueline didn't stay for the party and she left for a reception their 'uncle' had requested she would attend at the Russian Embassy. More work to look forward too, apparently some political game around 'golden showers' with a presidential nominee. She chuckled at last year's endless list of scandals, and she was only too happy to get some real truth on the matter. As a movie star, nobody was introduced in an easier way than she was and *Le Grand Monde de l'Elite* (The great world-elite) was now her own mundane domain that she was about to rule for years to come!

More than one bottle of champagne was finished in one late morning in William Lawless's Five Star hotel suite and while a spellbound Simon Averardo remained enthralled in the perfection of male physical beauty, Bill put away the small camera he had simply clipped amongst the hotel's expansive flower display overlooking a family of enticing Swiss dark chocolates. He knew his uncle would praise him for this last recording. He returned to his lover's open arms and Angelo welcomed more of his sexual prowess. By then, Simon had totally forgotten to warn his secretary to call off a very important business lunch, maybe the most important deal of his career.

46. FIORENZA, 1473 ANGELO

You didn't stop by
to charm me with a jaundiced eye
begrudging all other's fortune
I may have missed this time around,
green as I was, not of envy though. (Envy)

That same day, when he arrived at Careggi, Angelo Poliziano had a desperate look on his face. Maybe the last six hours had been an exhausting mistake. When loneliness crept in, he would visit the darker side of his desires and look for attention in the obscure alleys of the city. Hooded, he would sometimes stand for hours till someone would show up and mostly relieve him as fast as he had arrived. None of the fast encounters had any meaning and sadly, while keeping a small mask covering his face, he often recognized more than one city official. Even one of Giuliano's cousins had surprised him while Angelo had made sure the man never would see whom he had serviced. It didn't really make him happy, and the addiction was as gloomy as his own pure loving feelings for one man only, his soon-to-be legendary protector.

Angelo had made his way from the lovely garden terraces to the main residence. For a while he sat down at Giuliano's desk where he was always welcome, waiting but unable to pen down even a phrase and it wasn't like a writer's block.

What Giuliano had told him a few days ago had left his mind shattered. There was so much to talk about, and his emotions had now been stirred more than ever; answers were absent. Lorenzo had gone to bed after some intense discussions about life, politics and the future of his family with the threat of another conspiracy. His father and grandfather had already survived their attackers and he was planning no less. He had asked to be left alone.

Giuliano felt beguiled by the stars. He wanted to join those diamonds in the sky right then and fly off with his new friend, trespassing the borders of the Universe. He felt like distancing himself from his immediate environment, like moving to another planet. How would that be possible? Maybe GianLuca would have a solution. Angelo's needs were of a very different kind.

"I will follow your advice, my dear Giuliano, "Angelo said quietly. "It's been four years since we have sworn an everlasting friendship!" he was getting anxious to catch his friend's attention.

"Giuliano, may I talk with you?" Angelo softly tapped his shoulder.

"Of course, you may Angelo. Yet let us not forget that when one is that young, one makes promises that are outlasted by the maturity of growing up. So, forgive me, different and yet similar to my brother's, my thoughts about my life are evolving day by day! I for one, I would love a long and healthy life." He spoke while continuously gazing at the stars. "You have already witnessed my father's passing and besides the political pressures, Lorenzo at twenty-four is plagued, like our mother, with aches and pains. It just isn't normal. I fear that our family has a kind of a bad omen when it comes down to our health."

"I'm aware of this, my dear Giuliano. But right now, I do not understand what this has to do with my love for Lorenzo. Have I offended you or him or both of you?" he said in his own cunning, egocentric way, almost begging for an answer.

"No Angelo, you haven't. Do I need to explain to you that Lorenzo does have a wife, a family and a city, maybe soon a country to rule ... and on top of it all, at least one mistress?" He looked Angelo straight in the eyes. "Frankly, I do not see how he can have another lover when he is supposed to be supporting a law proposed by our own forefathers, a law against any actions between same sexes. This isn't ancient Greece."

Giuliano took a breath and continued. "The Office of the Night has become very strict and Lorenzo has already been dancing around the truth as some of our close friends and even one of our own family members have been picked up for their public involvement with younger men." Giuliano pinned Angelo straight in the eyes and the latter slightly trembled at the thought of even visiting a jail.

"Soon I'll be twenty and I'll be expected more and more to look into the affairs of the city. Lorenzo has planned to create an ambassador-like post for me where I may become the contact person for the great Monarchies in Europe to deal with. How tiring that will be," he sighed.

"The Medici banks in the North also need a boost and there is much work ahead of us. I can also see that you, Angelo, very soon, you'll be in a very important position linked to our family. But there have been snakes peeking at you and speaking of you in regard to your relationship to the most powerful man in Tuscany. And though nobody will dare to attack Lorenzo, you, Angelo, yes you might be eaten live!"

This monologue had clearly upset Angelo, scared but not ready to start crying in front of Giuliano, his best friend.

"You mean that Lorenzo can have a wife and children and a mistress and not a lover like in the days of Plato because that just isn't appropriate anymore?" He swallowed while Giuliano answered: "The Officers of the Night have no interest in Plato nor his theories and they will go after men of fortune who sodomize youngsters, under the age of twelve and so they should, if necessary, throw them in jail. The difference is that money will only bail out the wealthy adults."

"When there's a love between men, and I am speaking of an honest and honourable love, then you tell me it is unhealthy for my career and not right for your brother either, because he has to set an example and show society this way of living is wrong?" Angelo asked, his voice taking on a higher pitch. He looked at his friend, apparently offended and lost.

But Giuliano's attention was stilted, and he got drawn to an unusual late visitor. The local *Campanili* had announced midnight at least a half hour ago and he was surprised when he saw a horseman ride up to their residence. One of the servants opened the gate and accepted a note that he immediately brought to the *loggia*.

"Master, the servant from the Buontalenti Family has requested an answer if it isn't too late." Giuliano recognized the handwriting and quickly opened Andrea's letter. But Angelo, annoyed at the interruption, went off humming an old song from a poem he had written for the *Giostra*, which Lorenzo had won a few years ago. And then his own mind wandered off to one of his hero's own poems and sadness accompanied the words he softly whispered like a troublesome chant:

Bastave avermi tolto libertate
E dalla casta via disiunta e torta,
Sanza voler ancor vedermi morta
In tanto strazio e in si tenera etate.

(It is enough to have removed my freedom, to have distanced me from the road of chastity, without wanting my death in such suffering and at such a young age.)

Then suddenly, a feeling of unpleasantness came over him and it made him nervous. It seemed to him that since the foreigner had arrived, both brothers had been influenced greatly. It bothered him and made him worry about his own future. What would happen if his foreign visitor with all his worldly experience became truly close to Lorenzo and Giuliano? And what if he never left? While addressing the messenger, Giuliano's imposingly deep voice woke him up as from a bad dream.

"Tell Lapo and Andrea Buontalenti not to worry and that we will see to this first thing in the morning and please also remind them we are having a dinner in two days on the new moon at our Via Larga residence."

From the *loggia* he watched Andrea's servant leaving swiftly.

"A message saying friends of GianLuca were held up by the Officers of the Night and they are foreigners ... apparently they are innocent," he said.

Angelo immediately responded.

"You see, there are plenty of innocent men being picked up. It's ridiculous; this will soon grow into a dictatorship."

"Dear Angelo, your love for Lorenzo has nothing to do with the present political scene. Remember four years ago when I suggested you would meet with that astrologer, Marco Farini. Well, didn't he give you an accurate description of the facts and influences ... no?" Angelo sighed his eyes lowered.

"You have fallen in love with your protector, yes Lorenzo my brother, and obviously he is like a father figure. On the other hand, through your intimacy you may have helped Lorenzo release some of that lack of physical self-esteem.

Neither of us has been truly loved by our father, the way a father can love his children. Have you observed how animals behave with their new-born? They lick them, they touch them, feed them from their own body."

While his friend continued his monologue, Angelo cupped his head hiding in his hands and finally he wept. "Our father was making money like our grandfather in the back of his shop, with candlelight. It took a century for us to move out and defend our own ideas. Lorenzo and I want to live our future in different hues."

Giuliano spoke up very convincingly, yet it was feeding Angelo's melancholic mood even more.

"Lorenzo wants to have a happy family and instead he has been a politician at the age of fifteen. He also married for the same reasons. Fortunately, his love for the arts is always alive and not only in his poetry."

Angelo responded in a slightly jealous way: "He dedicates it all to the ideal woman and in his mind that woman is Lucrezia Donati. Is she really even a muse?" Angelo asked more seriously. "What a safe way to hide his real persona in a platonic liaison, unconsumed in his delicate poetry. Poetry I actually correct every way and embellish as he requests."

Giuliano straightened his back and said, "My brother is living in a dream when it comes to relationships with women. Underneath that poet lives a beast, and you know that only too well for you have shared his bed enough." Angelo blushed and his eyes slowly closed.

"And now he has set his mind on this woman once again, he will conquer her! Now tell me how many hours in a day Lorenzo can survive, first as a popular public figure, and as the man the foreign monarchy has named 'the Uncrowned Prince of Florence'?"

Angelo kept looking down to the floor while Giuliano finished his talk.

"Please reconsider your own intimacy with him and show him your dedication and nothing more. You are a brilliant man yourself and my family has offered you a unique protection and even a career. No doubt it's time to start looking at your own true colours and develop your unique talents." He spoke in a strong way making Angelo recognize he had yet another ruler in front of him, not just Lorenzo's brother. Angelo's face finally cleared up and he dived into Giuliano's arms. He wept.

"Look at you," Angelo said through his tears, "you have indeed outgrown your too short a childhood. Soon you'll be like Lorenzo with such wisdom beyond your own young years".

"Yes." Giuliano's answer wasn't devoid of cynicism. "Indeed, all three of us, we are already old men even before we turn into adults. Did you notice that Lorenzo has a few grey hairs, at his age?" Giuliano mocked. "But yes, my brother is wise, and I shall never be his match!" He shook his head.

They descended through a large stairway reaching his bedroom.

"Please tonight, take my Uncle Giovanni's room ... it hasn't been used since he passed away. I had it prepared for you."

"If you don't see me before, will you wake me up at dawn? I'd like to see Lorenzo before he leaves for the *Uffizi* (office)?" Angelo asked.

"Goodnight my friend!" Giuliano said and he closed his door while Angelo felt more alone than he ever had in his young life. He picked up a lute and quietly sang the verses of the last poem he had written in answer to his hero and lover.

47. GENEVA, 2018 SIMON AVERARDO

. . . on a yawning, ever-widening bottomland,
you split the marble of an ever-thickening abyss where no being can float harmlessly,
in a disarming Hades of fear that is not,
that is not even there
and never was nor will. (Dry Tears)

Simon might be totally lost in some unexpected schemes, but Elizabeth Von Weitweg-Freundreich had not forgotten 'the lunch of the year'. She attacked the office from her cell phone, one she used sparsely. Her complicit spy friend and favourite assistant Eveliebe and Siegfried's overly dedicated company secretary, jumped up at hearing her voice. Elizabeth had confirmed before by texting that her husband was truly tired and wasn't coming in today. All Siegfried's meetings were now cancelled, Eveliebe confirmed in a firm but friendly voice. Eveliebe had called Simon's desk a couple of times and left a message but no reply came.

Well after all, the Oslo people were expected at 1:00 pm for lunch and Simon had repeatedly told her it was a big deal. At 11:45 am she was growing increasingly nervous. She decided to call Jacqueline knowing that if Simon found out, her job could be on the line. Jacqueline had picked up quietly and had answered that Simon felt really exhausted today and she feared that he would stay home. Eveliebe knew a lie when she heard one and so she called the Averardo's residence where the maid answered, "neither Madame nor Monsieur had been at home . . ." Géraldine, Simon's personal secretary, burst into the room and locked the door behind her. Eveliebe sat back in shock.

"He's gone mad!" she claimed almost out of breath. "His wife and kids haven't seen him for at least a week and the cleaning woman, of all people, the cleaning woman claims she found him naked with that sloth, that 'actress'! And ... " her voice almost hit an operatic high C, " she'll ruin our company if this goes on and he had the guts to leave me a message on my cell to tell me he wanted Germaine fired. What does he care? I'll have to handle the press when she goes to tell her front-page story! We're lucky that the cleaning women don't walk around with cameras in their bags!"

"Oh, yes they do!" Géraldine responded. "We all have cell phones remember?"

Géraldine dumped another one of her many designer handbags on the Louis XVI armchair opposite her desk and lit a cigarette, while Eveliebe stormed towards the window to get fresh air to counteract the hazy room.

"I apologize." She lifted the *Gauloise sans filtre* (Gauloise cigarette without filter) and walked to the window while the other secretary dashed back to her desk to avoid inhaling any smoke while pinching her nose to the maximum. Eveliebe took out a handkerchief for disastrous moments like these and proceeded to spray it with some organic anti-anti something.

"*C'est scandaleux* (really it is scandalous)," Géraldine repeated.

"I agree, the only thing we can do is to call the guests, and tell them to just go and have a cheese fondue on a hot summer day? No, you must convince Siegfried to return to the office and to bring his wife back here," Eveliebe said.

"You are right, the two create miracles together and anyhow, this company exists because of Elizabeth, we all know that. Women like that soap actress can sink the boat but a lady like Elizabeth, and of course, us ... ha!" she was glowing like an all-feminine pride parade all on her own. Géraldine continued.

"We can save the boat from sinking. Now call them, Eveliebe darling, call them up right now," and she put her entire weight onto the desk, far more than any Louis XV could take. Skinny Eveliebe's fear that the exclusive desk might tumble, got her closer to the French door; she rushed out to call her old friend Elizabeth.

After a few rings she relaxed. Elizabeth picked up and Eveliebe released an as short as possible account of the present situation in the most delicate of wordings (with Géraldine interfering every five words and in seriously filthy language). The two voices in the office were so loud that Elizabeth needed to hold her cell phone away from her left ear. When both secretarial furies hung up, she pulled away her husband's sheet.

"Oh, my goodness, don't tempt me," she said when she saw his nostrils breathing fire.

"You look a lot more rested. I can see from that lovely imitation of the tower of Pisa?" she shrieked!"

Siegfried nodded 'yes', as he jumped up on the bed hitting his chest, pumping up and down on the mattress.

"I Tarzan, you Jane ... you woman, I now sniff you, I sniff you ..." and he ran up and down the room with wide-open legs as if a horde of monkeys were let loose. Elizabeth cracked up.

"Oh. *Désolé vraiment* (Really sorry ...), I have cancelled all the appointments we both have. Eveliebe thinks it's *'si incroyable, étonnant, vraiment extraordinaire* (so incredible, astonishing, truly extraordinary)' that she thinks we should have a second honeymoon. Now that's an option I'll take."

"Oh, darling Eliza, let's both resign and just have sex for the rest of our lives," he roared at her, pulling the sheets over their heads.

"OK, promise that for now we have an hour to get a new act together! Listen to this, it's quite a story," Elizabeth said.

"Can you believe Simon disappeared from the building and cannot be found anywhere? This morning the cleaning lady found him naked getting out of a rug with Jacqueline Kissmet behind the door, while refusing to let Germaine in. Of course, Germaine made it in her way, nothing would ever stop her. And there was the boss, *sans culottes* (without pants)!" Eliza continued.

"Next, Simon wanted her fired and if that happens, we'll have the press camping out in front of the building. This isn't just a *femme de ménage* (a cleaning woman); she directs the cleaning department, and she has a mouth like Niagara Falls."

Siegfried wasn't sure he heard well and looked astonished.

"I don't really remember her, and I didn't know Simon could lose it on his own territory," Siegfried said. "That doesn't sound like him at all. You heard what he sounded like when he hung up last night. That is really strange. Well, we can make it to the office in an hour."

He walked towards the bathroom and noticed the new clothes Eliza had displayed on the bed.

"... Oh really, a new pair of slacks and a shirt and sweater? Eliza, that is so sweet of you. All white, is that how you see me now, out of my shorts in virgin colours?"

"Oui, mon amour Un rêve de blancheur (Yes, my love, a dream of purity)." And while they laughed even more, he got into the shower.

She put on some make-up and a new black dress with a low cut back. The black and white couple, the one and the zero, walking chess players ready to step once again into the game, this time with their corrupt opponents, Benderberg, the Oslo people as Géraldine had called them.

This might prove an interesting luncheon. Eliza had told both secretaries she thought that the boss might arrive at the very last moment. By then they would have invented an apology, some family health problem. When the car turned at the roundabout towards Geneva, she admitted to herself a newly found strength; nothing like a husband and wife team. Siegfried took a guess at her reflection and he read the affection! Just then a new message on Elizabeth's cell phone woke her from more loving thoughts as Tchaikovsky's Waltz of the Flowers from *The Sleeping Beauty* ballet, announced Désiré Lesclau's short text; *'Trouble in Fiesole – impossible to reach trio – will fly to Florence today – watch out for all actors – e pericoloso sporgersi* (Dangerous to lean out)!"

48. GENEVA, 2018 WILLIAM LAWLESS

Schlep, schlep, schlep ...
that empty bag is getting heavier again
I do not ever see my father
There's nothing really, I need to feel ever again,
because mother, that man in the dark took my meridians
and then he took my chakras like in that story book he read me. (Schlepp)

The President's suite at a Geneva Hotel

Simon's mind still drugged from last night's surprise passion play with Bill sitting in his pupils, seemed unwilling to retreat. Bill had ordered an elaborate lunch to his suite ... after all, movie stars were allowed those contemptible privileges. William Lawless's 'President's Suite', was especially rented for the star, simply another proof of this immoral movie star status. More champagne would flow, caviar and smoked salmon were a part of a 'deluxe movie' he had dreamed up, one he wanted to outlast his still very much blossoming career.

It frightened him as much as he desired nothing less intense. Their physical attraction was terrific, and it really left a very scared Simon in the back seat. For the first time in his life, he felt like he was being programmed; as if he were starring in the abyss of a permanent porn series. Little did he suspect it to be that close!

"Do you ever wear clothes when you are at home?" Simon asked, not totally at ease with Bill's permanent anatomy display.

"Does it bother you," Bill answered shaking his cheeks. "I can get dressed but then I'll have to undress again, after lunch? Right?"

Simon swallowed and was getting concerned about his own sore muscles. He was afraid to get into the bathtub alone. To his luck, Bill's cell phone rang, and as he moved to the other room, Simon shut the door. He quickly sneaked into the luxury spa bath hidden amongst emerald green tropical plants about twenty feet away from the bed. The Lake Léman view was stunning and he was ready to take a nap in the warm lavender bubble bath.

Please, let's hope this is going to be the longest phone call for Bill ever.

At the DoWell Office Building

Meanwhile, an elegant black and white dressed pair firmly stepped into the main office entrance hall and it took the doorman a moment to realize who they were.

"Well, Monsieur and Madame Freundreich, aren't we looking smart today," he welcomed them, his face lighting up.

She blew him a kiss and the elevator took them to the executive offices. Arm in arm they kind of slouched like models towards Géraldine's desk. The secretary gave a loud account of her approval : *"Mon Dieu, Les voilà: c'est 'Bonny et Clyde', un rêve de haute couture et de charme requin* (Goodness, here they are, Bonny and Clyde; the dream fashion and shark tooth charm pair!)"

The couple made an entrance right out of a '007' movie. Géraldine lowered her voice; "The business meeting of the year is on and the monsters are on their way up." She rolled her eyes.

Géraldine had checked Simon's guests on the security video screen, and she found both men scary-looking to say the least. The taller one was bald, bulky and very muscular, straight out of the James Bond movies she was a fan of, and he certainly looked like the villain. She guessed he was from a country behind the former iron curtain.

She looked at Elizabeth and Siegfried. *"Bonne chance* (Good luck)*,"* she said*, "ils sont charmant comme la mafia italienne et la japonaise combinées* (they are as charming as the Italian and the Japanese combined)."

In the past, Elizabeth had never bowed to any businessman, so she extended her gloved right hand. Géraldine sucked in her cheeks as she made her announcement: "Elizabeth von Weitweg-Freundreich, Executive Director and her husband, scientist and co-Executive Director, Siegfried Freundreich," and she waltzed her way back out. Just those names will keep them busy ... her inside giggles became unbearable.

The two men advanced slowly and presented themselves, business cards extended. Siegfried showed them into the conference space transformed into the legendary New York 'Tavern on the Green' style lunch buffet. The balcony's automatic sliding roof and doors were another wonder of technology that seemed to have made its way in via their CEO's connections.

They all got seated under elegant parasols, made after the original of the London Ritz Hotel. After a few hesitant but unpleasant words from the bald giant who indeed looked like Bond's worst nightmare, Elizabeth lifted a glass of their expensive champagne; a toast to the possibility of an on-going collaboration. She offered Simon's excuses for being late due to his daughter's unpredictable health ... a grave allergy gave her breathing problems, she explained.

Eveliebe had snuck-in, making notes of some of the lies presented so she could arrange any needed manuscript later. She boldly hid an old mini tape-recorder in one of the exotic palm trees, that as she decided had no reason to be. Meanwhile, an ever-complicit Géraldine had sent a text message to 'that actress', with the entire story as it had unfolded.

Somehow, somewhere, he'll get this message, when out of the claws of that Jacqueline ... she pondered, not without a hint of jealousy.

The President's suite at a Geneva Five Star Hotel

In the fancy hotel suite, Simon was becoming more and more impatient. The cell phone did its usual mini concert announcement, but Simon didn't move, afraid he would get back into the claws of his lover, but this time it wasn't Jacky. He was wondering who was sending him a message as he relaxed in essential oils and the whirlpool brought his body slowly back to life. Bill had been on the phone for almost an hour ... Hollywood, no doubt. He dipped under water and just then, within seconds, two strong hands pulled him up.

"I saved you from drowning, ducky," Bill laughed, while wrapping Simon in a bath towel. Ducky Simon ... that's about the last name I'll accept. Nobody had ever dried him off. What was this, some kind of sex slave treatment? Bill was back on his knees.

"Didn't you mention lunch?" Simon asked. "I'm kind of hungry. You had a long call ... Hollywood?"

"You're right," he said, releasing his grip from Simon's hips. "Let's eat and I'll have you for dessert, twice and with whipped cream and a cherry!" Bill answered, returning to his *objet de désir* (object of desire)."

Simon shrugged. What is wrong with this guy? He's a living Miagra plant? Well ... only in his early thirties, why not? He threw on a bathrobe and picked up his cell phone; twenty messages! He looked at the last one and yelled out what his mother would have called 'bad words'.

"Damn, I'm supposed to be at a luncheon at my office. Bill, sorry, I have to leave ... this is one of the most important deals in my company's history."

Bill froze for a moment and cold-eyed, he turned around, pushing a glass of champagne in his hand.

"Should I accompany you as your official lover?" he joked, seeing Simon's eyes nearly popping out. "Only after a toast to our relationship surviving the darkest of nights." He crossed his arm over Simon's and they both drank.

"And you better get your little ass back over here as quick as you can! Take the helicopter back to your personal towering Tour Eifel!" He laughed out in a loud and outrageous way. He then grabbed Simon's head and kissed him. The bathrobe dropped to the floor and so did a very naked Simon. From the other room Jacqueline walked in, slowly followed by an equally glamorous woman in a very slick dress.

"Excellent work William!" the newcomer said, not even looking at him. "I have all the camera work from last night that will really please our uncle."

"Meet Bernice," Jacky said, "a miracle worker for any spy's mouth." She laughed out but Bernice didn't move an eyelash. With Jacky's help and very few words they got a portable chair quickly unfolded. The bathroom quickly looked a like a futuristic dental office. Bill carried Simon and laid him down on the chair, covering him up with a sheet.

"I'm glad he's had some cavities fixed," Bernice remarked.

"The last guy I had to chip, we had to drill a hole. This will be a quickie, mum fed him too much sugar, so we are in luck with a mouth full of cavities," was a cold remark. "When he wakes up, Jacky, make sure he takes this pill and he'll feel like normal. After this shot," and she took out a long and very thin syringe, "he won't remember a thing; only his own sex addiction to you both and whenever you are alone with him, he'll want just that. When the three of you are in the same room the effect will be different and he'll feel confusion instead."

Bill rapidly put Simon on the floor, dismantled the 'one minute dental office' and Bernice left an atmosphere behind far below zero. It was, after all, the uncle's requisite. Within minutes Bill got changed into a new suit. He combed some dark foam into his hair till it turned perfectly natural ... a dark auburn that changed his looks completely.

"Mission accomplished ... have fun sister!" And for a moment, a very brief one, she looked sad and envious of William. She had wanted to join him in the Caribbean, but that wasn't happening right now. He kissed her on the forehead and then briefly held her tight.

Jacky said, "Don't miss your flight. The cab is waiting on the side of the coffee shop. Call me when you get there ... deal?"

"I will," he promised his favourite sister and friend, and he ran off.

She quickly got her feelings back under control. That she had any left came as a surprise to her, and that they could still come to life seemed indeed a miracle. She was aware how manipulated they had both become. They had both accepted to serve a deep state that brought them money, glamor and maybe the fame they never searched for.

Her uncle had made her sleep with her half-brother when he was thirteen, she felt as if wired to him, almost like a twin.

But there was always more; she knew they had to serve their country and whenever Uncle Harry gave his OK, it was because she knew he loved her in his own unique way, wanting only the best for her. They were both serving a higher cause, one for national and now international security ... all terrorist-free! As he had taught her since her childhood, nothing could ever go wrong. So once again, she pulled herself together and looked at her watch. She undressed, her elegant dress slipped down, and she took a deep breath as she lay down on the floor beside the body.

Simon would wake up any minute now and he wouldn't remember a thing and she'd remind him that the lunch he missed was about to end and he might want to get up and meet his guests.

Oh, Uncle Harry, you're so clever. How fortunate William and I have been all those years! She closed her eyes and relaxed next to her victim .. .time for some real acting.

Back at the DoWell Offices, two businessmen sat back in their chairs and Siegfried impressed them with the details of the new programs. Elizabeth had absented herself briefly and was checking messages when, like a Wagnerian Walkyre, Géraldine stormed into her office.

"He's coming. Guess who called?" She lifted her chin to the ceiling. "Miss Kissmet, *bien sur* (of course)! I told her to inform him about the excuse for his absence and that now his daughter's health had improved slightly. I hope he doesn't get it all wrong!"

"Oh no, he won't." Elizabeth sighed, "He's used to playing any game he can profit from. He can lie like a real president." Then Simon thundered in.

"Well, that was quick," Géraldine said.

"Where are they?" he demanded in his usual arrogant way.

"Well, if it isn't our own Valentino," Elizabeth exclaimed while Géraldine hid behind her desk. "They're on the terrace and your daughter is allergic to pepperoni seeds in case these crooks want to know, it may stop her from breathing! But you are lucky and it's going very well. Siegfried has them mesmerized with the project and they now are waiting to see it with their own eyes. That part I'll let you handle. I think after this lunch, they'll even pay cash."

Part Two: white knight moves to take pawn, she thought as she turned her back to him and left him frozen; though instant thoughts of how to control the next move melted Simon's own ice quickly.

Elizabeth walked to her own office, the one she never used. Géraldine followed her in, saying, "You really need to be here. That's where the action is, remember!"

"*Ma très chère Géraldine* (my dearest Géraldine)," she satirised, "that's exactly why I took the luxury of staying in my old office below our apartment and that's where soon, my husband will return! I just claimed him back!"

The two grabbed each other's arms briefly and Géraldine replied.

"Bravo, you did it and nobody else could have! We just miss you here. The ambiance has become ... oh, so dark, so grotesque and Simon, totally absorbed by his ambitions. And then that woman on his mind; forget the family, he's sending them off to the Caribbean tomorrow. He'll have the whole of Geneva to himself to fuck that actress," she said in an exaggerated manner.

"You know that the cleaning woman claimed there was a man in the office when she first tried to get in the door? We can check the security video and then, ha-ha, I'll let you know. If there's no gossip enough in this place to feed all media, oh my goddess, we'll just all go under! The rumour is that he now likes 'trios' and Jacqueline goes 'under' a lot!"

*"Vraiment, Géraldine. That is, that is 'le ragôt du concierge' non (*Really, that's the doorman's gossip, no)?" Elizabeth joked while making her way back to the lunch meeting.

"Sometimes I feel I'm treated like a concierge, I can tell you that," Géraldine bitterly claimed, and she called security to send up the videos via the house WI-FI system. Ten minutes later a series of videos popped up on her screen and Géraldine had clearly typed in different time slots. After a while of fast-forwarding the videos, at first only discovering a dramatic scene between Elizabeth and Siegfried on the bench outside the building, she took a deep breath when she finally found the compromising material they were looking for. She froze the screen triumphantly.

There they are, that bitch, that whore... she probably brought her pimp. This tall lean man certainly looks familiar. Géraldine had a field day!

She ran from her desk into the lunchroom like a bull in a china shop, surprising Simon and his guests as much as Elizabeth and her husband. *"Mes excuses,"* Géraldine looked at Elizabeth and then at the other three men. *"Madame est demandée au telephone, et de toute urgence* (Apologies, but Madame is being asked urgently to the phone.)"

"Alors, je viens toute suite (So I'll be right there)," Elizabeth responded.

"I'll be right back." She glanced at both her husband and Simon, very much enthralled in their conversation with the giant, while Siegfried continued to pour more technical details on the table like salt and pepper on a meal. Nobody was about to miss the spouse whose stilettos were about to fire bullets.

"Tu exagères encore, Géraldine; cela ne pouvait attendre (You are again exaggerating Géraldine, couldn't that have waited)?" she giggled.

"Oh no, this couldn't wait darling," Géraldine said, her nose fuming like a Chinese dragon.

"Look at this! Let me bring up this image to 200%. The time is half past midnight or just ten minutes after you screamed at Siegfried," she exclaimed with her hand on her hip, a Mae West-improv speciality everyone had gotten used to. That man is Jacqueline's brother and you know who he is, no?"

"Should I?" Elizabeth answered, slightly annoyed at the star-studded addiction Géraldine had fed herself since her late 'television teens'.

"He is nobody else but William J. Lawless, who like his name, has a life devoid of any law. But hey, I don't just read the gossip columns on my favourite site 'Whodoeswho' on the Internet's popular 'SmackWho'." Elizabeth shook her head in disbelief that anyone could be interested in any of this.

"They leave the middle name out now because there's so much to talk and to write about the guy the press named 'the Sexiest Man of the Century' *Ma chère.* Even in the news they say he's linked to several of his female movie partners and the male babysitter of one of them even sold his story to, yes, another great website, 'DrearyNewsNoMore'. Well, the man has to be a beast, because that babysitter claimed he was pushed into a trio evening! *Et voilà*!"

Elizabeth said, "Look I know when a man is gay or bi-sexual when I see one! Géraldine, I started as a ballet dancer, remember? And in that world, we have a plentiful palette. Positively, I can tell you that Simon isn't in the same boat as your Loseless actor."

"Lawless," Géraldine intervened, "not Loseless". But Elizabeth could care less, and she went on.

"What Simon is though, is that he has become power sick, beyond all empathy," she didn't joke. "And I don't know how far he will go to keep that power. Then that woman may well be working for someone else, and who knows what she's got to hide; maybe drugs? Maybe a blackmail scenario?"

She was eager to quit the subject and get back to the meeting. But before she turned her high heels, she decided to ask Géraldine for a small favour. "Thanks, though. It will make me think, so save it to my computer will you, and see if anyone else appeared on the scene. Simon called to our car and I remember the exact time."

When she walked into the meeting, four champagne glasses were lifted and Simon handed her a fifth one, saying, "This is to conclude our first agreement and gentlemen, next let me surprise you for I have something to show you. Elizabeth and Siegfried, thanks so much for this wonderfully explicit introduction while I was with my daughter at the hospital. I'm going to show these gentlemen our downstairs lab and Siegfried, you're more than welcome to join us. I don't think this will be of much interest to you, Elizabeth".

Simon spoke out like a true CEO, and the closing phrase sounding indeed as insincere as they get. Elizabeth put up the sweetest of grins. "*Non merçi, mon cher Simon*, I'll finish the chocolate cake, this sauce anglaise is too delicious. What about you darling, you know the basement don't you?"

Siegfried looked at Elizabeth and then declined the offer to join the others. "Thank you," he looked at Simon. "I think I'll have some cake too; a big fan of la sauce anglaise."

Simon, pleased with himself, walked with his guests into the elevator and Géraldine pretended she didn't see him. Elizabeth said, "I cannot believe we just saved his butt. These guys smell like evil of the worst kind." She looked at her husband who came back quick-footed.

"They were at the Oslo retreat, I'm pretty sure of that. Faces look familiar though I don't remember exactly, but yes they were." Siegfried whispered.

"What was the emergency with Géraldine? She looked rather excited," he asked his wife.

"She checked the Security footage. Simon had visitors right after we left. Jacqueline brought an apparently famous actor of the dubious kind. Not that I care, but I have a hard time believing Simon would have an interest in men".

"Except if he gets drugged, like that time in Oslo. I told you some of the story already. And there's one thing you may have noticed; he is slightly misogynous," Siegfried added.

"OK, Sigmund Freud, none of us noticed! *Mon Dieu*, you know I'm not excited about the orgy department and any of their side branches!" She chortled, as she loved calling him Sigmund.

"You may have to prescribe sessions with a Swiss Mr Freud or Jung if you want to guide him through a psychoanalysis on his own and his family's past."

"Did you see his face just now?" Eliza asked. She stared at him with crossed eyes. "No, I don't mean the bags, it's clear Simon hasn't slept, but there is something wrong with him," she continued.

And Siegfried gave it more thought: "While you left with Géraldine, you wouldn't believe how he acted. Every other phrase he interrupted, as if he knew the subject yet he was making no sense at all, sort of like that British television reality show host." He laughed. "Simon was so scattered and he's so in command of his own material. By the way, last night when we were talking, I was too tired to finish the story about the visit in the basement office."

"Right Sig. Give me the gory details and soon I'll have to write a novel about it all." And she framed him with the sleekest of smiles. He frowned with a cute pout.

"OK. I'll rewind to last night before we left with the car. I told you the story about the basement lab and that we were watching the Renaissance episode appear. Where I kind of hooked off from the story before we arrived at the hotel last night? Well, three figures had appeared on the screen, all in Renaissance attire riding on horses. Then some dark forces, on black stallions, attacked them. It looked like one of these virtual games. One of the first trio was injured. Did we go to see that trilogy together, 'The Ring Lords' with those ghost-like horse riders living off humans?"

"I don't do movies without you, and you've been off – how long now? *Cheri*, I have no idea what you are talking about." She pinched a lip and instantly added some lip-gloss. "But I have read Tolkien, who didn't? Ghost riders you meant?"

"Right. On the screen downstairs in the basement, these ghost riders were really scary figures and the three guys put up a fight with such dignity, like they were some medieval knights defending a portal! Very impressive indeed and Simon was extremely attentive. He and Mouse ... ah, that nickname ... were changing levels of intensity while the fight was going on and they seemed surprised that those guys could really take on that much evil. Now I suspect this was one of those advanced video games where you kind of participate and you enter into a sort of virtual world."

He tilted his head and turned towards the sun, opening his shirt to catch some vitamins. What a gift the balcony had always been. Her thoughts wondered off immediately to a more physical inspiration than the story, "Vitamin D3, very good, you need to lift your arms, Sig, because that's where you find the most sensitive spots to absorb the sun's goodies! By the way D3 is an enzyme." Eliza had interrupted his trail of thoughts. Siegfried shook his head and continued.

"OK, so there were splashes of Light coming from the guy leading the battle. Eventually he crushed them by what seemed sheer willpower. It was amazing. He raised his voice and cursed the ghost riders. He then beheaded the virtual samurai who then disappeared into nowhere. Simon was very pleased at the experiment and told me with a very tense and cold look on his face that I had witnessed an inter-dimensional experiment where one could actually influence time travel within existing programs between existing players and virtual ones. One could confuse the traveler to the extent of, imagine, getting him/her frozen in time!

"The only weapon he said that could save that person would be his own capacities. Simon was convinced that very few people on the planet knew their true willpower and once freed from their own fear of not succeeding, they could indeed change many a reality and create a new one in an instant. Of course, it sounded a lot easier said than it could be done."

Sig still sounded as if he was impressed and he was, because as a young man, he had studied Taoism. "I first had doubts that this was an event in a real time, even outside our own, yet Since he was a child, Simon likes to play very advanced games, both with VR – and I've seen him treat his wife and daughters as if they were just toys. He can become like a cold reptile and then he turns around and goes about his business as if nothing happened." Siegfried sounded concerned. "He has nicknames for everyone. 'Artemis' speaks for you Elizabeth, clearly as Simon sees you as a very strong goddess-like woman and even though you make him uncomfortable, he does respect you. 'Mouse' works in the basement and in that episode in the basement, he called out the funniest names for this trio Simon had sent on some mysterious mission... like 'Left', 'Right' and 'Straight ahead'; Izquierdo, Derecho and Dritto!"

Elizabeth nearly tipped her own chair and Siegfried caught her foot in time to hold her back. "What's wrong darling?"

"Did you just say Izquierdo, Derecho and Dritto? These were the names Simon gave to these men, the ones he experimented on in another dimension? I'm not hearing this right, well no, am I?"

As often happened when she became really annoyed and extremely worried, she stuttered violently, and he got up and shook her gently by the shoulders. With twenty-five degrees Celsius of pleasant summer around them, she ran cold and stared hopelessly at her husband.

"Eliza, what's wrong? Speak up? Do you know these people?" he asked.

"That is the trio he asked me to investigate at the villa in Florence and that's why I had the meeting with the detective, who's now right there in

Florence. His last message read that there was trouble in Fiesole! You see, I wanted Désiré Lesclau, a private eye, to check on Izquierdo, Derecho and Dritto because they were to look for these 'important codes' that Simon demanded. I simply thought there were some numbers and letters and signs, symbols, *enfin ... tout court*! Ah, *mon Dieu quelle horreur* (In short! My god, this is horrible)," she exclaimed. "He may have tried to scare them too!"

She continued. "Now I'm getting an awfully confused picture. They have found a time travel device, but how did Simon even know it existed and how did he get to the trio, if it ..."

"Yes, Miss Shirley Holmes, do proceed!" Siegfried slipped some humour into their current developing drama.

"... if it wasn't for his political friend of course. This really has a bad smell, just like any MK Ultra-story, that good old fifties mind control program. Siegfried, we have to get out of here right now. You know, the end of the Désiré Lesclau's 'coded' message was 'to be cautious with actors ... don't lean out ... .'"

She had stopped. "Damn, I've got to show you something right now!" she said, nervously lighting her first cigarette of the day. "None of this makes sense." She exhaled. "I better get down to the basement and see what's going on there," Eliza said. "*Cherie non.* (Darling, no)," and Siegfried stopped her.

"You cannot just walk in; the codes are very complicated. You will not even get further than the elevator. Only Simon has the special key and once you walk in the corridors below you need a fingerprint and an eye code. Boy, that place is now like a vault".

"And vaults are there to be broken into, right?" She took out her cell phone to call Simon.

"No!" Siegfried nearly yelled. "Don't, not now! Those Benderberg – Oslo people are dangerous, can't you tell?" He took the phone from her and put it gently down on the table.

"I know another way and so do you, I can see it in your bright eyes!" he smiled. "Let's see who will get there first," Siegfried joked and they both ran like little kids into the office, cackling loudly like hens leaving their nest. An excited Géraldine, jealous but happy about their reunion, put both hands to her heart and just smiled like a happy granny.

Ah, Finalement (Finally), back together! The last of the normal couples, she thought. I wonder if they've stopped making those and we'll all continue this soap opera?

"Géraldine viens-ici, tu veux bien (Come here, would you please)?" Elizabeth said.

On overly high heels, she nearly tripped over the Miro design carpet before the phrase even finished. "Please play the video again and then fast forward to see what time these guests all left." But half an hour later when they had still found nothing, they looked at each other and nodded in agreement.

"The pigs, they had it right here," Géraldine exclaimed. "I just knew it; *un ménage à trois mon Dieu* (a threesome, oh my God)!"

Géraldine lifted her arms to their Michelozzo imitation office ceiling, and no blessing came down. She said, "Just like I told you this actor Lawless, I'm sure like the internet report reads, has these trio numbers going. Only there wasn't a babysitter here, only Simon."

Siegfried had no clue as to what this woman was talking about. While Géraldine continued to babble, he gently took his wife's hand and Elizabeth knew he was up to something. She turned around and smiled like a teenager, enough for Géraldine to get teary eyes and return to her desk a bit sad, because she loved to be *une complice* (an accomplice).

"Call me on my cell the minute Simon gets back up here Géraldine! We'll be quick," Elizabeth called out before they got into Siegfried's private office. He got out his key and then entered his studio apartment.

In the small kitchen, Siegfried fiddled around behind the fridge, unplugged it and then pulled it sideways. He pushed the thick wall panel to the side and there they were; in Simon's luscious, extravagant suite connected to his office.

"If the door had been forced, the alarm would have triggered the police right away," he said.

"Yes Mr Holmes. Goodness dearest, where is Watson?" she joked.

"No Watson needed; Shirley Holmes came along," he continued imitating an equally deep voice. "When Simon decided he had to have me work around the clock and needed to check on me as much, he found nothing better than to generously set me up in this little luxury bunker that, as you can tell is rather Hollywood 80s soap-styled. All paintings are originals and so are the Le Corbusier chairs!"

"The cleaning woman," Elizabeth remembered, "Did she get fired? They certainly didn't fix the place up; this is indeed chaos."

"Wait, Eliza. He's got a desk system called 'Meonly'. Remember he phoned me in the car and from this desk. You'll have never seen anything like this. This whole place is so up-to-date, the most advanced security control system existing!"

"So why does he have a doorman downstairs?" She munched on an apple she had picked from his kitchen table.

"He has become a control freak. He has the camera on all day in every room of the building and in the evening, he checks the whole video on his PC! I can tell he hasn't been in today. We may well have a ball if... ha-ha, he had one last night. Here is the private apartment's last twenty-four hours private viewing program and the camera eye moves as soon as anyone moves. If any guests were here, it will show!"

He opened the PC. "Simon got this unique system through a highly placed official in the secret service. See there's a laser-like beam that picks up all moves, each visual detail, even in the dark, and so exceptionally clear, as if light is accompanying the camera wherever it goes. He says he had it installed in case burglars got in, their identity would be registered, and they would be caught within an hour after the event. You see the date will be sent instantly to the local police once the game master, Simon that is, pushes the button. Only two people know the code and how to use it; Simon and yes, your husband!" He glanced at Elizabeth with a grin. Siegfried chuckled and typed in the code, the date and specified the time – 0:30 am.

What came next did hit them like a visual tsunami. It left them both speechless.

When the smallish screen lit up, they were left in a state of shock, especially Elizabeth who had never acquired a taste for pornography. First a faceless Apollo figure having sex with Jacqueline in a brutal choreography with perfectly matched violent moves, where penetration is always avoided yet the audience is carried away as it looks so real, like a true high-class nightclub act. Elizabeth sat tight, squeezing the cigarette box.

Behind the scenes they heard Simon's comments as well as the couple's occasional remarks. The big shock came though, when they saw the good-looking fellow dash, naked towards Simon and then raping him without any resistance with Jacqueline joining them.

Elizabeth remained totally stunned:*"Géraldine avait raison c'est l'acteur qui a joué dans 'Les Romains' ça alors* (Géraldine was right; it's that actor who was in the *The Romans!*)" That same moment her cell phone rang.

"Sig, on part! Vite, arrêtes tout, Simon est parti et il monte (Sig, we must leave; quickly stop everything, he's coming up.)"

Siegfried, who knew this technology well, set the program back to normal within seconds after he closed off the PC tower. He carefully replaced the kitchen wall panel joined to Simon's bathroom closet and put the fridge in place. He heard a knock on his door and lifted his wife's dress up to her waist and whipped her feet from underneath her to land on his single bed just as the door flew open.

"Well, you young people," Simon's tone sounded relieved. "Cannot leave you two alone too long now, can I? Hmm . . . I wish I could say I'd want the same for my wife," he commented with a haughty look on his un-shaved face.

Elizabeth had pushed down her dress and went in the bathroom. Her time to act, she thought. Simon continued, "You're right Siegfried, she's still quite gorgeous with that ballerina figure that has outlasted time. But you know I like them a little younger." Simon whispered loud enough for everyone to hear.

"You already know, I just dig Jacqueline, about twenty years our junior, a real horny bitch who would do anything in any position, well you know." Siegfried loathed the slimy version of the man he had worked with for decades and he now doubted he ever really knew. He felt sorry for him.

He's pitiful and he's badly in need of a therapist, he thought.

"I know, we have different tastes," Siegfried replied. "We won't talk about real love now, will we Simon. You did make kids with your first wife, no?" Siegfried looked him straight in the eyes.

"That's fifteen years ago and my priorities and my taste have changed since then. Of course, I do pay the on-going bills but that isn't all . . . !" he ping-ponged back. Siegfried pretended not to be offended and Elizabeth returned to the scene, breaking up their duet.

Oh, from what we just witnessed, we cannot really use the word taste, she thought.

"So how was the basement? Did you have the bulldogs sign the contracts?" she asked in a voice that was as insulting as possible. Siegfried felt like disappearing through the already thin wall. But Simon loved to battle Elizabeth.

"Ugly aren't they, but money has the best colour and when they have billions of dollars to spend and yes, they did go home a contract, open to negotiation of course. Amazing, no? But I must let you go because I have a dinner date and I must check my messages at the office ... you never know where cleaning women put their fat little fingers."

He laughed meagrely. "I had an intense night. And thanks to both of you it's all running along as it was planned. Have I been a bit hard on you two?" he asked in a childish manner.

"As for your Siegfried," he continued while he faced Elizabeth in a courtly manner that had her raise both eyebrows, "Well, I really needed him to finish the much-needed preparation to what has now become a 'highly classified', soon to be state, secret". His smile was as real as on any of the shows he so loved.

"And as for your extremely brilliant way of saving the luncheon and this billion-dollar deal, I couldn't have done it without you both. My gratitude will be eternally engraved in the Rolls Royce you will receive next week at your home residence. Geneva didn't have the latest model, so I've had it ordered five minutes ago! Don't you just love today's technology? One call from your cell, you get the newest model!"

"That's so typical Simon; win a billion give a million. Like we need a Rolls!" she cried out sarcastically.

"Yes, but it probably has full range camera installation to trace you wherever you are and with whomever in a world-wide radius! Didn't Scotland Yard start this system off?" Siegfried slipped in.

"Goodness Holmes," Eliza smiled, "you are a living library these days. So ... what about a cosy *tête à tête chez nous ce soir* (a cosy home dinner for the two of us)?"

She wanted to leave the building as fast as possible to check where Désiré Lesclau was to be found. What was going on in Italy? They both walked down and said goodbye to the secretaries. Eveliebe and Géraldine jumped up like twin sisters. The latter ran behind them, a happy mother hen whispering,

"*Olala, la Rolls*! And you know what he told me when I asked him what to do about our cleaning wonder, Germaine?" Eveliebe whispered.

"He said he didn't know what I was talking about and he never wanted to fire anybody since years and he wasn't about to. I called her back and she was stunned! Her answer was like... I suppose I had now better keep my big mouth shut. Well, I suggested that maybe that was the better solution. Germaine could have gone on for hours knitting a conspiracy sweater from the last twenty-four hours' myriad of events."

Both Elizabeth and her husband hugged her. They all took a deep breath as in a chorus and laughed, relieved at the present outcome. While they left the building, both secretaries had wiped the tears from their eyes. Their 'leading' couple was back together and ready to take on the world. At least it seemed that DoWell was once again in good hands.

49. FIORENZA,1473 MEMENTO

Never, never again will you be at loss for any information,
will you be lost at any time to any information center,
even in all Universes, Multiverses . . . Orgasmerses . . . (Dontyawannachip)

Meanwhile, Isabel and Florian had updated GianLuca about their time travel affairs and their trip through France. They had joked a lot because all three knew that this cast was involved in a scenario unfolding in 2018.

"What are you actually looking for in the year 1473?" GianLuca inquired, toning his own laughter down. "It isn't a shopping spree you're in. Milano's catwalk is still closed." They all joked around quite a bit, after all it had been decades, but nothing had changed between them, nor had their humour.

"Now that's becoming an out-dated joke, Flo," Isabel said in a suppressed voice, "and please let's be careful and not wake up our hosts; we have caused so much commotion in their quiet Renaissance lives they really need a rest from us foreigners. It's all about a decoding system that is to be found at the Medici's Fiesole Villa; we cannot put a name on it. I could feel it when we were there, in our last week, ugh . . . in 2018." They laughed once again.

"Tell me more about the Fiesole Villa. I was just there the other day," GianLuca inquired.

"There's a *grotto* (cave)," Florian answered, "with a statue, kind of dedicated to Venus, but very much neglected throughout the nineteenth and twentieth centuries. I think there are definitely some pieces missing. Architects have made alterations throughout the centuries. In these mysterious and dim caves, cool for the hot Tuscan summers, illusions and metaphorical god-like references to nature are intertwined with inventive handicraft of the period when Lorenzo's Uncle Giovanni had acquired the place." GianLuca remained attentive and pensive.

Isabel declared in a robust kind of way that "the reason we took the trio on this trip is complex. And yes, their names are Derecho, Izquierdo and Dritto …. you're welcome to smile. Let's say that they had been more or less trapped in this scheme by that illustrious Geneva-based Pharma, DoWell, the giant corporation that is partly a cover up for a Harry K operation … remember him?" GianLuca had his eyes wide open and Isabel went on.

"DoWell used these men to gather hidden information from the 2018 version of the Fiesole Villa. *Mon petit doigt* (my little finger) tells me there's a lot more going on inside those premises! I also suspect it to be an important star gate, at least into the Renaissance!" She finished her discourse.

"Does *votre petit doigt* (your little finger) have any information as to how I got here?" GianLuca asked and Isabel continued: "It must be a truly 'technical coincidence'; something to do with the fact that our world, as the three of us know it, is a free will zone. You, GianLuca, you have a karmic link to Giuliano, that's clear from what you told us, besides the obvious very similar looks."

Florian started yet another explanation. "My goodness, you could be identical twins if not for the hair colour and centuries-old haircut." They all laughed at this 'haircut'.

"Well, that's clear alright. When I'm back home … um … I'll check the astrology too! My take on it is that Giuliano brought me here, that he wanted me here; maybe like a game his spirit guides played …"

Florian picked up the line, "Simple facts; 1478 is the year he's supposed to be killed. Did he feel anything now, had he any dreams or visions? His family is one that battled ill-health from their forefathers onwards and gout was then a widespread disease. Now you know his leg was bothering him for a while, I remember reading that in the Florence library. The gout was a long male heritage in this family. That day, historically known for the Pazzi conspiracy, he didn't want to leave the house. The conspirators literally took him to the cathedral, right?"

An authority on the subject, GianLuca was aware of the historical background and nodded.

"Ask him about his latest dreams and you'll find out the compatibility with your dreams. Do you still write them down like you used to?" GianLuca shook his head.

"Oh, you don't. I also gave it up this last year. Answers seem to fall right into my laptop these days … I've missed it lately! Today, I have none and no web, aside from the one I fell into right here with this adorable lady! Haha" Florian joked.

"There's more to it all, Florian," GianLuca answered. "It isn't that easy," GianLuca continued, "maybe there's a cosmic storm of some kind, where some souls are connected to a space-time anomaly; maybe a black hole-like movement you cannot escape. You remember, you were a specialist on the subject of intergalactic exchanges and now I recall seeing a documentary about it not so long ago."

"I think we need to get up early and check that *bargello* jail as he called it. Don't you think so?" Isabel questioned.

"No worries, we'll have an answer before we go to bed, I promise you," GianLuca said as they watched Andrea's servant just sneaking by them and immediately running upstairs to Andrea's quarters.

"That's him, the young man Andrea sent off? Well, are you not going to ask him for an answer?" Isabel demanded impatiently.

But Andrea had already appeared on the balcony and waved at them with a big smile, putting up his right thumb. They waved back and slightly bowed their heads in reverence to thank him.

"He really is a sweetheart, isn't he? I could just take him back home with us," Isabel teased.

"I'd love to take Agnola too and I'm sure that GianLuca is ready for Fiammetta, no? We can make it a triple wedding," Florian sang along. "Time for a *grappa*?" he laughed.

But they were all yawning and ready for a new Renaissance dream … or were they expecting it to be a live experience?

50. FIORENZA, 1473 LA CACCIA & BARGELLO

And then, just then
when I smiled at the absence of the starry beauty of the unknown lover,
I always knew,
you turned my single sheet into the king size shawl and wrapped me in a love affair
I had envisioned seducing me out of all shadows of denial. (Shadows of Denial)

Giuliano found his brother in bed. "Writing poetry, no doubt?" he thought out loud.

"Have you slept well?" Lorenzo happily looked up from his little book. "Alone for once, I did indeed. I see your words worked their magic on Angelo."

Giuliano said, "He is of course, upset. Mind you he has a Pisces Moon in the fifth house of the child, the planet Mars in Taurus in the house of relations; at least that's what I remember! He has you on his mind day and night and your intimacy has grown into an obsession for him. You represent the seat of the gods, the Olympus to him, one god he wishes to give himself to so entirely there is no life left to live! He becomes like a controller not a lover."

Lorenzo gently kicked back the ball. "*Fratello* (brother), you still love astrology, a fine trait indeed!"

But Giuliano continued to express himself with a true concern.

"This cannot work," he continued, "but he works like a slave even when you tell him not to; if you teach him and not use him, he'll ..."

"You are telling me I'm using him, when it is Angelo who enters my chambers? We've already gone through this ..." Lorenzo felt, as usual, provoked.

"OK, what about sending him away and closing off your chambers, brother? I fear the truth has a different layer and you cannot resist this sensuous young body. Remember that afternoon, I have seen you change in front of my own eyes. I love you for who you are, and nothing will ever come in between us brother. Yet, you have two faces Lorenzo; look in that mirror and you may well agree!" He spoke up strongly.

Lorenzo stepped out of bed and he impatiently roamed the large room sharing his nudity with a splendid sun rising up gloriously from below the horizon.

Giuliano admitted he looked glorious, and the Sun only accentuated his sleek muscle tone; nakedness gave Lorenzo a different power indeed and Angelo was an accomplice.

"Alexander and many great rulers had a male lover and yet plenty of women and children. Italy is of a much greater concern to me than the few nights a month I have with Angelo. Just like you, he's only a year younger than my wife!" He stopped in front of Giuliano, and still fully naked, confronting him he started playfully pushing his forehead against his brother's, with the ruggedness of a Greek bull.

Giuliano pressed back, and he tried to lift him up with transporting strength.

Lorenzo voiced strongly, "A society where all life is valued; one where we can all live as we were at birth, different in our variety of so many of our desires, often forbidden by our society's laws. Yet, who has written these laws, and convenient to whom, are such laws? Didn't the Holy Book state: 'He created us in His own image'? I am not sure that is as much the truth as the Catholic Church isn't anything more than a political seat. It is a sin to kill, yet wars are still fought to conquer the so-called 'pagan' and to collect gold and treasures from the past."

Lorenzo spoke up while Giuliano leaned against the imposing four-poster bed.

"The Vatican is indescribably wealthy and as we both know, most cardinals have a mistress or young male lovers, or both. There men receive strange initiations and that is not only the case in Rome! I'm now glad they didn't want a Medici amongst them. You really don't fit in there. No other victim is needed to promote our family power; my marriage was sufficient!"

Giuliano threw a large linen cloth to his brother as Angelo walked in, turning his eyes away from Lorenzo. Angelo coughed, and Lorenzo smiled at him. "Breakfast is ready; and I heard you both had a talk so…"

"It's quite alright" Giuliano put his arm around his shoulder as he walked Angelo down. Lorenzo stepped onto the balcony, and he emptied a bucket of cold water over his body, dried off and got dressed rapidly.

"Let's go riding as we planned, Giuliano, we'll have something to eat later on." He took an apple and petted Angelo endearingly on the shoulder. "Morello, hungry?" he asked his horse, neighing happily. "Are you ready for a little competition Giuliano? And don't let me win like you did last time; that tournament four years ago did enough damage to my lower ego!"

They laughed and jumped on their stallions and rode off screaming like warlords. Angelo Poliziano's cheeks got wet as he watched both brothers. He picked up his master's lyre and his fingers plucked the sounds that redeemed his heart from his desires.

Upon their return, everything moved quickly. It left Angelo confused and wondering if he was of any use at all. He felt annoyed or was it the need for attention?

"Being wanted": is that a question or a frustration, he asked himself.

Upon returning from their outing Giuliano explained to his brother that two friends of GianLuca's had been picked up accidentally and thrown into the *bargello*. He promised to handle this quickly. Lorenzo called upon Angelo who took note of the event and of what he needed to do that same day.

"Oh no, my friend, not in Latin. Just brief reminders of what I have to accomplish today" and he continued dressing. Minutes after a light breakfast, a happy trio left Careggi for the city.

As Lorenzo's personal secretary, Angelo Poliziano had a new function in the Medici household. He thought that his busy schedule would keep him from disappearing within the rich carpeting at the Medici Villas. That was his only security when love had left a void in his heart.

That morning, Angelo had joined the Medici brothers at the *bargello*. The trio immediately caused quite some commotion. That early in the day, a visit by Florence's most charismatic leading knights would leave many surprised. The *comandante* (The Head of Police) seemed to be having great difficulty dealing with a very buxom young woman who banged her fist on his small office desk while obviously demanding the release of someone. Her voice had straightened his back and he nearly pushed her to the side when saluting Tuscany's two most famous brothers.

"What can I do for you gentlemen?" Angelo had withdrawn into the shadow of the wall and felt extremely uncomfortable at the imposing jail that had the weight of a government building and the daunting energy of a dark palace.

But the woman was getting slowly furious and imitated the *comandante's* voice contemptuously. "What can I do for you ...," she grinned while shaking her head and, lifting her breasts while sticking out her tongue.

Nothing too vulgar, Angelo thought while watching with hidden disgust.

"We have come second to this citizen, *comandante,* and we'll wait till you have heard her story. What is your name young lady?"

To everybody's surprise, Lorenzo had spoken. A rather amused Giuliano turned himself away, looking for Angelo to share a joke. But the latter had joined the bricks in the walls.

"Gentillisimo Lorenzo di Piero de Medici, Io sono Galessa, la figlia del padrone de la caccia (Gentle Lorenzo. I am Galessa, the daughter of the owner of La Caccia)." She bowed in an exaggerated courtly manner that neither suited her, nor the occasion. And oh, that lingo was a heavy one, Giuliano noticed.

Angelo tried to move out of his lack of self-esteem that made him feel like nothing but a part of the wallpaper and came forward to confirm that the woman's identity was true. She smiled when she seemingly recognized him. Fortunately, she gave no further explanation as to why he was a familiar face ... the image of the young poet fondling her brother was clearly engraved in her mind as were his more frequent visits of late, at La Caccia.

Lorenzo wondered if this wasn't simply all a comedy. But when she told her story, taking over abruptly, but most convincingly from the man in authority, her honesty rang the right bells in the young ruler's ears. As she finished, she went into the office and pulled out the man she called 'the third Englishman who is also here for trade'.

Giuliano wasn't the first to grasp the truth and he whispered in Lorenzo's ear that these three men inevitably had to be connected to GianLuca. After a short conversation with the totally amazed *comandante*, not even a paper for their release needed to be signed. When 'the other two Englishmen' were finally brought up from the basement cells, Galessa tilted her head proudly. Derecho had not noticed the men on their horses nor the fuss that went on in the inner courtyard and he hugged Galessa, who was glowing with pride. But Izquierdo had a memory the size of a palace and the paintings of the de Medici that came clearly to his mind. He walked up to the men, staring as in a daze.

"You must be Giuliano, you just look like a younger ..." he started to say, his eyes wide open. "I know, I look like your friend GianLuca," he smiled at him quickly. "My brother and I, we are truly pleased that this misunderstanding has been corrected."

The *comandante* had disappeared from the scene, or so it seemed. Lorenzo finished up the case by telling them that they would be invited to his residence in the Via Larga for a meal to correct this unfortunate happening. He nodded at Galessa who was about to start a new series of curtsies as they politely bowed out. Derecho briefly scanned Angelo, thinking his face wasn't unknown either ... from one of those history books no doubt, he thought.

They walked towards Via dei Pandolfini and Giuliano asked Angelo to accompany the three men to the Buontalenti residence. The poet certainly didn't jump up and down with joy walking along with Galessa and he did his best to ask as many questions as possible, so she could explain what had happened to the poor foreigners. When they arrived at Lapo's residence and Giovannino opened the main gate, the three men thanked Angelo, not knowing why, and the trio kissed Gallesa's hand, promising a visit before they were to leave the city of Florence.

Agnola was nearby and immediately checked what was going on in the front of the courtyard. She recognized Angelo Poliziano and greeted him with much respect. Thanking her for the family's warm hospitality, he confirmed that he couldn't stay, but that no doubt they would all see each other sometime soon. Before he left, he glanced at the other foreigners who were coming down and wondered why they all looked so familiar or, should we say 'alike'? When the doors closed, Angelo wanted but to run back quickly and return to Via Larga where he hoped Lorenzo was waiting for his new secretary.

Galessa had waited and followed him closely till, almost out of breath, she shouted out loudly, "You still like my little brother? Will we be honoured by your arousing visit again soon, oh great poet!" She giggled rather obscenely.

Angelo pretended not to hear as he pondered the fact that he had felt attracted to the man called Derecho; he quickened his pace and noticed a covered sky. His horse took the short road home and Galessa well, she gradually grew annoyed at the patches of grey clouds covering up the sun, right when she started a nice stroll back to the tavern.

51. FIORENZA, 1473 ALCHEMY

To lead you through narrow tubes
to that part you never dared to find,
where only I can hear, mad as I am? (Mad)

Cries of joy and laughter invaded the ground floor as Giovannino brought the new guests into the courtyard. Andrea was the first one to run down to greet them. He invited them to be seated while he called out to Agnola to wake up Isabel. Florian's antenna was sharp enough to pick up the early morning's event and quickly appeared on the *loggia*.

"There they are," he laughed out loud and he ran down, forgetting he was wearing nothing but his tiny briefs while Giovannino turned around in a dance of laughter.

"Imagine that no one less than Lorenzo and Giuliano de Medici made sure we were released from that dungeon. That was a scary enough adventure!" Derecho declared, glad to return to his latest patron. Izquierdo and Dritto pointed at Isabel, now hurrying down from the balcony, accompanied by Agnola.

"Look at the young lady who greeted us," Iz whispered to Dritto while pointing at Agnola. "She resembles her like a younger sister, no? Have you noticed they all have a look-a-like on this timeline ... weird, no?"

"Haven't seen any of our clones, I bet we need not have the same age either, haha ..." Dritto answered, without noticing how Andrea's page kept staring at him as if was looking at a more mature self.

"Isabel, you beat us from one dungeon into another one!" Derecho exclaimed, while opening his eyes widely when he noticed Agnola, who had shyly moved to the side. "Well, sorry we missed the Santa Croce appointment, but we can now tell you all about a Renaissance jail; once you're in you don't get out, not even with a twenty-first century device!"

Izquierdo insisted on telling them about their amazing adventure. As he started GianLuca watched Lapo coming down speechless, as he did in their first meeting, weeks ago. With quick steps, the patriarch of the Buontalenti family walked towards his newly arrived visitors as GianLuca gently took his arm.

Lapo came to stand next to GianLuca and he felt as if he was sliding into a world that had been so foreign till only a few days ago. Now he was caught up in staring at a newcomer, who was physically a younger version of himself, telling his story and GianLuca saw what Lapo was feeling. He was indeed looking at himself. Izquierdo seemed like a young Lapo, the age he was when he had his first son. For a moment Lapo was destabilized and he needed to sit down.

Meanwhile, at Andrea's request, Giovannino ran upstairs to bring Florian a light housecoat-like robe and Florian reacted with elegance and gratitude realizing he wasn't on a twenty-first century beach unwittingly offending anyone in his bloomers. To the contrary, he hadn't, because Agnola had enjoyed admiring his Mercurial looks and their eyes had met more than once. The complicity, mutual in their minds had wandered off to a place only they knew. Did they visit the same dream ... one they didn't dare remembering?

Isabel was aware of what was going on, but she proceeded like a Queen giving her undivided attention to Izquierdo's story. When she noticed that Lapo needed to sit down, the tight circle opened ever so slowly, and they all stared at their host. Only Izquierdo stumbled back and looked at Lapo's face. This man was indeed an older self and it left him totally defenceless; he felt like passing out and he wasn't the only one.

How come a veil was suddenly covering his eyes and then another one came down and another one? And when Izquierdo wanted to pull up the flimsy screen that seemed so swiftly to cloak his head, he was dancing around with all other faces in a feeble waltz of immaterial, even transient, images. He felt his own powerless body devoid of all present reality.

And then with unexpected speed, beyond all possible human understanding, eons away from all universal knowledge, still hidden to all the players in this grand game, in an unequalled iridescence of a constantly changing light spectrum dazzling in all its radiance, creating unseen glistening auric fields around each of his friends, GianLuca watched Lapo's arms extend into Izquierdo's shoulders to merge into a scintillating explosion of tiny flashes of memories where their necks intertwined and their faces changed into an abundance of new versions of the old souls they had been ages ago.

Within seconds, Agnola melted into Isabel's blinding blaze of a similar flame like splendour, like a psychedelic firework at Oberon's court of fairies. Dritto's head framed Giovannino's childish innocence and the kid's quick-witted eyes emitted rays of flashing brightness as his youthful smile gave way in a shiny lustre of high beaming incandescent brightness and childish love.

Derecho, all on his own, was levitating in a helix of phosphorescent effulgence... his longish auburn dark curls straightening in Angelo Poliziano's locks of raven black hair and their four eyes blinking rapidly as one.

Florian's statuesque beauty fused his athletic chest into limpid celluloid-like plasma, ebbing Lorenzo de Medici's face, shaped in a lambent spiral towards GianLuca's arching body, coruscating a glittering mass, spewing his limbs in the shimmering luminescence of Giuliano di Piero di Medici. And just then, Fiammetta lost herself in a lustrous golden rain of floodlit, diamond rays as she passed out on a green bed made up of gleaming emerald grass.

The entire Buontalenti Palazzo went up in an eruption of cosmic regurgitating forces with all ten bodies gravitating into a timeless patina that extended its plasma towards the Medici Palazzo in Via Largo, and then beyond the entire Tuscan valley.

The Medici Palazzo, Via Larga, that same moment.

By then, Angelo Poliziano had walked into Lorenzo's office as in a daze. The dream never seemed to have been so real. He looked at the heavy oak desk and he found Lorenzo engrossed in written requests from citizens applying for the few vacant positions at the Signoria. Lorenzo lifted his eyes briefly, but he felt heavy. He glanced at his lover and didn't find a smile.

"Take a look at this manuscript about the Pleiades. I would like you tell me more about it later in the afternoon when I have finished my meeting with the Podesta. Are you well Angelo, you are looking a bit pale?" Lorenzo asked.

"Until a moment ago, yes. I brought the people to Andrea's house," Angelo said, pleased that Lorenzo gave him some attention. Then he put his right hand to his stomach, almost immediately feeling drowsy. It didn't escape Lorenzo's notice.

"It all went very quick and ugh ..." he cramped up in a sudden pain that struck his belly. Lorenzo jumped up, taking a leap around the huge desk to catch Angelo but then he felt a similar energy and he dropped backwards nearly hitting his head against the large armchair. The guard in front of his open door heard a painfully suppressed scream and turned around approaching them, flabbergasted by a breath-taking and unusual light-fumigating scene in which he saw his master spinning in a blitz till an unknown force collapsed over him. Totally alarmed, the soldier ran out while Lorenzo froze and fell down to the marble floor.

Upstairs, at the same moment, Giuliano had been moving a small bronze statue of Jupiter. The head of Olympus carried his famous lightning-bolt in his hand, like an instant preview of what was about to take place. But Giuliano too lost his balance and he stumbled forward as if pushed by a cyclonic force, his hands covering his face as, on a flashing helmet of blinding starlight, Jupiter's sceptre flew into the air. And right then, all the citizens of Fiorenza saw the clear blue sky over their city transform into slowly changing hues of reds and purples until a night blue settled into a palpable darkness of scary tenebrosity. The last sunrays evaded the humongous gloomy dark clouds deceiving all possible angelic agreements of any promised saviour.

The bells from the campanile exploded in a chaotic hard metal-like concert when the sky broke open into a total blackness. A void of billions of fragmented strands of lost solidity, of non-existent fluidity in all dismantled spiralling frequencies of this unknown alien multiverse, was raining down on the entire valley. All consciousness gone, bodies floating throughout an indescribable cosmic chaos, no worlds could be shaped any longer.

52. GENEVA, 2018 HERCULES & VENUS

I look at you woman
as you glimpse the smile that once again, I am
I kneel to the dream you have kept alive;
to rest my lips
close to your womb's mouth into waves
of all unaffected... replay. (Replay)

"Champagne to celebrate our first... Rolls-Royce?" Siegfried laughed.

"*Mein Lieberrr, bitte* (my dearest, please) bring it to the bathroom because I'm running a lavender bubble bath and 'I vant you in it right now my *Erculo* (Hercules)', *maintenant* (now)!" Elizabeth giggled like a teenager.

"*Jawohl, meine Aphrodita,* vhere iz zhe *(Yes my Venus)!*" he imitated her German comedy act. He dropped his pants and she screamed. He wanted nothing more than to pamper every part she wanted him to nibble. They splashed into the big round tub drowning in kisses.

"Isn't the sign of Cancer a soixante-neuf, you know, that sixty-nine sign?" she pressed herself in a hilarious but sensuous way.

"Well, mathematically I could investigate this immediately..." and while he slipped under the bubbles, her first moans got cut off by Tchaikovsky's Waltz of the Flowers.

"Lesclau and in the middle of a pre-orgasm, how dare he?" she sniggered. Siegfried's head, dripping with foam, came up slowly from between her knees and she got out of the bath grabbing a huge bathrobe and picking up the phone.

"Thanks, darlink," Siegfried continued in a ridiculous slang, "you nearly broke my nooze gettink out of zhe bath with your long legs in my face and you could have killed me with one ztupid phone call." He sipped some more champagne but tuned into her conversation.

Of course, it was Désiré, her man in Florence. She pushed the speakerphone button.

"Ma chère, désolé! (My dear, so sorry!)" His voice sounded dreadfully worried.

"There is no way I can get into the villa the way you have described to me and I am under the impression that I am not the only one around here." He proceeded, "I have a hotel room almost right behind the villa and it gives me a good view. I also brought my laser lunettes, amazing, but I saw nobody come out yet. To keep anyone else from being housed here, I rented the whole place. I imagine you'll be flying over asap?"

"Well, let me tell you what Siegfried and I discovered right here in Geneva!"

Fifteen minutes later Sig started feeling drunk and the bottle was nearly empty. His wife gave Désiré a quick briefing of her own last twenty-four hours. Her husband clapped his hands.

"Brava cara, eccelente (Bravo dearest, excellent)!" he screamed.

"Désiré désolé, mon mari se soûle dans le bain et je vais louper mon prochain orgasme! Ne quittez pas ce poste et je te rappelle demain matin à huit heures et on discutera mon voyage. Bisous! (So sorry Désiré, my husband is getting drunk in the bathtub and I'm about to miss my next orgasm! Don't leave your post and I'll call you tomorrow morning at 8:00 am and we'll discuss my trip. Kisses!)" She hung up.

Another bottle of champagne tiptoed with Eliza into the bathroom. Siegfried wasn't in the bathtub and for a moment she panicked but she felt his hands on her breasts and he kissed her neck slowly till his hips discovered hers, willing to all rapturous abandon. Between the thick carpet and the warm lavender oils, they hardly found the sheets of their bed and the night was long, like the first week of a long-awaited marriage. This was indeed second honeymooning!

Simon Averardo's Office.

Simon woke up from a very long nap at about 7:00 pm. He hadn't checked his security desk yet and slouched tediously towards that control panel that existed like his second skin. It confirmed him as the almighty controller, and it made him laugh. He typed in several codes.

'Log in: please confirm your password'.

That had never happened before. He typed in the password again and the screen lit up. Did someone open his system; nobody but he and... no, Siegfried hadn't been in his office. The camera would have proven his visit. He checked immediately the afternoon tapes on a fast-forward mode and all the digital tapes were on time codes... nothing to be found.

Good, he thought, it's better we don't have more problems.

He set the timer on automatic and last night's film ran before his eyes. Little by little he got excited. *Damn, where is Bill?* He so regretted the absence of his boy-toy, but only a thought away the door opened wide. Jacqueline walked in and threw her summer coat on the couch and she didn't need to strip. He continued to watch last night's rape scene while she got on her hands and knees to execute just what he had become used to in the last few months.

When she had finished, he felt like taking her right at that moment, pushing her against the wall as he had done so often. She opened her purse and slipped a small envelope on the desk and the snow-white powder magically turned itself into straight lines. As she walked over to the shower it took but a minute to snuggle himself around her belly. He was so lost. She dried off coldly and walked back into the office.

To the stardust on the table, she had added TWX9, a specially prepared powder Uncle Harry had provided. That would knock him out for hours though his erection would stand for hours, an unfortunate side-effect she laughed at. She watched him, line after line until he was satisfied licking up the leftovers. He immediately forced himself on her and pushed harder and harder; and she almost felt sorry for herself.

He would rather join her anywhere but in the same Hades where he had been since his father had raped him for the first time in front of the brethren on that Friday 13th meeting at a castle outside of Paris. He had been a sacrificial lamb at only thirteen! Jacky knew every detail and she had helped him forget this trauma... a temporary healing seemed to have occurred when they were together. Yet she would also remind him they hid a lot more painful memories from their youth lingering under their superficial personality surface.

An hour later, two men walked in, the younger one a towering seven feet of athletic muscle. The older one, elegantly dressed like a banker or politician, sat down in the bigger armchair and looked at his pretty protégé. She was still beautiful after now almost twenty years of service. He had trained her well and he always protected her. The coke, TWX9 combination had its usual effect, sometimes it was devastating and even dangerous. And while the younger fellow extracted the CD from Simon's personal security system, the boss contemplated how he would get rid of Simon.

"It's all done sir, the last forty-eight hours all registered. I'll have the entire building back on screen at fifteen hundred hours, sir, that's your 9:00 am in DC. Anything else, sir?"

"No that will do, my assistant in Washington will work accordingly. Thank you, John, as usual, a great job," he said and lit a cigar. "Maybe you would like to have diner sometime with this young lady?" But John, politely declined, then finished his well-paid job executing the last orders.

"Ah, those Havanas," Harry puffed away,"in the old days Fidel would send them to me!" He didn't lie and he gestured with his signature, customary vanity.

"Dress up our little girl will you, John... there's a cool breeze tonight. Let's pull Simon more towards the checker-board carpet. And here's the game board; you know what to do." A few minutes later, John carried Jacqueline like a feather to the elevator and down to the parking lot. The dark Cadillac left the driveway and set off in the direction of the old town.

When, at seven o'clock, Germaine found the doors open, she was dumbfounded in yet another shock: one that wouldn't go away. This was the second time in 24 hours, Monsieur Averardo was found naked – but unconscious in a cramped position with a very erect penis stuck in a black and white checkerboard, on the floor. She called up security. The man ran upstairs and equally stunned, he immediately called the police.

Only this time Germaine had taken a picture with her cell phone just like her grandson had shown her. 'NewsdayBest' arrived at the same time as the police and Géraldine, who was the second person called by Germaine. The police urged her to cover up her boss with his large cape that she would find in the entrance closet. At least the newspapers wouldn't have to add little black squares to cover the boss's favoured parts! She hesitated to call Siegfried's home and decided to send a text message to both their cell phones, including the picture. She was sure that at one point they would call her back.

Siegfried Freundreich was still sound asleep, and Elizabeth wanted to surprise the man she loved more than anyone else. She'd get 'her' husband his preferred morning *croissant aux amandes*. Their favourite bakery, *Le Petit Pain Doré (*The Little Golden Bread) opened early, but most croissants were sold so she got the last two, a*ux amandes* (almond croissants) adding a crispy baguette. Their NosPresso coffee maker would do the rest and breakfast in bed was something he deserved after last year's madness. The 8:00 am news was on the radio and while the young woman behind the counter changed a one hundred Swiss Franc note, Elizabeth hardly paid attention to the local news. But this was another unexpected wake-up call.

"Simon Averardo, the President of internationally acclaimed pharmaceutical giant, DoWell was found unconscious in his office presumably under the influence of heavy drugs and taken to the hospital. The company's cleaning woman, by the name of Germaine Balet, who arrives daily at 7.00 am, had found his body undressed on the floor of his private apartment office. Apparently, his private parts were connected to a chessboard and the police started an investigation of this unusual case suspecting maybe burglars or a set-up by a competing company."

While a briefing was given on the company's success story, Elizabeth shook her head in disbelief and she quickly accepted the change. *"Merçi, à demain et bonne journée* (Thanks and see you tomorrow and have nice day!)"

"She left, running out of the bakery almost hiding in the bag of croissants.

"A demain Madame Freundreich (see you tomorrow)," the girl answered politely, surprised at her quick exit.

Oh, my goddess; the Press, she thought. I must call Géraldine. A tout prix (at all cost), *they mustn't come looking for Siegfried.*

The doorman Marcel was in a chitchat-mood. *"Bonjour Madame, vous allez-bien* (Good morning Madame, all is well)?" Elizabeth smiled. *"Encore une belle journée* (Again, have nice day)!" he added.

"Oh oui, une belle journée pour vous (Oh yes indeed, a nice day to you too)," was her final word, how annoying.

When she pushed the pin code to get to the private elevator, she noticed a black Cadillac pulling up in front of the building and the driver, one extremely tall man, got out and opened the door for an elegantly dressed older man. The elevator door shut and when she got to the last floor, she set the top alarm. Now nobody could even push an elevator button. They'd have to call the security at the front desk. Only she didn't know this man was a far heavier client than the local press.

The Nospresso machine, steaming hot, popped out small cups of coffee like a blinking hen. She sighed when the cell phone announced at least one message and, after the radio news, she felt she had better briefly check the last ones. Great. Simon, she thought; you were always an ass on a checkerboard! She poured the coffee into elegantly displayed nineteenth-century porcelain cups, the croissants on top of their silver throne surrounded by fruits and her favoured Algae Chlorella tablets. Oh, I almost forgot the flax oil for the green veggie juice. *Get down that cholesterol*... she copied a radio ad in a mini-mouse voice.

She walked into the bedroom and put down the plate on a smallish nineteenth-century table. She opened the terrace doors. A light breeze took her to a long snuggle. Siegfried opened an eye and hid his head from the sun peeking in. Grumbling, he stretched like a cat, howled and moaned when Elizabeth attempted to pull him up. He noticed the croissants and got in a good mood instantly.

"You shouldn't go out that early for food... and that's a lie," he said lovingly.

"I know those lies I can cope with! Bonjour mon amour," she meowed, making claws and crawling towards him. He lifted her up in a cascade of kisses.

"Two cups... we're actually having breakfast together two days in a row... wow. I think I'll marry you again," He joked around a little longer. The phone rang.

"The doorman," she said intuitively.

"I take it all back, no marriage if you answer."

She stuck out her tongue and answered in a shallow voice, "Cherie, they found Simon possibly on the verge of dying. He's in some sort of a coma with, yes, an erection stuck in a chessboard. That's what the message read on my cell phone, and the photo Germaine took, and that's what the radio announced before our breakfast! This smells like an act of vengeance if I ever heard of one. How improbably nonchalant!" She cried out laughing. The doorman's face appeared on the little screen and she picked up.

"Mes excuses Madame, mais il y un monsieur qui insiste vous parler. Il n'a pas quitté le parking; c'est urgent ? Que dois-je faire? (Allow me to tell you that there is a man who insists in speaking to you and he hasn't left the parking lot. What must I do?)" he asked in a nervous manner.

"Merci Marcel. Vous lui dites de m'appeler dans deux heures au bureau. Mon mari et moi, nous sommes occupés à prendre le petit déjeuner et nous ne voulons pas être dérangé!" (Thanks Marcel. Tell him to call me at the office in two hours. We are taking our breakfast and unavailable.)

The screen went dark. Those journalists, she thought, they'd get under your sheets if they could. *"Marcel annonce qu'un monsieur voulait nous parler, à cette heure* (The doorman is insisting that a man wants to speak to us. At this hour!)" Eliza added some more drama.

"You should have been *une tragedienne*, Eliza, it really is a second skin," he said mockingly. "I wished I could have seen you in your tutu and *on pointes."*

She looked away in mock disapproval. He continued.

"By the way, that article in *VIVRE* was so elegant, fun and the old pictures with you and Dame Margot Fonteyn, lovely, so classy. I bet you were even a better dancer."

"In those days, darling, nobody was a better dancer than Margot and Sir Frederic Ashton wouldn't even have allowed it! There's only one Queen at every court. Just look at history; when there were two, one lost her head!" She took a deep breath as she got rid of the cell phone. "Simon certainly is about to lose his! He must have overdosed. I read somewhere that all your muscles can stiffen in a traumatic state; whatever did he get himself into now?"

They looked at each other a bit concerned.

"We really ought to take a year off, you know," Elizabeth said, "DoWell owes you a lot of money on last year's overtime 'tableau' and I, well, I can resign today before the big news makes the world press." She repeated a decision made the day before.

"You will?" he asked while getting up and walking into the shower.

"Oh yes; I do own 14% of all European assets, we mustn't forget that you have still 11% in your contract. That means we can retire very comfortably. We'll sell the downtown apartment we have rented out since a decade and get a house in Provence. What do you think?" she said while she undressed to get into the shower with him.

"Only if we can have at least two bathrooms and three showers," he laughed as she tickled him.

The Cadillac remained parked in front of their building. The outside temperature had risen to a summer high. Harry Khope was sending off a few nasty emails. He was truly annoyed nobody was picking up the phone. A concerned doorman got really worried and he called upstairs leaving a message on the answering machine. When Siegfried pulled on his new summer slacks, he noticed the device was blinking. He had always approved of his wife's choice of old phones married to their answering machines like an electronic sidekick. At least we can still hear the voice and it's our choice to pick up or not. So, he called for his spouse's attention.

"Darling, listen to George, the doorman left another message".

She finished drying her hair and she stepped back into the bedroom.

"Madame, Monsieur permettez-moi de vous dire que l'homme qui voulait monter n'a toujours pas quitté le parking! (Allow me to tell you that the man who wanted to come up hasn't left the parking lot!)" His voice sounded grave.

"OK, that's it," she said. "We shall take a cab from the back of the building. I'm not going to have them put their nose in our business".

"Ah, Eliza, j'aiiiime femme forrrte (I love a strong woman)", he joked, and she took a typical Bette Davis pose.

"But I have an even less conspicuous way," he continued, "*le bus* (the bus!)"

About ten minutes later they ran to catch the bus towards Geneva's 'Place du Théâtre' and they carried just the right change to get their ticket.

53. FIESOLE, 2018 BACK TO THE FUTURE

Seaworthy society,
afloat aloof of all bewilderment
sustainable all in itself
in your fostered coats from worldly lining,
longing to know,
this is but a naught game
from one hinder in a media mist
no chaperons to clusters of respect,
and nursing natures almost found best bride. (Inner Voice)

When Dritto was the first one to wake up, he felt damaged or changed, confused and out of his body. No, it wasn't all that bad. He didn't have to be so dramatic. Yes, he felt scattered, but also aware enough that he didn't want to get out of this adventure. If there was ever any dream he wished not to leave, it was this one. He took a peek through his almost glued eyelids and noticed little by little that he was no longer in a Renaissance courtyard. A bit further he noticed that Florian was moving one arm after the other, ever so slowly and his legs were hardly stretching out. It wasn't the case with Isabel who seemed to have slightly lifted herself but had dropped back into the original position.

As for Derecho and Izquierdo, they seemed to share his same desire not to return to the twenty-first century. Dritto quietly unbuckled the safety belt that had kept him from falling off this travel-chair. No doubt this had saved the trio while they fought with the 'dark-vaders', a moment that he remembered only too well. He was in awe and curious to find out how he could still be here and yet have traveled to another dimension and remember everything; but especially, how in the world did he project himself into the Renaissance.

After looking at himself and then his friends, he realized they were all truly alive.

There was a slight mumbling coming from Izquierdo's chair and Dritto was hoping he'd open his eyes. He did. Within minutes, Derecho matched him and when an unhappy Florian moved his head towards Isabel, she seemed the only person who hadn't returned home. He wondered what had happened. All four men sat up and stared at each other, happy to be back but a bit surprised that they didn't accomplish their mission, at least so it seemed.

"We have to go back?" was the first reaction Iz gave.

Derecho wasn't sure if he had heard well; *'we're all going back?' His thoughts were scrambled.*

"That remains to be seen," Florian answered. "Isabel hasn't returned. We have just made an amazing jump back in time; well forward of course." He chuckled, almost embarrassed. "Here we are indeed and that wasn't exactly the way it was planned, right?"

"Well, we cannot just leave her there," Iz said, sincerely concerned.

"Leave 'them' there," Derecho corrected.

"Let's get some water and get to the kitchen first," Florian suggested. "We need to get some energy in our stomachs; one person should stay here."

"I will," Dritto offered graciously.

Florian smiled and the three went upstairs and into the kitchen. He boiled water to make some pasta while Derecho returned from upstairs with a bottle of water.

"It's strange isn't it," Izquierdo said, "You know Florian, I'm really happy we traveled back in time. These people were awesome, so kind and so hospitable. I am sorry we returned so quickly. Something amazing happened, no?"

"Yes, indeed by some strange phenomena we went through a black hole," Florian answered. "We could never have planned anything like it. Maybe I made a terrible mistake because I might have messed up the astrological calculation, maybe I missed out on minor degrees of some of the planets in the travel program. After all, in those days some of the planets hadn't even been discovered. I wonder if it matters that the Medici brothers, Andrea and his sisters were of the same generation with Pluto. But I am, I'll admit, a bit confused without an astro-wizard like GianLuca to give us further explanations! He did remind me that in 1473, Pluto hadn't been discovered, yet this planet has a very important influence because it rules life and death and all transformation!"

The tagliatelle was 'al dente' and Florian mixed them with what seemed now like last year's leftover pesto. He took the steaming pot down while Iz prepared dishes and silverware. All four men sat down and kept an eye on Isabel hoping the smell of the food might wake her up. But of course, it didn't.

"She stayed behind with GianLuca?" Derecho asked shyly.

"Yes, I imagine that's what has happened, a blockage of some kind. I must repair." Florian answered, hesitating to say anything more.

"My take is that because of GianLuca's relationship with the brothers, he'll take her to the villa, and they will find out what she needed to bring back. But how are they getting back?" Iz asked, while filling up every glass with some local spring water.

"Well, I'm going to have to get to my laptop to open the time travel device, and see what I can find out," Florian said.

Dritto looked surprised as he thought he could contact them in 1473.

"No, no dear Dritto," Florian smiled, "again I am no magician, but I want to see the configurations and then we must immediately take a look at the old cave that houses the statue. After all, we are right here. One of us must stay in the house and we must be very careful because it's a bright day, and after all, sometimes tourists come by the main gate and we do not want any extra attention."

Florian walked over to Isabel and checked to see if anything had changed. He held her hands, caressed her hair and gave her a tender kiss. He reflected on their last words, the explosion in the skies, and their past. It was time to act, and he moved towards the staircase. For sure, not much had been changed since his 2017 visit. He opened a side door leading to the garden below and Iz and Derecho followed. Dritto decided to sit with the last woman on Earth, he laughed at the idea. He was just fine watching out for Isabel's return; he did admire her. To reach the grotto, they either had to cross the first of the two smaller parks or walk on the upper terrace leading to the back of the gardens where the old cave was hidden away in the shade of the trees.

"You know your way around here?" Derecho asked.

"Fortunately," Florian replied, "I was invited to a party once and then the owner showed me around quite a bit. She hadn't been too revealing in her explanations of that part of the villa; magnificent renovations but no great research on a more esoteric level. Well, you know businesspeople today aren't always that interested if it hasn't got a historical and monetary value. To me a touch of spirituality is always welcome."

They now stood in front of the small cave with a side entrance, dirty, uncleaned and dark. There was the statue showing no signs of a goddess … if it ever had, it no longer did.

"Almost 500 years old, not too well kept," Iz mumbled, displeased, "not much we're going to find here."

"And yet," Florian replied, "and yet, the secret will be found right here. I do hope GianLuca can find out and with a strong woman like Isabel there …"

"Oh goodness," Iz exclaimed unexpectedly. "Talking of a strong woman, Elizabeth von Weitweg, *Oh mio Dio ti ho dimenticato* (Oh my God, I had forgotten you)! I have totally forgotten you." He repeated himself a few times, "It's been days."

"What, you forgot who?" Florian asked, while having his woman on his mind.

"I mean my Elizabeth; our employer, actually employers!" he screamed at his colleague. "Elizabeth Von Weitweg and Simon Averardo, I haven't called them back. Hopefully, they're not on the hunt for us."

Florian looked surprised and then recalled their story.

"I so need to get in touch with her," Iz said.

"I think we should wait a while," Derecho said. "Let's first see what Isabel is able to come up with!"

"Good thinking, Doh, that lady is also Isabel's half-sister and married to a scientific genius mind!" Florian answered.

"By the way," Derecho continued, "You need to know something. When we were on our way to Florence, we were attacked by ghost-like riders; the beings we eventually got to slay were extremely strange."

Florian waited and listened to their brief but convincingly scary story.

"Almost virtual you said, Derecho? So, is that the key?" Florian asked.

"It sounds like that program our secret services stole from the Chinese," Iz said.

"What?" Doh replied, "The Chinese?"

"Well time hasn't stood still there either. I mean we're not in Confucius's century," Florian reminded them. "It was something that was started under Mao Tse Tung and the Russians were involved, but the Agency found out and used it while adding it to their own MK Ultra programs, very much advanced in the early 60s."

"You sure went deep into it all, didn't you?" Iz remarked.

"Yup, I had to," Florian answered in a straightforward manner without any specific pride. "It's intricate ... you have no idea what they have become capable of. What you encountered that night with your 'Dark Vaders', well that was similar to a weather control program." Florian continued, "Iz you know about this don't you?"

Izquierdo assented, unhappily recalling some of his early study years and research.

"Today you can interfere with the weather, adapt the clouds, change the temperature and create floods, hurricanes and Tsunamis like a well-prepared meal. Competition grew strongly after the one that hit south Asia; remember Christmas 2004?" Iz continued to vividly recall images of destruction, relief services all over the east coast.

"Not to forget that last Puerto Rico hurricane, leaving the island without housing!"

Iz felt an old anger boiling and said, "The reasons for creating such weather disturbances are obvious only to the rulers of this planet. What we all experienced though is a well-planned disturbance through a virtually generalized fear program, maybe designed and close to perfection." He paused. "It slips into people's minds through their self-chosen addiction to entertainment devices such as video games, television, of course, and now the permanent media and phone systems and other similar toys," two pair of stunned eyes didn't blink.

"Now that doesn't change our problem. On the Medici's timeline, whoever triggered these phenomena, well, they must be totally unaware of our presence in 1473," Florian noticed.

"Derecho may appear slight, like a young adult, but he is mentally a lot stronger than you would expect and he had no problem resisting the images of evil projected against him. Eastern philosophers have said that what you believe is what you attract. Your courage, aha, your disguise of a fearless knight . . . and you didn't believe the attackers existed other than let's say in a video game, so eventually they had to exit the program." They all agreed while Florian proceeded.

"Look at Lapo's house where we all identified with our own physical mirrors. This storm, this cosmic event of uncommon proportions apparently absorbed us. But we still existed in more than one version. The ones in 1473 and 2018 are only two of them. We may also appear in different versions in our own century. There is a unique research program being developed and it will be fascinating to search for deeper perception on that level."

"Well, this sounds a little too complicated to me," Derecho joked. "Different versions; several Derechos right here on our timeline?"

"No Doh," Iz intervened. "Not right here, somewhere on planet Earth, it could be Alaska, Hang Zhou, Paris . . ."

"OK, I'll take Paris, that'll be cheaper than taking a hotel no? I'd love to contact my other 'me' around let's say, what about 'Le Marais district'," he clowned around.

"Gentlemen, gentlemen, this is serious business because it means that . . ." Florian interrupted.

"Yes, Florian. After that little fighting scene, it means we were being checked out. That also means that Harry Khope is involved because that's one of the programs he had sponsored in Switzerland! And to be precise, he brought it to the DoWell office in Geneva!" Iz quickly slipped in his five cents.

"What?" Florian exclaimed. "That would be rather unpleasant, and it will endanger our whole plan. He's a first-class Machiavellian devil, letting others do the work. Then his Agency walks in when the job is almost finished and then he takes his product to the . . ."

Iz said, "Right, let's not talk about *them.*"

"Can you all stop talking in riddles? If you mean the agency; I'm not totally dumb, you know me," Derecho exclaimed.

"Don't you think it is wise to return to the villa instead of hanging out in this cold and damp grotto? I don't see anything happening here," Iz said.

"OK, I'll stay and when I find anything new, I'll call for you guys," Florian answered. "Meanwhile, is there a way you can get in touch with Elizabeth von Weitweg? I wouldn't call the other guy. Also, make sure we all have our cell phones this time. I know we don't like to, but this is a state of emergency."

"Sure, and no, I wouldn't call Averardo," Iz said. "He's Khope's big friend and the DoWell top man. But I can call Elizabeth's secretary. She's big on espionage stories and social gossip with a lock on her mouth when her boss is asking questions. I'll get to it immediately."

Florian nodded and stayed behind hoping to find a quick answer to ... this mystery! He didn't have a clue yet taking a peek at the skies gave him a wonderful feeling.

54. FIESOLE, 1473 EVENTUS

You pulled me into your cave.
I felt lost for years.
Roaming around this world,
endlessly eloping labyrinths
till I remembered my own amygdala. (Smiling Voices in Limestone)

Andrea wasn't the first one to discover that there were fewer guests in their courtyard. He looked at his father breathing slowly while Fiammetta was still partly unconscious. Agnola opened her eyes, softly pounding her new friend Isabel on the shoulder and delicately removing her hair out of her face. Andrea looked down while chills ran all over his back when he noticed the absence of Florian and the other three men. He guessed that the last hour's event had swung their destiny into, at least to him, an unknown void. Maybe they were returned to their respective homes.

He had no idea yet how to cope with this. He was grateful GianLuca hadn't left! Giovannino ran straight into his arms but when he saw Lapo, not yet awake he immediately took him back to consciousness, his little hands gently slapping the man's cheeks. Andrea gazed at GianLuca who hadn't moved from a strange yoga-like position in the grass. Not sure what to do, he got up and turned him around. Isabel had been watching the whole scene and hardly found the strength to get up, but with Agnola's help, she finally did.

They knelt next to Andrea and Isabel put her hands on GianLuca's chest and told Andrea to pump while she closed GianLuca's nose and started breathing directly into his mouth. Agnola removed his sandals and started rubbing his feet. A big cough came up and she pulled back in time, knowing he hadn't been drowning so he wouldn't be spitting water into her face. He looked bewildered by this *deja vu.*

"I guess I'm still in the Renaissance, always a lovely lady to welcome me! Or should I check with the local doctor," he mumbled with a soft laugh. "You are all wearing such lovely outfits." It reminded him of his first entrance into the Renaissance at the Piazza Santa Croce not so long ago. It was Andrea who hugged him first. Lapo, still slightly out of balance stumbled into the table and attracted all the attention when the cups went rolling down in a brief orchestral interlude, sliding into the elaborate darkness that seemed to last an hour or so.

"Papa," Agnola ran towards her father. "Easy now papa, please sit down!" she urged him.

"Oh good, you're all well I see. Where is Fiammetta?" Lapo asked.

Agnola seated her father and finally noticed her sister's feet behind the bushes at the garden's back door.

"Oh Dio, aiuta (Oh God, help!)" Agnola screamed.

GianLuca joined her and the others ensued quickly. Agnola repeated the moves she had just seen her brother use on GianLuca's chest and her eyes asked GianLuca to use his mouth. While his face turned burgundy, he obliged. The response was overwhelming to both Fiammetta and to him. Even Agnola turned her head away and hurried into her father's arms whispering that her sister was now fine.

Isabel had taken Andrea's right hand and she wasn't sure if the events of the last day were the result of all that cosmic energy running their limbs into a confused limbo. But Andrea's eyes translated that perfect hunger a man manifests so strongly when he meets a woman he desires. He was pretty clear in his mind that this foreign visitor was that unique soul we all seem to wait for, sometimes for even more than a lifetime. It was her time to blush, but her commander duties took over, and her own nature isn't about to change. She immediately put her other arm around Giovannino, who had waited for the kindness of such a gesture from a foreign mama.

Fiammetta was holding on so tight that GianLuca could hardly breath. "How good to see you all survived this tremendous cosmic storm," she said, smiling.

But GianLuca had a few other ideas. "Do cosmic storms throw bodies into another dimension, Isabel?" he asked almost angrily.

She was surprised at the way her friend voiced himself till she realized the absence of Florian and the trio. She covered her eyes and tears started rolling ... she just couldn't stop. GianLuca moved Fiammetta to a chair and grabbed Isabel by the shoulders, but the result was feeble. She was close to hysterics. He turned around and looked for a carafe of water, and to the utter surprise of his limited audience, emptied one over her head.

She yelled out like a mad woman.

"Are you out of your mind? That water is bitterly cold!"

But she was back to normal and they both exploded in a loud laugh.

"Cold? The water isn't cold, and it is positively summer outside; no fridge as you may well know!" GianLuca joked while his face turned serious as only two knew what a fridge was.

"Any explanations?" he asked, not letting Isabel get away with a moment of emotional takeover. The Buontalenti watched in utter horror wondering if this was a dispute of some kind.

"Florian is gone. Haven't you noticed?" She replied not without anger in her voice.

"Oh yes, I did notice and where are the three other guys? Let's just hope they are all back home and not lost in some wormhole," he whispered. "But what about us and this kind family; what about the Medici brothers? They must have felt something. It could only happen to us if we all share a simultaneous connection, right?"

GianLuca paused before asking, "Would time traveling cause such an anomaly?"

"Are you shooting bullets at me GianLuca? Your eyes are about to pop out of your head. Do you think I was risking people's lives to come over here?"

Isabel's words had turned into steel daggers.

"Well, you're wrong to think I would risk anyone's life," she shouted, "because their bodies are still in our century, in the year 2018 and no, I didn't get you involved, nor searched for you, because I had no idea you were even alive! Does that answer your question?" She had raised her voice offensively, to her own surprise and that of two embarrassed sisters. Isabel's sudden tone of voice had shocked the entire Buontalenti family.

GianLuca stood back, though he understood her frustration. She panicked and without Florian she felt she probably couldn't get back. It would take magic to do so, or they would all be stuck in this century.

A moment earlier, before he had helped Fiammetta to wake up, GianLuca had neither an idea nor a troubled mind about remaining on this timeline. What was so different from the movie he was playing out in the twenty-first century?

Deceit and lies weren't only a Renaissance factor. And maybe with these legendary brothers he could help create a shift in consciousness. That inevitably would ripple in time and he thought it to be an exceptional gift after all to be right here and to be a part of such a possible turn in history.

But for now, he had a new family on his hands, and they were all waiting for an explanation. Isabel was crying and waving her hands like a woman who had lost her mind and then suddenly she stopped and walked over to Lapo, who with his daughters, attempted to make sense out of all this.

Andrea had dared to approach her and as he laid his hand on her shoulder again, she could feel the electricity one more time and she let her head melt onto his chest. He couldn't have asked for more because that was exactly what he wanted to do for her; be her friend and make her understand that even if she would be 'locked in time', he would love her everlastingly. And as she read his thoughts, she quietened down and his arm brought all the comfort for any century to come.

"I am so sorry, please forgive my behaviour," she said. "I panicked because I have taken a big responsibility on this special mission and I thought I had messed it all up, especially since I'm now without my companions. Forgive me, for a moment it felt I was about to lose all control. I'm so sorry, GianLuca, of course I didn't mean to insult you."

"It's quite alright, Isabel," GianLuca answered kindly, "everything will be falling into place soon enough, I promise you."

Agnola ran into the house and offered to take Isabel upstairs to change clothes. Isabel thanked her warmly and they left holding hands like sisters.

A slow breeze refreshed the garden's visitors and Isabel returned feeling more comfortable in a new gown while Agnola had dried Isabel's hair, now covered by a well-designed, multi-coloured silk scarf.

"That was quite something, those last few hours we had here," Lapo finally spoke up, "or should we say days?" and he did smile. "It hasn't been since the sad departure of my wife that we have had so much unexpected and mysterious things happen in our home. Do you think we have ghosts of some kind?"

"Oh no, Papa," Andrea answered.

"You heard Isabel confirm that this was a cosmic storm and ... what is that exactly, GianLuca?" Agnola asked.

"Well, let us not get more confusion on our plates than this change of temperature already did," GianLuca said. "Cosmic in terms of size: *Eventus giganteum cosmicae* (A gigantic cosmic event), a gigantic storm-like heavy disturbance from an astrophysical point of view, now multi-dimensional. My feeling is that the other time travelers went through a black hole and I have no idea how that even happened. I really have to sit still and contemplate what it all means."

He yielded to a greater mystery as he closed his eyes.

"You see, Isabel and Florian had set a goal by coming here. They wanted to bring a code back home from this timeline to theirs. It's a lost code that would simplify time traveling and make it available for more than just people in our world's governments who most of the time have rather dubious motives linked to their power games!"

"Dio Benedetto (dear God)!" Fiammetta called out.

"Does that mean that more and more people are going to come time traveling through this house? Papa, I believe we must seriously think of moving, maybe towards Napoli? You had a good rapport with the court there, didn't you?"

"Nothing like this," GianLuca continued in a joking mode, "please do not worry! The idea is that scientists and researchers would be able to travel in time for a non-political purpose."

At least, I hope so. If GianLuca didn't show any doubts in his heart, he was unsure nonetheless.

"You see, our secret services employ spies ... you understand the phenomena, yes?" They all nodded. "Something called 'The Agency', a bit like a fraternity who under the motto of protecting the country, is led by a few men connected to the rulers of our countries ... with the help of especially wealthy groups of businesspeople we call *cooperationis,* Latin for collaborations or, shall we say, 'corporations'?" He continued.

"They want to create, with the different governments, a program so they can control every citizen. Each country has their own similar 'organization' and they are supposed to work together world-wide and fight against so called 'terror-groups' whose goal is to disrupt peace through violent acts, but often the creation of those same governing bodies! A very sophisticated network has been created over the ages and it would make up an extremely long history lesson to explain the details to you. The bottom line is that a few countries on this planet ... I'm talking of course about the twenty-first century ... have sworn to find out more about specific secrets that especially the elders, the wise men and women from the past, encrypted in stone.

The story of our planet throughout the ages, the story of the 'creation of man and woman' ... nothing at all like women of the so-called 'holy scriptures'... is one where the sons of the gods, just like in your mythology, mated with the daughters of man ... or us humans. After these so-called gods had created such humans in the first place, they then enslaved them for different experiments!"

"And you're saying all this can be found in certain places, like here in our home?" Andrea asked with the innocence of a child.

"Well, it's a little more complicated than that. That one part of the Mediterranean where one says the man called Jesus of Nazareth, maybe the son of a king, was born, is called Mesopotamia. This fertile valley of the Nile and many more ... remember the Garden of Eden ... are a haven for centuries of secrets. Few have walked this Earth knowing the whole truth. Holy scriptures and books in India have acknowledged a similar story as biblical history offered. Paintings of similar esoteric and magical events, including the Noah's Arc section and the deluge can be found in their books as well as in the Babylonian written texts!"

Lapo was as always, excited by new information but this time his son and daughters had kept their attention span equally sharp.

"In our century, leaders are enamoured to rule the world in similar ways to Alexander the Great or Julio Caesarea or other legendary conquerors like Genghis Khan," GianLuca proceeded.

"They also do it through the invisible worlds and within cosmic wars no world citizen can visualize or understand because the citizens are never informed, and we remain distracted by the public lives of many famous artists and the elite we have created. The rulers have called in so many entities and their gods of old were not always the kindest ones. As such our world is being ruled by corrupt leaders seconded by entities who manipulate the law, re-write their constitution and want their citizens to believe whatever their media is proposing!" It seemed like an exceptionally long monologue, but their guest continued.

"They have created weaponry that can destroy this world... I cannot begin to describe the malevolent power, capable of rendering the entire human race extinct and creating more devastating wars outside the planet. Our world in the twenty-first century has become the orbit of lies and deceit, corruption and cosmic wars."

55. GENEVA, 2018 JUDITH'S TORTA

And you split below treasure ships of old,
sunken and forgotten
and ... in a splash of dazzling lights you split ...
and no sea, no lake as high as mountains of heavenly spheres
lowered to all heedless neglect of oblivious ego. (Dry Tears)

Izquierdo called the DoWell office, and he couldn't understand why it took such a long time to speak to someone. Finally, Eveliebe picked up a phone that didn't seem to stop ringing. She answered, and when he requested to speak to Elizabeth, she answered in a very irritated voice.

"If it is to get more juice out of our pharmaceutical mill and throw us at the world press, she won't talk to you. I can tell you that right now. For which paper do you write?" she asked in a very vindictive way.

"Oh no, Miss Eveliebe, I don't ..." he stuttered briefly, "I mean I'm not from the press. I actually work for Elizabeth."

"You do, and who are you exactly?" Eveliebe asked pertly.

And how come I don't know about this she bitched angrily. This last week has just been enough for me.

"Hold on I'll check if she is in".

She called Elizabeth who was handling the many journalists as professionally as she possibly could.

"You have a call, Madame Freundreich," she called out cynically, "and it's long distance from Italy."

"D'accord, j'arrive. Messieurs, je vous en supplie, un peu de patience! Je ne peux absolument rien vous dire de plus. Je ferai un effort pour organiser une petite conférence de presse dès que j'ai des nouvelles de la santé de Mr Averardo (OK, I'm coming. Gentlemen some patience! I can absolutely not tell you more. I will try to set

for a press conference as soon as I have news on Mr Averardo's health)", she announced as gracefully as she possibly could.

But the local press was annoying and adamantly growling like wolves, both in numbers and in eagerness.

"Nous voulons savoir pourquoi et comment l'érection du président de DoWell a troué un jeu d'échec (We want to know why and how the president's erection got into a chessboard)," one of them screamed out, more interested in a fine scandal than in knowing the truth, and nothing but the truth.

"Cela suffit vos ragot et questions bêtes, Mr Trouvert (That's enough stupid gossip questions, Mr Trouvert)!" Elizabeth declared, rather officially closing the shop.

"J'ai déjà donné ma parole. La discussion est terminée et j'ai dit mon dernier mot. Au revoir (I already gave my word. The discussion is over. I have said my last words. Goodbye)!"

And she turned her back and walked into her own office.

"Oh, those beasts," she called out, *"Eveliebe qui est au téléphone* (Eveliebe, who is on the phone)?"

"Un Monsieur, qui dit qu'il travaille pour votre gauche (A man who claims he works for your… left side), whatever that may mean?" Eveliebe answered in a high voice.

"Ah Mon Dieu, Izquierdo finalement (Oh my god, Izquierdo finally)," and Elizabeth picked up the portable phone and walked out on the terrace.

"Izquierdo," she repeated herself, "Are you well and where are you… on this planet?" she asked in a vivid and strained voice.

"Oui (Yes) Madame, it's a very long story, but we're fine, all three of us. I cannot talk right now, because I do not trust the phone line. Could I call you at the number you gave me in let's say… well you tell me in how much time."

"Of course, a very good idea… make it 30 minutes to get through the traffic."

When she ran by the secretaries, she told them she had an urgent errand to run, one to save the business. She'd be back in an hour and if Siegfried came in, he should call her urgently on her cell. In the elevator she suddenly remembered those eager journalists and she took the side entrance and ran for a taxi. She got lucky and twenty minutes later she rang the doorbell of an old friend and one of Geneva's finest art collectors, Judith Mannovsky. The door opened and the maid said that Madame would be in any moment and would she like to wait.

'Perfect timing,' Elizabeth thought.

"Can I wait in the office? I expect an important call," she asked the young Peruvian-looking teenager who proceeded to dust with a classical-looking *plumeau.*

*"Bien sur Madame, vous connaitre il camino (Of course Madame, I believe you know the way)," Juanita said in very colourful mix*ture of Spanish and French.

Elizabeth made her way to her friend Judith's study. The phone rang and she picked up right on time.

"Madame," Izquierdo said, "you must be an Olympic athlete running through Geneva at the speed of light!" he joked, and she was all too attentive to his next briefing. "Talking about light; we've never seen anything like it."

"Look Iz, we have a situation on our hands at the company and I'll spare you the details, but if the scandal hits the world press, we can close shop today. In any case it's all for the better because meanwhile we did find out about Simon's twisted schemes. Now, you time traveled didn't you and are you OK?"

"Oh yes Madame, we are. You certainly are with it and *au courant de tout*, Madame (aware of all)," he was glad to hear.

"Iz, don't 'Madam' me; Elizabeth is my name, even if it sounds like a queen, it's too tiring to be treated like royalty." she laughed.

"OK, Madame ... Elizabeth," he answered. He gave a quick rundown of their adventure including the attack on their lives.

"Now, is there a code?" she asked. "I will fly over tonight, that is, if I can get a flight. Let me call my husband right away. Call me back in five."

She reached Siegfried and he agreed he would stop by his travel agent and get two tickets with an open return.

'Time traveling, he thought, that would be a fun honeymoon; Tuscany in 1473. Why not, of course ... what about our clothing? He tittered.

When Iz called a minute later, Judith walked in and waved after she handed a full grocery bag over to Juanita. Elizabeth threw kisses and made a sign that she'd only be a minute. She overheard Judith ordering the maid to get the kettle on for some tea; perfect time for a nice piece of that organic *torta della nonna* (Grandma's cake). Judith was so good at making this Tuscan speciality cake herself – and in the old traditional way.

"We will be at the villa tonight before nine, so call my cell exactly at that moment and we'll figure a way in! *A presto*!" and she hung up.

Judith, delightful as she always was, shook her blond curls around and her golden bracelets demanded their own small recital.

"*Eliza, ma Chèrie* (my dearest)," she called out in a heavy but disarming American accent. "It's been weeks and I haven't heard from you. There were several calls for you!"

"So sorry," Elizabeth replied. "But it is a bit complicated as you can hear on tonight's news. I must get to the airport immediately and meet Sig and . . ."

"Oh goodie, goodie . . . meet your husband? That's a nice surprise." Judith loved a good gossip. "You've got to tell me all about it. I guess this isn't a holiday or a second honeymoon since you're not taking a suitcase," she joked.

"Oh *non,* no clothes, I almost forgot. We're like fugitives from the paparazzi. Can I borrow a pair of slacks and a shirt? I'll get some stuff at the airport. I've really got to run. Judith, it's a very complicated story and I cannot tell you right away because, well . . . trust me, I will admit I'm turning into a Mata Hari, it seems . . . and . . ."

"And your husband is 007?" Judith burst out in laughter. "Ah, he's such a hunk anyhow! Ah oui, but is he a worthy replacement for Sean Connery? Let's see what we have in our sport closet. Come along girl, you're the one in a hurry, not I."

She called Juanita from the first floor and ordered her to prepare a Tupperware box with two big sandwiches (lots of veggies!) and of course, two large pieces of her cake.

"You'll need them, the plane food is awful anyhow!" she said.

"Thanks so much, Judith, I'll call you from the airport!" Elizabeth ran to the car with a big black and white shopping bag containing food and spring water. Green slick designer slacks, a loose shirt and a light sweater were all packed in a ridiculously expensive travel bag. Judith's driver took her to the airport, and she made sure she made a few calls to find out if the proprietors of the villa were still on holiday. Siegfried was waiting at the counter. Less than fifteen minutes later the plane took off for Florence and they couldn't believe that Judith hadn't even forgotten the plastic knives and forks! Some luck as this was a 'seat yourself, no service on board' Schnell Flight; one of these cheap low-cost companies that struggle with high-priced strikes!

56. FIORENZA, 1473 COSMIC TIDES

The timekeeper rushes in to stop me from ...
dreaming away into more altruistic lives
I may not belong to.
There's no black hole I can timely pass through, apart from the
time-lapse between breakfast and dinner
Time, time, time ... time is making me dizzy ... (Food in time)

Giuliano sat up on the hard floor of the family's home, the Palazzo on Via Larga. Next to him that same small statue of Jupiter staring at him as if again, it had struck him with that lightning bolt, but of course it hadn't. He rubbed his head a few times and wondered if his brother and Angelo in the next room had experienced the same. He crawled and crawled and slowly got himself onto all fours. Within a seemingly endless minute, he was up and out, shaking himself out of what seemed like a permanent cloud of headaches.

Angelo's faltering entrance showed him he hadn't been the only one the gods had struck.

"Giuliano," he coughed, dancing in like a drunken sailor. "Please go immediately to your brother. He fell down when the cyclone hit us."

"A cyclone?" Giuliano asked while moving swiftly to the other room where he found Lorenzo scratching his head, still floored. He reached for his forearm and pulled him up with a forceful move.

"You old gladiator," he laughed, "Now I hear you're creating cyclones? What deal did you make with Neptune this time?" But Lorenzo couldn't laugh.

"This is the dream I dreaded. I've had it for years now; it comes and goes and then you appear but there's two of you." Lorenzo hesitated to continue until Angelo walked in.

"You understand what I mean, no? What is this related to?" he asked Giuliano who gazed through his own nearly tight eyelashes.

"Per favore Angelo, chiama Bruno dobbiamo inviare un messaggio con la colomba (Please call Bruno to send the dove with a message)," Lorenzo said with a sigh, "and have three horses prepared. We're going to Lapo's home."

Angelo couldn't believe he was being asked to join them and he quickly took his most intimate companion, a small booklet dressed in fine leather, to take notes. After all, history was being created right now and he'd better keep a record of it all.

The Buontalenti Residence

Isabel looked radiant in the wine-red dress Agnola had picked for her.

"Sorella de la mia Sorella (sister of my sister)!" Andrea exclaimed. "Really, they look like sisters, it's amazing, isn't it?" The ambiance took a pleasant turn.

"I'm a lot better now. You all are so kind," Isabel said, "Agnola, thank you for getting me into this beautiful dress. I feel like I'm in a Shakespearian play." She returned all compliments.

"Shakespeare?" Three voices asked at the same time.

"Oh no, not him," GianLuca begged with a smile. And of course, the whole family waited for an explanation.

"No, I won't tell you his very long story; simply, he's considered one of the finest writers from England but in another century from now, so we do not have to even think about him even though many of his plays were placed in this time in Italy!"

"How amazing, no?" Lapo said while he took a small message from the carrier pigeon Giovannino had brought him. "Here we have two beings who know more than 500 years of future culture and we have no scribe to pen it down."

Giovannino walked back on the scene with his infectious smile and he took Lapo by the hand. They walked towards the front gate. Together they opened the big wooden doors and three riders leaped off their horses. Andrea straightened his back and Fiammetta and Agnola sighed out loud.

"Gran Dio, ancora I Fratelli (Oh, good god, again the brothers)!" they all cried out.

Isabel guessed she was in, for yet, another historical treat and it had been worth waiting for. The three men stepped forward and Lapo introduced only Isabel.

"Madame you are indeed beautiful, exotic as any woman I have ever laid my eyes upon. You must, of course, be a friend to our dear GianLuca, no?"

He kissed her hand and Isabel felt his seductive warmth and a breath that reminded her that a powerful man had just appeared. She smiled without the curtsy the two sisters dived into at each encounter with Lorenzo de Medici. The future Prince of Tuscany greeted them in an equally jovial way, but the thrill from his hands stayed with her and so did his thoughts.

Giuliano had embraced both Andrea and GianLuca and he proceeded to introduce Angelo Poliziano as their friend, a poet and a philosopher.

"Where we are coming from, you are indeed famous, young man," GianLuca said as he shook his hand in an amicable way.

Angelo was surprised to feel at ease with the foreigner straight away, one he had so dreaded to meet.

"I'm truly delighted, sir," he answered, lowering his eyes, for he found the man opposite him very handsome indeed. "How sir, may I ask, how do you know me?"

"I have already read the wonderful poetry of *Stanza* (Rooms) – the great work you're starting to work on these days. Your poetry will greatly influence your times, you will see. I must offer my congratulations!"

GianLuca spoke in a very enthusiast voice and continued while Angelo Poliziano stepped back in awe of such clairvoyant abilities. But GianLuca whispered he had read it in his own century, which made it even more unbelievable to the poet, especially when GianLuca deliberately mentioned he would write a part in honour of his friend Giuliano at the next year's *Giostra*. Angelo's eyes fell wide open.

"But of course, you haven't come here to discuss the historical development of poetry but the storm that is on your mind as it is on ours!"

A true host, Lapo asked everyone to join him inside because on such a hot summer's day it would be cooler. Giovannino had already prepared some cool drinks made of different herbs and lemons. He brought them to the main dining area. Everybody sat down and all eyes were on GianLuca, now seated between both Medici brothers. Isabel couldn't believe what she saw; two of the greatest names in Italian history and one older twentieth-century version right next to the youngest, most wanted bachelor from Italy's most illustrious family.

If only Oliver Stone could see this right now, she thought!

In brief wordings, Isabel and GianLuca told their end of the story, including the disappearance of the four men. Of course, Giuliano and Lorenzo had met three of them at the *bargello* that very day and they were surprised to hear of their inexplicable departure. Then the brothers gave their account of the last life-changing event, confirming the simultaneous energetic changes in their own home and all over the Tuscan skies.

If Giuliano and Lorenzo were very open and made a serious effort to understand, Agnola was still discovering her 'sisterhood' with Isabel, while Poliziano understood far more of how it all worked. After all, his matter-of-fact mind dictated nothing had really proved that they all might be sharing a soul in another reality with the foreigners they had just liberated that day from the Florentine jail. With a name like Derecho, Angelo was left profoundly confused.

Born under a sensitive Cancer Sun, the young poet had trouble recognizing his own energy in a foreigner, let alone that of a time traveler. Something left him puzzled ... *maybe there was a lack of attraction. How limiting, he thought, contemplating his own thinking process. Must there be an interest in someone in order to listen to him?*

Lapo could identify slightly with Izquierdo. When observing the entire scenario in his own home, he had witnessed the Giovannino-Dritto and Lorenzo-Florian compatibilities. But he didn't always recognize the full physical attributes he expected to be so similar.

"Well, do you consider Florian as good looking?" Lorenzo asked with his customary, cynical grin when it came down to appearances and beauty.

"Oh yes," *Agnola* answered, blushing with her youthful charm.

"The physical appearance from a past incarnation isn't always totally apparent in the person and his new bodily appearance." GianLuca mentioned.

"We're not a 'bloodline connection', we are merely players in a very broad cosmic comedy! If you're in it, it may well seem a tragedy but if you can just be a witness, then it truly is a comedy!" He smiled disarmingly with Lorenzo in total agreement!

"Any chance of us visiting your world?" Lorenzo proposed with a good dose of humour.

"Well, that would be quite a tourist attraction," Isabel joked.

"Tourist?" Angelo asked, immediately thinking about how to spell that in Latin. His little book had just enough pages left for a rather extravagant series of notes being penned down as Giovannino had brought him ink and a feather.

"Yes, quasi forestieri (almost like visitors from outside); like people who come to visit a city; like making a discovery tour through the land or town or site, visits that are often done in groups," Isabel explained.

"In our world, people have created many offices so citizens can find their way about town and visit foreign countries, etcetera," she continued.

"I see," Lorenzo remarked, "you mean the citizens pay for it, right? It is like an 'academia' for research where one can learn about other countries? Well, it seems that in your world, everything is based on paying, from what I hear."

"And actually, so do we pay ... for everything, including high taxes to the city!" Fiammetta boldly said to everybody's astonishment yet with Lorenzo's smiling approval.

Giuliano said, "We must take some lessons from you both and use it for the benefit of the city of Fiorenza! Our treasury needs some new funds! We can tell you that!"

And he bravely continued, "Right, the next year's tournament must be well prepared. We need to announce such an event way ahead of time, so people can come from everywhere, even from the north or the south of Italy. But where would such visitors sleep?" he said looking a bit surprised at his own ideas.

"You see, that's what we call the hotel business and it is a really big market in our world," Isabel said. "People pay a fortune to be in a fancy place, an Albergo (*Tavern/Hotel*) with nice furniture and a bath, even for one night!"

Agnola laughed at the thought of a bath place in her bedroom. "It's a bit like our house at the present time." Agnola giggled. "We can open a *Gran Albergo* (a big hotel)," everybody laughed. But it did get Lorenzo thinking. GianLuca smiled at their 'tourist' conversation.

In the next three hours a heavenly conspiracy developed with three women interacting in a very twentieth-century manner with the five male citizens of Florence surrounding GianLuca, an apt game master making sure everybody got a chance to speak. The subjects varied from the role of the woman in 'their' future to healing professions, science and advanced technology, and eventually, a theme like time traveling. Lapo had made sure that his guests were provided with more drinks and though there was no time to prepare a feast, plenty of fruit and cheeses, as well as the traditional home baked bread and cakes were never absent from the table.

GianLuca explained some of the basics of a watch and a telephone and it might have been the highlight of the evening till Isabel made a toast to the incomparable mystery of the Universe and Giuliano got up for a brief speech.

"*Amici* (Friends), today I believe you have made history," Giuliano addressed his new and old friends. "You have come from our future and you have brought us so much information that it feels we need a lifetime to absorb it. I would like to raise our *bicchiere* (cups) to all of you here in attendance, that our lives may unfold free of fear and worries and that we may understand the essence of what GianLuca has called 'creating our own reality'!" Silver goblets clanked together, and happy faces shone from the courtyard and then Poliziano got up and with the speech of a teacher, he spoke.

"If only we could keep you good and kind people right here, but then we would have to hide you away somewhere as far as Cafagollio," the young poet suggested. "If not, the church might find out about your 'sacrilegious' information." Angelo had started to perspire a bit while he continued with the charm of a learned scholar, never forgetting what his teachers, Ficino and Pico had imprinted.

"Of what I have understood of your century, our future... well it all sounds somehow familiar. Not so much what you have called 'technology'... He looked slightly worried at the watch and cell phone on the table, "but also of the mere facts of how the powerful elite rule our society. It all seems to go back to the Atlantean days." He continued.

"As many a great philosopher claimed, the continent underwent tremendous changes – deluges; land masses moved and the gods played a grand game when humans believed they could use the same power and indeed the loss was tremendous, for continents disappeared and many shifted; you really should meet Leonardo!" A few heads immediately turned to each other.

Angelo was blushing when he mentioned that he had befriended an exceptional young man the foreigners needed to meet. He spoke of Leonardo da Vinci, who was working in the legendary Verrocchio's workshop where he was learning his craft together with one of the future great Renaissance painters, Sandro Botticelli. Of course, Isabel and GianLuca became excited, the thought of meeting one of the pillars of art and science was of course the icing on this Renaissance cake. The whole group around them was making cute little, funny remarks in their own vernacular that the visitors couldn't understand. It was clear they had no idea who da Vinci was to become. He was still only an assistant and history would show that many of Verrocchio's works were probably co-created by the very young genius.

"You know, you are right," Angelo said while approaching Lorenzo, "Leonardo is not even twenty-one and he has been exposed to an amazing array of technical skills including chemistry, metallurgy and even metal working. He has mastered plaster casting and leather working. You should see him in the *bottega* (studio/workshop) ,where mechanics and carpentry are never absent in the hands of such talented young men." He became so passionate that everyone understood that Angelo really admired Leonardo.

Lorenzo put his arm around Angelo and confirmed: "He excels as well as in the arts of drawing, sculpting and painting and even modelling! I believe he is the future of this country and I will support him!" His voice had taken a higher octave. Then GianLuca surprised Lorenzo greatly.

"*Eccellente, eccellente* (Excellent)," GianLuca said, "Indeed, he will become one of the greatest inventors the world will have ever known! And soon, he'll be joining your Plato society; Lorenzo you will be helpful to the young Leonardo, even rescuing him from the Officers of the Night! *Un bel discorso Angelo! Bravo, veramente bravo. Abbiamo capito tutto!* (What a nice speech. We understood everything)!"

Andrea seemed to want to change the subject. But GianLuca continued. "Do you know that Leonardo also refuses to eat meat?"

"And he buys caged birds to free them," Angelo interrupted happily, once again blushing. "*Dio Benedetto* (goodness), this is all to be found in your books on our history?" he asked enthusiastically. "Well then you will love meeting him, he's truly unique!"

Lorenzo and Giuliano smiled at him and they knew that the young genius would soon be in their midst. Hadn't their family adopted more than one great talent?

GianLuca remarked, "I must admit that we would love humanity to wake up one day to a different possibility... maybe a part-return to nature, even though we can no longer exclude the world of technology from our lives. Maybe we can continue scientific research and prioritize nature. What we call the 'machines', or any apparatus seemingly supernatural somehow, they have their own intelligence and with such a grand intelligence even connected to an invisible world, we must make peace, we must collaborate, we must exchange frequencies and grow."

Isabel sat back and clapped her hands.

"Wow GianLuca, now that's a real speech, one a president could captivate an audience with. Maybe that's what we ought to do when we get to DC." The subject they had avoided all along their fascinating, verbal exchanges; home bound... home, how and when? Giuliano had picked up their worried minds and recalled one of his last discussions with GianLuca. He switched gear in the general conversation.

"To go back to our conversation yesterday, I think, GianLuca, you were right. Your arrival in Florence at the time when I was doing the ceremony was indeed as Angelo now confirmed; at noon! Maybe that place in Fiesole is indeed an energy vortex as you called it. I feel we might be able to use it for your return, no matter how much we'd all like you to remain in our century, in our *cinquecento* (the fifteen hundred, as the period 1500 to 1599 is collectively referred to)."

He stated it trembling and GianLuca felt a plunging of energy. He knew his thoughts.

And for the first time he saw flashes of his own death and the different possibilities of change, while in Isabel's ears the name Fiesole rang a familiar happy sounding bell!

While Lorenzo quietly avoided interacting too closely with Isabel, she admitted he seemed a man full of passion, someone she could have been attracted to, a man of power.

Giuliano continued. "It will induce a similar sadness as if I were to lose Lorenzo, but we cannot keep you from living your destiny and I doubt it means you will stay here in Florence, at least not in our 1473. With your wisdom and experience you must help your own country especially if, as Angelo put it, you may well help avoid another Atlantean disaster!" Tears could have run down his cheeks, but he gained back his composure. GianLuca had followed the evolving story closely. Poliziano turned away and a sudden silence left all the women in awe of men showing their feelings, not a usual way of behaving in the Italian Renaissance.

Then Lorenzo got up, and with a contemplative look in his own watery eyes he spoke. "Giuliano, you surprise me more every day. How you have grown! It is you who should be crown king of Florence, no of Italy! Your heart is so generous and truthful as I doubt any ruler will ever be. How I do not want to give you up to any destiny where we need to part!" And he threw his arms around him and Giuliano merged with equal candour and veracity.

"Lorenzo," he answered to his brother, "let me take Isabel and GianLuca to the Fiesole Villa. We have a few more hours of clear sunlight left before nightfall. I should like them to inspect the grotto that houses the Venus statue."

"That's an excellent idea," Lorenzo de Medici responded in his princely manner. "Angelo and I can return to Via Larga and finish up some minor administrative work and we'll join you for dinner. Of course, I expect the entire Buontalenti family to join us."

Fiammetta and Agnola held on to Andrea and they could hide neither their excitement nor their sadness. But while Lapo and Andrea accepted the gracious offer extended to their family, they felt like weeping because in their heart they knew this really might become their last supper, even with Leonardo da Vinci in attendance!

57. FIESOLE, 2018 GROTTO

For if your windows and mine are the same on the screen of lesser fame,
playing the mirror game, then none of us is truly lame
even though we're almost all glued to the windows of your name
instead of our own even when we came . . .(A Bill for Windows and Gates)

At the Fiesole Villa, Dritto kept his eyes open while thinking he would love to smoke a pipe. *That probably isn't a good idea. What if Isabel starts coughing . . . will that complicate her return, or is that primitive thinking . . . ? I'll open a window.*

Meanwhile, Iz became eager when it was confirmed that Elizabeth von Weitweg was arriving with her husband Siegfried, the well-known scientist-turned-chemist for the pharma company she had directed for years. It seemed they were airborne for two hours, a short flight from Geneva. He quickly returned to the cave in the garden to get Florian. The last announcement made no impact on Dritto who looked as if he couldn't care less. He watched over Isabel and felt even more empathy.

I *cannot wait to get out if this mess. This poor woman, oiwee, she's still stuck. I liked the ride but . . . has it been all worth it if we can't bring her back?*

Derecho had returned to the villa where none of the confusion had subsided. Dritto looked at him, "What is going on?" he asked, "Florian is in the cave trying to figure it all out and now Iz said we're having more visitors?"

"Wouldn't you think that this is like an on-going television series?" Derecho said dryly.

"Please, stop it Doh, you loved every minute of our on-going series; remember the 'Dark Vader' passage . . . you are now a TV hero," Dritto called out singing an old television theme song in a high-pitched voice

"Oh, we're getting a bit jealous now, are we?" Doh answered jokingly.

"Hey, you guys, this isn't like kindergarten again, is it, and we're waiting for a former ballerina, *Frau Von Weitweg*, (Mrs Von Weitweg)" Dritto said cynically. Just then Florian and Izquierdo walked in.

"Did you mention Elizabeth von Weitweg? I did tell you that she is Isabel's half-sister, but you might have missed this," Florian said rolling his eyes in a funny manner.

Izquierdo's mouth fell open, but then little more would surprise him after their last journey.

"Does that make you her brother-in-law and we are the cousins?" he joked.

"No, but the two haven't seen each other for decades," Florian said, "... and now I really need to concentrate on getting both Isabel and GianLuca back here. I'm sure there's a way." Florian's mood sobered a bit. Iz remembered though, that Elizabeth's husband was very well read in digital technology; maybe he could help.

Dritto looked at his colleagues convinced there was a solution and said, "It's simple; Iz and Doh can take turns watching out here and I'll check the gardens whenever you need to be in that cave. Sort of like having a bodyguard; does that sound OK to you Florian?" Iz had agreed to check upon Elizabeth's exact arrival and he imagined she would be calling him any moment now.

"Sounds great," Florian answered. "I'll get right to the computer and don't be surprised if you see me run in and out. I'm going to take a digital picture of some of the details in the cave and put them on the PC. There has to be a mathematical, architectural solution as to how we can enter the lower parts of the cave."

He tried to recall some of the information GianLuca had given to him, some of which were descriptions by Angelo Poliziano. The young poet seemed to have been at many original ceremonies in that cave. Florian had a fixed image of the statue engraved in his photographic mind and he reflected on data from one of the books in the university Library from long ago.

"We have a few very serious matters on our hands. I don't even know why in the world they're flying over from Geneva," Iz said, "I presume something important must have happened. I'm going back to the house to turn on the television, maybe we'll get some info."

Meanwhile Florian had been downloading the pictures from the grotto and studying them from all angles with his advanced *ArchiTekGéant,* a program used for professional builders restoring ancient cities like Venice. It was a very broad and impressive program that gave him plenty of ideas and the missing pieces were slowly matching the image he had made of this villa at its initial construction.

What a pity I didn't get to visit the grotto with the Medici Brothers. I really regret that. There just has to be a way to get in there tonight. I just know it.

So, Florian returned with Dritto and they walked down a long elegantly dressed alley with, on one side, cypress trees and then a series of smaller houses on the upper roadside towards the gate. They admired some of the other traditionally built houses below looking down into the valley, but they were of no immediate interest because they had been restored and adapted in the last two centuries. They would find no answers anywhere but in that cave. Both men entered and continued their exploration.

Izquierdo stood outside on the balcony leading to the gardens and thought they were all very lucky that the owners were away. But some commotion at the front gate caught his attention. He hid behind a few trees next to the first house. Two voices sounded familiar.

Should I check ... what if the owners have returned? That'll be a scene, especially with one strange person in sort of a coma and another one in the smelly cave.

When a cell phone rang Derecho looked behind him and he heard someone run, and for a moment he got scared.

"Iz what in the fuck ... are you doing, scaring people and ugh ..." Derecho shouted out.

But Izquierdo had started running towards the main entrance.

"Elizabeth, just a moment, it's a long run to get to the gates!" Iz screamed through the cell phone. Derecho ran behind him and looked surprised at the foreign couple eagerly taking a peek through the metal gate. He got his little device out, pushed a few buttons and the gates opened.

Izquierdo looked at him with surprise.

"You could have told me?" Iz said.

"No Iz ... how do you think we got in again ... papa Dritto's wonder box?" he laughed as he put away his remote. They shook hands with both the Freundreichs and started to give an account of the last few hours.

"We have more surprises for you, Elizabeth." Derecho happily announced. "But did you have a good flight? Are you hungry?"

"*Non, mon cher* (No my dear). We're just fine but you seem *en pleine forme* (in great shape) and of course, my husband Siegfried is here to assist you all," she answered smilingly.

"Time traveling is becoming to you both. So now to business, I brought Sig because he is a true technical wiz and we may need his help. He also worked on the original program you were nearly killed in."

"Remember the dark ghost riders?" Siegfried asked, "Yes, that was my program. I hope they didn't make you suffer too much."

Elizabeth lifted her eyebrows; both Izquierdo and Derecho were left flabbergasted. She continued, "You do not have to worry; the owners of the villa aren't back for another week. They told me in person that they have the most sophisticated alarm system you can possibly dream of and I shouldn't worry." They all laughed.

The new guests approached the cave as Florian and Derecho appeared from the bushes. Introductions were easy. The visitors were instantly taken by the guys' innate charm and they followed them in total confidence as they entered what Iz had called the 'travel room'. Elizabeth nearly fainted when she recognized her sister Isabel.

"Is she going to be all right?" she asked, and Florian answered, "I'm working at finding out how to return her to her 'home station' because she has her own code linked through her DNA with the travel system and I don't know it. We were transported back in time through some kind of a galactic storm that quite possibly ejected us from a black hole, at least, that is what we presume happened. Well, it brought us back ... but only four of us."

"Siegfried, you said your name was; maybe you'd like to look at this right away, now you have met your sister-in-law?" Florian asked with a smile." Follow me".

Siegfried sat down in front of the big screen.

"Ah, you're using *'ArchiTekGéant'* program. Well, I'm afraid Renaissance buildings aren't a great platform for that plug-in. Can you get to *Archmaverick* 2018?" Siegfried asked. Florian nodded 'yes' and clicked a few rounds of buttons and a stored credit card number took care of it.

There it was. Siegfried started playing around with the new shapes and forms appearing on the whirling screen. The others had joined them and his wife, while Iz and Derecho looked in amazement at how ancient buildings could be restored in a matter of minutes . . . at least on a computer program. After a while they all left to visit the famous cave and now Derecho stayed behind looking at Elizabeth's sister. *This movie sure knows no end.*

58. FIESOLE, 1473/2018 PARALLEL REALITIES

You've cast a spell with your long walk along the Styx
up to my ancient temple where men worshipped the oracle
around the blessed of all fires
where Sybil and her virgin graces,
no fortune tellers they were,
pleaded a part of human destiny. (Lost Flavours of a Pleiadian Filibuster)

Giuliano de Medici got off his horse to open the gates. Isabel and GianLuca followed him as he jumped back on and they rode uphill a little longer while admiring the beautiful residence his uncle had left to both brothers. They didn't get into the house, something Isabel would have loved to do ... maybe another time. He took them towards a shady spot in the upper garden. For a moment they all turned around and looked at that amazing view of the old city.

"There is our special cave, *bello no* (beautiful, no)?" Giuliano said and suddenly he stopped, and he shivered at the thoughts that plagued his mind.

"You're leaving aren't you, GianLuca – tonight?"

Giuliano's mood flipped to an early grief and both men turned silent.

"My dear GianLuca, if you feel this place as I do this very moment, then we can indeed create an exit or even re-activate an existing gate."

"I'm willing to set it up with you, yet not without having Isabel joining us." GianLuca answered while his throat tightened.

Isabel picked up the tension. "Well," she said, "Lapo's family will be here very soon, no? If this is going to be a farewell, let us have a party; *facciamo una festa* (let us have a feast)!"

For a moment Giuliano smiled whole-heartedly.

"Come with me to the house and I will order the servants to start preparing the evening meal. Maybe you'd like to refresh yourself first. Come, if you please."

"If it's all right with you both, I'll just stay here and start checking it all out, after all there's not that much time. Have you checked out the skies?" Isabel pointed upwards.

Clouds were masking the sun and they were hoping that it wouldn't start raining. This apparently hadn't happened in years. In Tuscany, summer storms were a rare phenomenon, Giuliano had confirmed that he didn't remember witnessing even one. While they left, Isabel approached the slick statue of Venus making an odd contrast to the grotto. So unusual, she thought; much more an earth mother like Vesta than a seductive Venus; of course Vesta didn't expose her breasts.

The fountain below was running and she guessed this water came from the mountains. She shone the sleeve device's pocket light onto the back of the statue. She discovered nothing unusual and continued her research, moving into a larger space, where the walls were slightly humid. She couldn't figure out the smell... sulphur came to mind.

Like the oracle at Delphi, she pondered. Intricate place, where to look first? If only Florian were here now; he is so quick with...

But something had caught her eye. "Ah, bird droppings," she shrieked and wondered if any of them would be flying in or out and what if these were bats? Before giving it any further thought she was following a line of... more bird excretions. It took her to a small swirling staircase, but not a usual one for there were no real stairs. She stopped afraid she would slide down. She heard voices in the back.

"Isabel, where are you?" GianLuca called out.

"Right here, follow the bird poop," she laughed.

Giuliano took him by the arm leading him towards the spiralling corner.

"Well, we never go there," he confirmed, "at least I don't. We usually just throw flowers, a little bit like an offering for good luck to the goddess. But the main part is located right behind; just be careful and lower your head."

They tried to squeeze into a smallish vault while GianLuca held up a torch and there it was, right in front of them, depicted within a marvel of colourful mosaics and tiny gemstones. A proud Hermes statue held a shining light in the centre of an eight-pointed star, encircled by the zodiac. His divine adolescent body was leaning onto the symbols of the planets as known only to the most ancient of civilizations. the symbols of the planets as known only to the most ancient of civilizations.

I've never really given it any thought, Giuliano reflected, because the few times I came here, I sat on a bunch of pillows, but of course I knew Mercury/Hermes was right underneath us. I took it as a good omen.

Meanwhile, Isabel pondered... if we could only email this discovery to Florian, I'm so sure our friends are at the villa looking for a way to bring us back.

"Right and they will be working at it in a parallel way, trust me!" GianLuca intercepted her thoughts. "There's got to be a coding that makes this cave into a stargate but how in the world are we going to find out?"

"Angelo will show you the ceremony he and Lorenzo have done on several occasions at the full moon. I'm sorry we don't have one tonight," Giuliano contemplated.

Isabel sighed, "No, it's actually a new moon, at least that's what Florian had mentioned to me before he... left."

GianLuca watched Giuliano. He knew that those two brothers had a solution they might not even suspect having.

"You must trust dear friends, something exceptional will happen, especially after this day of mysteries," Giuliano said, "it is as if we all have started off something new, as if we have opened the first door and tonight, we may well get to the main gate and let's hope that we may witness yet another miracle."

Fiesole, 2018

Siegfried and Florian were going ahead as if they had been teammates all along and Elizabeth smiled happily at this new complicity.

What a handsome brother-in-law he'll make. What a pity that Simon Averardo had to be such a dissociated crook. Another understatement she told herself. He too had once possessed a brilliant mind like this young man, Florian. Well, here we go again... good old Star Wars... while she continued mumbling to herself as if she were on another planet...

She said, "If there's no darkness, how could light be defined as light and how could man evolve and transform his ancient destinies if there is only peace? I mean the challenges make us who we really are, no?" and she blew a few small clouds of nicotine in the air while immediately opening a window to air her involuntary pollution attack on her new friends. "How complex can I get? And am I blabbing away at such an important moment of research?" she apologized.

"I agree," said Izquierdo, surprising her while she shrugged, blowing more smoke towards the windows. "I mean I agree what you said about ... ugh ... Madame ..."

"Goodness, I'm talking to myself again. Don't let it happen to you, Izquierdo when you are approaching seventy!" she almost apologized.

"Ha-ha, seventy, you are just making that up!" Iz exclaimed.

"Second Saturn return will give you about ten years less than your age, Elizabeth!" Florian said without blinking an eye from the screen. Siegfried also shrugged one more time; it seemed the thing to do at those occasions, especially discussing a woman's age ... never a great idea! "And imagine that I almost lost a goddess to a time travel design in an obscure underground atelier, sponsored by Dark Vader, Harry Khope!" Florian said.

"Please gentlemen, do continue your compliments; after this is over, I might have gained back my teenager's confidence and my girlish figure!" Elizabeth said, squeaking.

"Oh, oh fishing for more compliments milady, but you'll have to stop smoking too!" Derecho joked, as he took her for a few waltz steps.

"Well, I *reallee is surprised at ya judgement of my nicotine addiction*," she joked in a thick US southern accent. "*Where have ya all learned such a sophistication son, and such subtieeel dancing feet, honeypie? Might you all have been on those southern ballroom floors?*"

"Well ma'am, I just had a fancy dancing grand'ma and she, oh oui, she knew how to get them dancing steps going, I can tell ya that. But you see I ain't some fancy ballerina like you, we're just gonna do some salsa stuff ..."

"*Well now ya all, ya all come here and luk at this*," Siegfried's Mississippi drawl wasn't as convincing as was his discovery. It certainly made up for it.

"Yep, there's more to this little cave than meets the eye," Florian said.

"See this very narrow opening; it's got to lead down and not up like the staircase shows. This villa was sold in the sixteenth century by the Medici family to yet another Italian family of considerable wealth." Florian continued,

"The same happened a century later, to their famous residence in Via Larga, the current Via Cavour, to the Riccardi family who fortunately respected the style and when they expanded the building, they continued to renovate and embellish.

The architect's ego brought more decoration and covered up much of the villa's esoteric past. Yes, nothing is exactly what it appears to be!"

"Let's go and check it out! What happens to Isabel; what if she wakes up?" Siegfried asked with genuine concern.

"I'll be here!" Elizabeth answered. "I haven't seen her for decades. I'll do anything to speak with her again, even to stop the ... smoking habits!"

Better late than never.

She lit another cigarette. "I'll stay too," Dritto said, "Maybe I can get a special tango lesson?" But she didn't waltz around, and he shut up and turned on the television in the side room, hoping to find a news channel.

Within five minutes Izquierdo returned. "We really need some strong light in that ancient cave, and we have to cut the creepy vines growing from deep within. It looks like nobody really ever went into this place for centuries!" he said while his attention briefly went to Dritto, who had found an international news channel.

"This cannot be true," he screamed out, "Elizabeth you must see this!"

She hastened, suspecting the worst and yes there it was. The popular talk show host, a French woman in her late twenties, stood in front of the Geneva DoWell office narrating a rather wild story, one Elizabeth knew only too well.

...'*trop bien coiffée* (too good a haircut)' she thought; these actress-turned-journalists... bimbo doll look-alikes, in Russia, China, and in Western Europe. She was annoyed at their looks, the news and all it stood for.

The very blond speaker went on announcing how "... the president of one of the worlds' fastest growing pharmaceutical giants has been summoned by the local authorities. For now, his lawyers announced he would be still recovering in the hospital for at least a week. Mr Averardo, the CEO was unable to give any comments nor was any member of his family or staff. Two strange coincidences have demanded some more attention from the local authorities as firstly two famous actors were seen in the building the day before the incidents, as witnessed by the night porter.

A second speaker continues that world-renown former Secretary of State, Harry Khope was held up at the airport before leaving that same day and his car had been seen in the vicinity of the DoWell offices. Many questions were asked by the local news channel and none appeared on the international media!"

An eager Eveliebe appeared behind the journalist and Elizabeth just started praying they weren't going to interview a secretary or the cleaning woman, but the soap opera found a happy follow-up when Germaine, certainly not embarrassed 'to tell the truth, and nothing but the truth', proudly confirmed that "what was happening on the top floor wasn't always meant for the public eye! None of us had any idea; we had all briefly noticed that visiting 'actress'." And Eveliebe had smiled and waved to the camera hoping someone might notice her.

Wow, I didn't know she could even talk ... this domestic .., let alone in a perfect French, Elizabeth had judged while becoming more and more annoyed at the present happenings. I hope nobody found out where we went. I can just read the news headlines; 'Hollywood sex ring reaches out into a hot Swiss pharmaceutics cover-up for time traveling devices to get you to the Italian Renaissance and lost in a cave!' She shivered at her own sarcasm and hoped the news channel had some fashion to divert the television addicts!

And while the cameras showed Simon Averardo's office and a few more familiar faces, mostly stunned secretaries in hefty discussion and some photos of his wife and children and with Jacqueline in front of a Swiss Hotel, the news presenter finished up her story. "... No response has come from Mr Averardo's family, out of town during the present discovery of the scandal.

Their lawyer and spokesman have denied any knowledge regarding the present discoveries. Other names mentioned in this new scandal include popular Hollywood star, William Lawless and his half-sister, equally popular actress Jacqueline Kissmet, who have checked out of their Geneva hotel suites this afternoon and apparently left the country. Late News Updates on our award winning Eleven o'clock news."

When the commercials popped up, Dritto turned off the television and stared at Izquierdo, who said, "Gotta sit down a moment. Dritto can you hand these flashlights to the other guys? They're kind of waiting for these."

"Sure Iz, sure ... don't worry they didn't even mention us," he said and went off.

"Well now you know as much as I did when we arrived here this afternoon," Elizabeth said. "Iz, the fact that you are working for me will save you all and we'll figure out an easy scenario. You heard of undercover double agents?" she giggled. Tchaikovsky's *Nutcracker* waltz interrupted all conversation and she picked up her cell phone.

"Désiré, heureusement (Désiré, lucky us)! Où t'es? Quoi, devant la maison, tu veux dire sur Via Beato San Angelico. OK, pas de problèmes, je t'envoie Spiderman ; ayez un peu de patience la villa est à 300 mètres d'où tu te trouves (Where are you? In front of the house; I'll send you Spiderman; be patient , the villa is only 300 m away).

She explained to Izquierdo that he needed to fetch Dritto for his magic touch at the front gate. He ran out and this time took a bike he had found behind the garden house.

Sister, you have no idea what is going on while you're having a Renaissance time of your life, she thought while looking at Isabel, still peaceful, so close on her armchair and yet far away.

"Sorry, but I think Florian is the one to go in first, he's the thinnest and I'm too tall," Siegfried called out while he heard Dritto running off and Iz returning to the scene. The grotto was about to reveal its mystery.

"Keep the lantern up, there's only that staircase ... it must have been built that way after the Medici period. We're going to need a few tools to break down the sidewall. Is anyone available?"

"Yeah, I'll go," Derecho happily announced getting out of this humid and spooky place. Meanwhile Derecho had picked up Désiré Lesclau, Elizabeth's detective.

"Have we met?' Désiré asked.

Désiré introduced himself but Derecho shook his head and ran off to the kitchen to look for a garage key.

That's the only place I can think of to find some tools.

"Colourful place you have here, Elizabeth and I hope this lady is still alive," Désiré said as he walked into the place.

"Oui bien sur, c'est ma demi-soeur elle est encore en 1473 (Yes of course, she is my half-sister; she remained in 1473)", Elizabeth answered.

"S'il te plait, assiez-vous Sherlock. L'affaire est bien plus compliquée que j'osais penser (Please sit down, Sherlock; this affair is far more complicated than I dared to imagine)!"

Elizabeth gave him a quick update of what had happened in the last 24 hours.

He sat back quietly and admired the verve by which she held herself. He decided to give them some more information on the subject.

"Well, that all fits in beautifully now doesn't it. I have some news too! Before the villa was sold to the current owners, a certain Godfroid Brockechild, married to the granddaughter of Georg von Blaublut und Rotgrab, briefly was the proprietor. Georg was big pals with, yes, the father of Harry Khope, who as you may know is German-born." He took an air of conceit and grinned.

"At the end of the Second World War when the biggest secret service of all times was founded in the USA, Georg gathered some of the most important scientists, psychologists and surgeons and took them over the ocean. The insider who gave me the information said they were flown out of Switzerland on a government plane. We have found out that Georg helped Khope to develop an amazing network that experimented with ... mind control."

"Incroyable mon cher tu n'as pas perdu une minute (Fab darling, you haven't wasted a minute). Bravo!" Elizabeth exclaimed in a happy voice. "We now have to pray that Isabel is returning soon. I have a feeling that we're all going to have to spend the night here."

"Pas de problèmes, ma chère (no problems, my dear)," Désiré said, "later I will return to my hotel, because I have a room on the top floor and I get to watch the villa; it will be safer than an extra private eye watching out for you all! By any chance, is there any water around? *Naturale per favore* (Still water please)." He smiled and she showed him to the kitchen.

In the grotto, Florian was vigorously breaking down a hollow wall with Izquierdo, while Dritto and Derecho took turns in an echoing concert of banging the past down! Siegfried was, well ... too tall.

"Quick get us more lights, we're on to something," Florian shouted in a slowly growing ecstasy. "Damn, the staircase isn't holding up, get back you guys, it may collapse!"

And as he spoke, Florian went down in a pile of bricks and dust. "No light, damn!" he called out.

"Are you hurt and how far down?" Siegfried's baritone voice echoed through the cave.

"No, I'm fine, I think I landed on some kind of mattress, maybe twenty feet down. I'll need a rope to get back up and you need to give me light and a big broom; we're surely close to what we came to look for!" he shouted back, his voice resonating as from a dungeon.

59. FIESOLE, 1473/2018 HERMES & LEONARDO

Tantalizing nothingness,
sponge to my void
taking the last drop from my lips
in a shallow embrace that vanishes
with the tribe of the uncommon,
to reappear behind the veiled inner eyes,
whimsical fibers of pagan leaflets,
road signs to ancient untouched roots. (The Void)

Lapo and family had arrived at the Fiesole estate.

They never have parking problems here. Isabel was thinking when they saw them walk up the long staircase to the garden terrace... splendid in those slippers and stockings, in this Renaissance summer; at least there's a breeze here in these Fiesole hills.

Agnola ran to Isabel and as they touched hands, she suddenly broke into tears; she felt ridiculous in this apparently permanent state of watering eyes.

"Oh no, dearest Isabel, don't worry, I'll be all right," Agnola stuttered through her handkerchief. "It's just, well, we have just met, and you are like my own sister and I know, I just know what this feels like..." Her sister Fiammetta just walked in and immediately held her in her arms. All three teary women fell into a commendable silence that was deeply sad. Andrea looked at Giuliano and his conversation preferred a quiet voice.

"At least, Giuliano, you'll be here with us and every time we meet, we'll think of them all, our time traveling, otherworldly family." The chills rubbed his veins.

"Come on now, come on," Lapo expressed with a paternal hug to Giuliano and then GianLuca, "it isn't all that bad now is it."

But he was suppressing more emotions ready to cascade down and he continued to talk as quickly as he could.

"GianLuca has brought us different insights, offered us so much knowledge and information and well, we only need to study it and develop our own lives with a higher purpose in mind." He continued, "Giuliano and your brother Lorenzo with your academy and together with Master Ficino ... there must be a way to bring such higher knowledge to the masses, or ..."

"Oh yes, when the masses are ready my dear Lapo," Lorenzo de Medici's thundering voice welcomed them all from the top of the staircase. Everybody stared at him in total surprise. A gentle wind caught his open shirt emphasizing his athletic physique. He looked so different from just those few hours ago. It wasn't only his mood but the total aura around him.

The three women were not indifferent to his manly, extremely sensuous appearance that took away all attention from the face he himself had declared common, but never without interest. And yes, in this light he did remind them all of the handsome Florian – and Isabel saw no commoner in front of her. In a lady-like manner, Isabel stepped forward and offered both her hands. He kissed them with theatrical gesture, though she felt he embraced her eyes at the same time and for a nanosecond, they both knew this could have been a fatal attraction.

GianLuca broke the spell and turned to Lorenzo while Isabel now offered her right hand to Angelo Poliziano after he gracefully picked up and arranged her long skirts. "I have read your works ... they're magnificent. You are indeed a true poet!" she softly whispered in his ears while his cheeks turned their usual red.

For the first fifteen minutes, chitchat continued to fill the air and while Angelo made sure a table was brought out and refreshments were served to their guests, Bruno and a few more servants added a few comfortable benches and eventually a simple table decked with a healthy-looking display of fruit, cheeses and dried meats. Lorenzo spoke.

"We love coming to my uncle's estate." He continued, "The way the sun settles below the western horizon is a magnificent spectacle and it happens almost every evening of our weekly visits." He took a long breath. "And every morning it rises again and where we have left off the night before, we pick up our thread and we sew our daily coat of life."

"You are such a poet," Fiammetta whispered loud enough for him to hear. "Dear Lorenzo, allow me to make a toast to such a beautiful phrase, for we mustn't allow our hearts to be saddened by the departure of those extraordinary beings; our friends and our family from the future."

Both GianLuca and Isabel looked at each other and wondered why everybody was so convinced that they were leaving. He admitted being a bit excited at the idea of returning, yet he had grown used to this rather non-invasive techno-free life, with these kind friends. Now it all seemed so cosy here that he no longer felt the need to continue his travels. They all lifted their *bicchieri* (cups) for a toast and enjoyed a wine of a most unusual taste.

While they all briefly stared at their glasses, Giuliano described the dinner party's ingredients. "Ah yes, quite a wine, it was brought to us from the area of Toulouse by a friend of our father well connected to the French court. I believe actually it is close to the region around the city of Bordeaux."

"Now my dear Angelo," Lorenzo changed the subject, "would you kindly do the honours and take our friends to your special place in the grotto?" he asked. Angelo straightened his back and was a bit surprised while Lorenzo looked his brother in the eyes, slightly uncomfortable.

"All of the guests?" Angelo asked and he looked at Lorenzo once again. The latter had risen ... a stature of a god.

"I mean that you should take Isabel and GianLuca, sadly without their three friends," he spoke softly, and everyone could see that he carried himself as a true ruler.

"Yet, let's first have a moment to enjoy these dishes, no?" Angelo proposed.

"Of course," GianLuca said in a grateful way. "And maybe dear Angelo, you will enchant us with one of your poems!"

We're not really in a rush to get off and on the planet. But then again, I hope that Florian and the trio are back and at the same place. Isabel nodded in the silence of a co-conspirator.

Angelo stood and recited, while on the side, Bruno was playing the lute ever so softly. Poliziano spoke gently:

"Le gloriose pompi e fieri ludi
della citta che 'l freno allenta e stringe
a' magnanimi Toschi, e I regni crudi

di quella dea che 'l terzo ciel dipinge,
e I premi degni alli onorati studi,
la mente audace a celebrar mi spinge

(My darling mind urges me to celebrate the glorious pageants and the proud games of the city that bridles and gives rein to the magnanimous Tuscans, the cruel realms of the goddess who adorns the third heaven, and the rewards merited by honourable pursuits; in order that fortune, death, or time may not despoil great names and unique and eminent deeds.)

They were all surprised when GianLuca got up and congratulated Angelo with very loud applause and a few more meaningful words.

"*Sei Magnifico* (you are amazing), you have the touch of the most sensitive of poets and your hidden meaning is of the finest!" Angelo had no answer. "Your well-hidden description, further on in your book, of Lucrezia, Lorenzo and Giuliano's mother, is outstanding. To compare her to Leda, who by Zeus gave him Castor and Pollux is just brilliant. Now who is Castor and is Giuliano now Pollux?"

The small group laughed, but was unsure what to think.

Angelo said, "Dear friend from other worlds, you prove us right as nobody has read my unpublished poems. They will hopefully appear good enough to be used in a manuscript. As you know, I will name the whole, *stanze* (rooms)," Angelo was proud and continued, "But not one soul knows this and thus you really have read my books. This is truly amazing; if we had any doubt, if 'I' had any doubt, I can but agree that you have come from the future or you are a ghost in my house." While the small audience laughed, he remained stunned and GianLuca gently embraced him and whispered that he had read his works at the university. Angelo, still in awe, was charmed by the encouragements.

While slowly, a variety of conversations divided the table in little couples discussing many subjects, Giuliano was watchful of GianLuca speaking to his brother more about the manner the world was ruled in the twenty-first century, resulting in the new wars. Sadness had invaded his space.

GianLuca did his best to concentrate, because on his left, Fiammetta had laid her hand on his, and his palm gently covered hers. A bit further, Isabela had fashion stories for Agnola, and the way 'haute-couture' had found its own path throughout the centuries, especially in Milano. The light dress she wore at present could very well be a twenty-first century model! "Everything goes on our timeline and a woman can wear whatever she likes, only the *stoffa* (cloth) has evolved tremendously and some of the most inventive creators of clothing are actually the Italian 'couturiers', pioneers in such matters."

She went on explaining how men were even wearing dresses, though less stylish or traditional than what Lapo wore the night before. Agnola was flabbergasted and the idea that women had the same freedom as men, made her totally uncomfortable. When the women's movement came up, Isabel refrained from more controversy even though GianLuca compared the transvestites to the men dressed as women in the Greek and Roman tragedies, to him they were all artists. Here nobody was offended.

Angelo and Lapo were talking about Plato and GianLuca jumped in with some 'modern' or 'Machiavelli' ideas to make sure that Master Lorenzo didn't feel left out. Eventually the name of the god of all travels and winds was mentioned when all heads turned to GianLuca.

"What? Hermes, you said?" GianLuca asked with a twinkle in his eyes. "Didn't Angelo's teacher Marsilio Ficino call Hermes/Mercury the patron of your academy, he who was described by Virgil in his *Aeneid* and ... stirred the wispy vapours from the clouds so the truth could filter down from heaven, penetrating our minds with no blinding light. *Emanatio, conversio et remeatio* (Emanation, Rapture and Return); am I right Angelo?"

Angelo Poliziano got up once again startled by his soon-to-be departing guest, so he answered: "I have noticed more and more how well versed in Latin you are, *Gentillisimo* GianLuca. I shall now weep even more than all others should you depart so soon, for what you know of my teacher is known by few!"

"Ah yes, but you see, you will write about it and so will Lorenzo and other men of wisdom and knowledge. Again, I have simply studied this material in university. There is no magic here, not on my behalf." GianLuca had answered with a relaxed smile, happily for he felt change was indeed in the air and a trip soon to manifest.

Out of nowhere came a voice, "What we will need now is the real magic and alchemy of Hermes Trismegistus!" These words did not come from GianLuca, and Angelo now proudly introduced a very special newcomer: *"Ti presento, Leonardo di ser Piero da Vinci* (May I introduce, Leonardo da Vinci?)"

Fiesole, the Grotto 2018

After his unexpected landing, Florian had to push most parts of the broken staircase to the side and with the aid of the lanterns he now discovered a small pond or was it a fountain? There was water everywhere, but he brushed wildly and noticed it slowly went down and little by little, a large circle was revealed.

And finally, there he was in all his mosaic splendour: 'Mercury', the messenger of the gods.

"Got it. Got it! Get me a camera in here so we can film this and, Doh please get to the coding program and figure it out on my laptop. The eight-point star has to be a sub-program, my personal code is *étoile.* Siegfried, can you write down this stuff?"

"Of course, Florian I can," and he took out his never-absent notebook.

Dritto had to run back and forth from the house where Elizabeth was getting curious.

"What's going on there? Have they found anything worth the *déplacement(the trip)?* I cannot leave Isabel on her own, what if she wakes up?"

But Désiré, the gentleman he had always been, encouraged her. "*Vas-y Elizabeth* (Go for it, Elizabeth), maybe you can actually help them."

"I doubt it, but I am really curious with my husband out there. After what he told me about what those creeps in Geneva had going on in their 'underground lab' under Simon's supervision, I don't trust any of these experiments!"

She waved her left hand like an Italian princess and walked out into the dark garden. Realizing she had no flashlight, she returned, swiftly picked one up, and a bottle of San Pellegrino water.

You never know... someone may be thirsty.

When she reached the cave, she could hear Florian's voice echoing through.

"Wow this is amazing, sorry... you should try to get down here," he called out. Iz couldn't wait, and he had used a rope he had found in the garage, one long enough to reach the first big Cypress tree and he climbed down. "After all, this isn't Jurassic Park!" he told his old friend.

Better not, Elizabeth thought, and she looked at Siegfried handling the small digital camera. Oh, these guys, they so love the technology, guess we are just lucky, especially today!

"There's the real goddess, yes that is Venus," Elizabeth said. "I was sure the one at the entrance was Vesta. In Roman mythology she's the keeper of the heart and she's at the entrance while fickle Venus devoted to beauty and money is hidden right below!" She peeked in the cave with a big light showing the treasure.

Typical, Elizabeth pondered, the seduction right below the heart; hum . . .

"What else?" Siegfried asked.

"Give us a moment," Iz said. And Elizabeth and her husband heard some mumbling from Iz and Florian who were moving something like pretty heavy stones. They had been cleaning parts of the floor mandala they had just discovered and now Siegfried could record a clearer image.

"Got it," Sig howled down. "Doh has left for the house to fetch your second laptop and he'll be right back.

"Why don't you just break the other part of the staircase so it's out of the way?" Elizabeth asked.

Sig momentarily stared at his wife, surprised at her remark, "Sweetheart, are you an architect?" he joked, "Part is a ceiling to the place below; we don't want to lose our friends buried underneath tons of bricks!"

"*Ah non, non, non . . .* Siegfried, she insisted, her usual teasing self, "I don't mean that little staircase, I mean the one a bit further, in the garden, on the side. It's made of wood! *Vraiment messieurs ou est donc votre tête* (Really gentlemen where is your brain?)" she said equally joking.

"OK, so Florian stays down," Siegfried proposed "We'll get Désiré to join in, and no, we won't use forks and spoons. Our cars carry a few tools and there's a lot more to be found in the villa's garage."

Elizabeth decided to get Désiré and she ran back to the house. Minutes later the men were breaking down a staircase that wasn't at all what they had expected it to be.

"Oh yes, this is really, really old! Like hardly post-Etruscan! That's where they were living, here in Tuscany." And he continued to load up Florian's laptop with the freshly filmed material. Within less than twenty minutes they all looked down, holding up five lanterns, noticing that the ground was shaking slightly. Fortunately, nature remained on their side and the unexpected earthquaking stopped! As they continued to search diligently, each of the men went down and joined Florian for a short while, till they all got out and sat on the grass around Doh, who was having the time of his life searching for any possible code that could serve either Florian or Siegfried.

Meanwhile, Elizabeth had returned to the villa taking turns with Désiré to watch Isabel. The entire team was busy while the church bells up the road rang eleven times. Suddenly, it occurred to Elizabeth that she could do some research herself and though she hated doing it on the internet, she found what she suspected to be Florian's computer, opened right next to her sister's laptop. She got online.

After checking the web and avoiding the publicity ads and unnecessary sales interruptions, she discovered several sites. She got excited ever so briefly.

Never in the world am I ever going to be a computer whiz, she grinned.

She continued till she found a very lacklustre page without many colourful pictures and tourist information. After a brief scanning, a large description and history referring to more esoteric findings, she noticed within an eight-pointed star the words: Hermes Trismegistus!

Bingo, she smiled, let's get on with the show! And one of her favoured songs kicked back in. Oh Mercury, I do miss you ... she laughed thinking about that last concert Freddie Mercury had given, and she had attended, three decades back.

60. FIESOLE, 1473 LEONARDO DA VINCI

Mythology or not,
You all have visualized me and
For the game, my name,
is not Apollo
even if you truly all have been my muses
And I am so grateful that you have… imagined me. (Lost Flavours of a Pleiadian Filibuster).

"Yes, Hermes Trismegistus," Leonardo sighed and continued, "A complex subject you have aborted. He, who though invisible, is to be found everywhere, connecting the gods with the humans and bringing the knowledge so our minds can be challenged."

While the table remained silent ready to absorb the latest 'news from the sun', GianLuca was beaming, whilst also looking stunned and fascinated by da Vinci's intervention.

"Hard nut to crack," he laughed while knocking on his own skull, but da Vinci didn't blink an eye. He had no time to joke and he didn't even smile, nor did he want to let on to anyone that he understood what was actually going on even if Angelo had explained the situation earlier. After he greeted the hosts, he was properly introduced to each of the people in attendance. The young genius sat down quietly and rolled out what seemed to be a map.

To the foreigners, his uncomplicated behaviour seemed astonishing. Angelo had provided Leonardo with pen and ink. Everyone withdrew in his shadow for a moment, and they gave space to the man who would one day be the author of the most mysterious smile on earth, the 'Mona Lisa'. As da Vinci spoke, you could hear a needle drop.

"Always ready to get in our own way, we humans. If we could only take time and sit still, listen to our inner voice; if we would connect with nature and allow our own higher knowledge to filter through like our winged friend Mercury."

Giuliano approached and spoke in total agreement.

"On every journey I take, even a horse race with Lorenzo, we halt for a quiet moment in nature," he said with an infant's smile on his face. "So, the songs of the birds alone can bring us to a perfectly peaceful place, quite unlike my very busy brain."

"Their frequency changes your brainwaves, you see?" Isabel agreed. "Since our twentieth century, several scientists started agreeing that the quietness and 'noises of nature', the sound of birds balances both sides of the brain. Today, you are still lucky because you do not have the frequent interruptions, we on our timeline are surrounded by." She continued, "Music is often a daily disturbance in our homes, in offices, public places like the *negozi* (the shops), even on the streets." The group looked slightly confused but da Vinci had already some picture in his mind.

GianLuca now spoke up, "Remember we explained to you, a bit, last week how technology has taken over our lives, or worse, our television entertainment boxes distract us from paying attention to the self and the personal healing we so need to address?"

Isabel joined in the conversation and said, "One of the keys to all the answers can be found within each family lineage and of course, our other incarnations if you believe, and like to call upon such possibilities."

"Do you mean it is not healthy to play our instruments, for example the harp or the lute?" a confused Fiammetta asked, her eyes both astonished, almost annoyed.

"Oh no, not at all, to the contrary," Isabel answered. "Your wonderfully soothing instruments, the beautiful ballades you listen to at your weddings or other festivities, carry a unique frequency. The future will be different with unimaginable distractions coming from all kinds of loud sources. But forgive me, I mustn't try to explain."

You are centuries away. Oh, how I would just love to stay with you all and teach you more, but I don't think destiny will take us on that road, Isabel pondered while letting go of Agnola's hand.

Isabel stepped out of her daydreaming moment and said, "I mean how could we influence you to the extent that you will comprehend your inner 'technology' so well, that you can indeed change your present reality?"

Isabel had touched the core of the subject and Lorenzo's voice, soft as it rarely was, surprised everyone at the table, and he agreed, and he believed one could indeed change one's reality. "Angelo, we must show our foreign friends something that may help them find their way back home," Lorenzo affirmed.

"And that is why I summoned our young friend Leonardo, to explain to him the present challenge and I trusted that he would come up with a valid solution," Angelo answered.

Surprised at what he just said, both Isabel and GianLuca got up. They watched both Giuliano and Lorenzo exchange a unique eye contact and GianLuca felt like an accomplice.

"GianLuca and Isabel, please join Angelo and Leonardo in visiting the grotto. I will gladly continue talking with our other guests. Forgive me..." Giuliano said as he turned to Lapo, "The place is rather small, and we cannot all enter, especially not men of our size" and he smiled, but Isabel felt awkward in excluding anyone at all.

Angelo led the way with Leonardo, while Giuliano hooked both Isabel and GianLuca's arms. Isabel was thrilled beyond words. They were actually walking behind this genius. She hardly could keep her thoughts to herself and GianLuca's eyes showed an empathy and understanding, while Giuliano had equally evaluated this moment in time as totally unique.

"I'm concerned. We all may discover what you came for and then after such a moment we will not see you again will we?" Giuliano asked in a curious way and GianLuca could feel the strength in his grip on his arm and he laid his right hand on his shoulder.

They reached the back of the upper garden and entered the narrow looking cave. Leonardo offered his hand to accompany a now very excited Isabel down into the pit. She thought about the last time she had walked on these premises, in the Medici family's far-ahead future of 2018. Giuliano took a second torch and followed Angelo and Leonardo as all five descended. In a less than elaborate setting, they pushed a bunch of pillows to the side and he removed several layers of bedding revealing the centre part of the smallish room. Angelo called it the academy's 'sacred space'.

Between a near life-size statue of Venus/Aphrodite and a smallish fountain positioned right opposite a complex circular design, they admired these small bits of coloured, mosaic-like stones that made up the shape of yet another god in an unusually distinguished way.

"You recognize of course the messenger of the gods?" Giuliano asked.

"Yes, the mosaic depicts Hermes (also known as Mercury), the son of Zeus and Maia." Angelo continued, respectfully, nervously lowering his eyelids as if Hermes himself was present.

"Indeed, Hermes's mother has been said to have been Rhea or Cybele or Maia after whom our month of May was named." Leonardo slipped into the conversation. "The names don't really matter. That woman bore the messenger of the gods."

GianLuca said, "In the Emerald Tablet, this woman has been written up as the nurse (*nutria ejus terra* (Earth is its receptor, the womb)... no?"

"Will you ever cease to surprise me, GianLuca?" Giuliano commented in perfect reverence to what GianLuca just claimed. Leonardo proudly continued and he held everyone's attention.

"You may notice then that the Hermes layout is all semi-precious stones like amethyst, alexandrite... here it turns red because of the torches... and a different beryl, like Emerald and Aquamarine, with a variety of coloured quartz."

GianLuca had knelt down and let his fingers slide over the mysterious signs and symbols.

"Magnificent," he said. "Astrology is my favourite hobby, but I'll admit being very limited without my own world's technological travel and search device that contains our libraries of knowledge. Well, it looks like a big flat book."

Giuliano and Angelo shook their heads in disbelief that such a thing could exist (the flat metal box full of encrypted data GianLuca had explained just a few days back) and Isabel softly giggled her way around the conversation. Only da Vinci's eyes and ears took on another focus. Intuitively he knew it was time to find a solution for the foreigners to return to their world, and that moment was to be very soon.

"Let us not lose our focus," Leonardo announced almost coldly, and rightly so.

"You're right, there might well be a key right here," Angelo mentioned, as he pointed at the symbols contained in the outer circle.

"Giuliano will you go ahead and start off the experimental process?" Angelo asked.

"I'll help you; we have done this long ago in one of the ceremonies. Please just mirror GianLuca and put your hands right on the inside of the outer circle and, at the same time as he does, turn the discoid counter clock."

As both GianLuca and Isabel had expected, the mosaics gave way only slightly until, with a tiny click, the entire circle dropped down gently about half a foot deep. In its place another circle started to slide very slowly, about three inches below the outer ring that formed a new three-dimensional wheel. An old manuscript GianLuca had studied long ago suddenly came to mind. There were formulas created for magical rituals and now he realized that the 'ancients' used that kind of indescribable magic. These were no longer coming from a bag of tricks. This was a part of a well-designed ceremony and da Vinci and Angelo had the knowledge, the science and consciousness to carry it off. They knew that they were on the right track.

Isabel looked at GianLuca, who had a smile on his face, and she had no idea why he looked so confident. Then Leonardo spoke in a solemn voice, "Hermes Trismegistus: Hermes or Thoth: thrice the greatest; he who also took the soul back and forth from Hades, ruled by Pluto to transform that soul and when Pluto is paired up with Saturn/Kronos, your soul may well travel through time."

Very appropriate, Isabel thought. Back and forth in time, please let's do this!

GianLuca had hunched over and finally got down to the floor figuring out the degrees he noticed encrypted above each of the twelve houses, just like in an astrological chart.

"Giuliano, please turn the lower plate again," GianLuca said, "maybe both Angelo and Leonardo can help, and I will turn the middle one."

Rather surprised, both men wrapped themselves carefully around the mysterious device as GianLuca requested.

It took a few minutes till GianLuca called out, "Stop!" They all looked astonished and wondered what was to come next. Even Isabel got the chills. Only da Vinci knew what was coming, how this ceremony was to end, how all was to evolve. His mathematical brain had it well calculated and he knew this plane well, for he was one of its frequent flyers. All the others distanced themselves from the newly found 'pit' and GianLuca reached out for Giuliano's hand.

Angelo got really emotional and Isabel could hardly contain herself. She took Angelo's hand and he turned his head away from the two other men, now holding Isabel firmly in his arms.

Isabel spoke, "I should pay my farewells to Andrea and his family, I know, and we want to thank Lorenzo and ..."

Lorenzo interrupted and said, "You are telling us last night that it will be our choice to lead Tuscany and Italy. If we rule through terror and the struggle of power, or if we want to bring a greater awareness, bring a higher education and the creation of a new value system the future will be a different one, right?"

Giuliano's face looked as if he assisted in the drowning of his own soul. Angelo climbed out of the pit and they could hear him call the others. He spoke clearly and affirmed, "We'll have to be quick, because I know as in days of old, that the fumes will manifest rapidly."

"Do you remember what happened that same noon when you arrived at Santa Croce?" Giuliano asked GianLuca. "Remember I explained to you that Angelo and I were having a private ceremony at that same time?" da Vinci knew all the details as Angelo had given him.

"Those fumes are connected to a kind of magical gate, like in Delphi," Leonardo commented. "It will have a hallucinating effect to take a human being out of his limiting thought patterns and therefore free the way into very different realities and enter another world. That's what I suspect; better I feel will happen."

"And I guess we'll have to move quickly, won't we?" Isabel asked. "The prelude we had this afternoon may well extend itself in another cosmic storm and our friends are all going to feel it very strongly."

While he listened and lowered his eyes, da Vinci agreed, "That's also what I feel."

Lorenzo had now descended into the grotto. "Angelo has explained already in his briefing what you have discovered, and I suggest that we quickly say goodbye!" he said in his regal but urgent manner.

"I must tell you, dear GianLuca, that only Mercury could have sent a messenger like you, maybe from the Pleiades, where our real mother Maia was born," he said in a laughing way. Leonardo's eyes had softened, and a brief regret made its way into his heart. He wished he had known them longer because with those foreign visitors he would have had so much to discuss and discover.

Leonardo addressed GianLuca, "You will now return and take with you Isabel, because you are both needed on that timeline where, as I understood from our conversations with Angelo and the brothers, on our planet Gaia, the people have to be warned not to recreate the Atlantean phenomena and catastrophe! Please remember this always!" he sighed, trembling as he held GianLuca's hands.

Even though Isabel had a few more thoughts to convey, she understood what a confusion the previous night's stellar commotion had caused. She therefore refrained from any further comments. She smiled and turned to Leonardo and said, "We were honoured to have met you. I just wanted to tell you that you must never forget where you came from and trust that when the time comes to leave Italy, your good fortune will lie with the king of France and he will take care of you till your very last day on this Earth." She then refrained from any further comments.

GianLuca also coughed and spoke with a dry throat, "A Pisces Moon will pull many human souls into this fantasy zone we call the astral plane, in an astro-psychic maddening anomaly, as many celestial bodies exploit us, like devilish mutant pranksters, away from heavenly guiding lights."

And as he paused, Lorenzo, who had followed every word up close, took the baton.

"Thank you for all the time shared with all of us and to have reminded us of the tremendous work we have in front of us. My closest ally is 'your presence' in my beloved brother, Giuliano. Yes, we must change the future as you have warned us, and no doubt we can create another version. Let's hope it may become a change to be read in your history books. I pray it will. And if not, then we need to be a part of another library in the Universe, correcting the countless amoral deeds humans have allowed to happen!"

He smiled once again, but his own sadness was predominant. "My brother Giuliano will guide me, as you would if you had remained amongst us! We will call upon you when we do our full moon ceremonies and pray for your well-being on that other timeline you have called 'parallel'!"

Leonardo stepped forward and his handsome face looked enlightened and enchanted as he spoke a last time.

"You have woken up in me a frequency I knew I possessed, but dared not believe in. You both remind me that we are all incredibly beautiful and full of unforeseen powers. You have inspired me, and I feel I can help our world to fly like Icarus! My eternal gratitude to you both!" He stepped to the side and bowed his head in sincere humility and honest empathy.

Then Giuliano's brother solemnly took GianLuca in his arms with a tremendous power that left him briefly out of touch with the present. He was gentle with Isabel, but with her twenty-first century education she did nothing less than to kiss him heartily on the lips with an almost hypnotic effect on the man's loins, even then, profoundly stirring his brainwaves. He could no longer hide his attraction to this very 'free woman' he had met too briefly.

He swallowed and then turned towards GianLuca a last time. His last brief touch was whole-hearted and then he stepped away. He would never show tears under any condition, happy or sad. But this time he did turn around.

"May Mercury and the whole pantheon of gods be with you both, with your friends and family!" And as the future 'Prince of Tuscany' waved his way out, he did not look around and lifted his eyes to the heavens. Angelo and Leonardo stood a few feet away, and the Buontalenti quartet endured a semi-frozen state.

61. FIESOLE, 2018 HERMES TRISMEGISTUS

I never thought I was to witness
the most unexpected of universal holidays
in the most changeable of nanosecond mysteries
and live my own life first and then with you. (Your Chair)

They could hear the church bells and Elizabeth realized that in a half an hour it would be midnight. She turned cold for a moment, thinking that some magical spell might well manifest right under her nose. I better stay here she had told herself while wondering if she was going to get used to mumbling loudly when she was alone.

I may just have to watch my words, in public at least. Hmm . . . time for a cigarette, or not.

Izquierdo and Florian were on their knees cleaning parts of the mandala, in awe of the multitude of gemstones.

"That outside circle, look Iz," Florian said in an excited way. "It looks like one big astro-game and . . ."

"I got it. I got it!" Derecho called out triumphantly. "Oh no, that's when I love high tech really, really high-tech, my friends! Now Florian, turn the inside counter-clock, it's gotta move." Surprized, both Iz and Florian followed Derecho's direction.

"Turn, ever so slowly fellas, really slow!" he indicated. "Now it may be a bit stuck, over the centuries, that's to be expected. But push it downwards; my guess is that somewhere it'll click into place and move another hidden device."

"Excellent, Derecho," Siegfried called out, also on his knees looking down.

Seconds later the click came. Nearly in a trance, they could feel the plate moving to one side and then further down. By adding more of their weight, little by little, down it went. They withdrew instantly as if some snake-like monster had jumped from an infinite past right at them ready to swallow their heads. But what they saw left them speechless. A second circle of symbols appeared right below the first one, only inches away.

"Wow, that's really out of this world!" Siegfried screamed while he moved the flashlight closer to the newly discovered, smallish pit.

"It sure has a strange smell," Izquierdo announced with a slight cough.

"Sulphur! It is sulphur, that stifling odour, no? Giuliano had mentioned something similar," Florian nearly complained.

"Well, we didn't expect a fancy perfume now, did we sir," Iz laughed at his own silly remark. "That's like in the Greek, hum ..." Florian said.

"At the Delphi Oracle, Florian. You said it," Siegfried caught his thought.

"You gotta check this out guys," Doh called out, almost in a happy panic. Siegfried had moved with the laptop, activating a few more parallel programs.

Izquierdo suddenly needed to get out of the cave.

"Look at this, the way it's turning, and you only added the 'free self-search' program to it," Iz said to Siegfried.

Elizabeth ran back to the cave. She was calling out loudly, "It's almost midnight!"

"So what?" Doh said.

"What?" she said, ready to hit him on the head in a joking manner.

"Female intuition, that's what it is." Doh apologized.

Not without pride, Elizabeth said, "*Hermes Trismegistos* is the greatest Hermes in three versions, you know when it all happens? Yes, the magic happens at ... midnight."

"Oh Mademoiselle Elizabeth," Derecho replied in a mocking way. "Elizabeth you are the genius linking us all! There it is of course, triple ... TRISMEGISTOS; the triple circle!"

"With the right degrees on each sign ..." Siegfried commented. "Florian you better get up here, this is surely going to inspire you to get us the right codes."

"But what's that smell, the discomfort of a fart?" she suddenly asked in an amusing comedy voice. Nobody paid attention. But Florian didn't reach the staircase. He began to lose consciousness while a stinky mist started to invade the cave.

"Get him out of there! Can't you tell? Get him out! He's got a strong allergy to smoke," Siegfried shouted. Dritto and Iz kind of stumbled down and carried him up as the whole group quickly moved outside coughing until they were able to breath fresh air. They stretched Florian out on the grass and started pumping his lungs.

"He's going to be fine," Iz announced gratefully. "That gas makes you want to..."

"... hallucinate..." Florian whispered, as he peeped through his thick eyelashes.

They all sighed when he opened his eyes.

"Look at the sky, does that look more and more familiar... right guys?" Florian called out, still on his back admiring the almost fluorescent colours the clouds seemed to shape themselves into. Displeased, Dritto was the first to be put off.

"Oh no, not again," he prayed. "Not again, please. I just wanna stay on this planet in this century!" he cried out laughingly.

Derecho, now left in charge of the laptop, hadn't moved from Siegfried's side. He put it down. "Is this a similar event as last time we were together, that night at Lapo's?" Dritto now asked. The latter looked at Florian and then he walked over to Izquierdo as quickly as he could and said, "Maybe we should get back to the house... Isabel might get back before we know!"

It didn't take more words for Elizabeth to run back and the bells rang midnight. Chills crawled all over her body. *Goddess, lucky I'm wearing sports shoes*! *We're close, she thought.*

This is going to change our worlds! Was Cinderella waiting for a full moon to wake up?

62. FIESOLE, 1473 COSMIC TWINS

If love is what you feel for me,
let it be for love's sake only
as I won't love you for your looks or smile or sweetest of ways,
seducing reflections, in ponds the Gods set up
for our eyes to rest into each other's dreams outlasting all eternity
in all exalted amity. (The Difference is . . .)

Fiammetta and Agnola forced their bravest appearance. Agnola thanked her 'twin sister' as she had labelled Isabel and the two promised to think of each other on each new moon. Agnola told her to hang out a sheet of paper on the full moon and then to write on that page the next new moon so that all she wanted to accomplish was propelled into the ether and she herself might even get the message like an empty bottle on the waves of the endless sea of consciousness, mailed out through the cosmos! That did it, and in a very tight hugging session, Agnola also allowed her tears another free flow. Isabel took off a golden chain with a small pendant and put it around Agnola's long neck." I will always be with you."

GianLuca and Fiammetta had an equally speechless moment, as their desire for one other had been so profound and spoken. His thoughts and hers melted in an unrequited dream of a divine union, at least in this Renaissance Florence. They wrapped each other in their deepest thoughts and the outcome was a sky without any romantic limits absorbed in all Renaissance literature.

"I will write you over the lines of time on that new moon and I will love you always and we will appear in each other's different realities and dreams again for I do love you, Fiammetta," GianLuca whispered in her eager ears.

"So, will I . . . always love you and maybe we will see ourselves in another century in a different fashion!" she said smiling. And she kissed him on the mouth and then held his hand to her heart and left. As both sisters now departed, Fiammetta turned to Isabel. "Thank you for taking care of him and be happy on your timeline and embrace Florian for us all!"

She smiled, her head tilting sideways as if the weight of tears was gathered all on one side. And on her way out, her brother waited for her, as did their father. Lapo made all efforts to be as formal as possible, extending invitations in a funny burlesque-like way for his new friends to return any time and Andrea burst out laughing which brought the ambiance an octave up from the heavy solemnity and, once again, with the humour their conversations in the past had so benefited from.

As true gentlemen, they said farewell to Isabel as if they had known her for ages. Andrea stood in front of her as he briefly felt like a teenager who was hoping to seduce his foreign language teacher.

"I wish you much happiness; my greetings also to all your other brave companions. You will see them very soon and that is how it should be!" Andrea covered up his own irrevocable *tristessa* (sadness).

"Brother, I'll miss you; may we dream another adventure once again!" GianLuca swallowed as both men separated. Giuliano had been sitting in the corner. Silently his eyes were now closed. And just then Angelo stormed in.

"Giuliano, you have to come back up, we cannot lose you to another century!" he shouted out, putting up both of his hands begging GianLuca to release his friend in the endless farewell. *"Ti prego, vieni con noi* (I beg you, come with us)?"

"Angelo, ti voglio bene e Leonardo grazie per tutto; sei incredibile (Angelo, I wish you well and Leonardo, thanks for everything; you're great!)" GianLuca said. "Be well in these coming years; you will have a grand life. Be warned that if your desires cause you trouble, don't doubt that you have all it takes to reach for your own 'inner guidance modality'. The universe never will let you down!"

Leonardo's body got the chills just by hearing him speak; he knew now why he had to be here at this very moment. It would change so much for all those in attendance and he could hardly believe this was actually happening.

"When your loins are stirred with confusion and an uncontrollable passion, don't land in the *bargello*!" GianLuca declared looking at Angelo and at Leonardo, rather unasked for. "But be at ease no matter who you befriend, yet with your love for men, it may be wise not to bed the powerful elite! Also do not stay in Milan too long and be careful the day the French king will invite you!" While he shone with truthful intentions, a sobbing session seemed close.

Both young men, the poet and the inventor, ran out like heroes from a Greek tragedy.

"My friends of cosmic and comic times," Giuliano joked, "I have just imagined you back in your 2018 Florence, but somehow this time you will not land on the Piazza where you departed, but on the land where my Uncle Giovanni's Villa was built, in Fiesole. I can hardly believe that I can be speaking of a place we are at right now. In little time, yet in more than five centuries, you will fly in like a cosmic bird."

A last-minute surprise came when da Vinci showed Giuliano his latest design of huge wings on a man's body; he wanted to give it to GianLuca to take back to his century. But that was impossible, and Giuliano quickly stuffed it in his shirt; or . . .! He sniggered.

"Well, so be it," Giuliano said. "Let us hope that with the help of our Hermes you will manifest your travels into being. May love and friendship guide you wherever your path will take you unconditionally!" While chills invaded his entire body; Giuliano had no more words left. His left hand actually discovered a note from his friend GianLuca to both brothers.

They went back to work. Giuliano and GianLuca now tackled the triple mandala brilliantly, its inner zodiacal belt shining forth. All three sat down holding hands. There was an instant glow coming from them all and GianLuca's arms started to shake slightly. Both men's eyes turned upwards and after a nearly violent arch they curved their upper bodies like rising snakes.

Right below them, within the Hermes figure, the emeralds shone stronger and stronger, bigger and bigger and Mercury's eyes flickered a fiery red, sparks of titillating fuses. Isabel felt as if she had collapsed in an avalanche of stones, as if swallowed by an ethereal smog veiled in the transcendent mist while she watched GianLuca's face fuse with Giuliano's, disappearing in the bottomless pit below them and in a new series of fireworks of explosive crystals within the blinding rays of mystic lights. Isabel dived into an inscrutable abyss of spiralling strands of dancing figures intermingled with scenes from all the travels she had ventured those last few weeks.

Outside the grotto, Angelo Poliziano prayed to the entire pantheon of gods to allow his beloved friends to return to their own century and not to take Giuliano. Fiammetta found comfort against Lorenzo's gladiator torso. Agnola held onto her father's hands while Lapo wrapped her in his arms. Leonardo pushed himself against a big tree and held on tight and close by, Andrea was still sadly staring at the sky, when an effervescent rain of multi-coloured layers of expansive rays suddenly exploded above their heads and the clear blue starry heavens darkened with clouds speeding past each other and worlds melting into one another in divine coalescence. Andrea's hands wanted to cover his eyes, and while the others turned their heads away from this indescribable empyreal event, Lorenzo and Andrea grabbed the light explosion, deeply wishing it to benefit their time traveling friends while leaving the Buontalenti and the Medici families, in 1473 Tuscany, with a wealth of sprouting seeds for a new and safer future.

Leonardo da Vinci, the young man who released birds to their freedom after he had bought them at the Tuscan markets, this rare genius who preferred life's experience over Latin, sank to his knees thanking the heavens for this implausible encounter. Meeting these time travelers would now change all of his work, whether art or original scientific research.

History would one day acknowledge what GianLuca had incited him to do. His ideas for central heating systems, the designs of parachutes, automatons, mechanical war tools and helicopters were to be second to none. Very few original paintings and anatomical designs could match his human intent and understanding of the magical ability of nature and the dynamic process and function of the organism of both man and woman. He would serve this world with his utter brilliance; he would excel in coding the soul's essence with the colours of his paintings and his blueprints would predict a future as these time travelers had shown him.

A voice downhill called him and he happily recognized Angelo. He slowly walked down while leaving behind the most amazing spectacle he could ever have imagined. He knew, deep in his heart, that one day all humanity would be able to travel in time. May I never lose my focus; he promised himself not to. I shall remain private in all my intimate actions and as GianLuca had suggested, I will control my own desires and let nobody ever know that I love those built like myself, as this century is not ancient Greece, and I will not be judged dangerous for my taste and preferences, landing me in a jail like the *bargello*.

Who could ever blame me for my love of men, for I love each genuine human and will need to keep this to myself, for few men are not abusive of their power; I will never go public and as such, I will protect myself and those I love and care for.

Leonardo looked down at his favourite city, *la bella Fiorenza* (beautiful Florence) and that very moment he indeed knew one day he'd fashion phenomenal creations. There would be jealousy and traps to get him away from his life's goals and as the foreigner had told him in a very precise way, he would end his days at the French court... a long way to go. Soon, he would even share the same patron with his faithful Angelo now awaiting him at the foot of the hill and together they would continue their new journey for a few more weeks in quiet harmony and with a touch of youthful love and eternal friendship.

63. FIESOLE, 2018 OLYMPUS

How few the gestures we don't fake,
in all grandeur from core detached,
the diamond framed in golden lace of drifting wounds
on lanes of dissociated, future pasts. (The Kings and Queens we were)

Befogging fumes grew out of the cave quicker and quicker and the valley below the city of an almost dormant Florence remained drenched in a complete fog, as if the fall season had assaulted the summer. People and cars bumped into each other, and the honking became so frantic that many of the houses on the Fiesole and the San Domenico hills turned on their lights. Windows opened and closed rapidly when a drenching rain came down within a sticky steam of fizzy purple particles of light that then evaporated fearlessly into a dusty haze of trembling lightning bolts that shook up the whole city.

Seven clouds mingled around the upper garden at the Fiesole Villa as if discussing the last hours' events, witnessed along the lines of time. The sturdy Cypress trees were tenderly waltzing sideways, their longish green fingers fanning the foggy veil away with Elizabeth holding on to the window frame, the wind playing a game as in a hairstyle commercial. She hardly dared to look anywhere else but silently watched over Isabel's body not knowing whether to do something or to continue being still. A ciggie would certainly help. She searched her bag and she contemplated the health of the person on the chair.

The men outside fought against what first seemed like seasonal bad local weather, maybe some kind of a hurricane of lightning specks exploding in their faces yet leaving no trace of their unearthly passage as in a Carol Lewis fairy tale.

Derecho continued to handle the laptop with a zesty professional agility under a broken umbrella. Florian, still a bit drowsy, crawled over to him.

No one else paid attention to him, so he pushed himself up. In the middle of the computer screen, the three circles from Mercury's mandala continued to spiral at the most erratic speed. And then like in that famous da Vinci drawing, one man appeared in the middle of a triple circle spinning around between planetary signs till the computer gave out in an ebullience of splashes of DNA-like formations, dappling the atmosphere in the entire upper garden.

Five, star-scattered men held their breath as if awaiting Zeus to free Prometheus from his mountain chains. Then the clouds disappeared and right above, a celestial brush painted a starry night sky close to Orion's belt, in the vicinity of blinking Sirius, twinkling Maya and all of her Pleiadean sisters. A long feather of iridescent light tore the sky in two and the heavens imperceptibly blended with the darkest of nights.

It wasn't until a very heavy coughing caught Florian's attention, that it occurred to him it was one of his companions. Standing above the freshly made gap he looked down. He ran around the mound nearly sliding back down into the grotto they had nearly totally destroyed a few moments earlier. Prometheus and Hermes had joined hands. He beamed cheerfully for as he had hoped, there was his old friend.

GianLuca slowly stretched out and stood up. Not a Frankenstein monster come alive, GianLuca smiled when he saw Florian and uttered with much emotion a few words nobody could hear clearly. He repeated them, enabling his own speech to find a natural rhythm ever so slowly.

"One black hole that was! How beautiful! And now I find again my oldest friend, my little brother Florian? Just couldn't wait to get ahead of us all now, could ya?" he joked, feeling his good old self almost back in place. He looked around and sadness briefly shaded his eyes.

"And Isabel, she didn't make it?" GianLuca asked with fearful eyes staring around the cave and garden.

"Oh no, she definitely must be in a much more comfortable position than you. I can explain. Let me pull you out of there and we'll go to the house, where it all started," Florian said.

"We're right here boys … having a good old time down in the pit?" Derecho called out, with three other men laughing unreservedly while a high-pitched female voice screamed her vocal cords off the planet. It was Elizabeth's commanding voice echoing throughout the premises.

"She has returned, come here, right now. Isabel is here! *Elle est là*!" Elizabeth was so excited, she just couldn't stop screaming. She forgot to close the window and the cigarette had flown outside. She looked back at her half-sister in a very slow wake-up state while four men entered step by step checking out that they didn't interrupt any 'girlie-girlie talk'.

And then Isabel had her eyes wide open and she noticed Dritto, Derecho and Izquierdo and she named them all, looking at Siegfried with question marks in her eyes.

"I'm your sister Elizabeth's husband, Siegfried Freundreich and I'm truly glad to meet you back on Earth; and so is Elizabeth!"

But Elizabeth was sobbing away and covering her face with mascara running down her cheeks and a box of Kleenex at her side. Isabel got up and hugged her before even addressing her friends. Iz tried to figure out how Isabel had returned.

"After all those decades, you and your husband helped me get back over here?" Isabel asked in total surprise. Eliza answered, "Well, they all worked together with Florian," and Florian walked in with GianLuca.

"The party is over Isabel. We have him back!" Florian roared, still ecstatic. "Let's now have a real party!" Florian quickened his pace and Isabel fell into his arms but there was no doubt possible that Cupid had worked his arrows long before, maybe even centuries back, leaving behind a Renaissance attraction wearing her chain and pendant. But now this life on this lifetime counted and now family was back together. Isabel remained dumbfound but happy.

"You've met my sister and brother-in-law, it seems" Isabel said.

"Oh yes, and they've been extremely helpful, though no doubt they will say they hardly did a thing, right?" Florian said with a big grin.

GianLuca sat down on one of the 'dentist chairs' he noticed for the first time.

"I have a medieval cavity, doctor Isabel. Would you check the wisdom teeth," he joked.

"We have all lived an extreme adventure and we have left behind some wonderful people, some extraordinary human beings. Lapo's family was extremely saddened by the fact we had to return to our timeline, and they wanted you to know how grateful and happy they were to have met you all. And then Leonardo da Vinci was devastated upon our departure. He took to heart all you told him, Isabel," GianLuca said, and he sighed. It wasn't a jetlag he was coping with. In his voice rang a melancholy like a Radio Nostalgia.

"We have loved a man and a woman in 1473. Giuliano de Medici, simply myself on their timeline and I had almost fallen in love with one of Lapo Buontalenti's daughters. I so cherished their family. Who knows if we may see them again throughout other travels, maybe in our dreams?" GianLuca paused.

"We have made new friends from our own century, of all places in the Renaissance, as if we were visiting a museum like our visit at the *bargello*." The trio giggled, loudly clapping hands and thumbs up.

"So sorry that you guys missed out on Leonardo who had the genius to touch the right buttons in the cave!" Florian said.

"How amazing," Dritto laughed out loud. "Now your CV can mention you worked with da Vinci and you broke a code!"

"Very funny," an entire choir lifted their voices, "That novel wasn't his best one,"

Elizabeth announced. "And now the wonderful surprise is that I have found Isabel. *Je suis totalement comblée* (I am totally fulfilled, as we say in French)!"

"I guess we can do the dishes tomorrow," Derecho said, and they all looked at him, rather curious of the next joke.

"*Le jardin* (the garden)! It's a mess, but we'll get the repair done professionally so the owners won't notice any time traveling left-overs!" Dritto joked.

"Don't worry, that's the last thing to think about," Elizabeth announced. "I still have Désiré, my private eye, who will help us. He'll find the right people to restore our Venus temple!" Elizabeth had more than one arrow left.

"While you gentlemen were having a good old time digging deep in the past," she smiled, *"Moi, par contre en 3D* (Me, instead in 3D)," she laughed, "Well, I called up the wonderful hotel right above us and Désiré has ordered two large double bedrooms and four single rooms, all first class! DoWell is inviting you all and our Sherlock, Désiré, will be pleased not to have to spend the night alone while keeping an eye out for all of us."

Elizabeth von Weitweg was so relieved that she took to a waltz in the back of her mind and she looked at her Siegfried with the pride of a university graduate; as if he were once again twenty-one.

64. WASHINGTON DC, 2018 H.K., THE GAMEMASTER

Slow moves on the chessboard that isn't yours?
Black Queen wavering, kipping Horse,
lost Tower, Runner fell, Royal pretence: King stuck
You're speaking in tongues to H.K, the King's jester (Scary Traps)

"A cleaning woman! One of our great politicians, an octogenarian of international repute; how can it be that he was stopped and interrogated at Geneva Airport for questioning?" a man in a very dark suit screamed over the fax-phone line he preferred using when it was a busy day at the lawyer's office. He continued, his voice hitting more operatic levels.

"Don't you, 'but sir' me; I am a senior Senator. I can get all of the information from another source too if you cannot be more precise, Bill. And no, I do not have a direct access to Harry Khope's personal line. And let me be more precise: do not, I repeat, do not call here ever again and leave some urgent message for an asap call back! Get it? This isn't a Hollywood set where you all snap your fingers when you want a tissue or a make-up assistant or a fucking blow job! This is a serious political office and stop the 'buts and the sirs,' I said . . . and . . ."

Bill's voice on that landline phone had finally raised his own tone and he wasn't sweet any longer. "What if the Washington Post prints a picture with your naked ass on top of me, Larry? I'll send it right out if you cannot control your innate nastiness!"

There was an unexpected silence, but to Bill this was an equalled victory. He hadn't been in the business that long, but Uncle Harry had surely taught him the tricks of the trade. He wasn't about to throw his career away because he had been on the *scène du crime* (crime scene) in a Geneva office as if on a CSI-TV series. The man who used the cover name 'Larry' sighed.

He wanted to throw the phone against the overly white wall, but then he bit his lips and answered venomously.

"What in the fluke do you want from me Bill? I can only get you the phone number by tomorrow, OK? This is top-level secret information. And where in the fuck are you now?"

"I'll call you back tomorrow morning at eleven! Better have his cell by then, Larry Crow or no more DC parties with big dicks and hot chicks!" The line went dead and Larry's hairpiece had moved side-ways. Bill watched his sister in the Napoleon III armchair and he was concerned with more than just their careers.

"He hasn't called us once since we left Geneva. Who would have thought that something odd like this would happen?" Bill asked. "The pictures of Simon on the web are frightening. I am really concerned about what will happen when the taped material hits the world press. Internet has become such a powerful tool. Remember when Pallas Stilton, that Cheese factory heiress, was all over the web because her lover had a camera when they were in bed?"

"Many gossip papers believed it to be a publicity stunt. I want to speak to Harry and find out if he has that recording or the DVD and if so, who may have a copy? It couldn't be on the company's original hard disk, right? You told me Harry's assistant erased all material after he copied the security tapes. Hmm ..." William Lawless sounded annoyed.

"Well, I guess we'll have to wait for tomorrow for an answer," Bill continued. "That Crow is the only politician I know scared enough to get me whatever number I need. He owes me big time since that movie party where he ... oh, I'll spare you the nasty details." Bill smiled maliciously.

"Yes, please do. I have had enough of those kind of career stories in our obligatory off – screen adventures," Jacqueline said, and she closed her eyes while he turned on the television for their favourite late-night show that featured hilarious jokes on today's politicians.

Harry Khope's office at DoWell.Inc. in Washington DC. (That same day).

DoWell.Inc. was not Harry's favourite place for a meeting. The leading East Coast branch was hard to reach, and he preferred a building where he could reach the elevator from the basement. No need for public display. He even disliked going to the White House, avoiding public places with the media vultures always hiding behind a column or maybe disguised as a leaf on an Oak tree beside the Oval Office windows! He hated them all with that 'raw killer' passion. He was greatly upset about the way things had gone at Swiss customs and he had no idea who had warned the airport control that he was taking a flight out of Geneva.

It messed up his stopover in Paris and he missed a privately chartered plane a friend and Hollywood producer had waiting for him. Long trips were a drag and he avoided being recognized as much as he possibly could. One of his insiders at a French club, *Mon Palais*, had some news for him. He needed to build a new future for the agency, because the old ways and tricks weren't doing it as they had in those last fruitful and busy thirty years.

Normal, Harry thought, what goes up must come down! Time to develop some new plans.

And he felt his stomach ready for a nice meal and his heart smiling at the next evil plan he would have. He went back to the time he had dated that wonderful actress, in the sixties that was. Holly had become a popular writer and yes, she had helped him start up the New Age Movement, a deeper phase of his Mind Control Programs. What a laugh that had been; communities just biting right into the 'new spirituality' bait. Vegetarians, macrobiotic freaks, organic food addictive gurus with their dazzling chanting and even that unhealthy vegan-soya craze.

Ah ha, his inside jitters made him burp loudly, all by his own masterful hands with, of course, some inspirational help from his favourite Holly MacSlaine. Of course, he still was generous to his friends, especially an old mistress like her. He made sure she was awarded more than just an Academy Award and he spoiled her equally successful brother. Her books became a series of bestsellers, and some inspired more ET-like stories to hit the market allowing new faces to show who they were, so he could again simply crash them.

After all, the film industry would forever be in debt to him since he used enough of their stars as couriers and sex-slaves while the government was picking up the training and travel bills! He was proud to have earned his place in the pantheon of the pernicious. Some called them 'evil gods', but to Harry good and evil were on the same ambiguous side of that one malevolent coin.

When he had started the 'Grotto Gatherings' in California, the world elite had only joined because all those in attendance were but politicians who only cared to fortify their positions. Then there were the newcomers who wanted to belong so badly to the biggest club of them all, that they didn't mind traveling from the four corners of the planet to this celebration, a once-a-year gathering like a *La Court des Miracles* (Court of Miracles), teaching an evil 'course of allopatry'. His concept had been so unique that many requested a repeat performance and no doubt the presence of the Hollywood and entertainment industry had helped.

He brought a few specialists on board, some shamans; others, true witches who knew how to play the dark forces. 'Live' offerings were made to the old Sumerian gods like Bel who ruled order and destiny! The so-called ancient deity's name was called out in a very dark ritual and Harry had delighted in the human sacrifices needed to inspire the higher forces to merge with some of the world leaders. The High Priestess was an amazing woman. He baptized her the Queen of Hades and she was a distant cousin of a... president! What a laugh he had at his own well-planned intrigues.

He had always been attracted, since his early childhood in Germany to that invisible world he thought of as his greatest ally. All the great dictators like Stalin used the dark forces to manipulate the crowds. Stalin had collected one of the world's biggest esoteric libraries and he had grown so enamoured of the dark side that he never trusted any human, not even his own bodyguards... at the Kremlin he changed every night to another bedroom with new private guards in front of the doors.

Harry had never needed magic tricks. He had simply remained, as much as possible, the man behind the scene, 'The Puppeteer of the Presidents'. He had retained something on each one of them from paedophilia to murder, you name it, and yes, he had created it for them. Some of the most popular politicians secretly loved muscular young men (often out of the sports world) they themselves had sponsored, while many preferred women from the world of entertainment. And only Harry could provide them with under-aged virgins, sometimes the daughters of fellow politicians or movie stars, and all in total discretion.

His film archives had grown into a building. Yes indeed, he had gathered proof on each one of those power-hungry people. They didn't even have to be a Freemason anymore. He just had to reprogram some of them like in that movie which still had him laughing out loud, the *Manchurian Candidate*, no not the sixties one, but that new version ... *good acting,* he admitted ... *but nothing like the original with his old friend Frankie.*

There were more and more 'revelation of the method' movies and it didn't bother him a bit. He would live well over 90 and who would ever dare to take him to any Court of Justice, even with humanitarian groups claiming his past proved him to be a perpetrator of war crimes. Nobody had the guts. He had enough cards in his deck to make the highest placed politician cover his back any time he wanted, and in every country needed. There wasn't one successful leader who didn't owe Harry a favour even if some of them took years to fall through the mazes of his very intricate long-time game. It was the greatest game of all time and he was the greatest, the best hidden leader the planet had ever known.

He had a great talent in developing sex-stories for each one of his clients. Yes, the sex stuff had been such an easy toy. Even those happy idealists, married within an exemplary, traditional family, ha-ha, they all had a hidden life. He would free them and then feed them enough opportunities to not just live their hidden passions but to simply grow into their most secret addiction. He knew that once he got them possessed by an entity, or even better, a group of discarnate souls, their multiple adventures would take them back onto Harry's road of total control.

At the deeply hidden, MK-Ultra headquarters, he had seen enough when at the height of sexual ecstasy, two or more beings would merge, and their untold stories channelled new scenarios. They would open gates beyond human comprehension, and they could attract very much-unwanted companions from invisible worlds and from other timelines. Very few knew how to resist and those who refused would never make a career beyond the local newspapers. In his late twenties, he had studied well the complex human nature. It was obvious we all had a kind of a mother or father issue ... or both.

At first, his MK-Ultra programs had caused a scandal with many inside politicians, but later the world's government leaders thanked him because in the end he gave them what they all wanted; power over their adversaries and pawns ready to be sacrificed on the bigger chessboard of this so very well manipulated 3D world!

It had all started one day in 1953. Using underground programs, the secret services manipulated the brain function through external electromagnetic stimuli with the intention to control and then remotely actuate the human, like turning on and off a television set. Now in the era of advanced technology it gave him even more strings at his fingers than ever before and he was eager to control and train a brand-new staff.

He was happy about Bill; he had taught him from early childhood, just like his sister. To both of them, Harry was like god and they were his favourite children, his personal 'Adam and Eve'. In them, he had planted undetectable seeds of permanent submission thanks to Doctor VonWeltsturm's Z-chips.

He had saved the professor, well-known from the Nazi pantheon, now under another name, from prosecution. Once chipped, there would be little chance for reprogramming ... as in never! One day, Bill Lawless, written up to be the new Gary Grant, would also have a chance to become the first totally programmed president. *"We certainly worked at it," he thought, "thirty years went by in a sneeze," he had told a colleague, an insider-spy at the United Nations.*

He once had prepared a much more mediocre actor, but his wife had been such a convincing collaborator they had become one of the most popular presidential couples ever, liked everywhere, even in Buckingham Palace. His vice-president had been a major player and he had agreed from the beginning to use his own sons for some awful experiments and then of course his granddaughters were next.

Most of his 'subjects' were planned for, and they all landed in high office. But they didn't always develop as he had hoped. Emotions were the boundaries they couldn't control and only one made it to the White House. In those days, unfortunately, some of the programs had serious flaws and those heavy traumatic experiences needed to program people like in the fifties and sixties, were now no longer required. The nanochip was on the market to the highest bidder and an injection was sufficient, even a 'flu vaccine, the doors to other realities just swung wide-open.

Eventually I'll have my own private army of robots, because that's what they were, nothing more. Harry had calculated in cold blood.

Cunning as he was, he had made sure that a wide variety of religious choices was made available so people could believe in non-truths and be dependent of some higher force or a god figure, higher than their own petty lives. He always knew that he had made his own choices very early! As the human value system was going down the drain already, billions of people were looking for a way out of television's Lala-land and the obviously entrapping material world. The world society was so easy to program.

He felt relieved as if on a well-deserved holiday now that *BookUface* or *Spitter*, the cell phone's equally annoying program, or the *I-Flod* had created new highways for total control. Soon there would be the *I-Nail* that would connect all users to the *HighClouding*, a system that, of course, was again totally controlled. Why would he even consider the word 'compassion' when today's crowds simply walked in with their eyes open, glad to slip into the mouth of the lion?

The sooner they do, Harry thought, the better; Sodom & Gomorrah every day!

In less than a decade nobody would know the difference between a real actor and a programmed one, between a genuine sportsman and one designed for stadium-pleasing mega events. Top prize winners preyed on fame and recognition in all branches of this material world; many were ready to sell their souls for a moment of glory in the limelight of the grander stage of existence. Worldwide, the Performing Arts Academies on the television had become their best recruiting centres ... it was going to get easier from now on!

Yes Harry, you really did a great job these last fifty years; I guess there really should be a sort of Nobel Prize for Evil, he giggled inside, because it isn't really all easy to play the evil guy now, was it? I must call my kids as they might have seen that ridiculous alert at the Geneva Airport.

"Is that you Jacky, this is Harry calling," he said in a jolly relaxed voice. He knew when not to use 'Uncle Harry' because that set off a different program; *'izthatyou Jacky – (pause) – this is Harry calling'* – launched them into what he called their *'quiet/original mode'*. He rarely ever used it except when a new killing was the real reason for the call. This time he was pleased he could. "Oh Harry, oh that's just wonderful. Are you all right? We ..."

Chatterbox she is, he immediately reflected.

"Yes, of course dear, you saw that I was, shall we say ..." and he hesitated briefly, "that I was held up briefly at the airport. Nothing really important happened and as you know I don't carry weapons or drugs ever," he sniggered.

"We sure are glad you are well, Harry, and here's Bill who wants to say hello. We had just been looking for a way to contact you," and Jacqueline passed on the cell phone to her sibling.

"Hi Harry. Good to hear you're well, we were concerned." He followed up his sister's conversation. Harry replied in his most charming voice... he was always surprised he had one.

"You must never worry, my dear Bill, but it's kind of you both to think of me. Very few people do on this Earth!"

"Harry, I hope I didn't make a mistake," he admitted, hesitating. "I... I have called Larry Crow because he was so appalled that they stopped you and then I kind of made him feel like 'he better get me a number where I could reach you'... you know, like a hotel where I could find you. I hope you don't mind?"

"No, this time I will forgive you this mistake Bill," and he raised his voice ever so slightly. "You mustn't forget that I travel so much that it's a bit hard to catch up with me. And I do always call you and Jacky, and you never need to call me, nor do you have to worry about calling me." He did sound a bit tedious, Bill thought.

"We will actually have a day visit together in the Bahamas soon. Simon will not be able to make it this time. From now on, I will give you the number of an answering service and you can always leave a message. It checks in automatically, every day and wherever I am, it connects to my laptop. And don't worry about the 'film' they talked about on the news. It has disappeared... mysteriously of course, ha ha." His laughing had the quality of a *Friday 13th* movie."

"So, take good care of yourself, both of you and stay out of trouble! Here's the number on the text message; *adieu mes enfants* (goodbye my children!)"

Bill put the phone number deep into his memory bank as did his sister. They hung up and deleted the last phone message and then destroyed the cell phone.

Harry looked satisfied and he chose an old bottle of his best bourbon and served it in an antique crystal glass with a real 18-carat gold rim; the one that Winston had given him after the Hiroshima disaster. Then three men came in, one seemingly in a very tired mood. The other two in black suits left instantly, nodding politely. Simon Averardo sat down, wondering if he had entered another nightmare.

"My dear Simon, how annoying. Really? I didn't even want to talk to you. But OK, for old times' sake, I do hope you're feeling better." He rattled along in a disinterested manner.

"We have to have our little talk, since we couldn't have it in Geneva," Harry said in a cynical voice, slightly tinted with the disgust a landlord might have over a tenant being late paying his rent. "Of course, you are aware about your addictions; the sex and the drugs. Here let me share this footage of you in action."

He turned around and a click on his laptop opened a video on the life-size wall screen. Harry grinned as he left for a brief stop in his private restroom, hidden behind the library door. Simon dropped his head onto his chest, ready for another coma. He knew very well what he was about to look at and it could turn him over to eternal slavery. Now he just hoped he could still get something out of it and escape a public trial and more press.

"Harry, I truly don't know how it all evolved so quickly into such an intense story, all within one month," he almost stuttered his way into the conversation. "Come on, you know me; all this wasn't really me, all the sex stuff and the drugs! I mean, I am grateful that you had sent Jacqueline but it never occurred to me that…"

"…a dream could outlive its own subject's family, Simon?" Harry asked with that scary grin on his face that made him look as if he walked straight out of that horror movie.

"You know that you're not the first one to make this confession… with different words? I know you generated interest for our time travel business, and it isn't so much the way you led the project, as the need to make as many public appearances in the presence of at least one famous actress. After all those years your closest, long-time collaborators have turned against you. They have started procedures against you, some are resigning and selling their assets, like the Von Weitwegs, who sold over twenty or more percent. And then that cleaning woman, totally supported by your secretaries… they blew the whistle and made your story sound like the New York Philharmonic on a world tour!"

Simon slowly shrank into the designer chair opposite the big Harry K. He didn't even dare to suggest turning off the embarrassing DVD with nude bodies endlessly copulating. He just hoped nobody else had seen it. But he was wrong.

"Then without any comment whatsoever Mrs Averardo filed for divorce ... she somehow got some excerpts from this tape? Ouch! And now your ex-spouse refuses to speak to you, her husband and the father of her children?" His eyes shrugged deviously while Simon was again hiding his head in both hands.

I really planned this one well. Sorry, Harry thought, you are no longer required in this role!

"The board of directors has called you *persona non grata* my dear friend. You're lucky I had the basement cleared before the press received the official statement by Mr and Mrs Freundreich a week later." He sighed heavily. "To your great luck, I am able to employ you for another job as long as you remain incognito. Here's the address you will visit tomorrow. She's a dentist and she will give you all the necessary information as to where to go undercover and what will come next."

He actually looked him straight in the eyes before he continued in a different voice, on a vile tone.

"She will create new fingerprints too; a whole new dossier with another name and another life of service to our great New World Order! You are indeed lucky I saved you!" He had firmly dictated his way through Simon's head. A technique Simon loathed, the way his dad used to humiliate him. He so hated to be told what to do.

Incognito! Just shut up, he was talking to himself, silently, again and again.

"Let's say that a talented man like you must get a second chance, don't you think so?" Harry smirked. "Now you still can handle a gun, no? Your records led me to believe you were very able with weapons when you did your military service. You had an automatic gun, a Luger, right? You may want to pick up your old hobby but that's for later, don't worry; we are not developing you into the next Oswald, ha-ha, we're not ready yet with training the new JFK!"

And he laughed at his own vicious jokes and nearly convincing lies.

Simon was on his knees without a boxing ring to fight from. Now he was going to have to please the boss like never before. He was finished playing the president of a big company. He might as well leave for a waiter's job, but the thing was, he knew too much and they would always find him wherever he would try to escape to.

"Another point I need to make, Simon, a bit of a tough one. I must insist you don't contact Jacqueline or Bill. You understand that we cannot jeopardize a major film career because you seduced them." Simon almost choked.

'I seduced him? He cramped up '... when he ...'bite your invisible lip, bite Simon, bite so you can stay awake and in some kind of a self-control ...

Harry was so pleased; he had trapped his own victim and he had caged him well, in gold and there would be more enticing sex and drugs, whether Simon wanted it or not.

He'd be in the middle of it all. Simon had no idea about the training program he was about to undergo.

Maybe one day he would be fit to shoot a president who had been a former lover. Oh yes, it was all on tape too with very spicy close-ups. What a soap opera series that would be! Ouch, he thought, I'm sure *Flatnix* or *SnowTime* will want to buy the story!

What a scheme I am thinking up. Just brilliant, Harry, ah ha. Self-congratulatory, like a president we all know; it does sounds like it, no?

And he put on his traditional burdensome grin and turned off the laptop. Life is great, he thought ... at least from the top of my pyramid!

65. GENEVA, 2018 THE LETTER

Whereabouts . . . for both of us
sliding back and forth in worlds
as parallel as all paths we crossed,
an echo in reverse
of sprinkling that mirror into
billions of stars,
in a fortuitous mizzle of aeonian particles of us . . . (Mirror of the Wall)

Elizabeth and Siegfried relaxed on their balcony. "A toast," they announced. "What an amazing Red Chianti, great choice, darling!" Siegfried said. It was the only present they brought from the small airport duty free shop in Florence. There had been no shopping time when they departed from Fiesole. Désiré had made sure all evidence from their adventure at the Medici Villa had been removed and they had left a clean cave in a much better state than when they had entered it. The owners would never find out who had done the cleanup, indeed, a small present in exchange for the discoveries they had made.

All protagonists of last month's stirring time travel conspiracy, except the now illustrious trio, were happily sharing a great dinner on the terrace of the Freundreich's residence overlooking the political capital this Swiss city had once been. They would exchange stories into the wee hours, still not believing it was all over; or was this only the beginning? How had such amazing historical encounters even taken place? The staggering Medici family, the overwhelmingly kind Buontalenti family and artists of the likes of Angelo Poliziano and then one of the world's greatest artists and inventors: Leonardo da Vinci.

"Can you believe that in the *Cinquecento,* that man actually invented the helicopter and the tank? And the minor toys like a calculator and solar power.

He mastered on his own hydrodynamics, optic and civil engineering. How much of a genius can you be?" GianLuca couldn't contain his enthusiasm. All the dinner guests were in total agreement.

"Yes, his concepts were so ahead of their time," Isabel confirmed with a huge sigh. "I so wished we could have taken more time to talk to him. Maybe we can one day... visit him in his last years at the French Court before he passed away." GianLuca nodded in a very serious manner.

Florian continued, "Yes, what an extraordinary artist and human being; do you know that at his funeral he insisted that beggars would follow his coffin and then the court and his royal friends had to follow; just a reminder of the real world!"

Elizabeth didn't budge from her sister's side. Their first exchanges had grown into a real family friendship. GianLuca, Isabel and Florian, were once again inseparable. Their other new friends, Iz's trio, had received a very generous payment from DoWell Pharmaceutics the same day they returned to Geneva and Elizabeth had made sure it went through quickly before an international court case started or before the press extended the DoWell's story into a bombastic national television series.

Derecho and Izquierdo had promised Siegfried to stay in touch because one day they might like to work together on a similar project. Dritto had decided to stick around Tuscany for a while, a province he now loved even more. Désiré had quickly produced a kind of professional report to show all costs on their adventure, leaving no expenses uncovered. All three seemed to have gone their own ways.

Upon their return to Geneva, Elizabeth and Siegfried had issued an official statement, avoiding *à tout prix* (at all costs) a press conference, especially since Simon had disappeared without even a note to his former wife. Hours before they submitted their resignations to the international board of DoWell Pharmaceuticals, they had cleverly sold all their assets back to the company losing less than 0.75%. Freedom wore no price tag and Elizabeth especially couldn't wait to get out of the DoWell business, quite aware of what the organization owed them.

Isabel's plan to move the next fall, indicated they would all return to Tuscany. GianLuca had decided to live less than an hour from Florence, hoping to assist his friends in finding a new home close by.

"I'm glad we're doing a potluck dinner," Elizabeth said, "I didn't really feel like cooking". But her hubby replied, "Darling, I'm mostly cooking, no? That is true, I'm once again cooking like in the good old days, right? Your personal cook!" Siegfried smiled and as usual, she giggled.

"I'm sure we'll have too much food; you know these parties. I only ordered *hors d'œuvres* and that wonderful *Tarte à la Mousse au Chocolat Cru, je ne pouvais pas résister.* (The raw chocolate mousse cake I couldn't resist)," Elizabeth answered dramatically. The doorman rang.

"What a surprise, our trio is here!" and Siegfried got up to answer the door.

Isabel, winged by Florian and GianLuca, embraced all three men waving their capes around.

"We couldn't resist getting dressed and here's some more great wine." Dritto hugged Siegfried while Elizabeth welcomed Derecho and Izquierdo.

"You are looking stunning Isabel," Iz said.

"Et toi aussi, quel chique (so do you, how chic!)" Elizabeth smiled and continued, "I am so happy – at my age, it's a gift to have a family, no matter what anyone says".

"A toast," Siegfried announced while popping a bottle of French Champagne by the name of some widow.

"Look at the sunset, just another great gift and to have survived this amazing adventure... I bet we are still thinking about our Renaissance friends, no? I know, so do I," Florian said.

Isabel and GianLuca nodded, and the latter continued, "After checking the emails... oh what a list that was... I noticed on the international news that one local Newspaper had given minor attention to the fact that Sir Harry Khope... yes he's a Sir now, well, he had been stopped at Geneva Airport's customs only last week. As for the temporary closing of the DoWell offices, neither national nor international news channels mentioned anything. He sure hasn't lost his pull, has he?" Izquierdo noted.

"And yes", Florian said, "the story hasn't ended; of course not, how could it?" He threw both arms up in the air making a pose from a Greek Tragedy. "A man with a master plan to keep this world as stupid as possible; this master puppeteer... even after his death he'll be around!"

"Yeah," GianLuca joined in, "we ought to check into that creepy Benderberger group, Siegfried. At least you're a witness and we better make sure you're not in the news ever!"

"*Absolument pas* (Absolutely not)!" Elizabeth agreed, "I have no intent whatsoever to lose my husband to a bunch of conspirators!"

"Well said," Dritto and Derecho sang in a happy chorus.

While they munched on the *hors d'oeuvres*, Elizabeth whispered that she had convinced the company to buy back their apartment. They would invest the money in a small house somewhere in . . . Tuscany.

"Oh Eliza, how clever," Isabel exclaimed. "That's such good news. The area between Castellina and Radda in Chianti . . . and, of course, on the way to my darling Sienna . . . close to our Lorenzo, and as *magnifico*. We must all go and check it out together and . . . maybe revisit a few of the Medici's residences!"

"Yes, we had better find one of their best hidden fortresses if we are going to take on the New World Order," Florian said. Six pairs of eyes fixed on him and slowly approached, booing with lifted claws ready to devour the vampire's victim.

"Boo, boo," the trio grumbled continuously. "Go away, you extra-terrestrial spy, we want a quiet life!"

"Well then vacation is off," Florian laughed and continued, "because GianLuca and I are setting up an underground movement to battle this new takeover of the planet by unsolicited entities, called upon by secret societies, world governments and . . . all their club friends!"

"Count us in," Izquierdo gladly confirmed laughing out.

"Oh yes? Did you think I'd consider that option?" GianLuca pretended in total disagreement, but nobody trusted him on that question.

"I know you, *carissimo* (beloved one)," Isabel said. "Even if you find a local Fiammetta, you'll still be wearing Robin Hood-y shoes, won't you? As for you, my co-pilot, if you leave me out of this project, we will never time travel again and you won't see her either." She giggled, "If we're going to play this next game against 'grand evil' together, I want a new wardrobe."

Champagne glasses accompanied more laughs.

"My love, you just pick some of my old costumes and take them along on your next travels!" Elizabeth commented.

"And I'm going to retire, which of course doesn't mean we cannot be joining the home team, right *mon amour*?" and she gently bit Siegfried's right earlobe.

While two amorous couples took a kissing session for granted, GianLuca and the trio finished their champagne looking down from the balcony. Newly filled glasses were emptied ever so slowly as their thoughts returned to another century.

GianLuca demanded another toast. For a few seconds he stared into a Seven Sisters star cluster right above their heads and his throat closed down.

"Here's to a magnificent memento, to all you wonderful Renaissance friends, to my sweet Fiammetta, and to Agnola, Andrea and Lapo; to Lorenzo, Angelo, Leonardo ... and to you my dearest Giuliano!" He paused and took a breath and his smile briefly turned sad.

"May we dream up new games and new roads to cross along the lines of time in at least ... our galaxy"? There was more than one pair of teary eyes while they finished their Tuscan delicacies.

Amongst the unopened mail on his desk, Siegfried had noticed a picture on the back page of that same day's Universal Tribune, announcing that a 'Former Medici Villa in Tuscany's Fiesole is for sale'. He turned around and glanced at a beautiful wooden frame, with an original Leonardo da Vinci. How in the world did that ever get here?

Siegfried shrugged while thinking back to last year's adventures. It appeared he had missed episodes of an enticing television mini-series and he regretted not being a part of such a big-time travel story. At least not yet: "Am I right, Leonardo?"

Fiorenza, the late fall of 1473, Palazzo Medici

On a timeline known as the *Cinquecento*, an elegant hand was drawing a face of an unusually gorgeous, yet invisible model. That young artist was thinking of a beautiful woman he so cared for and yet never got to meet ... Caterina, the young pale-skinned slave from the Middle East, said to be his mother.

He gazed in the mirror when a kind hand combed his handsome curls. The strikingly athletic man's soft caress relaxed Leonardo. He stood up gazing at him in an almost mysterious way as they strolled toward the largest room of the ancient Palazzo.

"I will protect you, and your genius will flourish, and you will be free to come and go," Lorenzo said.

"My gratitude will know no boundaries and I will honour your family the best I can," Leonardo replied. Lorenzo de Medici wrapped Leonardo da Vinci's graceful hands in his.

"Let me share this handwritten letter." He looked the young artist in the eyes and there was a sadness he could not hide. He continued.

"Before leaving back to his future, look at this gracious memento our timeless friend GianLuca has left my brother and me." With a smile and a thrill in his voice, Lorenzo read out aloud.

Dear Giuliano, Dear Lorenzo,

It was an exciting time having been able to visit both you and Giuliano, the Buontalenti family and all our dear friends on this amazing Renaissance timeline. No doubt we have all been taught many a lesson. For most of us on the path of higher learning, the understanding how life truly functions, will remain a mystery. As humans, we have always battled the lack of love and self-esteem.

Our personal frustrations may inhibit us from getting out of the bigger drama, a victimhood we have lived for eons. While each individual is born with such unique capacities, we judge pretty badly our fellow citizen. We can hardly avoid landing in an ocean of emotion, because that is one of the lessons we have come to learn.

We had better all become good swimmers with many navigating abilities beyond our own deep personal doubts. I have high hopes that, unusually gifted as de Medici family and friends have been demonstrated to be, you dear Lorenzo, as a ruler, you can indeed make a huge difference. You will influence generations to come and why not reflect right now how to bring awareness to the people.

I am so looking forward to witnessing a real change in our human history, one where we can strive for a greater awareness and equality and thrive in the goodness of all of our souls.

As such I close off this chapter, one in which I remain moved to tears for I believe in the greater good of mankind and I pray that a phoenix, winged with new leaders from the ashes of our earthly past, will take us all together throughout time beyond the manipulation of those who chose hate over love.

Today, on a more personal note I am truly aware, yes convinced, that we all have lived a manifold of lives, possibly on different timelines. These last months, our ageless friendship will forever remind us that the encounter of our souls is engraved, ad vitam aeternam, as a shining memento of the love and humanity we have laid like a ley line between our centuries to choose and to keep alive as a never-dying flame of hope for all generations to survive on and to keep alive this amazing Terra!

With loving care,
Yours always,
Jean Luc Médecin (GianLuca de Medici)

THE END

Made in the USA
Columbia, SC
23 July 2021

42295536R00262